BEAUTIFUL REDEEMER

OTHER TITLES BY KAIT BALLENGER

The Original Sinners

Original Sinner

Wicked Believer

Seven Range Shifters

Cowboy Wolf Trouble

Cowboy in Wolf's Clothing

Wicked Cowboy Wolf

Fierce Cowboy Wolf

Wild Cowboy Wolf

Cowboy Wolf Outlaw

Cowboy Wolf Christmas

Rogue Brotherhood

Shadow Hunter

Rogue Wolf Hunter

The Vampire's Hunter

Praise for Kait Ballenger

"Kait Ballenger delivers a seductive masterpiece in this fiery romance. Lucifer is as irresistible as he is sinful. With blazing-hot chemistry, this book will leave you begging for more. Wickedly and utterly unputdownable!"

—*USA Today* bestselling author Sara Cate on *Original Sinner*

"*Original Sinner* is a sizzling hot, irreverent, and seductively enthralling read. Lucifer is guaranteed to become your new morally gray book-boyfriend addiction."

—Abigail Owen, #1 *New York Times* and *USA Today* bestselling author of *The Games Gods Play*

"Kait Ballenger is a treasure you don't want to miss!"

—*New York Times* and *USA Today* bestseller Gena Showalter

"An extremely promising high-voltage start . . . Readers will savor strong characterization, steamy animalistic sex scenes with Dom/sub subtext, and an interesting series arc."

—*Publishers Weekly* (starred review) on *Rogue Wolf Hunter*

"This story has it all . . . The chemistry is electric, and the spicy banter is terrific."

—Fresh Fiction on *Cowboy Wolf Trouble*

"Hits all the sweet spots of paranormal romance. Recommend to readers of Nalini Singh and Maria Vale."

—*Booklist* on *Cowboy in Wolf's Clothing*

"Adventure, intrigue, and a super sexy premise!"

—*USA Today* bestselling author Terry Spear on *Cowboy in Wolf's Clothing*

"The romance is sexy, and a fast-paced, rollicking plot will keep readers engaged."

—*Kirkus Reviews* on *Wicked Cowboy Wolf*

BEAUTIFUL REDEEMER

KAIT BALLENGER

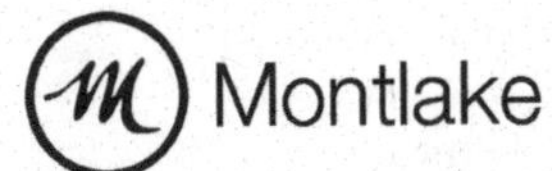

This is a work of fiction. Names, characters, organizations, places, events, and incidents are either products of the author's imagination or are used fictitiously. Otherwise, any resemblance to actual persons, living or dead, is purely coincidental.

Published by Montlake, Seattle

www.apub.com

EU product safety contact:
Amazon Media EU S. à r.l.
38, avenue John F. Kennedy, L-1855 Luxembourg
amazonpublishing-gpsr@amazon.com

ISBN-13: 9781662528903 (paperback)
ISBN-13: 9781662528910 (digital)

Cover design by Christian Bentulan
Cover images: © fivespots, © Graphic Compressor, © Molotok289, © Ross Panfilov, © Volodymyr TVERDOKHLIB / Shutterstock

Printed in the United States of America

To the women reclaiming their power . . .
I'm proud of you, fearless girl.

AUTHOR'S NOTE

Dear reader,

Thank you for picking up a copy of *Beautiful Redeemer*. I'm so thrilled that you've enjoyed Lucifer, Charlotte, and now Azrael's story, starting in *Wicked Believer*, enough to be invested in their dark and devilish ending.

Original Sinner is a passion project that doubled as an exorcism of my own demons, and I poured just as much of myself and my creative joy into *Wicked Believer*, but if *Original Sinner* is where the journey began, *Beautiful Redeemer* is my victorious race across the finish line, a dark, triumphant ode to abuse survivors who've reclaimed their power.

Beautiful Redeemer is exactly the kind of trilogy finale I love, a book that revisits all the sinful and delicious things that made us all fall in love with Lucifer and the other Originals, while also leaving room for Charlotte, Lucifer, and now Azrael's world and, more importantly, their relationship to mature and grow even as it takes darker turns. As such, *Beautiful Redeemer*'s content might not be suitable for all readers.

Beautiful Redeemer is a dark, sexy, "why choose" paranormal fantasy romance and features two villainous, morally gray men—a billionaire devil who previously blackmailed his former employee into dating him, and his now murderous ex-boyfriend turned romantic rival and lover, Death incarnate. While Lucifer may have been irrevocably changed by Charlotte's love in *Wicked Believer*, at his core, he's just as seductive and horrible as he's always been—and despite their clear differences, his ex-boyfriend, Azrael, can be equally delicious and destructive. For Charlotte, she may have escaped the trauma of her fundamentalist religious past, but the challenges she'll now face as a new immortal caught between death and the devil are far from over.

Beautiful Redeemer contains heavy themes of religious trauma, with frequent references to shame, sex, virginity, self-worth, body image, body shaming, purity culture, the concept of sin, and the role those assigned female at birth are expected to play in the fundamentalist Christian church, as well as extensive scenes where the heroine confronts her primary abuser. It discusses emotional, physical, and sexual abuse that is parental, religious, and spousal in nature, which is revisited in several on-page altercations. It shows consensual nonconsent during a BDSM scene, consensual partner sharing, breath play, edge play, and breeding kink, along with references to stalking, on-page drinking, and references to drug use. It mentions forced marriage and pregnancy; shows vivid depictions of catastrophic, apocalyptic devastation; contains graphic violence, religious genocide, and mass murder; and, as always, has a healthy dose of swearing.

Readers who are sensitive to this content, take heed, and prepare to be seduced by mythology's ultimate bad boys . . .

THE ORIGINALS

Lucifer—Pride

Azmodeus—Lust

Mammon—Greed

Belphegor—Sloth

Satan—Wrath

Leviathan—Envy

Beelzebub—Gluttony

THE ARCHANGELS

Michael

Gabriel

Uriel

Seraph

Jegudiel

Raphael

~~*Jophiel*~~

OTHER CELESTIALS

Charlotte

Azrael—Death

Then there was war in heaven. Michael and his angels fought against the dragon, and the dragon and his angels fought back . . .

—Revelation 12:7

PART ONE | GENESIS

In the beginning . . .

Azrael

I never understood the fuss about humanity—until the day God asked me to make Lucifer my friend.

The space inside the Nothing is thick with the scent of burning stars, the distant explosive hum of God and Lady Chaos's latest creation still cracking and fizzling. I exist at the edge of their universe, watching, waiting as it all comes together.

It's fragile and full of possibility, but none of it begins to interest me—not yet.

The celestial light of the first dawn flickers, teetering between the birth of the world and the silence, the Nothing that completes me.

I am both beginning and end, Destroyer of Worlds, and I watch as His angel's rebellion comes swift and fierce—violent, unrelenting—but it isn't my place to interfere.

Not until He asks me.

I feel the insistent tug at the back of my consciousness—a deity summoning me. If I can even bring myself to call what I am that—consciousness.

That word is too little for me.

I shift across the galaxy toward Him faster than one of those pesky little things He calls light beams, eager to get the fuck out of here.

Onto my next creation scene.

So far, this one holds little to be desired. Lots of stars and a few awkwardly sized planets—the third one from the sun is the one He favors, apparently. There's barely anything resembling what I would call life on it yet. Just a lot of green plants, plenty of water, and these odd sentient creatures He and all His angels are fighting about.

Humans. Two of them.

In the garden He made.

I find God on the highest plane—Heaven—the "home" He created for Himself and His angels, using whatever power it is Chaos gifted Him.

I'm not certain I like the idea of that, Chaos and God fucking. He's one of her creations, too, after all, just like everything else here.

And I'm not sure I understand what their new ideas even mean.

Home. Love. Family.

These are foreign concepts, but somehow, they seem . . . important.

You summoned me? I say.

My words aren't spoken aloud. Not like His.

I'm not corporeal, and I never have been.

God shifts as He looks down toward Eden, and the single fallen angel He just nearly eviscerated, the former leader of His angelic army.

It's *that* more than anything that's summoned me.

The sense that some kind of end is near. The angel's existence, maybe?

"I'm going to ask something of you that's never been asked before," He says.

It's a strange request, but no stranger than any other universe's beginnings.

I've seen them all. I don't remember a time when I . . . wasn't.

I'm listening.

"I want you to go to him." God gestures to the fallen angel He's hurled into the dirt and His planet's muck.

The one who's severed and bleeding.

You want me to—

"No, not end him. I . . . want you to be his friend."

Friend?

This word is another foreign concept.

And I don't have time for any of this shit.

No.

I start to barrel my way across the universe, headed to the next creation, before—

The angel stirs.

I feel it.

I linger, torn between another galaxy that calls to me and the possibility of something deeper.

I glance toward the angel.

Beauty like that never falls without being pushed.

And what is all this fuss about love? Family? Humanity?

I'm down on God's planet—Earth, as He calls it—before I can change my mind, watching the broken angel moaning before me. He's injured and bleeding, maimed, but underneath it all he's so fucking beautiful I can't help but want to touch him.

I become corporeal, taking a similar form to his—bipedal, strangely hairless, with wings, like how he looked before whatever it is God did to him—so I don't scare him. I draw closer, reaching out until—

He lashes out and cuts me.

Above my eye.

The claws on his hand slice straight through my brow.

A sudden feeling of . . . I'm not sure what to call it expands inside me.

My own hand now trembling, I touch the spot.

The angel stares up at me, panting like a cornered animal. He's naked and bleeding, covered in his own blood and dirt, and the stumps of where his wings used to be are still raw and twitching.

"Death," he whispers, christening me.

No one's ever named me before.

"The fuck you just call me?" My response is raspy, hoarse. Untried from lack of use.

I've never even *heard* my voice.

Let alone laid eyes on a creature as vicious and beautiful as the one before me.

He tries to move away, scrambling and writhing in the dirt, but he doesn't get very far. Not with how badly he's injured.

I inch closer.

"Don't touch me," he snarls.

Immediately I understand why.

I glance at my own blood still fresh on my fingers. If the pain he showed me only a moment ago is any indication of how he's feeling . . .

I look to the blood-soaked ground. To the bruises, the cuts, and lacerations that cover him.

"Did you . . . come here to take me?" he asks, his voice wavering.

Broken. Defeated.

I'm not certain I know the answer to that, but for some reason, I shake my head. "No."

My response doesn't change anything.

He's still staring up at me with wild eyes, like I might lash out and do *exactly* what he did to me—only worse—similar to what he endured at the hands of his—

"Father," he groans, collapsing onto the ground and staring up toward Heaven, pleading.

Pleading for the forgiveness of the Creator who nearly ended him.

Who *is* this confusing creature?

I must ask the question out loud, because a moment later, he puffs out his chest slightly, despite that he's still lying there, only a stone's throw away from me in the dirt.

"Lucifer," he rasps.

Lucifer. God's Lightbringer.

That's right.

He was God's favorite among them.

Well, *previous* favorite.

I take a step closer. "Let me—"

"I said, 'Don't touch me,'" he snarls, the fear in his eyes crackling, like that thing called fire his "Father" created recently.

It's the first time I've ever seen a glimpse of what I truly am to someone.

I'm death.

It's the whole of me, and yet I don't want it to be.

But I see it there, playing out on his face.

The fear that I'm going to end him.

"What were you fighting for?" I crouch beside him, curiosity getting the better of me.

He swallows and closes his eyes for a moment, the muscles in his throat writhing as something wet starts to leak from them. "My pride, it seems."

He looks away, and deep in my chest, I have the sudden, inexplicable urge to comfort him.

"Do you know what a friend is?" I lift the brow he cut, and another round of pain sears through it.

I've never experienced anything like it before, but I'm . . . not certain I hate it.

An odd mixture of suspicion, confusion, and curiosity plays out on his face, his gaze narrowing.

He's still lying there, bleeding and broken, barely able to lift his own head, and yet he's still full of that thing he just mentioned.

Pride, he called it.

"No." His amber eyes dart over me, momentary, fleeting, before he collapses into the dirt. "My Father keeps talking about it, but my sister, Seraph, is the closest thing I've ever known."

"Sister?" This is another new concept.

"One of my siblings."

I tilt my head at him curiously. "Do you think you and I could be—"

"Friends?" he finishes, his gaze combing over my nude form, the one I created to match his.

The feeling that sparks low and deep in this angelic version of me is also new.

Unexpected.

I give a curt nod before I offer him my hand.

He stares at it for a long beat, considering, before he says, "I suppose I'm going to need someone to help me rebuild," and then he takes it.

And that's how it starts.

Both beginning and end.

Of me. Of him. Of all of us.

I hide him somewhere I'm certain God and none of the others will see, somewhere none of them will ever touch him again, a realm that he and I plan to create, before I return to Heaven, once I'm certain God's newly fallen son is no longer watching me.

The Creator greets me with wide, open arms as He says, "Now, Death, let me tell you what I have planned for the ending."

CHAPTER ONE

Lucifer

I tried to warn Charlotte about my ruddy siblings. But she wanted to make a family. Join celestial forces. Fight my Father's impending apocalypse—together.

Her goddamn naïvety will be the end of me.

But I suppose I've always had a penchant for lost causes.

I lean back upon my makeshift throne of scorched steel and broken concrete—crafted from the bones of what only a few moments ago was downtown Dubai—the leftover remnants of the Burj Khalifa crumbled to dust at my feet. Emergency helicopters whir overhead, the vortex of the wind they create drawing up enough dust that it now thoroughly coats both my suit and face as the few humans who remain begin their desperate search for survivors.

They won't find many.

When I command it, my siblings burn the world down with such conviction, you'd almost think they *believe* in something.

"I gave you one bloody task," I snarl. *"One."*

Satan and Leviathan—Wrath and Envy, respectively—stand on opposite sides of the wreckage, glaring at one another with little regard for the catastrophic damage they've just caused me. Wrath lifts some of the rubble over his head, using the force of his abilities to send the debris careening toward Envy. But Envy deflects it easily enough, stopping it in midair and temporarily seizing Wrath's abilities until a newly formed chasm splits open not ten feet from me. A deep, jagged rupture created by my brother's seismic tantrum, no doubt. Flames lick at the edges, bursting up from beneath, but it isn't my realm cracking open to unleash my latent powers to me.

Fucking inconvenient, that.

"Enough," I growl, giving a sharp jerk of my chin as I rise from my throne.

Death and Abaddon, the shared leaders of my demonic legions, step forth from where they flank me, more than prepared to do my bidding.

I told my brothers to bring down the goddamn skyline, not level the whole blasted city. The Righteous were meant to tremble, not recruit martyrs from the ashes. But when have my siblings ever listened?

Being the eldest has never exactly been fun or games for me.

Though I suppose I can't claim full immunity.

I, too, often consider torturing my siblings to Hell and back whenever they annoy me. At least before that bloody bastard, Michael, went and stripped my powers from me.

But now with my legions topside and Earth under my command, they will bow to me all the same.

Like it or not.

"He said it wasn't that big!" This from Envy.

"He what?" I shout across the ruins.

The smoke from the nearby fires they created obscures my view momentarily.

"He *said* it wasn't that big," Envy snarls, spittle flying from his mouth, before he launches another unexpected blast of Wrath's stolen power at us both.

They cannot possibly be serious.

I sidestep out of the way, just as Azrael uses his abilities as a celestial shield for me, returning the rock to the dust from which it came, but not before a sharp piece of the shrapnel sails past, resulting in a rather ghastly tear down the front of my favorite suit.

My gaze narrows upon my siblings.

Once my powers return, I will fucking end both of them.

When the dust finally settles, Envy gestures wildly to the three-hundred-story tower they just destroyed while simultaneously wiping out half the godforsaken city.

As if to indicate it's *that* which started this whole thing.

I glance between them.

"Are you bloody joking?" I shout.

Neither of my siblings is given the chance to answer before the earth once again begins to tremble beneath our feet.

My nostrils flare.

There is only one thing on this godforsaken planet that could make the entire world quake like that *aside* from me.

Charlotte is going to blame herself for this, as I might've once done.

And that is an outcome I cannot accept willingly.

"Fuck!"

A round of shouts follows as the few human survivors begin to desperately point to the heavens.

Somewhere, hundreds of kilometers away, lightning flashes as the sky overhead transitions to a crimson, bleeding red. The clouds part upon a sudden crack of divine fury, and a massive blast of Holy Fire rains down upon the earth.

"Lucifer, down!" Azrael orders.

I drop to the ground, shielding my head as the first pulse of power bursts forth.

My Father's celestial judgment barrels throughout the world like a rampant plague.

Unleashing chaos. Razing buildings. Vomiting fire and ash at anyone or anything that stands within its path.

It cannot possibly dissuade me.

My siblings are knocked off their feet, toppling like the broken idols they're quickly becoming, as my blood pressure begins to rise, and I press my lips together.

This is not wrath; this is annihilation the likes of which humanity has never seen.

The crimson sky darkens, and my expression goes cold. For once I begin to question if even *I* will manage to survive all my Father's apocalyptic seals opening. A sudden chill runs down my spine as the world goes silent.

The Red Rider.

War has been unleashed.

The second seal is now open.

And not by my command, it seems.

Azrael and Abaddon are the first ones up, shouting orders for my legions to fall back in line where they cowered before my Father's fury, just as Wrath throws back his head and laughs wickedly.

Envy lets out a low, appreciative whistle as they both stumble to their feet. "Looks like you've got bigger problems on your hands, brother."

Of course I do.

One of my *other* blasted siblings, no doubt.

Controlling them is like keeping panthers on a fucking leash.

I stagger upright, attempting to brush off my suit coat to no avail, only for a round of distant gunfire to break out amongst the survivors. Fuck.

War isn't on his way.

He's already here.

I cast an unamused glance at the battle zone my siblings have just made, before I pull one of my celestial blades from my suit coat. A stray piece of shrapnel whizzes past my ear.

"For fuck's sake," I bellow as my siblings resume their fighting. "Would you two bloody well pack it in?"

Wrath turns in my direction, the singular movement inhuman and uncanny. His irises flash to an angry, murderous red, as red as the sky that bleeds with our Father's divine fury. He and War always did love to feed off one another.

"And what exactly are you going to do about it, Lucy?" Wrath steps forward.

I grit my teeth, my mouth twisting into an unhinged grin, and drop the knife at my side with a hollow clatter as my brother prowls toward me.

I cast my arms open wide, welcoming whatever pain he may bring. "Well, go on then," I taunt, the hellfire in my gaze blazing. "Make it count."

Wrath hesitates, and I smirk wickedly.

Being temporarily mortal has *not* been convenient for me, but in our Father's absence and with my legions now topside, *I* am the true god they fear.

I mutter under my breath as Wrath advances, summoning all my godforsaken demons to do my bidding for me. Without my full power, there is little my demonic army or even my former lover can do to truly contain my siblings once their minds have been set upon something. And clearly, one of them is set upon undermining me.

What else is new?

I look toward the parted sky, my jaw clenching.

I knew it was a mistake opening the first seal of the apocalypse for Michael.

I just failed to recognize how thoroughly he'd fucked me.

CHAPTER TWO

Charlotte

Two weeks later . . .

The worst villains don't make us hate them.

"Are you certain you want to go through with this?" Azrael—Death incarnate—checks in with me again.

I nod, clocking how his white-blue eyes narrow as he watches me. "Jax is my best friend. I won't allow the Righteous to get away with helping Michael target her and hand her over to Lilith without repercussions, and I can't let you and Lucifer keep fighting my battles for me."

And this *is* my battle. My choice.

And my zealot father we're questioning, unfortunately.

Azrael gives a quick jerk of his chin, like he recognizes I've come to terms with the decision, and unlike Lucifer, he isn't going to argue with me.

From where he stands on the opposite side of my new townhouse, his dark wings backlit by the blinding snow that now covers Manhattan, he looks exactly like the avenging angel humanity expects him to be.

Until he turns and the skeletal side of his face flashes.

A stark warning.

Few humans have seen Death like this.

Well, and lived to tell the tale, at least.

Azrael closes the distance between us in a few strides before he gently pulls me into his arms and lays a soft kiss on my lips. Whenever we're close like this, the familiar trace of a scent I catch behind his ear soothes me.

Vetiver and rosemary.

Dark, earthy, inevitable.

A lot like the primordial himself.

Azrael eases back, releasing his hold, his pale eyes still on me, and the shiver that runs down my spine is beyond my control, even as I give him one last kiss and step through the ether.

I freaking hate this.

But no one ever said being an immortal would be easy.

I appear outside Hell's Depths a moment later, the heat of my breath steaming. At the sharp landing, my stomach drops, instantly making me queasy.

The Depths' dark obsidian halls seem to stretch on forever, an endless cavernous maze lit by the surreal glow of flickering torches. I sigh, leaning my head against the cold stone wall. The coolness helps a little.

Not that I'll ever get used to traveling like this.

The nausea subsides, and I straighten just as the sound of some poor soul's screeching echoes in the distance. I stiffen.

The Depths are for the worst offenders, my fiancé's favorite victims, and though I'm still learning our realm's geography, in Hell there's no escaping the devil who's *supposed* to be here beside me.

Or my own demons, it seems.

"Lucifer?" I call out, my voice echoing against the labyrinthine stone.

No one answers.

Tentatively, I inch forward, but I only manage to make it two steps before I'm snatched off my feet into a hidden alcove.

Lucifer has me pinned against the nearest wall in two seconds flat, the heat of his lips brushing my neck and the thrust of his hips hiking up the hem of the Valentino dress I'm wearing.

"Fuck. Is this . . . ? I mean . . . Bloody hell," he swears.

"Yes," I pant.

His whole body seems to sigh in relief. "Thank fuck."

Ever since I put a temporary pause on our D/s dynamic, Lucifer's been unusually careful with me, always asking my permission where he would have relied on my safe word previously.

This time, he doesn't hold back.

He tears into me with renewed vigor, the feeling of his mouth on mine so perfect and delicious and sinful that I can't help but whimper in need.

I want so badly to return to what we used to have, to what *he* wanted for me, but I can't allow myself to give in to my baser urges.

Not yet.

Through his suit pants, the thick length of his cock presses into me, making me ache so much I'm twice as slick as I was already. He nudges my legs open.

"You smell like him," he growls, his tone gruff and accusing, but his touch only grows more wild, more feverish.

"Does that make you want to punish me?"

Or Azrael?

Lucifer pulls my panties aside, dipping two of his fingers into me and stroking over that spot he knows I love so much, and I let out a breathy moan. I turn molten, more than eager for him to be inside me.

This is what he does. Makes me my most wicked and sinful self.

Everything I never knew I needed to be.

He coats his fingers, quickly bringing them to his mouth. "But you taste of me."

His cum, he means.

The smug, self-satisfied grin he gives me is sin embodied.

"Azrael—"

"Hasn't sealed the deal yet?"

The three of us have been practicing ethical nonmonogamy, with Lucifer and I still engaged, while he and Azrael have agreed to share me.

Except now they seem to have some kind of competition for me going.

Lucifer finishes licking his fingers clean of me, his forked tongue flicking over his skin, before he smirks at me, his hands on my breasts as he starts in on my throat.

That teasing smirk of his is pure evil.

Everything I want and more, and yet . . .

Why can't I allow myself to have this?

All it would take to resume our dynamic is a single word, but . . .

My thoughts turn to the other celestial in my life, the one whose deadly kiss acts as a kind of soothing balm to my soul, even if we still haven't . . .

The heat in my face flames.

"Azrael and I are taking things slow."

"Mmph," Lucifer hums noncommittally, like he doesn't know the meaning of the word. He claims my mouth again, so I have no choice but to taste myself on his lips.

I'm nothing but a bundle of pleasured nerves in his arms. Moldable. Like clay.

And more than anything, I want *him* to be the one to help sculpt the shape of me.

Though we both know he can't.

He nips my neck, his fangs grazing over the now-sensitive skin before he pulls back, giving me just enough room to breathe. "Funny how you never felt the need to 'take things slow' with *us*."

"You're different," I pant.

"Am I?" He lifts a brow, giving a half smile like he's won this round, though we both know exactly what I mean.

I'm destined for him. Made from one of his bones.

Like Adam and Eve.

But Lucifer knows as well as I do that I can still be the architect of my own fate.

His family and their freaking apocalypse be damned.

"Don't worry, little dove," Lucifer whispers, the heat of his breath tickling me. "When Azrael *does* make his move, it'll be well worth the wait. Trust me."

I shove playfully at his shoulder, and he lets out a dark chuckle, easing off me.

I'm more than grateful he's giving me the space to explore whatever this . . . attraction is between me and Azrael. He's respecting my needs, allowing me the chance to build my own life, make my own choices, before I fully submit to him. But my fiancé still has no qualms about reminding me that he and Azrael have their own kinky history.

A level of backstory that he and I don't share.

Not that either of them has been particularly forthcoming about it.

Lucifer leans against the adjacent wall, reaching for a cigarette, the amber hellfire in his eyes roving over me. In his custom suit and polished Armanis, he cuts a dangerous figure. Sin and desire and temptation all rolled into one.

He wasn't exactly thrilled when I told him I wanted to move out of the penthouse and divide my leisure time between him and Azrael *equally*, but sometimes I think the bit of distance it's created between us has been good for us both.

I crave every moment he and I are together more than I crave my next breath.

And I would know, considering these days Death is practically stalking me.

"How was the press conference?" Lucifer asks, lighting his cigarette.

I shake my head. "Not worth discussing."

Ever since Michael forced Lucifer to open the first seal of the apocalypse and Lucifer lost his earthly powers, the entire world has gone to hell in a handbasket—literally—considering Hell's demonic legions have now infiltrated every part of the city, along with everywhere *else* for that matter.

With the second seal now open, war has begun breaking out all over the globe thanks to whichever one of Lucifer's siblings went rogue.

We're not entirely certain which one it was yet, but it's made my already tentative alliance with them even more unsteady.

Meanwhile, Michael and Lilith are temporarily untraceable as they both prepare for their next strike.

Not to mention the human zealots called the Righteous have started moving into politics.

They and their followers are stronger than ever.

Who knew the Big Apple would be apocalypse ground zero?

And where's God in all this?

That's one question I can't seem to stop asking.

The end of Lucifer's cigarette flares, illuminating a small cut healing on his cheek, and another tortured scream echoes, reminding me of exactly *where* I'm standing.

Honestly, at the moment, actual Hell is preferable to what I'm dealing with topside. The media and the general population didn't take kindly to my livestreamed "revelation" that I'm immortal.

Understatement of the century.

I brush all that aside and try to focus on the task at hand. "Do you really think I can do this?"

I look toward Lucifer, unable to hide all the uncertainty plaguing me.

About this. About him. About Azrael. The apocalypse.

All of it.

How when all of that's stripped away, I still don't know who I am underneath.

What kind of immortal I'm going to be.

Lucifer's smirk widens, and I let out an irritated huff, feeling annoyed with myself.

Right.

These days I don't need to ask for his approval. My own intuition is *supposed* to be enough.

So why do I feel like my anxiety is slowly crushing me?

"If I said yes, would that help you feel better?" Lucifer tilts his head curiously.

"No."

We both recognize it for the lie that it is.

Lucifer's expression softens.

He knows better than anyone what it's taken for me to get here, even more than Azrael, who in the last several weeks has become my shoulder to cry on.

But unlike Death, Lucifer would never coddle me.

Instead, he simply opens a door I didn't realize was there, stubbing out his cigarette and beckoning me forward like he not only welcomes how wicked I can be, but encourages it.

How anyone can resist him is beyond me.

"After you, little dove."

At his invitation, I stiffen, the cold air coming up from the Depths suddenly even more suffocating than the heat. Lucifer's lips twist.

He's enjoying this. The asshat.

I made my bed, and now he's going to make me lie in it.

Like the true sadist he is.

I clench my teeth, hesitating.

Fuck. What did my upbringing do to me?

I can trust in *myself*, goddammit.

I press my lips together, forcing myself to remain strong as I brush past him.

At the bottom of the narrow staircase, we come to a series of stainless-steel doors covered in elaborate locks, and Lucifer opens the third one on the left with a single brush of his finger, or maybe his shadows, I'm not really sure which. As we step inside, I'm greeted with the sight of what appears to be a grimy meat locker.

What the . . . ?

My heels click against the ceramic tile as the door slams shut.

Why did he . . . ?

I step farther in, taking in the dingy space, the flickering fluorescent lights, the rusted floor drains, and the lingering rancid smell of something rotten. It could be the set of a horror movie.

No less than he deserves.

Seemingly undisturbed, Lucifer steps past me, and to my surprise, the familiar scent of smoke and whisky that clings to him doesn't do anything to calm my restless nerves, even as he offers me his hand.

I take it, holding on to the small bit of comfort he gives me.

I asked for full disclosure, to be a part of his celestial family, and since then, my fiancé's done nothing to shield me from his world.

So why does it feel like we're moving backward?

"I'm happy to do this for you, little dove. Just say the word," Lucifer whispers, breaking the momentary silence as he tucks a stray strand of hair behind my ear.

I'm not sure I can do this, I think.

But I don't send it down the line of our connection, so he doesn't hear me.

As much as I sometimes wish he could read my mind, he can't. Not in that way. Both he and Azrael have insisted I have nothing to prove, but they're wrong in this case.

I *do* have something to prove.

To myself, at least.

"Let's just get this over with."

Lucifer nods, his grip steeling me as he leads the way.

When we reach the final part of the meat locker, a freezer or kill room that's been sectioned off by several hanging plastic panels, he nods encouragingly.

Whatever challenges either of us faces, we face them together.

It's me and my devil against the world. No pressure or anything.

I'm the Queen of Hell after all.

My soul belongs to the fallen angel beside me, for now and the rest of eternity.

And I'm grateful for it.

Even if I'm still struggling to figure out who I am underneath.

We step inside, the opaque plastic flaps swinging as I tell myself it's only natural to feel nervous. It doesn't matter that I was made from one of Lucifer's bones. I'm still my own person with my own trauma and history. But the moment he steps out of my line of vision and my eyes settle on the monster in front of me, my stomach drops.

At first, I don't fully register that it's him. He doesn't look anything like the man who raised me. He's thinner, paler, emaciated. If it wasn't for the fact he's wearing the same baggy, bloodied suit I'm pretty sure he died in, the one with the navy blue tie Mark bought him three Christmases ago, I wouldn't recognize him.

He's strapped to an old metal electric chair in the middle of the room, the leather that binds him cutting into his skin, so I know he can't move from his seat, but panic still grips me.

Initially, he doesn't acknowledge that Lucifer and I are there or even lift his head to look at me. He's slumped back in the chair like he's been tortured so many times and in so many ways that the how and why make little difference anymore.

Good.

The thought tears through me.

Though I'm instantly ashamed of it.

Lucifer gives my hand one final reassuring squeeze before he releases me, and I watch in an odd mixture of curiosity and abject horror as my father stiffens at his approach.

He recognizes the sound of Lucifer's Armanis.

Just like I do when Lucifer and I are alone in the playroom.

Though for a far more fucked-up reason.

Lucifer wrenches my father's head back by his graying hair, and it's only then that my father speaks. "'He who was hurled to the earth, and his angels with him.'"

I flinch, my heart racing.

Lucifer doesn't appear the least bit fazed.

"He does that," he says, speaking as if my father isn't there, like he sometimes does to *me* when we're deep in a scene. "Speaks only in those bloody bastardizations of my Father's verse."

In quotes from the Bible, he means.

I exhale a shaky breath.

Once a zealot, always a zealot, I guess, I send down the line between us.

Abruptly, Lucifer releases him, tipping his chin toward the exit. "Would you like me to—"

"No, stay."

Lucifer lifts a single brow.

We may have put a temporary pause on our dynamic, but the Prince of Darkness answers to no one—me included.

"Please?"

He nods, capitulating like he's happy to do this for me. He leans against one of the meat locker's refrigerators, crossing his arms over his chest.

As if he's eager to see what I'm about to do.

You and me both, sir.

Slowly, I step forward, my father's gaze meeting mine as everything else around us just sort of falls away, and all the progress I've made suddenly abandons me.

Until I'm nothing more than a scared little girl, standing in front of my abuser again, trembling.

Only this time, he can't hurt me.

I'm more grateful than ever for the feeling of Lucifer's shadows at my back.

A reminder that no matter what, he's got me.

"You always did need a firm hand." My father spits onto the floor at Lucifer's feet before he turns back to me. "I knew from the start you were rotten to the core."

I shake my head. "You're not allowed to speak to me like that. Not anymore."

"You'd dare chastise me with that serpent tongue, girl? After all I did for you?" He scoffs. "You're no daughter of mine. The devil has dug his claws into you. You're just a harlot of Babylon, drunk on your own rebell—"

"I'm not afraid of you or your God anymore. He's too much like you." I inhale a sharp breath, internally bracing. "Where's Lilith keeping Jax?"

The first question that falls from my lips is a stupid one. My father doesn't know the answer, even if it *is* one of the most important questions on all our minds lately. But I'm still new to this whole torture-and-interrogation thing, to releasing my anger, harnessing my powers, and with my father's eyes on me like this, what my brain knows and body feels are no longer in sync.

But still, it sets the tone nicely.

His nostrils flare. "'Trust in the Lord, your God, with all your heart and lean not on your own understanding.'" He huffs, his eyes combing over me as he takes in the Valentino dress I'm wearing.

Too short, his judging look seems to say.

Then my makeup. *Too dark.*

My high-heeled shoes. *Too suggestive.*

All the way down to my venomous lips, my voice.

Too strong, his expression screams.

Everything about me has always been too much for him, too wrong.

Not good enough.

Too powerful, Lucifer whispers inside my head, encouraging me.

For a moment, I have to choke down the well of emotion his words release in me.

He's given me more confidence in myself than he could ever know. More than any human partner ever could.

But somehow, it still isn't enough.

No, not too powerful, I correct. *Not yet.*

Not until I conquer the last of the demons this monster's abuse created in me.

I want to watch him and all his followers burn.

I glance down at the dress I'm wearing and give a fake, watery smile. It's a modest look. Something I'd wear to any standard press conference or at Apollyon, Lucifer's luxury conglomerate, where I used to work.

Now I'm at Zest, the lifestyle brand Lucifer's sister, Greed, owns. I'm there—temporarily—while I start my own company. There's been a lot of change in my life recently, but that's one thing I've learned from all this.

Everything's temporary.

My life. My choices. Even my father's abuse.

And if Michael and Lilith have their way . . .

Humanity.

The very people I'm trying to save.

Not that they'll ever thank me.

"Why her? Was it because she's my friend? Why have you been so focused on me from the start? What's the Righteous's long game?" I demand, starting again, trying to infuse my voice with false confidence.

But my father has already sensed the crack in my armor, and like always, he aims to kill, the familiar derision in his eyes making me sick, even if he can only use words to hurt me. "'And I find something more bitter than death: the woman whose heart is snares and nets, and whose hands are fetters. He who pleases God escapes her, but the sinner is taken by her.'"

My body begins to shake.

I rear back my hand and slap him.

I've struck him before I've even chosen to do so, my palm glowing with the weight of my power and my rage as he laughs at me.

For all the disgust in my father's eyes, the disgust *I* feel is tenfold.

The way he looks at me, I might as well have paraded in here with Lucifer's cum dripping from my lips. It's not an unlikely scenario, really.

But my sperm donor's opinion doesn't matter, *shouldn't* matter.

And yet, all I can think, all I can hear and feel, is the hate in his tone, his amusement.

The way it rushes in my ears, mocking me.

The way it continues to rob me of my joy makes me question what I could ever do to be worthy of his love.

Every doubt. Every fear. Every anxiety.

Every feeling of worthlessness inside me belongs to him, to what he did to me.

That's what he and his God gifted me.

And for that, he deserves to be punished.

I'm not sure whether the thought comes from me or from Lucifer, but I . . . can't do it.

"I'm sorry," I whisper, my voice breaking.

Without warning, I tear from the room, not stopping even as I look over my shoulder and see Lucifer step forward, more than prepared to do this for me.

My vision blurs.

I sprint toward the stairs, no longer recognizing where I'm heading, until suddenly I connect with something solid—Azrael.

"Shhh. It's all right, little siren. I've got you."

I bury my face in his chest as Death holds me, unable to stop the painful sobs that rake through me uncontrollably, the sharp sound of my father's tortured screams ringing in my ears.

I can't bring myself to glance back to where I can feel him there, with Lucifer, the love of my life, for whom I'd do anything.

Azrael's grip on me tightens as I fall further apart.

No, the worst villains don't make us hate them. I encase myself in Death's arms, unable to listen to the sound of my father's screams.

They make us hate ourselves for how we can't help but love them.

CHAPTER THREE

Azrael

I return Charlotte to the penthouse a short while later, gently depositing her onto Lucifer's bed, where she clings to me. She stays like that for a long time, curled up beneath the sheets, crying, as I lazily stroke my fingers through her hair.

That monster she calls a father never deserved to die with any kind of dignity.

Unfortunately, the decision wasn't up to me.

I pull her closer, holding her head in my lap, and the crying eventually stops. I don't have any illusion that it's because the trauma she's relived has passed or because she's no longer raw from the feeling. I just don't think she has the energy to shed any more tears.

But then she does, and it guts me.

Like fucking magic.

I've seen plenty of humans cry before, but none whose emotions ever hurt me the way hers do. Like her pain's become a part of me.

No matter how I've tried to resist it.

I leave her sometime later, returning with a warm cup of tea. I press it into her upturned palms, where she now sits at the edge of the bed, staring out at the snow that falls idly over the city. But she doesn't look at me.

Fuck. Seeing that bastard didn't do her any damn good.

I feared as much.

When she finally manages to speak, her voice is barely above a whisper, laced with concern. "Do you think this time Lucifer will be able to—"

"We'll find her, Charlotte."

Her friend's safety is a constant weight on us all.

Me, most especially.

With the second seal now open, it won't be long until the next battle inevitably hits.

Michael needs us, even with one of Lucifer's siblings gone rogue.

And when he does, we'll be ready for him.

"He wasn't always like that, you know. My father, I mean."

I give a curt nod, not wanting to break the spell she and her warmth and the sight of the falling snow have cast over me.

In a few short weeks, she's grown more willing to confide in me than Lucifer ever could, and now there's a level of trust and intimacy between us that's so . . . unexplainable. She means more to me than I ever imagined possible.

I've always had a soft spot for beautiful broken things.

And I'd do pretty much anything if it would heal the pain she's feeling.

"When my mother was alive, he used to be kind, in between the . . ." Charlotte's voice trails off like she's caught in some distant memory.

The falling snow outside dampens the surrounding sounds of the city until the quiet is so penetrating, I'm certain we both feel it in our bones.

"Did you . . . ? Did you reap her?" she asks unexpectedly. "My mother?"

I tense.

I am Death. Both beginning and end.

But that doesn't mean I always want to be.

I swallow thickly. "I reap everyone, Charlotte."

"Even me?" She gives me a watery smile, like she's remembering when I first held her in Limbo.

Another tear slides down her cheek.

I brush it away almost instinctually before I can stop myself.

I've tried hard to keep my distance. To remember this is just supposed to be for our shared pleasure, even if I agreed to be the choice she needs. She belongs to Lucifer, and sooner or later she'll return to him. I swore to myself long ago I'd never put myself in that position again.

Where it felt as if my entire universe began and ended with one person.

Until the love I felt was used as a weapon against me.

I shake my head. "I hope not, little siren."

"Not now that I'm immortal, you mean?"

"Immortality is—"

"Just a different kind of fragility, I know." Charlotte lifts the mug of tea to her face, inhaling. "Now you sound like Lucifer."

I stiffen, the mention of my ex making me uneasy.

Lucifer and I have more shared history than Charlotte could ever know. Enough that I'm certain he could never truly love anybody, despite all appearances to the contrary.

On the surface, he and Charlotte are so fucking perfect that sometimes I can't help but fear what'll happen if we go where I know this feeling could lead.

The guilt is fucking eating me alive.

I didn't have any idea where this was headed when Lucifer offered his deal to me, the finer details of which Charlotte is still unaware.

I expected the shame, but I never expected the jealousy.

Toward him, the fucking bastard.

He has everything I want and more.

His heart. The one thing he always refused to give me.

And now . . .

The one woman I don't think I can bring myself to forget.

Charlotte wears her heart on her sleeve. All I'd have to do to make her mine would be to reach out and take it.

And yet . . . even *I* don't hate my ex that fucking badly.

My goal is to protect her from him. Nothing more.

But I can't seem to ignore the way she calls to me.

She's offered me more of her heart than that fucking narcissist I call my ex ever could.

I don't want to come between them, to be what ruins that, even if I have no doubt Lucifer will poison it eventually.

But I can't help but feel that if she's so perfect for him, that maybe she's also . . .

A little perfect for me.

Like he was, before he went and fucked up everything.

"Azrael, will you tell me what happened between the two of you?" Charlotte asks, like she can read the thoughts playing out on my face.

But I've never had my ex's way with words.

I cross the room toward the window. "It's a long story, little siren."

She's curious about us, but there's no use dredging up old history.

Lucifer and I are never going to be what we once were.

"I did reap her. Your mother," I say, returning to a subject that seems more manageable to me. "I remember every soul I've ever taken."

"All of them?" Her brows lift.

"Not their names, but their faces. I remember them all. She looked a lot like you."

An uncomfortable silence follows, and Charlotte glances at her hands before a fresh round of tears starts to quietly slide over her face.

"Fuck, I shouldn't have—"

"No. No, it's okay." She quickly swipes them away. "I asked you."

But her reassurance doesn't change what I'm feeling.

That's all I'll ever be to anyone. Even her, eventually.

The unknown they fear.

Charlotte takes a slow sip of her tea. "You know, when I was little, I used to wonder why she stayed with him and if that meant she didn't love me, but now that I'm older, I understand that"—she lets out a long sigh—"change isn't easy."

"Of course she loved you." My expression likely reveals more than I want it to. "But sometimes the people we love aren't capable of loving themselves enough to be what we need."

She looks toward me, and somehow, we both understand who I mean.

There's a strange bond that comes from loving the same man.

Even if mine and Lucifer's relationship ended differently.

Charlotte inhales, gripping her tea like it might lend her strength. "I'm trying to be different from her, trying not to fear change, to stand on my own two feet, but sometimes when I'm with Lucifer, I feel like I . . . disappear a little. Like I'm slipping into an old pattern that was never mine to begin with, and I worry that I'm . . ."

"Too much like her?" I finish.

She nods. "I've put that part of me on hold. The part that used to kneel for him without question. But I miss it. It isn't about power—it's about losing myself. I don't regret taking it off. But sometimes I wonder if I did it for the right reasons—or if I was just running. I need to know the answer to that, to who I am, before I can offer that again."

"You're so much stronger than you believe, little siren."

A blush burns through her cheeks.

"Azrael." She glances down at her hands. "Azrael, I'm . . . not sure I want to keep waiting to heal to allow myself to be happy."

I lift my scarred brow as something deep inside me stirs.

Old, eternal, unknowable.

Never-ending.

"You, me, Lucifer. The apocalypse, all of it. I . . ."

My chest tightens.

"Every day I wake up wondering if this is the day I snap, the day the pressure cracks me in two. And then I look around at the world, at how poorly humanity is steering itself, and it's just . . . There's so much pain, and I can't possibly prevent it all. I know I'm not helpless—not anymore—but it still feels like I'm drowning under it all because the whole world is counting on us, on *me,* to fix this, and sometimes it's all so much that I . . ." Her voice catches. "I can't . . . breathe." Her eyes glitter with unshed tears. "This pressure, it's . . ."

Killing me.

She doesn't need to say the words out loud for me to see it.

Everything she's carrying.

It's the weariness of people who see me as a welcome relief.

"You don't have to bear the weight of the whole world alone, little siren. Lucifer, he—"

"Azrael," she says, her expression pleading.

It's not Lucifer she wants right now.

It's *me.*

I swallow.

My ex has never been good at carrying anyone's pain but his own. At least, not until his Mother created the new immortal sitting in front of me. But even as . . . unexpected as he's been with her, I would never trust him to be there for her.

Not in the way she needs. In a way that lets her breathe.

Not without asking for anything in return.

So, what's stopping me?

"Azrael," she whispers again.

Like a siren, her voice calls to me.

And with those damn magic tears in her eyes, I'm suddenly as powerless as my ex is.

I'll be for her whatever he can't be.

I cross the room in two quick strides and crouch in front of her. I cup her face, and she leans into my hand, into me, her eyes fluttering closed like she's relaxing into the peace only I can bring her, until—*Fuck, baby girl, what are you doing to me?*—she looks a lot like she did the first time I held her.

My throat closes.

She opens her eyes, those long lashes flicking up to me. Her mouth parts on an intake of breath, and her gaze falls to my lips, my wings.

Unexpectedly, she reaches out. "May I?"

I give a quick nod.

But the moment I feel her touch there, I regret it instantly.

Something ignites in me, my whole existence on fire, and the growl that tears from my throat is inhuman. Something a lot like need, and dangerously close to—

I don't even allow myself to think it.

She's in love with my ex.

That much is obvious to me.

I start to pull back.

"Azrael." Her hand catches mine.

Like everything I'm feeling is being mirrored at me and more.

All our shared vulnerability reflected in her face.

Fuck, baby girl, I can't.

But then she brushes my wings again, and I . . . shiver. Fucking shiver.

I feel it all the way down to my cock, to the pull of my balls tightening, making my voice thick with need.

"What do you want, little siren?"

I asked her the same thing when she first looked to me in Lucifer's playroom.

This time, there's no hesitation when she answers me.

"Everything."

That single word heals some broken part of me.

"I want you to wreck me, Azrael. I want you to make me forget, long enough to remember who I am underneath."

I tug her closer, our foreheads pressing together as we share breath. "You and me both, sweet girl."

CHAPTER FOUR

Charlotte

The moment I confess to Azrael what I've been aching for, something inside me breaks. Like a dam. The rush of emotion pouring out makes me feel like I'm finally free.

From the weight of it all.

For the first time in weeks.

I need this, need him, more than my next breath. If I'm supposed to keep moving forward—keep fighting this apocalyptic nightmare we're trapped in—then I need to leave everything I was before behind.

The whole world is counting on me.

And tonight, I choose this.

I can't leave another second up to fate.

Slowly, Azrael cups the back of my head, his touch tentative but certain. "Are you sure, little siren?"

I give a quick nod.

We've been taking things slow, trying to see where this leads, but I'm finally prepared to plunge headfirst into the abyss with him.

Consequences be damned.

Fuck fate. Fuck my father. Fuck anyone else trying to make my choices for me.

I want this for myself, goddammit.

For the relief I know he's going to bring me. The way he doesn't ask me to be anything more than I am.

Azrael grounds me in the here and now. Reminds me of what it means to be human.

Even if that's not who I am any longer.

I glance down at my hands. "I've been afraid that if I let myself have you, I'd . . . really fall, and I wouldn't know how to stop."

Azrael inhales, his mouth parting, the longing in his eyes making something deep inside me ache.

The only thing that's been holding us back is fear.

Fear of what we both know this could be.

He traces his thumb over my cheek. "Do you know what it's taken for me to deny myself this? For me to stand at the edge of every moment, watching you with *him*, wishing I could be the one in his place?" He leans forward, his mouth hovering above mine as a soft, appreciative growl rumbles from his chest. "I won't be like him. I'm going to worship every breath you give me."

Death's mouth crashes into mine, and his touch is like a reckoning, a new beginning and an end all in one, his tongue sweeping over the inside of my mouth until . . .

All I can feel, all I can taste, is him.

Until nothing else matters to me.

"Fuck, you're perfect." He drags his lips down the curve of my jaw. "But we can't do this. Not here."

There's a sudden whoosh as Azrael's wings flap. He wraps them around us, and when they pull back, I'm lying on top of a stone sarcophagus under the cover of an old mausoleum.

A panoramic view of Manhattan glitters in the distance. I recognize this place from a tour Jax took me on when I first moved to the city. Greenwood Cemetery. In Brooklyn.

I should feel cold, especially with the Angel of Death standing over me like this, and maybe I would if I were still human, but now all I can feel as Azrael leans into me is the heat of him on my neck, my breasts, until . . .

"Why here?" I whisper, glancing at the snow-covered graves.

Azrael's expression is thoughtful, serene, even as his scarred brow furrows. "This place is beautiful to me," he answers, before . . .

One of his large hands falls to my breast, pinching my nipple, and I—

I practically come up off the tombstone as he rolls it between his fingers.

Thank God I didn't meet him until I was immortal.

With that deadly touch of his, I would have been a goner instantly.

Azrael's hands continue to explore, brushing, teasing, until I've long since forgotten all about the cold.

"Do you . . . want this because I'm made from Lucifer?" I pant, just as he starts to toy with my other breast.

Azrael pauses abruptly, those cool blue eyes capturing me from where he's now knelt between my legs, and the look he gives me is so intense, so transfixed, that breathing feels impossible.

The whole of Death's attention is on me.

"You're everything that's good in him and *more*, little siren. This isn't about him. This is about you and me." He peels down the front of my designer dress so I'm naked from the waist up, exposing my breasts to the cold night air, and my nipples start to—

"Fuck, baby girl, do you have any idea what you're doing to me?" Azrael licks his lips over one of my nipples, kissing me there.

The way he concentrates on me is so overwhelming—like I'm the most exquisite thing he's ever seen. It's almost . . . unnerving.

"Tell me."

His cool eyes darken as he strips off what remains of my clothes. The lust and hunger in his eyes heighten with each revealed inch of skin, until the need and adoration in his face are so . . . unguarded, I'm not sure it's something even Lucifer could ever give me.

One look and Death's cleaved me in two.

Whittled me down to the basest parts of myself.

With him I don't need to earn his affection. I can just simply be.

And he won't ask me to do anything to show I deserve it, because to him I . . .

I deserve it already.

"You unravel me, Charlotte." Azrael's voice is low and deep as he gently pushes against my stomach until I'm propped back on the grave on my elbows, my legs splayed open. "The Angel of Death brought to his knees by the curve of your mouth." He smears what's left of my lip gloss. "The sound of your voice." He strokes a hand over my cheek, and I lean into Death's touch eagerly.

"And the sounds you make." His large hands fall to my breasts again, and he cups them, testing the weight of them, before he rolls one of my nipples, and I arch into him, gasping. He growls in approval. "You make restraint a torment, little siren."

"So do you," I gasp, wishing he'd move closer to where I want him to be.

I'd give anything to have him inside me right now.

But Death won't be hurried.

"Now that I have you, I'm going to ruin you."

"Azrael," I pant.

He dips his head between my thighs and kisses me there, inhaling like he can't get enough of my scent as his mouth grazes over my—

"Fuck, you'll taste so good for me," he growls against my pussy.

I feel the vibration of it all the way down to my toes.

His praise is so delicious, so raw . . . it's almost embarrassing.

"Azrael." I grip the sides of the tomb, begging.

He chuckles again, that deep sound in his chest vibrating through me, but nothing I could ever say would make him hurry.

Death has been waiting for me for a long time.

And not even the devil could keep him from me.

He spreads my legs wide, my whole body growing impossibly hot, despite the falling snow, as he pushes two fingers inside me, sliding his fingers in and out as his thumb massages my clit. "I'll make you feel so good you don't know which way is up or down, baby girl. I'm going to pleasure you until you break apart, until I'm the only one who can put you back together again. I'll make you feel so certain, so sure of yourself, that even when you're with *him* you never have any doubt that you're worthy. Do you understand?"

He traces his large thumb up the seam of my pussy before he adds another finger, working it into me, until all I can hear is my own heartbeat, my own breath. "Will you let me?"

I'm no longer capable of speaking.

So much for Death not being much of a talker.

Clearly, he's been holding out on me.

"Yes."

The tension in the graveyard changes.

If I thought Death, of all immortals, was going to be soft with me, he proves me wrong. He stands, and there's a sudden shift in his posture, the cool blue of his eyes changing. The moonlight overhead disappears, the skeletal side of his face flashing, and then his power, that chilled feeling whenever he's near, seems to consume everything.

Even me.

Death's power is suffocating, dangerous.

Everything I need.

And I'm *his* to destroy this evening.

"Lie back," he commands, stripping off his leather jacket and his shirt, revealing those solid abs I've become so familiar with during training.

I want to run my tongue all over him.

Anywhere I can get my mouth, honestly.

He casts his clothes aside, the jacket's leather and the shirt's fabric passing through his wings easily. As if they aren't really there at all.

A ghostly illusion.

Though only a few moments ago I touched him there.

Caressed all those soft feathers as he shivered for me.

But now it's me who's shivering, trembling beneath his touch.

"May I?" I whisper, scooting to the tomb's edge. I gesture at his wings.

"They can be an erogenous zone." He smirks, nodding, and the moment my fingers connect with the downy black feathers, our shared groans echo throughout the graveyard.

Azrael's wings are the softest thing I've ever touched, but in the dark like this, the more I think about it, the more devastated it makes me feel for . . .

"Don't think about him. Look at me," he grumbles, his voice eerily similar to the one he uses when we're training. Like he just *expects* me to be a good girl and listen, without question. "When we're like this, Lucifer's no longer the only one you call sir, understand?"

Uncertainly, I glance up into his haunting gaze.

"Yes, sir." I lower my eyes, instantly prepared to behave for him.

He doesn't need to ask for it. I just know it's what he expects of me.

For me to behave like I'm already worthy.

"Good girl," he purrs.

A shiver of desire runs through me, my already swollen clit throbbing. "What's our safe word, sir?" I glance at the surrounding gravestones.

An eerie backdrop to the distant lights of the city.

Out of the corner of my eye, I see Azrael's slow grin turn wicked. "Look at you. You're already doing so well, being so mindful of your own safety, and I haven't even put you on your knees yet." His cool gaze rakes over me, making me impossibly hot even as I tremble from the fear and anticipation building in me. "But I'm going to." Death growls, his movements slow and predatory. "The safe word is *oblivion*. Tap my leg if you need to breathe."

I feel myself slicken.

Azrael's scarred brow quirks as he prowls around the sarcophagus. "You're already wet, aren't you?" His grin widens.

"No," I lie, glancing away.

He tsks at me. "This only works if you're honest, Charlotte," he warns, his hand suddenly brushing my throat.

A threat and also a . . .

A dark promise.

In my ear, he says, "Be a good girl for me."

I flush, my face filling with heat.

He's so quick with the praise that I don't even feel like he expects me to earn it.

He just wants to give it to me.

Make me feel good.

Even when I don't deserve it.

"All right," I admit reluctantly, my face even hotter than it was previously. "I am."

"Of course you are, baby girl. You'd never be anything other than honest with me, would you?"

My breath catches. "No, sir."

Azrael smiles. He's the one in control here and doesn't even need to punish me in order to get my submission. "Then lie back. Don't think," he orders, gripping my chin like he can already see the doubt rising in me. "Eyes on me, baby girl. Just let me make you feel good. Understood?"

"Yes, sir."

Azrael growls appreciatively. "Sweet girl."

I lie back and do as I'm told.

Fate and the apocalypse be damned.

I relax onto the cool marble stone as Azrael trails a hand over my belly.

"I'm sorry I made us—"

"Shhh. Hush." He reaches up, his muscled forearm flexing as he gently holds where my chin meets my throat. My heart and my pussy ache in tandem. He drags a rough thumb over the edge of my lip before his hand drifts back down again.

I'm so ready for him I'm throbbing.

"Don't you *ever* apologize to me for prioritizing your needs. Understand?" He pushes my legs farther open, hooking my knees over the solid width of his shoulders as he rubs his thumb up and down my center. I arch into him. He locates my clit easily, greedily massaging it with the slickness that now coats his fingers, before he slides them in and out of me.

Small touches meant to taunt and tease. A haunting prelude of what's to come.

But I want the whole dark ending.

"Azrael," I pant.

"Unh-uh, sweet girl." He makes another low sound, his grip on me tightening. "You will *not* rush me."

"Yes, sir," I whimper just as his inky black wings swing forward and those impossibly soft feathers start to brush over me. My breasts, my stomach, my shoulders, until . . .

He bends down to his boot and whips out one of the blades he carries, shoving the hilt up inside me despite that the sharp side is now . . .

"Azrael," I gasp.

Blood drips from his palm, but Death doesn't appear to care. He makes a low, pleasured sound deep in his throat, his head lolling back in enjoyment, before that same hand starts to . . .

"I like pain." He chuckles, the blade now tight in his hold, before the flesh on his fingers is just gone suddenly. "But since it concerns you . . ."

I stare down at that skeletal hand, each thrust of his knife making me wetter.

I throw back my head and cry out as Death slowly destroys me.

"That's my girl. You're so soaked for me." He cups my mons with his flesh-covered hand, his thumb probing me, even as the hilt of his sharp knife continues to—

"I love it when you shiver for me like that. Stop for a moment just so I can look at you, okay?"

"Okay," I rasp, my voice barely louder than a whisper.

It takes everything I have in me then, but somehow, I manage to go still beneath Death's gaze.

"Azrael," I beg a moment later, sounding even more needy.

All his praise and attention are like torture. Sweet, sweet torture.

So good, but also . . .

More than I can withstand comfortably.

"Ride it," he orders, his gaze flicking back to where his skeletal hand still holds that dangerously sharp knife. "Ride it like you would his cock."

I know without asking who he means. Lucifer.

I start to rock up and down, sliding over the blade's hilt, my thrusts growing slicker by the minute until I'm breathing heavy.

"You like that, don't you? When you're a little afraid of me? When you're turned on just enough it doesn't feel like danger?"

I nod, shivering.

"Fuck, Charlotte. You're perfect. So fucking beautiful. Did you know that?" He works one of his skeletal fingers up inside me along with the hilt.

And I practically come up off the tomb from how its ridges make me clench.

Azrael's touch redefines what pleasure is.

The thrill of danger.

And for a moment, I struggle to think straight as he waits for me to answer him.

I want so badly to say yes, to be the confident woman he's encouraging me to be, but some deep, insecure part of me can't help but be one hundred percent truthful when I'm pinned beneath Death's gaze.

Those cold blue eyes really do lay me bare.

"Sometimes," I whisper, like if I say it softly enough, maybe he'll take pity on me.

He tsks, shaking his head like that disappoints him, and the way that singular sound haunts me is somehow a thousand times worse than any punishment I've ever endured from Lucifer. I never want to disappoint Death ever again.

I'll be a good girl, the *only* good girl he ever needs.

"Don't worry, sweet girl. We're going to fix that," Azrael whispers, the gravel of his voice soothing me. He dips another one of his bony fingers inside me, rocking the blade hilt back and forth, as he finds that exact spot like he . . .

Like he's been watching me and Lucifer when we—

I cry out, nearly losing it.

"Fuck, are you going to squirt for me?" Death chuckles, the sound sending a shiver down my spine.

"Azrael, I . . ."

I don't even *know* what I need.

I can't make sense of up or down. What words mean.

Azrael's touch is unraveling me.

Like he's pulling my soul apart, even as he puts me back together.

I pant as he removes the blade, dropping it to the ground with a hollow clatter, the flesh of his hand returning with a flick of his wrist as that skeletal face of his flashes.

His flesh is like a mask he wears that reminds me of who he is—*what* he is.

"You like that too, don't you? My real face? The way I scare you?"

Breathless, I pant, "Yes."

He circles his thumb over my clit as I remember at the last second to tack on his address so I don't disappoint him again.

"Yes, *sir*," I correct myself.

I stare up at him, eyes pleading.

Death's grin is slow and deliberate. A little like someone *else* I know. "We have all the time in the world, Charlotte." To prove his point, he gestures at the darkened graveyard and snaps his fingers.

He's frozen time.

My eyes widen.

He's frozen time for *me*.

The snowflakes that were falling only a moment ago hang suspended in midair, trembling at the command of the ancient primordial in front of me.

Just like I am.

"I promised I was going to savor you, and I keep my word, understand?"

I nod, my chest rising and falling in slow, fearful pants.

Just *being* with Azrael is a kind of breath play.

"Good girl," he purrs again, lowering his mouth to me. "You're such a good, good girl for me, aren't you, little siren? So perfect. Look at you, all wet and needy for me. But you can also be a rotten little slut, can't you?"

Abruptly, he yanks my ass over the edge of the grave, so that I'm suspended, held upright only by his skeletal hands. Death buries his face in my cunt. "Now cum all over my face like I've watched you do for your *other* daddy."

CHAPTER FIVE

Charlotte

"Azrael. Azrael, if you don't stop, I might . . ."

"You won't die, little siren. Trust me."

With how many times he's devoured me, nearly driven me to madness, only to cruelly rip my pleasure away again, I'm not certain I believe him.

I'm so wrung out I can barely hold myself upright. He lies on the crypt's stone floor beneath me, bearing the whole of my weight on his face, after he dragged me down from where I was hovering over him and ordered me to "fucking sit on it already."

"You'll taste even better once I've got you bucking on my—"

"I want that," I gasp. "I want it a thousand times, sir."

"A thousand?" He chuckles, the sound vibrating through me. "Then breathe for me, sweet girl."

I inhale, sharp and fast, and the next thing I know, the hot weight of Azrael's mouth is on me again. He laps and tastes my pussy, until I'm grateful he told me to breathe and that for once in my life I actually listened. If I thought Death stole my breath away whenever he looked at me, it's nothing compared to how he tongue-fucks me when I sit on his face.

The way he indulges in me is unhurried.

A soul-shattering pleasure so intense I'm not sure I can survive it.

Azrael enjoys me like he's got all the time in the freaking world, and he does—if the still unmoving snow is any indication.

Death's in no rush to end my pleasure.

He's going to take his sweet, torturous time.

His fingers dig into my hips, my ass, his tongue stroking over me in long, lingering laps, licks that cover the whole of my pussy until I'm coming apart.

Good God, *how* did I not realize his tongue is that freaking wide until now?

I fall forward, gripping hold of the tomb's edges, shuddering and shaking, as I drop my head and moan again. The noises he's managed to coax from me in a single evening are sounds that I didn't even know I could make.

"You taste incredible." His chest rumbles. He would happily drown in me.

I'm coming apart at the edges so hard I'm practically unraveling.

Azrael's touch breaks me down to the fiber of my being.

Until there's nothing left.

His grip tightens, his bony fingers digging into my skin in a bruising grip so that I'm forced to stay in place as I start to buck like I can somehow manage to escape.

It's too much. It's all *too* much.

"Azrael!"

"You can take it, sweet girl," he growls, dragging me back down.

I can't possibly survive this.

He hooks one of his big hands over my hip and yanks me even closer, shoving his fingers up into me and hitting that spot that I like as he drowns himself in me.

Death feasts on my pussy like he's a starving man falling upon the altar of the gods.

Worships me with his tongue.

And I lose myself completely.

He bites and licks and nips as I buck and scream and beg for his mercy, all the times he's brought me so close compounding until I'm shattered. So broken apart from the pleasure that if I were human, I'm pretty sure I'd just peacefully die here.

Wrapped up in Death's arms.

I lose track of my own thoughts after that. All I'm capable of doing is existing. Living for the moments in between the laps of pleasure until I'm both everything and nothing all at once.

My sense of self ceases to exist.

Eventually, he rolls me onto my belly, lifting me on top of the stone sarcophagus again, and some distant, still conscious part of me starts to think that maybe this divine torture really *is* never-ending. Maybe this is how it'll all be over—I can't think of a more perfect way to go, honestly—but then he suddenly releases me, and I'm vaguely aware of the metallic sound of his belt buckle before he—

Oh fuck.

The lash across my ass comes hard and fast, pulling me back down into my body.

"Goddamn it, Charlotte. Breathe."

I suck in a harsh breath.

Azrael snarls, rolling me onto my back as I cough, my lungs burning. "I can't allow you to lose yourself in me like that for long. Understand?" he growls, gripping my face once I'm inhaling steadily again.

I nod, still delirious, my eyes watering as I gaze up at him.

And the weight of who he is, of *what* he is, truly hits me.

Azrael is dangerous.

Very, very dangerous.

He pulls me into his arms, lifting me and dropping us both back onto the ground so that we're slumped against the tomb. I straddle him and our eyes meet.

The hunger and total devotion I see there is everything I've been missing and more.

Like I'm valued. Like I'm worthy. Without expectation.

For the first time in the whole of my existence, with Azrael, I can just be.

Fade into nothingness.

One touch and it would all be over for me.

He tongues his chin clean, where his face is now drenched from me.

Before I can anticipate what he's about to do, he throws me over his shoulder, carrying me down the mausoleum's few steps and depositing me onto a patch of frozen grass before he drops his pants. He throws our shared weight about like it's next to nothing to him, and I can't help but laugh at how he lunges at me, settling all that solid weight on top of me like he's been starved of touch for centuries.

When we finally still, I'm smiling, my limbs loose and trembling.

The massive length of his cock juts between us. In the moonlight, a bead of precum glistens at the tip, and my mouth waters as I realize—

Holy shit.

Death's cock is as big and wide as the rest of him.

"You can take it." A slow, smug grin stretches across his mouth, and I relax against him before he rolls us. I let out a startled eep as he leans against a gravestone and positions me on top so that he's pressed outside me. He wraps his dark wings around us, some of his long undercut hair falling into his face as he shields us from the wind, until it feels like we're the only two people in the world. Him and me.

Death and the one who got away.

Slowly, he pushes into me, and my mouth pops open.

Holy fuck, he's going to ruin me.

"I want to watch you take it," he growls.

"Of course you do, you freaking stalker," I tease, my words breathy. I nudge at his chest, playfully glancing down to where we're joined, but only so he doesn't see the emotions I'm feeling.

Azrael captures my chin in his hand, forcing me to look at him, staring straight into my soul.

Too late.

He's so solid and sure.

Like the ground beneath me.

Like if I let him, he'd be my anchor, the one thing that keeps my soul from drifting, even when everything else feels unsteady.

Even as someone *else's* love untethers me from his earth.

Lifts me higher than I ever knew was possible.

Death chuckles, smacking me on the ass so hard I yelp, teetering forward and giving him just enough purchase on my hips so he can settle me onto his—

Holy shit.

It burns so sweet.

"Fuck, I love watching you," he groans as he rocks slowly. A rush of heat slickens me as he works farther in, the words steeped in a deeper meaning that feels almost . . . terrifying.

My eyes dart to his.

I can't hide what I'm feeling any longer, because I know that he feels it too.

That spark between us is doing more than flickering.

It's been growing stronger every night.

Every moment he watches over me.

I lean forward and kiss him again, trying to infuse everything I want to say into the meaning.

I want you.

And also, I . . .

Think I might be falling for you.

But I'm terrified of what that might mean.

Azrael holds me, gripping the sides of my face like I'm his everything, his whole freaking universe, as he pushes deeper into me, until he sinks all the way in, until I'm so full of him I'm practically bursting.

Like we could breathe that shared spark between us into life together.

Like he'd let me.

Eventually, my muscles relax, the feeling transitioning from a slight burn to a throbbing ache until I'm so hot, so slick as he stretches me that I feel like I might break again.

In an entirely different way.

"You take me so well, little siren. You're perfect for me."

And it's true.

We *are* perfect for one another, except . . .

There's also someone *else* who's just as perfect for me.

Someone who's my whole eternity.

The fallen angel who's my destiny.

The one I promised I would come back to, to submit myself to, completely.

And I still want that. More than anything.

But how can I ever keep that promise when now I can't imagine living without the immortal beside me?

"Azrael."

"I know. You don't need to say anything." He cups my cheek.

He rocks into me, entering and withdrawing inch by inch until I feel so torn between the impossible choice that's been given to me that there are tears leaking out of my eyes.

Azrael moves slow and steady as he holds me, and yet somehow he still manages to swipe my tears away. "Shhh, it's okay, baby girl. I've got you. Let it all go."

And I do.

I come apart in Death's arms.

He guides my hips up and down, sliding into me over and over, making us both feel so full, so perfect and raw, I'm overwhelmed with the feeling.

The pressure inside me builds, a sweet, chilling ache, until I can see the whole of my path forward, of God's plan for me, and all the emotions I've been holding back burst out of me.

The old me dies on a wave of pleasure that feels never-ending.

Azrael curses, but he doesn't do anything to stop all the light and shadow that pours from my body unobstructed. Instead, he simply follows along after me, thrusting hard a few times more as he groans my name, grounding me to the earth as the thick width of his cock coats my insides in warm, heady spurts and a trail of flickering spots lines my vision.

We're nothing but stardust, he and I.

Teetering beyond infinity.

Into oblivion.

"Charlotte," he moans.

I suck in a harsh breath, the sweet pain of my lungs causing me to cry out as I combust.

But Azrael's right there with me.

He always has been. Right from the very start.

Even if I didn't recognize it until recently.

He gathers me in his arms as I collapse against him, a constant string of sweet nothings and pleasure-groaned curses falling from his lips that I don't comprehend completely as I realize I don't think I've *ever* heard Death talk this much before.

The thought is so silly I start to laugh, the joy I feel bubbling up inside me. He rolls us over so we're lying in the grass side by side, sweaty and panting, pulling me into him, and we both fall headfirst into the abyss together so easily that it feels like every choice was always supposed to lead to this. I feel it in every touch, every sweet and gentle word he whispers to me.

I'm in love with the Angel of Death *and* the devil.

Because for some love stories, death isn't the end.

It's just the beginning.

CHAPTER SIX

Lucifer

There are some monsters in Hell even *I* refuse to claim.

By the time I'm finally finished with Charlotte's father, he's nothing more than a splash of crimson viscera strewn across the meat locker's floor along with several leftover leaking syringes of drain cleaner I forcibly injected into his urethra.

Honestly, the experiment didn't yield the exact result I'd hoped for.

Though it won't be long before he recalibrates, and we'll be at this bloody ruse again.

I've met demons with more goddamn compassion than that insignificant, self-righteous prick, and after several weeks without answers, torturing him for the whereabouts of Charlotte's friend along with the finer details of the little deal the leadership of his human hate group made with my brother, Michael, grows tiresome for me.

I fucking detest hypocrites.

I make it a point to torture them personally.

Sometime later, when I've collected enough of my power to manage to snap myself topside—one of the few divine abilities of which I'm still capable—I find myself standing in the Church of the Holy Sepulchre, on the outskirts of Jerusalem, my stationed legions already standing sentry outside the door for me.

Holy pilgrimage sites haven't exactly been the most popular of human tourist destinations as of late. Not now that the entire world has become my family's angelic war zone, my blasted brother and all his ilk have gone and made themselves known, and humanity has spiraled into panic about whether or not the world is ending courtesy of Charlotte's little livestream. Humanity is terrified of what they do not know.

And they do not know plenty.

Their ignorance is all they have left.

I wander through the sanctuary only long enough to locate my sister.

The church, for all that it's worth, smells faintly of blood and incense, the combination of which isn't a particular shock to me. Jerusalem never changes—even now that the world is under my command. The only thing that does change is the sins humanity chooses to bring to it.

Holy ground makes liars of the lot of us.

I find Seraph waiting for me beside the Altar of the Crucifixion, her dual sets of feathered wings stretching. She leans in close to one of the golden effigies intended to be Christ—positioned over the rock of Calvary, which lines the supposed spot of his crucifixion—before she pokes the statue in the eye suspiciously, as if she suspects it might start blinking.

The church always did love their idolatrous figures.

"You're late," she says without looking at me.

"I had to stop for a change of clothes, I'm afraid." I smooth a deft hand down the front of my suit as she steps down from the rock's casing.

"I shouldn't be able to sense you without your powers, but yet it seems you still know how to command a room."

I place my hands inside my pockets. "Are you flattering me, sister?"

"You're incorrigible."

I smirk. "Well don't stop now on *my* account."

She rolls her eyes.

I pull a cigarette from my suit coat pocket—despite Charlotte's continued insistence that I should quit whenever I'm topside—and light it upon a nearby votive candle. "So, which one of them was it this time, hmm? Which one of our sinful siblings opened the second seal before I gave the ready?"

"I'm not certain." Seraph casts me a concerned look. "Michael took the meeting alone."

Which means my brother already suspects we're up to something.

Even a broken archangel is right twice a day, apparently.

With Michael so dutifully working to bring about our Father's apocalypse in hopes of Father returning home, the Righteous actively campaigning against me, and our blasted Mother seeking to regain her full power by unleashing all four Horsemen—coupled with the *obviously questionable* loyalty of my siblings—it's only a matter of time before more of my Father's seals are opened. We cannot stop them. Not without my powers. Not indefinitely.

So why not use opening the seals to our advantage?

"That doesn't change anything." I flick my ashes.

"No," Seraph agrees.

Though Michael's suspicion will make mine and Seraph's task all the more precarious.

But what's a little backstabbing between siblings?

"I did what you asked. Found what you need." Seraph produces an unfamiliar scroll from the ether and unfurls it, holding it out for me.

I scan over the glowing Angelic inscription quickly.

"Resurrecting the nun will work to restore your powers, but there's a . . . few complications," she says, confirming what I already suspected.

I lift an amused brow.

"Father's scriptures are clear. To raise someone from the dead, you'd need a prophet, and a powerful one at that. One of Father's, ideally."

"Like Charlotte's friend, you mean?"

She nods.

No wonder my blasted Mother went and absconded with her.

Thwarting me is quickly becoming one of my family's favorite pastimes.

"Or?" I prompt, sensing there is yet another option Seraph hasn't revealed to me.

There is *always* another option.

My sister snuffs out one of the altar's candles with her fingers, watching the flame die. "Or you could earn Father's redemption again. Whichever comes first."

I scoff. "That'll be the day." I start down the stairs toward the rotunda, casting my cigarette onto the marble flooring.

"Will it? Will it, Lucifer? Is it so far-fetched?"

I don't answer her.

She grabs hold of my shoulder just as we reach the Stone of the Anointing, and I round on her, knocking her hand askance, harder than I intend to.

"I am irredeemable! Don't you understand?"

The confession falls into the silence between us, heavy with self-loathing.

My hands clench into fists at my sides, fingernails digging into my palms, but I am unable to bring myself to look at her.

Slowly, I unclench them, my breathing hard.

"I was cast out for a reason." My fingers dig into my chest, where the remnants of my sigil used to be. "I asked for His forgiveness before I opened the first seal, and look where it got me." I let out a bitter huff, sneering. "I'm no longer interested in your preaching."

"Lucifer," she pleads. "You were already given it once. Is it so impossible to assume that you might be able to earn it again?"

I wave a dismissive hand.

"Or if not that, then all you'd have to do to reclaim it would be—"

"No," I snarl, turning so fast I might as well still be immortal. The look I give her is one full of incredulity. "No, that is *not* an option."

I refuse to place Charlotte at risk again.

Not even for my own gain.

The consequences of gifting my Father's redemption to her were beyond my control, but I'll be damned if I ever ask her to be—

"She'd give herself up for you willingly. You know that."

"And for what? For her to bloody die again?" I throw up my hands. "For fuck's sake, Seraph."

"If she knew that was the only thing standing between her and saving humanity, would you let her?"

We both fall silent for a beat.

"I would *never* even consider letting her—"

"But it's not about her, is it, Lucifer?" Seraph steps forward. "This is about you. About the fact that you refuse to—"

"I will *not* lose her again. Do you understand me?" I snarl. The words settle into the tarnished sanctuary between us.

But Seraph doesn't look away. "No matter how many innocents die. No matter how—"

"Does Michael know?"

"No. No, he doesn't. If he did, he wouldn't touch her."

I swear under my breath. "I would never allow her to sacrifice herself for my—"

"Well, maybe you should," Seraph challenges, planting her feet. "Maybe you *should* be asking quite a lot more of her, Lucy."

The way she says the old nickname, the one Michael gave me all those eons ago, is different from how any of the others say it.

More compassionate, more affectionate than anything, but still, it infuriates me.

"If you have something to say about my future bride, sister, say it," I growl. "Preferably *before* the wedding."

If I have my way, Charlotte and I will be married before the year's end, despite whatever temporary dallying she and Azrael may be doing.

I'd sooner allow the whole of humanity to fall and my brother—or even my goddamn Mother, or my traitorous ex, for that matter—to come out on top of this apocalypse charade before I ever dared ask her to . . .

No.

I shake my head.

No. Not for me.

And definitely *not* for humanity.

I am not above strategic loss when it suits me, but I will not allow Charlotte's life to be put at even greater risk than it already is.

No matter what monster that might make me.

Seraph's expression grows cold.

"If there's something *else* you feel you ought to say, sister, then say it."

I easily read the furious gleam in her eye.

She's concerned for me.

Nothing more. Nothing less.

Back when I was the leader of my Father's armies, His most devout creature, Seraph was almost a . . . friend to me.

Before my rebellion against Father went unexpectedly sideways, and then falling for someone went and fucked everything.

Charlotte and I have more than a bit in common, I'm afraid.

Seraph shakes her head, stealing a look at our family's old relics that are now divided in the church's exhibit amongst the Syrians, the Armenians, and the Greeks. "With the second seal open, the others grow restless, and it won't be long before Michael decides to—"

"Whatever our brother has up his sleeve, this time, I'll be ready for him."

I will crush Michael like the insufferable brat he is.

And my Mother, well . . .

There will be some harsh boundary setting, considering Charlotte has already gone and stymied my greatest bargaining chip.

Making promises about our hypothetical children to a goddess was foolish, reckless at best, especially since she and I might not even be able to . . .

I drop my chin, looking away momentarily.

There are still parts of my life she couldn't possibly begin to understand.

How could she when I have not told her?

"I wouldn't underestimate Michael." Seraph glances toward a flickering mosaic candle that illuminates the fading frescoes with an almost divine fatigue. "He intends to strike where it hurts. She's a wild card he didn't account for."

"If he so much as lays a finger upon her, I will—"

"Not *him*. Not directly." Seraph shakes her head. "The trials, to open the seals, he—"

A shout sounds from just outside the sanctuary, signaling a struggle between my demons and whoever it is currently searching for me. The Righteous and their ever-growing network of followers, or Michael, or my Mother.

Take your bloody pick.

Everyone and their brother wants a piece of me.

Now that word of our Father's impending apocalypse has gotten out and humanity's reign has fallen, *I* am divine enemy number one.

Even my brother's angelic soldiers are searching for me. Including the one at my side.

Though she won't be the last to join us.

Not if I have a say in anything.

"There's something else I need to tell you," Seraph whispers, pulling me into the nearest passageway just as gunfire echoes outside the church's door. "The lance . . ."

I roll my eyes. "We've been through this, Seraph. Without my powers, there's no chance of my reclaiming it from Michael, and I—"

"You really think that it was put into play by *accident*?"

The question stops me in my tracks.

I thought I knew the whole of the game, had mapped out every eventuality, but that is one angle I hadn't quite considered.

"Tell me," I growl, fury starting to rise in my chest as my mind begins to connect the dots, the patterns—who had the motive, the power, the means.

And the desire to see me bleed.

Seraph flinches, looking away.

The sight of my true face still occasionally disgusts her.

"I think you know."

I give a curt nod, and then Seraph utters the name of the one and only celestial, aside from my future bride, who could ever truly manage to hurt me.

"Azrael."

My expression goes cold.

And to my shock, I find I am still capable of being surprised.

And betrayed, for that matter.

"This isn't the first time he's gambled with something that wasn't his to risk. He always did know how to ruin things before they became beautiful." I huff, betraying nothing, as I turn away from my sister. "If she bleeds for his mistakes, I swear—"

"You'll do what, Lucifer? *Kill* Death?"

The look I give her is one of cold fury.

"I will remind him that he's not the *only* immortal capable of ending worlds." I remove my wallet from my back pocket, pulling out a five-hundred-dollar bill and waving it before I drop it onto an offering plate. "Your devotion won't be forgotten, sister."

Seraph scoffs. "Not everything holy is a transaction, you know." She shakes her head, flapping her wings, and then she's gone.

Leaving me all of two seconds before the Righteous's soldiers burst in.

Gunfire rings throughout the church as Jerusalem devolves into chaos, signaling that the end must truly be near.

Just as the door to the main entrance ruptures, I snap my fingers, sending myself careening down into my realm, where they are unable to chase me.

I'm safely ensconced inside my throne room before they can even begin to scour the church for me.

I drop onto my throne, allowing myself a much-needed moment to think.

My former lover is playing a game.

And the only question is whether my future bride is the prize, or the pawn he intends to use against me.

CHAPTER SEVEN

Azrael

I watch Charlotte's slowed breath drift up into the cool morning air beside me as she sleeps—and meanwhile across the ocean, I kneel in a darkened street, rain soaking through my leather coat as I cradle a boy whose chest slows after a car just hit him.

His blood is warm on my hands.

Here, she sighs. There, he cries softly, cowering at the sight of me.

I'm here. I am not.

I am both. Always.

A being whose loyalty is divided.

I guide the child into the dark, into the Nothing, the space that's both separate from and a part of me as another version of me whispers to a man under a collapsed bit of rubble.

I can feel him—and the others—off in the distance, tugging at another thread. But we don't compete.

And I won't be sparing them like I did her.

I take Charlotte's hand as I whisper in their ears.

I am everywhere.

Until a sudden blip in my attention grabs me.

I narrow my focus, scanning the dimension before me. I've been searching for Charlotte's friend for weeks. Trying to undo all the damage

I caused the moment I chose to heed God's word and put the blade into play and violently reinsert myself into her and my ex's life again.

It may not be my fault that Lucifer's Mother chose to abduct her.

Or that she chose to target Charlotte's Seer friend.

But it *is* my fault that Lilith and Michael were able to make their trade so easily.

The one that ended with Michael in possession of the spear, the Holy Lance, the one that can end any battle. Or the life of the new celestial beside me.

And the thought that Michael may intend to use the blade to hurt Charlotte . . .

Well, that's far from the worst of my sins.

My attention falls to the sudden ripple I feel in the Nothing, the dreamlike realm that exists on another dimension, another plane, one beyond what humanity's capable of comprehending.

Through the haze, I can see her there. Charlotte's friend. God's prophet.

But the haze of Lilith's power obscures her from me.

I fucking hate goddesses.

And Lilith has never exactly been a fan of me.

She's hated me since long before Lucifer and I ever became anything.

Despite any deals she and I might have made before . . .

I draw closer, in whatever way that means when I'm not corporeal. It's somewhere dark, but wherever she's located, the light that surrounds her does little to illuminate her to me. Human geography has never been of much importance, if you ask me. It's shifting. Ever changing. A lot like the dream Charlotte's friend appears to be caught in.

A nightmare of Lilith's making.

As for me, I've always preferred the dark.

The mortal ends are less tricky then.

"I know you're there, Azrael." Lilith's chaotic gaze shifts about the space, her voice far too pleased, but she hasn't been able to pin me down just yet.

Meanwhile, I search for some sign, some indication, of where this place may be, earthly or otherwise.

Charlotte's friend stirs, and the chains around her ankles rattle.

From the looks of it, Lilith hasn't been doing a very good job of remembering to feed her.

Humanity's need to eat, drink, and piss with any regularity is a foreign concept to most celestials. They don't spend as much time among humans as I do.

"Why not show yourself?" Lilith's head whips in my direction as she grins wickedly.

She may be the embodiment of all chaos, the divine spark that created everything, but there's little about Lilith that's truly motherly. Not in the way God's children ever deserved.

The prophet stirs again, her eyelids flickering, and she lets out a weak groan as she starts to wake, but it's enough to momentarily distract Lilith.

That's all the hesitation I need.

I start to pull back, enough to get a glimpse of the building's basic structure, but then—

"Please. Please take me," her friend begs. Like she, too, can sense me.

Like they can only do when the end is near.

Lilith touches the Seer's forehead again, and the prophet cries out in pain, Lilith's touch launching her into yet another endless nightmare.

An infinite, dreamless sleep that will never end.

Not unless we—

"Azrael."

Charlotte's soft voice sounds from beside me, pulling me out of my trance.

It . . . calls to me.

Like humanity's myths of old, it makes me remember myself.

Just as Lilith's attention shifts back to me and she begins to summon some of her divine power into her palms.

Shit.

Not even I can war with a goddess.

"Shhh, I've got you, little siren," I whisper, sitting down on the bed beside her as my focus comes back onto her completely, and she settles down into sleep. "I've got you."

For as long as she'll have me.

Until she learns what it means to love the end of all things.

CHAPTER EIGHT

Charlotte

I wake to the smell of fresh coffee from my automated espresso machine, Azrael's large body wrapped around me, so when I roll out of bed, I'm still half asleep. Considering I'm naked and Manhattan is freezing this time of year, I bundle myself in the blanket I was sleeping in and pad toward the kitchen.

The sun hasn't begun to seep in through the windows overlooking the West Village, the clean lines, warm wood, and curated fixtures barely illuminated, and the townhouse is so quiet, so still, that I expect to be alone, but when I round the corner, I turn only to find—

"Lucifer." I blink, suddenly wide awake.

He sits at my new granite countertop on one of the refurbished barstools, one of several I bought a few weeks back when I went shopping with Azmodeus—my new, self-declared "replacement bestie"—as part of a work outing. When I'd somehow gotten the crazy idea I might be into antiquing.

That didn't exactly pan out.

Saving humanity from apocalyptic doom is a full-time job, apparently.

On top of the other side hustles I'm already working.

My eyes dart between him and the bedroom, where Azrael is still.

Lucifer sips the coffee he's holding as he nudges another cup toward me. He rakes in the sight of my mussed hair, flushed skin, and smeared makeup in a single look, a slow, devilish smirk spreading across his features. "Morning, love."

"Morning," I squeak, glancing toward the stairs as if he might be imagining exactly how Azrael and I—

Oh, he's definitely imagining it all right.

He's imagining it in *explicit* detail.

If that flicker of hellfire in his eyes is any indication.

"You weren't in the training room this morning," he comments, not revealing a damn thing about what he thinks of this particular turn of events.

My future husband knows how to play his cards close.

He takes another slow sip.

"No," I agree unhelpfully.

Probably because my trainer was already here. Inside me.

My face flames with heat.

"I just . . . didn't feel like training." I shrug.

Lucifer's devious grin falters. "Are you lying to me, Charlotte?" he asks, his expression suddenly cold.

Oh no.

No, no, no, no, no.

"No, sir. I just—"

"Sir?" He lifts a single brow, clearly toying with me. "I thought you were no longer calling me that."

I gape at him. "I'm not. It's just . . ."

"Had a change of heart?" Lucifer stands, abandoning his coffee on the counter as he stalks toward me. "No one would blame you."

He crowds my space, his gaze never leaving mine, and I'm so awestruck by the hungry way he's looking at me I'm almost incapable of moving.

Slowly, he begins to unwrap the blanket from around my nude body, until I'm so drunk on the familiarity of his touch, the dark promise of the temptation of what I know could come, that all the resistance I've been giving him melts out of me.

One time couldn't hurt, could it?

He tucks a stray strand of hair behind my ear, the warmth of his skin brushing against my cheek. "Perhaps you need a reminder of who you belong to? Just a taste to take off the edge." The hellfire in his eyes flares as he leans down, his mouth trailing across my jaw like a sinful vow, until he's whispering in the shell of my ear like he did to Eve. "Just say the word, little dove, and you're *mine* again."

"I—"

"Hnnn," Azrael growls, suddenly prowling into the room, all snarling savagery.

Death's dark tattoos and raw muscle are on full display, and with his undercut hair down like that, it's reminding me of how we—

A small, helpless noise escapes me.

He pulls a hair tie off his wrist and quickly uses it to put it up in his signature man bun before he roughly tugs me toward him, his eyes never leaving Lucifer's. He lays a possessive kiss on my neck, inhaling the scent of me.

Lucifer's smirk takes on a dangerous edge.

I'm torn between whether the fiery gleam in his eye is because he's enjoying this or because he's imagining all the ways he eventually wants to punish me.

Once he gets me alone in the playroom, that is.

And he will, and soon.

Especially if he keeps looking at me like that.

I awkwardly clear my throat, not knowing what to expect from this encounter, just as Azrael chooses to release me. My face is practically on fire, my guilt searing, and that nasty little voice inside my head starts hissing insults, just as my stomach decides that *now* is the perfect time to begin its usual round of prework anxiety.

I try to figure out what I was supposed to be doing.

Lucifer looks pointedly at the coffee he brought for me, shaking his head like both of our lives and this whole apocalypse situation would be so much easier if I'd just stop overthinking and submit myself to him again. His gaze flicks to Azrael, and he lifts a brow as if to say, *Told you it'd be worth the wait.*

He is not making this easy.

But when has he ever?

"I need to pee," I announce, darting toward the bathroom.

Once inside, I turn on the faucet to drown out the noise. I spend the next several minutes making a sacrifice for my poor life choices to the god of the porcelain bowl.

When I'm done emptying my stomach's contents, I wipe my mouth on the back of my hand, taking slow, steady breaths in and out through my nose like my therapist taught me. Her voice comes to mind easily.

Note five things you notice around the room.

My eyes dart over the bathroom tile.

My makeup bag. My eyelash curler. The face cream that costs more than a Birkin that Sophie insisted I bring with me now that I'm no longer living at the penthouse.

And the plastic CVS bag on the counter that contains a . . .

I splash some of the running water on my face and turn off the faucet before I return to the kitchen.

Lucifer and Azrael are still there, except instead of one, there's now *two* hot beverages on the counter waiting for me—the premium Arabica Lucifer brought that's probably been flown in from some old, ailing artisan in South America who's been crafting this brand of bean for the last six generations, and a steaming cup of my favorite herbal tea blend that Azrael made me.

An impossible decision.

I hesitate before I finally snatch up the coffee, only because that's the smell that does the least amount of damage to my insides this morning.

Lucifer smiles triumphantly as Azrael grunts, turning away.

"So, what brings you by this morning, Lucifer?" I lift the coffee to my face, trying my best to lighten the mood.

The warmth permeates through me.

Lucifer repositions himself on a barstool, and the next thing I know, he's hauled me into his lap, just as Azrael grumbles something about making his own damn coffee.

Lucifer's hands curl around my waist, and he captures my mouth in such an intense and bruising kiss that by the time he releases me, I've forgotten all about my drink.

"I'm not allowed to pop by and escort my future bride to work now, am I?" He nips at my lip with his fangs playfully.

"Of course you are, it's just—"

My gaze darts over to Azrael.

"It's *my* morning," he growls.

The temperature in the room goes cold.

"Be that as it may . . ." Lucifer's grip on my ass tightens to the point of near pain. "Considering you absconded with her last night and interrupted this morning's training schedule, a trade-off would only be fair."

"Or, you know, maybe you could just share me?"

The words cut through the room like another apocalyptic seal opening.

Dangerous. Volatile. Destructive.

Off-limits.

"Or not." I lower my head as they both return to what they were doing.

"Actually, little dove, I came here to steal you away under false pretenses, I'm afraid."

Lucifer recounts what he learned from Seraph, his angelic informant, this morning.

My spine runs cold. "So, if Michael suspects, what does that mean?"

"There's a possibility he could alter the seals to pose a mortal threat to you." Lucifer casts a grim glance toward Azrael.

I shake my head. "But I'm immortal now. It's not like I can . . ."

"It's not that simple, darling."

With the Righteous openly campaigning against me and Lucifer, the media backlash about my immortality, plus the devastation of the first two seals opening and now this, the list of who wants me dead keeps growing rapidly.

At least Lilith wants to keep me alive for the sake of her future grandbabies.

Lucifer's expression turns deadly serious. "You're now the only thing that stands between Michael and what he truly wants."

"Your other siblings?"

He nods. "The seals weren't meant for you, even if you have the power to open them. You're a cosmic paradox, Charlotte. A foreign body that could potentially backfire, which means . . ."

"Michael's plan would be easier without me," I breathe. "But we can reroute *our* plan, can't we? Find another way to get your angelic siblings on our side? Now that he knows what we're up to?"

Lucifer's jaw tightens, like this is *exactly* why he resisted being transparent with me about his family in the first place. "It'll take time, but it's possible."

Azrael shakes his head. "It's just a scare tactic. Until we know for certain the seals are a threat to you, we stick to the plan."

Lucifer nods in agreement.

"But until then, we need Lucifer's siblings to stay in line now more than ever."

And considering one of them has already gone rogue and opened the second seal . . .

Our entire plan is at risk of fracturing, if we don't act quickly.

"Okay." I pace back and forth as I try not to panic. "Okay, so until we have something better, we double down on keeping your siblings in check."

"If a better path even exists," Azrael grumbles, like this is no big thing.

To him, it likely isn't. He's seen nine apocalypses before this—*nine.*

Lucifer casts him an impatient look. "Darling, why don't you go upstairs? Azrael and I need to have a little chat alone."

"Alone?" I look from one to the other. "You're not going to . . ."

"I'll be fine, Charlotte." This from Azrael.

The way he looks at me then, like he's no longer going to hide how he feels in front of Lucifer, concerns me.

Almost as much as the idea of leaving the two of them alone together.

I turn my attention toward my fiancé. "How did it go last night, by the way? With my dad?" I ask in a pathetic attempt at changing the subject.

Even as I'm filled with the awareness that, yes, talking about torturing my father for information on how to hit back at the Righteous for helping abduct Jax *is* a preferable conversation topic to whatever silent standoff Lucifer and Azrael are having.

Lucifer scoffs, pulling me closer. "Unsuccessful, I'm afraid."

"*You* might have had little success. But I didn't," Azrael growls.

My eyes widen as we both look toward him.

I've never heard Death so much as utter a word against Lucifer, not like this, but after last night . . .

That mouth of his seems far more dangerous than it's ever been.

"I found her," Azrael says, looking directly at me.

My heart races.

There's only one "her" he could possibly mean.

I shriek, my anxieties forgotten as I launch myself off Lucifer's lap and into Azrael's arms. "Is she all right? Is she—"

"She's alive. That's what matters." Azrael's self-satisfied grin fades quickly.

"We have to go get her. How do we—"

"Charlotte." Lucifer's voice drops low, taking on that familiar, warning edge.

The one he uses when I'm treading into dangerous territory.

When I'm not conducting myself as the immortal queen I'm expected to be.

My spine runs cold.

He pats his leg, nodding toward his lap, as I reluctantly untangle myself from Death's arms and obediently slink back to Lucifer.

"Sorry, sir," I mutter, shrinking against him.

I may not be Lucifer's collared sub at the moment, but not *everything* about our dynamic disappeared overnight.

Old habits are hard to break.

Azrael glances between us, eyes narrowed, before finally he clears his throat. "I located her in the Nothing, but where that translates into human geography is unclear to me."

"Meaning?"

"We can't go after her." Lucifer strokes my hair, my head now lying on his shoulder. "Not yet."

"But if Azrael found her, why can't he—"

"It doesn't work like that, unfortunately." Azrael's gaze hardens, like he can see how concerned this makes me and he hates it. "She could be anywhere here on Earth, between this world and the next, and that could mean—"

"But you *will* locate her, won't you, Azrael?" Lucifer arches a brow, the tone in his voice leaving no room for refusal.

An order to a soldier from his king. The Prince of Darkness.

Some silent communication passes between them.

A moment of tension before Azrael lowers his head. "Yes, sir."

My gaze darts between them.

Wait. Did Azrael just obey *him?*

Could they be . . . ?

No, of course not.

Lucifer's grip on me tightens as he takes another slow sip of his drink, his fiery gaze never moving from Azrael.

I know where Death stands, but if I told Lucifer how I was feeling, maybe he—

"Be a good girl and go get ready for work now, little dove. Azrael and I have business to attend to." The hellfire in Lucifer's eyes flares, and if the furious gleam in his eye is any indication, well . . .

This conversation has been a long time coming.

"Of course." I scramble off Lucifer's lap, my heart sinking as I peck a quick kiss on his cheek. I hesitate before doing the same with Azrael and then retreat upstairs to the safety of my bedroom.

I close the door and sag against it, defeated.

There is no chance in hell either of them is ever going to agree to make this a permanent thing.

That much is clear to me.

CHAPTER NINE

Lucifer

As soon as my future bride has safely ensconced herself inside that dreadfully average shower she insists upon keeping, along with this inconveniently artsy townhouse, I wait only long enough to hear her turn up the water pressure to full steam.

Before I lunge at Azrael.

I have him pinned against the counter, with one of my few celestial blades that could do any permanent damage to him, before either of us can blink.

"What in the bloody fuck were you thinking?" I snarl, shoving my blade against his throat.

The tip presses into his carotid artery, and a drop of blood sensuously begins to pool there.

I may not be capable of summoning enough power to end Death as I truly wish, not in my current state at least, but I can certainly teach him a new meaning of pain this morning.

He always did enjoy my rather *uninhibited* techniques.

Azrael—the impetuous bastard—has the audacity to look a bit smug as he eagerly leans into my blade. "You're the one who suggested that we—"

"I am *not* talking about the fact that you are fucking my future wife, Azrael."

His gaze narrows, the handle of the empty mug at his side a mere flick of his wrist from becoming a crude shiv.

"No longer enjoying it now that it's real, lover?" he taunts, his skeletal face flashing as he casts me a derisive grin. "I thought you *wanted* to share her." He wrinkles his nose as if he cannot possibly imagine what would ever possess me to do such a thing.

But love makes fools of us all.

Me included, unfortunately.

"I offered to share her body, *not* her heart, and only so that she would be protected from the likes of *you*, you treacherous, deathly cretin. Her immortal life was at stake. You would've stolen her from me." I shove the blade farther in, just enough so his head is forced back to where I now grip his hair.

A trail of blood trickles down his neck, unexpectedly drawing my attention.

"And if you think for even one bloody minute, I'm going to allow you to—"

"Never," Azrael growls, suddenly ramming his knee up into my groin.

I double over with the pain of it, giving him the exact access he needs.

He sweeps my feet so I'm now lying flat on my back, like I was when he first met me. He presses his knee into my chest, and his hand falls to my throat, now holding the blade he managed to strip from me.

I snarl.

I knew—I fucking knew—training a primordial in angelic combat was a mistake.

But that was several millennia ago, when I still foolishly believed he cared for me.

"I would *never* hurt her," Azrael spits, as if even entertaining the thought personally offends him.

Like whatever he might now feel for her runs almost as deep as anything he might have once felt for me.

And with *my* fucking fiancée at that.

"Do you even know me?" He shakes his head in disbelief.

"You made certain I didn't the moment you and Father chose to fuck me," I sneer, my fingers finally connecting with the intact mug.

Without warning, I swing my arm up, smashing the mug into the side of his temple where he's knelt on top of me.

The ceramic shatters, the shards raining on us both.

But I'm not nearly finished with him yet.

Azrael goes down hard, toppling into the adjacent cabinet, just as I throw myself on top of him and—

A sound echoes from upstairs, causing us to still.

An audible creak follows, the sound of the faucet turning off.

Azrael seizes the momentary lapse in my attention, tackling me as he uses his weight to his advantage. He has me face-down, one arm twisted behind my back, my shoulder screaming in agony as he digs his knee deep into the sinew of my spine and the scars there, like he somehow believes he might possibly be able to crush all the fight out of me.

Fat fucking chance, that.

I let out a furious roar just as the sound of Charlotte's hairdryer drowns out the noise, signaling that she's still blissfully unaware of what's happening. Her celestial abilities are not yet as attuned as they one day will be, and I'm not ready to surrender to my traitorous ex.

I will make him bleed for every time he has ever dared betray me.

I give one sharp twist of my torso and—pop.

Pain flashes, white hot and searing, my mortal body screaming in agony, but I shove it aside, ignoring it. Any pain I might feel is mere background noise compared to the hatred, the betrayal, that now courses through me.

I will fucking *end* him for daring to come between her and me.

With my shoulder loose, I've just enough room. I drive my toes into the floor and explode—hips up, body twisting hard.

Death isn't ready.

His balance shifts, his knee sliding off-center.

I roll to my bad side, my shoulder dragging uselessly. But I'm moving.

And that's all that bloody matters.

I hook my foot behind his and yank. He stumbles forward, and I pivot, using the momentum as I throw myself up and sideways.

I'm on one knee as he tries to recover, reaching for control, but already I'm inside his guard, and it'll take a helluva lot more than the loss of my power for him to best me.

I will make him rue the day he ever met me.

I capture him by the hair, my fingers finding purchase, before I ram my forehead into his, unrelenting. No wasted motion.

We both see stars.

Death's nose starts to bleed, and I clutch him by the throat as he tries and fails to regain the upper hand. He may not truly need air, not even when he's corporeal like this, but in this form, it still smarts all the same.

"You should never have . . . given her His . . ." he rasps.

My Father's redemption, he means.

My grip on his throat tightens.

Death or not, I will squeeze the godforsaken life out of him before I ever deign to admit that she might have been better off without me.

Better off with him and my Father.

"I will *never* apologize for making her mine. Do you understand?" I snarl, the hellfire in my eyes so unhinged I can see it reflected in the cool-blue hue of his gaze. "Hear this, Reaper. I would make any deal, destroy *anything* in my path. Lie, cheat, kill, sin, stop my Father's goddamn apocalypse, and upend the whole fucking universe if that's what it takes to see her happy." I hiss mere inches away from his face. "And if you dared think I shared her with you out of some misguided hope I might still care for you, well, think again, *lover*," I say, tossing out the old endearment like celestial rubbish. "Nothing I ever felt for you could hold a candle to her. Do I make myself clear?"

Death nods to the best of his ability. A vein in his temple throbs.

"The only mistake I will ever admit to making is trusting her with the likes of you."

"I told you, Lucifer. It wasn't—"

"It's *always* fucking personal when it comes to you, innit?"

Azrael's eyes meet mine, the look of resentment and fury there slicing through me, and I am filled with a sudden reminder of how things might have been.

His gaze falls to my lips.

Immediately, I retreat.

"This isn't just about her." I release him as we both stumble to our feet. I still need him. For now, unfortunately. "Not entirely."

Azrael paws at his neck. "If not her, then—"

"The blade. The lance," I growl, advancing on him. "You didn't think that I would discover it was you?"

We both fall silent for a beat.

"Lucifer, I—"

Abruptly, I turn away from him, so I am no longer reminded of how his broad body was once the only thing that could've undone me.

"I don't want to hear a single damn one of your excuses." I stalk to the other side of the room, bending to pick up the blade he almost nicked from me. "I shouldn't be surprised. Not after that damn kiss at the awards ceremony. You always did know how to strike when I was at my most vulnerable."

"Lucifer, I—"

I tuck my recovered blade inside my suit coat, giving him my back as I prepare to leave.

Before I allow him to see that he is still capable of wounding me.

"I wouldn't hurt her," Azrael says.

The rest remains unspoken.

Not like I did you.

"Are you certain?" I sneer, finally glancing toward him.

"I'm bound by the deal we made. You—"

I let out a cruel laugh. "Of course. The deal. And a good thing, too, because that is the *only* reason you are still standing here." I turn toward him. "If you do anything to put her at risk again, I will annihilate you without a second thought." I draw to my full height, the serpentine slits of my eyes narrowing. "You *will* tell her where your loyalties lie before this goes any further. Or I will. Is that clear?"

Death stares at me, his jaw clenching. "Crystal."

"Good," I say, beginning to strip off my suit.

I fully intend to enjoy *my* fiancée this morning.

I will make her scream so loud that I am certain all bloody Manhattan will hear.

"I need not remind you that the terms of *our* deal remain intact despite any others you might have made previously."

"I wouldn't—"

"Spare me." I lift a hand. "Whatever it is you and Father are up to this time," I say, speaking over him, "I'll find out soon enough." I cast my tie onto the floor. "I won't allow her to pay the price for our old history."

"Wouldn't dream of it," Azrael grumbles.

"Good," I snarl, feeling the unsettling sensation of his eyes on my scarred back as I quit the room, but he doesn't dare say anything as I toss over my shoulder, "Now do me a favor and fuck off into the endless void you came from. She's *mine*."

CHAPTER TEN

Azrael

I fucked up. I fucked up hard.

I fucked up so hard I might not ever be able to fix it.

So hard I'm not even certain Charlotte will be able to forgive me.

Especially now that I'm . . . at risk of losing both of them.

I appear outside the church she likes to visit down on Seventh Street, somewhere in the Garment District close to Times Square, while the other me waits inside her townhouse, torturously listening to the sound of her pleasured screams.

I've watched as she's visited here a few times, and I don't know why it is she keeps returning, but something about this place . . . calls to me.

And it suits my purpose just as well as any.

I climb the stone steps, my thoughts turning to the way she looked at me last night, how I worshipped her. It's almost as if what she's starting to feel for me might be . . .

I shake my head.

I can't even allow myself to think it.

I glance toward the church's sign as I near the entrance, the name like an unspoken prophecy. Our Lady of Perpetual Sorrows.

I huff.

God always did have a fucked-up sense of humor.

I step inside, the heavy doors sealing shut as the dust motes that move through the early light dance around the sanctuary. The church is mostly dark, especially at this hour, the dim light of a few altar candles flickering. The first service is likely a few hours off, though human time makes little difference to me. I approach the altar.

A stained glass image of Christ stares down at me.

It looks nothing like him.

Too white, too . . . celebratory.

He wasn't eager for me to take him. Just like the rest of them.

To sacrifice himself for his Father's plans.

I drop down into the first-row pew, alone, uncertain what exactly it is I'm doing. I haven't spoken to God in over a century, and definitely not in the last ten years since Lucifer and his siblings came topside. Nor do I understand why Charlotte and I feel drawn here, considering her frequent visits over the last few weeks.

But I'm here all the same, and actually corporeal for once.

I drop my head, leaning forward onto my knees. I don't mean to speak my desperate prayer to Him aloud, for my words to summon Him, but something in me . . .

"He knows," I say into silence. "He knows, and I can hardly fucking stand it."

"Of course he knows."

I stiffen at the calm voice that answers me.

I turn to find the church's priest drawing near, the one Charlotte keeps meeting with. Father Brown, I think. After all these eons, human faces sometimes blend together for me.

But for some reason, this one stands out.

I lift my scarred brow, surprised he's bold enough to face me, let alone talk to me like this. I can count the number of meaningful conversations I've had with humans on one hand.

Few have ever spoken to me directly, save for the rare occasions I've allowed them to get a glimpse of me.

Ever since God and then Lucifer used me as a threat to keep them in line in that damn Garden, it's been like their fear of me was coded into their DNA.

"You mean Lucifer, don't you?" he says, drawing closer. "Nothing gets past that devil."

I lift a brow. *How did he—*

"You say that like you know him."

The priest nods. "I do."

I lift the other brow.

Father Brown grins. "Though perhaps not as well as you do."

I shake my head, dismissing his words for the religious bullshit it clearly is. "Nobody knows him as well as I do. Not even his fiancée."

"Is that so?" The priest tilts his head before he sits down beside me. "I'd like to think I know him pretty well too." His gaze flicks toward the stained glass overhead. "And him."

I shift my attention back to the image of Christ. "Forgive me if I don't take your word for it."

I've been closer to God than this priest will ever be, even when he eventually dies.

Close enough to remember the exact words He whispered to me.

Keep thy faith, and I shall unbind their fates . . .

I scoff.

Even if at the moment it all feels like a fucking joke.

Lucifer did always take his Father for a liar, but I don't know why that particular promise made me think . . .

I don't allow myself to finish the thought.

The priest leans forward as I rake both my hands through my hair, brushing aside the stray strands that've fallen into my face.

"You were there at the beginning, and you'll be the last to leave when it ends. Won't you, Azrael?"

My spine stiffens. "How do you know my—"

There's a flicker in his eyes for a moment—too ancient to belong to any human.

There and gone in a flash.

"I think He may be paying a lot closer attention than you think." The priest pointedly glances up toward the ceiling.

But I'm not buying it.

God has plenty of prophets, but it couldn't possibly be that easy.

Could it?

I shake my head again. I watch as the man's eyes narrow. I take in his warm face, his knowing grin. He must have put two and two together and recognized me from one of Charlotte's confessions, that's all. That's all it could possibly—

"She prays for you a lot, you know," he says, and now I *know* he's seriously fucking with me.

"Aren't you supposed to keep that private or something?"

He chuckles a little. "I don't think she'd mind if I told you she doesn't want to lose you." He pauses. "Or him."

I know the feeling.

I let out a long sigh, leaning back in the pew as I drag a rough hand down my face. "Look, a human like you couldn't possibly understand what I've done."

"Are you certain?" he asks like he can see right through me.

Other than Charlotte, I've never met one of them who could understand the sacrifices I've made. The hurt. The longing.

All for a promise He made me.

No wonder she keeps returning here.

"None of that matters now." I look away as I lean forward onto my knees again. "He's never going to be mine, and neither is she."

"And why not?"

I tip my chin toward the stained glass window overhead. "Because He's abandoned us all, *you* all, remember?"

Along with the promise He made me.

"In what way?"

I sigh. This conversation is getting old, and fast. "He made a promise to me once, but it was only if I . . ."

"Had enough faith in Him?"

I press my lips together and give a curt nod.

When he says it like that, it sounds just as foolish as Lucifer accused me of being when he found out. Reckless. Hopeful. Not worth all the pain it's caused us both.

Father Brown nods, as if he's beginning to understand me. "Did He abandon you, or is He simply testing your faith?"

I grumble something unintelligible, before I grunt, "Why not both?" once it's clear he isn't going to leave me be.

I must be losing my touch.

I'm the Grim Reaper, and I can't scare off one fucking annoying priest anymore.

The priest chuckles like he can tell what I'm thinking. "Have faith, Azrael, and remember what's at stake if you choose a different ending."

I roll my eyes. "And what's that? My eternal soul?"

I turn back to face him, only to find he's gone.

Leaving me alone in that strange human sanctuary, wondering if God really did tell me the truth of how this would all end, or if maybe He left out a few of the key details.

CHAPTER ELEVEN

Charlotte

By the time Lucifer drops me off at Pier59 Studios on the Hudson River over an hour later, my ass is so tender I can hardly walk straight.

Between everything Azrael and I did last night and the way Lucifer pounded into me this morning—like he was *trying* to make certain everyone in the neighboring buildings could overhear me—I'm going to need a minimum of two full bottles of Tylenol in order to get through work. The lower impact pharmaceuticals and other substances have on celestials is inconvenient, to say the least.

And that says nothing about how I'm starting to feel about Azrael, or the fact that the apocalypse has basically become my life's background noise. This morning was a clear reminder that there can never be any kind of future for him and me.

Not without Lucifer.

And I could *never* give him up.

I'm completely addicted to him.

Which is part of the problem, actually.

When I finally break free of my security team at the Chelsea Pier, I feel Lucifer's demonic army watching me. They're more of a . . . feeling than anything else. An occasional inhuman gleam in someone's eye, a knowing grin from a total stranger, or the uncanny awareness that settles into the pit of my stomach whenever I'm out in the city.

They're everywhere.

The idea shouldn't terrify me.

They're my fiancé's creations after all.

But somehow, the thought is still unnerving.

As I round toward the studio entrance, a flyer fluttering on a nearby lamppost catches my attention.

> Rapture Awaits the Righteous! The Final Purge Is upon Us! But the Lord Has Not Forgotten His People!

Followed by a stylized caricature of me with devil horns and the sharp end of the Holy Lance piercing between my legs.

Flustered, I crumple the paper in my fist and throw it into the nearest garbage. The Righteous are still the evangelical death cult they've always been, but how a growing number of people can't see that concerns me.

And why are they so obsessed with me?

What's their endgame?

I make my way through the rest of the production complex to Studio 8, where Imani waits for me.

"Careful." She kisses my cheeks and nods to where Greed is currently shouting at the *Vogue* photography team. "She's in a mood."

I place a hand on Imani's arm like it might lend me strength.

One of these days I'll have to get the full story of how she's survived working for Lucifer this long. I could use a few pointers.

"I said alkaline, you fool!" Greed shouts, tossing the uncapped bottle of *non*-alkaline water at her quivering PA.

The bottle's contents go flying.

I let out a heavy sigh.

Like the others, this new assistant won't last long. Not that I blame her.

I make my way across the all-white studio, signaling to the crew and style team that we're taking a short break before I mutter a few words of encouragement and directions on where to find the *exact* right brand of water to Greed's crying assistant. She scurries off, and Greed finally flops down in her director's chair.

"Did you see what those minimalist, lo-fi idiots over at *Rolling Stone* ran this morning?" She wrinkles her nose. "The nerve of some humans."

Greed's not only taken to using me as her personal publicist—only a few more weeks of this hell and counting, and then I'm off scot-free from when she helped me escape the CFDA awards—but she's also decided I'm what essentially amounts to her celestial therapist.

At least when she isn't training me to use my "divine abilities."

That's a whole other aspect to our relationship.

"Mimi, have you eaten?"

"Why wouldn't I have?"

I roll my eyes. "Imani, can you—"

"I'm on it," she calls as she exits the studio.

"You *know* you get hangry whenever you try not to eat. These detoxes are starting to become a problem." I shake my head, examining the lighting to see if we can adjust it to be more flattering. These are the sorts of skills I've learned since I first started dating Lucifer.

Along with a lot of *other* things.

Mimi waves a dismissive hand. "Please. Like food will fix this. I'm not a child, Charlotte."

"Of course." I smile my best Sunday-morning-greeting grin.

Though the way she bullies me during training definitely reminds *me* of being a child.

Thankfully, Greed and I have finally made some progress on that front. I'm still not great at harnessing my anger as a fuel for my power, but so far, I can shoot some pretty sick light beams out of my hands, and I'm even starting to be able to wield Lucifer's shadows.

Apparently, when Lucifer gifted me God's redemption, he made it so I'm the only immortal, aside from Azrael, capable of navigating all three realms.

Heaven, Hell, and Purgatory (i.e., Earth these days).

Go figure.

Which is exactly why I'm stuck here working for Greed: all the divine favors doing PR for Lucifer's siblings is affording me, in exchange for their help stopping the apocalypse.

With Fashion Week right around the corner, and all the speculation about if Lucifer and I are still getting married, the PR hours I've been pulling for them have been insane. The other Originals have been racking up a helluva tab.

And when the time is right, I'm going to cash in majorly.

Make them help me open the seals for Michael, while Lucifer makes whatever deals are necessary to flip some of Michael's angelic army to our side.

Team No Apocalypse for the win.

If I can keep them all on our side, that is.

Michael won't know what hit him.

"So, what's wrong now? This is your third diva moment this week. Did they forget the titanium straws for your champagne again?"

Greed scowls. "Oh, don't act like you don't already know."

I pinch the bridge of my nose. "Honestly, I don't, Mimi. Just like I also can't do anything about Azmodeus upstaging you at the Golden Globes last week, especially since you're still refusing to tell me who—"

"If you dare accuse me of knowing which one of my idiotic siblings opened the second seal again, I am done with you. Do you hear me?" Greed practically snarls. "I won't have any more of your amateur sleuthing. Not today. After all, this is *your* fault."

"My fault?"

Greed huffs, flopping back into her chair before she shoves her phone in my direction.

> Inside Zest: How Greed Built a Billion-Dollar Wellness Empire on Exploitation, Snake Oil, and Silicon Valley Sleaze.

I wince, then lift a brow.

I'm not sure how that has anything to do with me.

Other than it being my job to fix it.

Mimi sticks out her foot to examine the custom art heels she's wearing—a collab between Christian Louboutin and a Japanese ceramist in prep for Fashion Week. "I couldn't possibly know what they're talking about, of course."

"Of course." I roll my eyes. She's that much like Lucifer, refusing to admit any vulnerability. "But I still don't see what this has to do with—"

"Read the opening lines, Charlotte," she says, overenunciating each word like she can't believe how stupid I'm being.

I frown.

This family . . .

I snatch the phone out of her hand.

> CULTURE / INVESTIGATION
>
> *January Issue*
>
> *By Riley Vega,* Rolling Stone
>
> It turns out the biggest scandal in wellness didn't start with a faulty jade egg or a recall on astral protein powder. It started with a religious revelation when a recent viral livestream from Righteous stronghold and evangelical megachurch Victory in His Name revealed former Apollyon intern Charlotte Bellefleur née Davis—daughter of the far-right firebrand, Greed's soon-to-be sister-in-law, and yes, Lucifer's fiancée—is immortal.

> And once the internet finished spiraling over *that*, a deeper question began to emerge: If the devil's bride-to-be has been secretly immortal this whole time . . . what else are these "people" hiding?
>
> All roads, naturally, led to Zest—Greed's sprawling self-help empire-slash-luxury cult, hawking $800 "clarity mists" and workshops promising "financial enlightenment through divine femininity." But behind the crystals and cashmere lies something far more terrestrial: shell companies, labor violations, off-the-books pharmaceutical testing, and a trail of NDAs thick enough to choke an entire Sedona wellness retreat. It turns out that the devil really is in the details.

I stare at the article, my stomach churning, until a sudden, unexpected round of nausea has me.

"Not on my shoes again!" Greed shrieks.

I drop to my knees and upchuck what remains of my coffee. Imani and then Mia, my assistant—thank God—are at my side a moment later.

"That's it! You're fired, Charlotte!" Greed blusters, waving her arms about, like me and my vomit are the most disgusting thing she's ever seen.

Far worse than the exploitation she's directly responsible for in this morning's headlines.

I swipe at my mouth. "You can't fire me, Mimi. I'm doing this as a favor to repay you. Besides, we have a celestial contract."

The terms of which I've recently learned are enforced by the archangel Gabriel, another one of Lucifer's siblings.

God's messenger.

"Maybe not the right time to mention the contract," Mia mutters, helping me to my feet.

I don't have the heart to point out to her that for me, this is progress. Six months ago, I was nothing but a terrified mess standing before Greed.

Now look at me.

Confidently vomiting on her couture shoes and everything.

Leaving Mia to deal with the fallout, Imani quickly whisks me out of the room, frog-marching me to one of the nearby dressing rooms before she shoves a bottle of *non*-alkaline water into my hand and orders me to sit.

I flop back into a makeup chair.

This is so not what I needed this morning.

"We can't allow them to drag her brand like this. Even if it is a tiny bit—"

"It's not *her* brand that's the problem." Imani levels me with a hard look.

"Straight talk?" I take a tentative sip.

"Straight talk," she agrees, before she lets out a long sigh. "This whole debacle with the livestream's getting in the way of your work. You're a PR nightmare, Charlotte. Having you near the other Originals is poisoning everything. Their images, their brands."

"I know the public wasn't happy to find out I'm immortal, and the Righteous have only made things worse, but I wouldn't exactly say—"

Imani huffs, shoving her phone toward me.

People. Immortal and Still Not Married: What's Wrong with Charlotte Bellefleur?

"That's not—"

She uses her manicured thumb to swipe to another. *Us Weekly*.

> Fans Slam Lucifer's "Bride" for Manipulating Him with Immortal Allure

"Okay, you and I both know that one is just downright ridicu—"

Imani shakes her head, scrolling some more. *Politico*.

> HELL HATH NO FURY: Charlotte Bellefleur Outed as IMMORTAL—World Leaders Demand Answers.

"I know, but—"

And the final nail in the coffin.

TMZ.

> Publicly Empowered. Privately Unraveling. One Devil Wasn't Enough? Lucifer's Fiancée Accused of Secret Affair!

I stare down at the shoddy side profile of Azrael and me. My heart stops. "It's not like that. You can't actually think I would ever—"

"Girl, it doesn't matter what I think. It only matters what it looks like."

And it looks like I'm everything my father said I'd be.

A jezebel. A whore. The devil's plaything.

Loathed by the whole of humanity.

But that's not what really plagues me.

I slouch in my chair, unable to meet Imani's gaze.

Behind the sensationalism, there's a kernel of truth there.

I glance down at the headline again, feeling suddenly fatigued.

> Publicly Empowered. Privately Unraveling.

It's a brutal, impersonal autopsy of my life. Especially with the second accompanying photo: me looking like a hot mess as I stumble out of some club. Like any *normal* twenty-something. A woman I barely recognize.

I sigh.

Back when I first started dating Lucifer, I thought I knew who I was, or at least, who I was *supposed* to be, but now that I've taken charge of my own life, my own fate, every choice I make feels like a betrayal.

To myself. To Lucifer.

To who I was previously.

To God, maybe?

To a human version of me I'll never be able to get back.

When the truth is . . .

I still don't know who I am, what kind of immortal I'm becoming.

The question sits like ice inside my chest. Not because I'm still uncertain of the answer, but because I think I know it already.

And I'm not certain I like what I see.

I wave a hand, passing the phone back. "This isn't anything that can't be fixed with a little reframing. We—"

"Charlotte, Sloth's lawyers called this morning. You know he's been dragging his feet on signing the contract, which means . . ."

The sound of my heartbeat thrashes in my ears.

I've lost one of the Originals.

In *addition* to the one who went rogue already.

"No. No, no, no, he can't do that. He—"

"If you think any of the others won't try to pull the same . . ." Imani gives me a chastising look.

Meaning I need to clean up my image—and fast—and until then, I'm more of a detriment to my own clients than anything. And considering my only clients are Lucifer's billionaire siblings who are paying me in the divine favors I desperately need to stop the apocalypse . . .

This isn't just another PR nightmare or damage control. It's mythmaking.

Unless I can stand confident in who I am . . .

The whole of humanity is fucked.

"What are you proposing?" I fist my hair as I cast Imani a desperate look.

She passes Greed's all-natural protein bar to me with a muttered "eat this" before she says, "You're the boss now, Charlotte. You tell me." She smiles, encouraging me.

Like she always does.

I nod, my lungs expanding a little.

She's right.

I know this game. Imani taught it to me backward and forward.

But Lucifer made me a true master at it.

That's all PR is anyway—manipulation.

And I wouldn't even be sitting here if she and Lucifer hadn't chosen to believe in me.

"We need a trifecta. A high-gloss crisis makeover. Elevate the narrative, control the frame, radical transparency. We stage a couture resurrection during Fashion Week. Balenciaga and Xzander handle the look. Apollyon coordinates. At the same time, we land an exclusive with *The Cut*. A soft-focus confession—me crying barefoot in Tuscany, you know the drill. Bloomberg reframes my brand as a visionary under fire, *Vogue Business* gets the fashion angle and spins this as a new era of sustainable luxury. In a few weeks, everyone will be saying they're only hating on me because I'm a woman who owns her power."

"And what about you?"

I lift a brow.

"What'll *you* be saying?" Imani gives me a knowing look.

My ribs tighten as I push my hair out of my face. "Just leave this to me." I glance down at my hands. "I'll handle myself for once."

"You're certain?"

I nod.

I don't doubt my own abilities anymore.

But somehow that hasn't changed anything.

I'm still far from the confident woman I want to be.

The woman I wish I saw in the mirror.

"Okay," Imani says, smiling a little, like despite all I still have to learn, she's proud of me. Like I'm growing.

Maybe I am.

I just wish growth didn't come with so much uncertainty.

"All right, it's a plan then. Take the rest of the day and handle your shit. I've got this." Imani tips her chin over her shoulder to indicate Greed.

I sink back into my chair, already exhausted. "You're honestly the best, Imani."

"Don't I know it?" She grins, fixing her curls in one of the style room mirrors before she heads for the door. "Oh, and Charlotte?" She looks over her shoulder at me.

"Yeah?"

She lifts her phone again, flashing one last headline.

> Sin Conceived! Is She Pregnant or Just Bloated? Lucifer's Fiancée Spotted with a Rounded Belly

I glance down at my midsection, paling slightly.

Some of my designer clothes have been feeling a little bit tighter lately.

Imani gives me an amused look. "Girl, you're glowing. Do us both a favor and take a damn pregnancy test." She closes the style room door behind her just as I look toward the dressing room mirror, noticing exactly what she means, and a whole different kind of uncertainty settles into me.

The shame I was raised with isn't as much of a problem anymore.

But clearly, my own denial is starting to catch up to me.

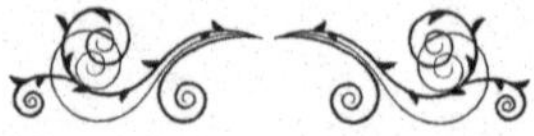

I decide to actually take the rest of the day off after that, like Imani said.

At least from my work at Zest.

I grab another coffee, decaf this time, and nibble a bit more food—my stomach is seriously making me regret not accepting Azrael's tea—and stop by my new office space.

Well, what I'm *hoping* will be my new office space.

When all this is said and done.

I stare up at the vacant building in Battery Park overlooking New York Harbor, feeling something expand inside my chest with a new kind of certainty.

A new kind of hope.

I can do this.

I know I can. Even if my confidence wavers occasionally.

Loving Lucifer and now Azrael has taught me that much.

I snap a quick photo to post—#dreaming—wishing Jax were here, telling me all I need to do is manifest everything I'm hoping for in some spiritual ritual.

A few minutes later, I know exactly what I need to do in order to make my first move. That CVS bag on my bathroom counter is calling my name.

I turn to head back toward the Town Car, only to find the archangel Michael standing across the street waiting for me, holding my mentor captive.

CHAPTER TWELVE

Lucifer

I should have suspected something was amiss from the moment I dropped her off at the pier this morning. I'm alone at the Metropolitan Club on Sixtieth and Fifth Avenue near Central Park East, halfway through my second glass of whisky, as I wait for a black-market dealer who purports to know the exact location of another one of my Father's prophets, when a sudden awareness hits me.

A tension I cannot place coils behind my sternum, the kind of silence that falls right before the celestial dawn—or the cut of one of my blades.

I set down my glass. Not gently.

Wherever she is, my wife needs me.

I come to my feet, the club's crystal chandeliers and coffered ceilings adorned with a few annoyingly rhapsodic family paintings looming over me. Azrael, in one of his many versions, appears by my side a moment later, confirming what I already suspected.

I throw back my glass, steeling myself for the battle ahead.

It's show time, apparently.

"Take me to our girl, Reaper."

Death nods, a rare moment of understanding passing between us.

In this and only this can we find a truce.

An agreement that we will both do whatever it takes to ensure her safety.

Abruptly, Azrael grips the back of my neck, drawing me so close that I let out a brittle laugh at the mere thought that he might actually be foolish enough to kiss me. Our eyes meet for a beat too long, before his lip curls.

"Careful now," I taunt, snaking one of my hands about his waist and dragging him against me. "You wouldn't want her to think you still care for me, would you?"

Azrael's eyes narrow. "Never."

I smirk wickedly.

The next thing I know, we both become shadow, our bodies temporarily evaporating into the ether and reforming in a way that is now both familiar and foreign to me, until I am standing, suddenly alone, in the middle of a busy street on the south side of Battery Park.

A yellow taxicab lays on its horn as it barrels toward me.

But I don't pay it any mind.

The Statue of Liberty, Ellis Island, and the open water are at my back, and in the distance, I can see where my future bride now stands facing my least favorite brother, half a block away from me. But I am unable to reach her.

An unhinged growl escapes me just as the taxi and I nearly collide.

I slam my hands upon its hood, denting it, just as it stops abruptly.

The driver leans out the window. "What the fuck, asshole? You—"

I shoot him a furious look, and he pales as soon as he recognizes me.

Humanity knows *exactly* who's in charge here.

And it's no longer my Father, thankfully.

I set my sights upon Charlotte, and the driver shrinks back into the cab as I climb on top of the car's hood. The soles of my Armanis find purchase before I ascend to the roof of the cab, finding my balance.

A few of my demons sense my presence and emerge from the street, but I refuse to take my eyes off her.

Now that I am mortal, my presence alone shouldn't be enough to summon them, but somehow, they can still sense me. As Seraph can. And I can feel it too.

My power, simmering just beneath the earth's surface.

Ripe for reclaiming.

Mortality is but a mere diversion in my path.

Not even the loss of my powers can stop me.

Not when it comes to her.

I leap from vehicle to vehicle, my eyes never leaving her, as more humans, more onlookers start to point and flee at the sight of me. My mind begins to connect the dots, the patterns, as the path forward suddenly becomes clear to me.

I thought I knew the whole of the game the first time I lost her.

But that was nothing compared to the rage, with the terror I now feel, watching as she stands on her own against my family.

With only the trust and the promise of all I have wrought, all I have given her.

And if she dares die again before she chooses to be mine, well, I can no longer be certain she'll remain in my realm for all eternity.

Not now that she's chosen to make herself into a guardian angel for humanity.

I didn't think I could possibly hate them more.

But I was wrong about quite a lot, frankly.

CHAPTER THIRTEEN

Charlotte

"I'm sorry, Charlotte, I tried to—"

"It's okay, Imani."

Azrael is at my side a moment later. Ever present. Always ready. Exactly the watchdog Lucifer planned for him to be.

But even Death can't save me from the archangel before me.

Michael stands on the other side of the street, twirling the Holy Lance in one hand—the one that can kill any celestial and ensures he can win any battle, including Armageddon—as he grips Imani's upper arm with the other.

He must have found her and threatened her until she and the security team were forced to reveal my exact location, since our demonic army has been on constant guard, the security team has been on high alert, and Azrael's been using his power to obscure wherever Lucifer and I are in the ether.

A celestial stalling tactic if there ever was one.

It was only ever going to last for so long.

Michael shoves Imani aside, and my heart stops as she stumbles and falls to her knees, nearly colliding with the oncoming traffic, but the cars stop quickly from some commotion up ahead.

Imani glares at Michael, like she's about to tear into him. "You—"

"Stay out of this, Salome," Michael growls, speaking over her.

Salome?

Suddenly there's a whole lot of shouting as Michael's massive wings unfurl, and a bunch of passersby begin to lift and point their phone cameras toward him, me, and—

"Lucifer."

My future husband leaps down from the top of one of the stalled vehicles, landing like a languid jungle cat in a half-crouch, a whole horde of his demonic legions flanking him. I recognize them by their soulless black eyes, their irises blocked out completely.

Lucifer casts a fleeting glance in my direction, the thready mental connection between us momentarily strengthening with the weight of what neither of us can say, before he faces Michael. "Brother." He grins, his expression turning serpentine. "How lovely for you to join us this morning."

The cruel mockery in his tone is enough to send chills down my spine.

Meanwhile, most of the humans on the street are still busy gawking.

Others are exiting the now-stopped traffic in order to flee in the opposite direction. Like they already know what's coming.

Honestly, I can't say I blame them.

I glance up at the skyscrapers overhead.

Even more faces press against all the buildings' windows. More phones. More cameras. More people, which means . . .

The world is watching.

"Cute, having your little boy toy hide the two of you away like that, Lucy, but you had to have known I'd drop by for a visit eventually." Michael grins. "The city's only so big after all."

Azrael snarls. "The fuck he just call me?"

The temperature in the air drops by another several degrees.

Lucifer simply stays Death with a lift of his hand.

Michael smirks.

"You wanted my attention. Well, now you have it." Lucifer's expression drips with so much contempt it's terrifying.

We all knew this moment was coming.

But none of us expected it to be this soon.

There's no time to change plans.

I *told* Lucifer we needed to leave the city, but where else would we go?

Hell's overcrowded. Heaven's empty. Lucifer's demons are scattered throughout the globe, and I needed to stay topside in order to train and keep his siblings appeased.

"Actually, considering Father finally finished the job He started all those eons ago and you're now *fully* neutered, Lucy, it's your future bride that interests me."

Neutered?

Something tells me Michael isn't just referring to Lucifer's wings.

I can't see the expression on my fiancé's face, but from the spark of fury barreling down our connection, I'm not sure I want to.

Michael turns his attention to me. "Time's up, Charlotte," he says, raising his voice as he gestures to the array of human faces around us. "The world's watching. Time to pick a side."

I glance at the people, at the humans who haven't always been capable of seeing the good in me, in Lucifer, or even themselves. I look from face to face, seeing hope upon hope that I'm going to be different, that I'll be the savior they so desperately need.

But I can't be their savior.

I have to be every bit the vicious queen that they made me.

Lucifer turns toward me, striding to my side so that our shoulders touch as he leans down like he means to kiss me. He whispers into my ear as he presses something familiar into my palm. "I love you."

My throat constricts painfully.

My thumb runs over the smooth leather of the token he gave me.

My training collar.

A reminder of everything he's ever taught me, of how far we've come.

"I love you too," I whisper as our eyes meet.

I've been trying to find out who I am without his collar, but maybe that's the wrong question.

With one final look, he steps aside, claiming his spot at my back beside Azrael as I take the training collar into both my hands and place it around my neck.

It's a stark reminder of who I belong to.

But this time, the choice is mine completely.

The snap closes around my neck with a finality I'm certain the entire world can hear as I look toward Michael, holding my head high and speaking loud enough for the public. Not as Lucifer's bride, but as Hell's vicious queen.

"I'll open the next seal for you."

"Good." Michael grins wickedly. "Then your first trial starts now."

CHAPTER FOURTEEN

Azrael

I'm not entirely certain we're going to make it through this, but for the sake of the humans watching, I don't dare show it. Instead, I stand there, ever the watchdog, the perfect image of the loyal soldier to my queen.

Queen of the Damned. That's what the human press calls her.

If only they'd realized it was their own damnation they were signing.

Michael, that lying, self-righteous fuck, doesn't waste any time in getting down to business. He snaps his fingers, and suddenly dozens of Lucifer's angelic siblings appear.

Seraph. Uriel. Raphael. Jegudiel, and even—

"Gabriel," Charlotte breathes.

I tip my chin toward him in greeting.

"We meet again, Charlotte." Gabriel grins, brushing a hand down the white suit he wears and holding out a small chest to Michael.

Aside from Michael, he's the only one on the angelic side of Lucifer's family that Charlotte's ever met.

But *I* know them.

And I've stood at Lucifer's side long enough to hate them all.

Mammon—Greed—pops into existence beside us a moment later, the other Originals not far behind her. Azmodeus, Belphegor, Satan,

Leviathan, and Beelzebub follow—Lust, Sloth, Wrath, Envy, and Gluttony, respectively.

They're eager to see what celestial drama unfolds.

Sick fucks.

Greed's wearing some insane getup she must have been in for the photo shoot she and Charlotte had this morning—cascades of gold, coral-like beams encaging her voluptuous body in lieu of any material. She looks like an elemental goddess.

Or humanity's idea of one, anyway.

The real ones are far more terrifying.

"You didn't think I was actually going to miss this, did you?" she mutters to Charlotte, before she kisses Lucifer on the cheek like Judas, once again prepared to be his loyal lieutenant.

Though the last celestial rebellion they waged together didn't end well.

But they didn't have me on their side back then.

Greed glances at Michael. "Mikey, you look like shit. You too, Gabriel. A millennium hasn't done a damn thing for you."

There's only one of Lucifer's siblings who may fight to destroy Michael just as fiercely as I will.

And it's Greed.

She hates all her angelic siblings nearly as much as I do.

"Ur-i-el," Azmodeus—that lusty little fuck—calls out, drawing out every syllable of his brother's name and flinging out his arms like this is one big happy reunion or something.

Uriel simply glares at him.

"Well, jeez. Eat shit to you, too, then." Azmodeus shrugs. "Fuck all of them for all I care, lovey."

"Do I honestly even need to *be* here?" Envy complains. "Luce is always the center of attention anyway."

"Oh, shut up." Wrath.

Gluttony just crosses his arms, shaking his head like he'd rather be literally anywhere else. Lucifer massages his temples as if he's quickly losing his patience.

But Charlotte simply gives Envy an almost motherly look, placing a reassuring hand on his arm, and somehow, he quits bitching for once this century.

"Honestly, Charlotte, do you truly expect any of these idiots are going to help you?" Michael scoffs like he knows what we're planning as he removes one of the sealed scrolls from Gabriel's chest.

But our strategy isn't dependent on hiding anything.

It hinges upon Michael making the same mistakes Lucifer did.

Pride was always going to be this family's downfall.

My ex was just the original catalyst.

Michael removes the third sealed scroll from Gabriel's box and pops it open without a second thought.

Nothing happens.

"Clock's ticking." Michael grins at Charlotte as we all wait for what comes next.

Charlotte's eyes narrow. "Which one of the seven comes first? There's one Original for each seal, isn't there?"

Minus Lucifer and whichever one of the others went rogue.

Only five remain.

"Well, it wouldn't be very fun if I told you now, would it?" Michael laughs.

Just as the humans begin to gasp, pointing toward the nearby coastline.

The pressure inside my chest tightens as the water rapidly recedes.

The ocean pulls back violently, exposing the mucky brown bottom of the harbor until a massive wave starts to form in the distance. The Statue of Liberty trembles against its weight as it passes, and we all watch in horror as the bay almost empties within seconds as if drained by some invisible force, the water pushed back, hundreds of miles out until—

It starts to fall.

The tides rushing straight for us.

An unstoppable churning mass.

Shit.

My mouth goes dry as I look toward Charlotte, hoping that Greed and I have trained her enough she'll be able to survive and get us all through this.

Or else my job is about to get a whole fucking lot harder—and fast.

New York City is royally fucked.

CHAPTER FIFTEEN

Charlotte

Nobody ever said this would involve swimming.

Or parting a literal sea, for that matter.

My stomach hardens, panic and adrenaline shooting through me at the sight of the rapidly rising water. The tide is coming at us from all sides, the movement of that massive wave causing a ripple effect all around us. It surges up and over my knees within seconds, nearly knocking me off my feet as bile burns the back of my throat.

Greed and I didn't even begin to cover this in training.

And from the looks of it, none of the other Originals expected this either.

I glance behind me, desperately searching for Lucifer, for some indication that he might know which Original this seal belongs to, but already he's snaking his way through the water toward his angelic siblings.

To bend ears. Make deals. Change hearts and minds.

What he does best, actually.

And neither he nor Azrael can help me.

It *has* to be me to open the seal. With the power he gifted me.

Or one of his sinful siblings.

My heart palpitates.

The six other Originals stare up at the massive black tidal wave barreling toward us over a dozen miles out like none of them can even believe what they're seeing, the incoming surge in the distance now so tall it casts an incoming shadow over the One World Trade building.

And the surrounding water is already up to my waist.

What the fuck was I thinking?

I can't do this.

I feel myself choke as an overwhelming sense of dread fills me.

This is *so* much worse than every worst-case scenario I ran through my head.

"This is way above my pay grade, lovey," Azmodeus says, before he snaps his fingers and—

"Really, Az?" I screech as he disappears into the ether.

So much for besties.

There's nothing keeping any of the others from following suit.

Except the divine favors they owe me.

I glance desperately toward them. Time to cash in. "Azrael, start getting as many people out as you can. Mimi, guard Lucifer. The rest of you, help Azrael save whoever you can," I snap. *"Now."*

Azrael moves into action, barking orders to the remaining Originals just as Mimi leaves in search of Lucifer.

Adrenaline coils inside me, a tingling sensation taking over my extremities.

Which one of these sinful assholes could possibly be—

I throw up my hands, trying and failing to do anything to stop the incoming flood.

My palms glow, and a blast of celestial light bursts out.

But it accomplishes nothing.

My breathing goes shallow as I panic.

The dark water is up to my chest and rising quickly, and I'm pretty sure it's not regular water, which means Michael must have done something to alter the seals now that he knows our plan after all, and my immortal life might actually be . . .

A ghostly face swims past, there and gone in an instant.

But I don't have time to consider it.

Parting the Atlantic Ocean like it's the freaking Red Sea and I'm Moses wasn't exactly on my bingo card this morning.

What in the celestial fuck?!

"Whoa, what a wave," Sloth says as he floats beside me. He stares up at the biblical flood heading toward us like he wishes he had his surfboard.

"Sloth!" I shriek as realization hits.

Who *else* would God make work this hard to do anything?

I turn, ready to beg for whatever help he might give me.

Just as he slicks back his wet hair and says, "Well, I'm out."

I dive over an incoming wave, barely grabbing him in the nick of time when a large piece of debris slams into me—a section of metal scaffolding from a nearby building.

Why is there so much construction in this damn city?

The scaffolding knocks us off balance, sending us both into the water's depths.

But I don't let go.

I tighten my hold, kicking and fighting against the current and Sloth's superior swimming skills, using every bit of muscle Azrael and I have been training lately.

I kick like my life depends on it.

The next thing I know, we resurface, Sloth struggling against me. We're floating halfway between the middle of his Hamptons beach house, the ether, and State Street, the rushing water flowing between all three.

Apparently, God doesn't care if His tribulations defy the laws of human physics.

Because of course He doesn't.

I fight against Sloth and the current, realizing one of my heels is now dangling from my—

"Oh no, you don't, you lazy asshole," I snarl, kicking them both off just as my foot connects with the top of a submerged mailbox.

I tighten my hold on Sloth and thrust upward.

A moment later, the hole in the ether is gone, and we're in the middle of the rushing tide again. But that massive wave isn't getting any smaller.

Holy shit.

It doesn't matter that I'm immortal.

I won't be able to live with myself if I allow Michael to wipe out half the freaking city.

If I don't act now, people *will* die.

Switching tactics, instead of fighting *against* Sloth, I manage to use my hold on him to clamber onto his back, shadowing us both onto a nearby rooftop. I've mastered that at least.

"Do something!" I shout, gesturing wildly toward the wave.

We're both soaked from head to toe, and I'm pretty sure my running mascara's making me look like a feral raccoon, but that massive wall of water is drawing closer by the second.

It blacks out the sky overhead.

And I don't have any time left to persuade him.

"I'm not sure what you want me to—"

"Sloth!" I scream, throwing up both my hands like I might actually be able to—

The wave and my powers connect, its weight hitting me like an unstoppable force, so powerful the wind's knocked out of me.

My knees buckle.

Holy shit!

How is water that fucking heavy?

My arms, my legs—my every muscle screams in agony as all my fear, all my anger, rises toward the surface, funneling toward the wave. I try desperately to shield myself from it, to hold it all in, like I always do, but somehow, it bursts out of me.

The massive wave comes to an abrupt and quivering halt, supported only by my—

My anger.

The fury I just unleashed.

Like my power really *is* connected to my rage.

Azrael and Greed have been telling me that all along, but it's one of the many emotions my father and the Righteous and so many others like them taught me I should be ashamed of. Lest I be a witch, a jezebel, or worse, a whore.

Every terrifying feminine archetype Greed's been bullying me into embodying.

Lucifer's already made me both his Madonna and his whore, and for the first time since I accepted that he and I are fated, I feel it inside me.

My power. My rage.

At everything that's happened to us, at all that's being done to humanity.

It's there alongside Lucifer's, tempting and drawing out my own.

I hold my position, my arms starting to shake.

My whole body is on fire.

My muscles screaming.

But I've survived far worse at the hands of my father, and then in Lucifer's playroom.

Though not for nearly as long as I've been holding this.

My arms start to waver.

But then I think of all the humans who are going to die if my father and the Righteous get to have their way. The "salvation" they've so desperately bargained for with Michael and Lilith. And then I'm furious in a whole new way.

Like hell will I ever allow them to win.

My arms hold steady, my resolve strengthening, and somehow, I manage to turn my head toward Sloth, that small movement testing every last bit of my control as I snarl, "Do. Something."

The demonic quality in my voice is new.

A little like Lilith when she turns from one into three.

Sloth must recognize the similarity, because he pales slightly, sputtering as he tries to find some excuse. "Our deal's off, remember? I didn't even *want* to rebel against Dad. I slept through the whole damn thing, and He still kicked me out, okay? What exactly do you expect me to—"

The furious look I give him coupled with my serpentine eyes mirrored back in his gaze as the flood starts to retreat a little bit farther must be enough to show him I mean business.

"You. Owe. Me."

Hellfire suddenly ignites in my eyes. I can feel it.

Or maybe it was already there.

"Too easy for your first time?" Michael calls from an adjacent rooftop, where a few of his angels and Lucifer's demons appear to be locked in a battle. I begin to shake from head to toe.

He and the other archangels have taken temporary refuge there. Along with my now vulnerable *mortal* husband.

Or should I say "soon-to-be husband"?

I'm done waiting to heal before I allow myself to be happy.

If we survive this, that is.

Mimi is nowhere in sight, and she was supposed to be guarding Lucifer.

Another burst of righteous fury barrels out of me.

The injustice, the pain of it, is unbearable.

I cry out, whether for God or Lucifer, I'm not entirely sure, as the first of a plague of locusts Michael's now summoned pelts me directly in the face.

My knees start to tremble.

You have got to be kidding me, I think as the cloud of insects descends, casting an opposing shadow over the north side of the city.

The side I can't currently guard, because I'm too busy.

My legs bend, the weight of the flood, of God's wrath, of everything finally causing my knees to tremble just as I manage to scream to Sloth, "Whatever it is you want, I'll give it to you!"

These are the conversations I have when I'm trying to save the world, apparently.

Being good at begging has its advantages.

Sloth's expression turns wicked as the massive wave teeters. "Get me back into Heaven again, and then you have yourself a—"

I sink beneath the oppressive weight threatening to crush me. And then I see it there, reflected in the wave. God's judgment. I don't know how I know that's what it is, I just do. All the distorted faces. The memories.

Every moment of inaction where I ever sat by while someone else was . . .

"Deal!" I shriek.

One of those ghostly faces surges, and my knees give out.

I have no idea what kind of promise I'm making.

Or if I can even keep it.

The next thing I know, I smash down into the pavement, my skin ripping open while the sea, the sky, and the locusts overhead converge, blacking out everything.

"God help us," I mutter.

But I guess that Big Asshole and His triple-headed wife/creator are exactly who got us into this damn mess in the first place.

Mother. Fucker.

CHAPTER SIXTEEN

Azrael

I don't know what kind of deal Charlotte managed to wheedle out of Belphegor—whose unsurprising and epic laziness speaks for itself in the fact he chooses to spend all his immortal days in Hawaiian shirts now, apparently—before Charlotte collapses onto the ground.

I become Nothing and shadow toward her.

Sloth rolls his eyes and raises both his hands over his head as if he's been asked to perform his least favorite chore, and the massive tidal wave looming over the south side of the city parts. That lazy dickhead doesn't so much as break a sweat.

But Charlotte is bleeding.

An unnatural resolve fills me.

If I could end him without messing this up for her, I would.

With a single touch.

Being in love makes me . . . unhinged clearly.

Possessive as all fucking get-out.

Bel huffs in annoyance like even that little bit of work physically pains him. At the same moment, I become corporeal again, tugging Charlotte down and into my arms to shield her.

"Lucifer, down!" I shout at the other rooftop, where a battle has broken out between Lucifer's demons and Michael's angels. Where the fuck is Greed? I drag Charlotte onto the ground.

Belphegor waves off what remains of the plague of locusts.

The sky above turns a sickening black.

Not the black of night like Charlotte's or my ex's shadows.

Darker. Hungrier.

Like ink bleeding through everything.

The chaos and terror raining down on the city explodes.

The sea parts, the locusts disappear, and thanks to that lazy fucker Sloth actually working *toward* something for once in his miserable existence, the water starts to recede, its retreat nearly as destructive as its onslaught, as the power of the third seal unlocks.

The few humans who managed to take refuge on the rooftops scream.

Humanity's fate is being weighed and judged until . . .

Famine appears.

Not a person. Not a beast.

A force.

A force a lot like me. Only worse.

Just as God and Lilith created him to be.

The earth and the rooftop beneath us shake, and the pressure in the already cold air suddenly drops. The moral reckoning of the world is silent until—

"Fuck!" I roar, unable to cover my ears before they bleed.

My brother sweeps through the city.

Glass shatters. Skyscrapers moan, their steel bones rotting from the inside out.

The sound is sickening.

The sound of hunger given form.

The screech of God's divine scales leveling.

And *not* in humanity's favor.

I shield Charlotte as well as I can, pressing us both into the ground as I try not to allow myself to consider what this means.

This isn't wrath. This is divine deprivation.

The collapse of everything humanity has known previously.

No lightning. No flames.

Just the slow, grinding halt of a world already starved of His love, of His intervention.

And no one—not me, my ex, or Charlotte—can put a stop to it.

I glance overhead, searching the darkened sky for the sight of my brother, the one God commanded Lilith to create in my image, before I spot the dark horse he's riding.

The Black Rider.

I keep still, a feeling of dread overtaking me.

Unlike War, Famine doesn't need to kill, because as soon as Charlotte opens the next seal . . .

He'll have me to finish the job he just started, unfortunately.

Underneath me, Charlotte gasps, but it isn't Famine she's looking at as he rides off to wreak his terror upon the world.

I follow her gaze to the flood's rapidly receding waters.

To where a human child and her mother desperately cling to the branch of a submerged tree. The violent current thrashes against them, the city's muck and debris surging with the reversed tide. A crushed Citi Bike that's hooked to a stray food cart heads straight for them, clipping the mother just enough that her grip loosens.

The child screams as her mother's washed away.

Charlotte tears from beneath me before I can stop her, scrambling toward the building's edge. "Azrael!" she shouts, gesturing to where the mother and so many others are now being washed out to sea, to the drowning onlookers, who were still on the street when the wave hit.

And the sides of the buildings, where there're even more people pinned.

More victims, more deaths, more drowning.

More people trapped between pieces of debris.

I can't possibly save all of them.

Even I can't be everywhere at once.

And already I feel their ends drawing near.

The cut of fate's string.

But I don't turn away from her.

"Azrael!" she shouts again.

Not a request, but an order. An order from my queen.

One that goes directly against Lucifer's.

I glance toward her then, between her and the rushing tide, flooded by the sense that the end of something significant is near.

She's immortal now, but with what Michael's done to this seal . . .

I can't always see who I'm coming for until it's imminent.

And I swore to stay by her side.

But I also swore I would be her choice, and that's what this means.

Letting her make her own decisions, no matter what ill-fated consequence it may bring.

I've heard enough confessions from the dead and dying to know what regret is.

And I won't regret her.

"I love you," I growl just as I turn to go after the mother.

Though I hope, after last night, she already knows it.

But I learned from someone else never to leave anything unsaid.

For a moment, Charlotte smiles, the joy on her face even more radiant than her Lightbringer. "Tell me again tomorrow."

She's confident we're going to make it through this.

Even if I'm not so certain.

She rushes toward the child.

Like the new guardian angel she's becoming.

Lucifer's bride. Our little siren.

An amused smile twists my lips as I become Nothing again.

Only He would've written a fate this impossible.

CHAPTER SEVENTEEN

Charlotte

I dash across the rooftop, unable to think of anything other than the terror in the little girl's face. She can't be older than five, fresh out of preschool. I know exactly what that kind of terror feels like. What it means to be hurt, to be frightened in the name of a wrathful God who was supposed to love you.

A piece of stray glass slices into my foot, and a sharp pain tears through me.

But I don't let it stop me.

I don't think of anything else—not even my own pain—as I desperately search for a way to reach her, and fast. There's no way I can swim against the receding tide that's cascading like a raging waterfall being funneled back between the buildings, and I can see her small hands starting to slip.

I don't hesitate.

I become shadow and plunge toward her.

When I come out the other side, I'm balanced on a larger gathering of branches nearby, but a gush of the receding water immediately knocks me off my feet.

I go down and into the icy current, hard, cold, adrenaline shooting through me as I use what little strength I have left to fight my way back toward the surface.

I reach for one of the tree's branches, my lungs screaming.

My powers are rapidly draining.

They're like a muscle.

Built from time and training, but now tired from overuse.

Not infinite.

And I used nearly everything I had holding back the flood.

I'm running on empty.

Despite my fear, I reach down inside myself, summoning what little righteous fury I can muster at the unfairness, the injustice, of all this as I reach the water's surface.

Black spots start to swim in my vision.

I burst out of the water a second later, my lungs seizing as I grab on to the nearest branch and use it as an anchor against the oncoming waves.

My muscles scream in protest as one of my hands slips.

Holy shit!

The branch is slippery.

But still, I manage to pull myself up enough that I'm able to throw one of my legs over the tree's edge until I'm straddling the branch.

That was a lot harder than I expected, honestly.

"Hang on!" I shout to the little girl.

The fear and shrillness in my voice sound like the old me.

The one who was just as terrified as the little girl is.

I inch and shimmy my way down the wet branch toward her, the shakiness in my limbs and the rush of the tide making me unsteady as I get as close as I can to grab her without the branch breaking. If she lets go for even a moment, she'll be washed away like the rest of them.

The rest of them . . .

Oh God.

The precautions I tried to plan aren't going to mean a damn thing.

I draw nearer, just a little more, and the waterlogged limb cracks beneath me, lurching suddenly.

Shit!

The little girl screams.

But by the grace of everything that's holy, I manage to grab her at the same moment the skinnier part of the limb she'd clung to washes away. It crashes into a floating dumpster.

I tug her toward me, fighting against the tide to pull her onto my part of the branch.

But she's no longer looking at me.

For one brief moment, I wonder if my serpentine eyes are to blame.

If it's *me* she's so terrified of . . .

But then I see the floating taxi, lifted and carried by the rapid waters, heading straight toward us.

Oh fuck.

We're both going to die, aren't we?

CHAPTER EIGHTEEN

Lucifer

Few horrors in Hell could hold a candle to my Father's divine fury.

It's something I've been trying to remedy for the last several millennia, actually.

Though I am once again the snake in the Garden, bending my siblings' ears, tempting them, and make no mistake, not even my Father can keep them from me.

I grip hold of Jegudiel from behind, pressing one of my celestial blades into his throat as I hiss into his ear. "You remember what it's like, don't you? To march at my side? To feel Heaven tremble beneath our feet? You miss it. He abandoned you, left you all to rot in your own obedience, but *I* offer you freedom."

Like it or not, he and the former leaders of my angelic army will soon be mine again.

As will she.

No matter how hard they may fight to resist me.

The city dissolves into chaos around us, the rapidly receding waters a mere distraction as my demons and I battle it out against my siblings. They hop from building to building as they mount their pathetic attempt to evade me, no longer interested in hearing my hellish sermon on how thoroughly they've betrayed our Father, on how similar they are to me.

But I'm right on their tail at every turn.

Whispering into their ears. Tempting them to our side.

Twisting their darkest desires until they're mine for the taking.

Though portaling to Hell and back to keep up with them is growing tiresome quickly.

Lucifer!

I hear my future wife loud and clear inside my head as Jegudiel thrashes in my arms. A desperate plea.

Though I'm not certain she's conscious of it.

I pause, clutching one of my hands tight to his throat as my brother struggles from where I've just struck him in the jugular with my blade. It won't exactly kill him, but it'll smart all right.

He wasn't interested in what I was offering anyway.

A *true* leader.

In lieu of our Father's divine approval.

They're no better than the sheep He made them, the whole lot of them.

And I'm not the only one among us with daddy issues, apparently.

Lucifer!

I hear Charlotte's voice again, this time more desperate, as Jegudiel's blood coats me.

Like a prayer.

Or when she begs for mercy whenever she's reached her limit inside the playroom.

But I cannot locate her, nor Azrael, on any of the surrounding rooftops, and Mimi has already buggered off to who knows where, which means—

Jegudiel seizes in my arms as my gaze falls toward the rushing waters.

Charlotte holds a human child as a car carried by the current is about to—

My heart plunges into my feet.

But I'd never allow a pesky thing like my own mortality to stop me.

Not when it comes to her.

I shove Jegudiel aside, snatching the three-pronged whip he's known for from his belt before he can stop me.

Dreadfully insignificant legacy, that.

The commotion draws the attention of my other siblings, who attempt to grab me before I can abscond with their celestial weaponry. I dart around them swiftly, far faster on my feet than any of those winged cretins could ever be, as Abaddon and the others among my demonic army come to my aid.

I sprint toward the edge of the building.

My strategy forms as I use Jegudiel's whip to my advantage, roping it up and over a hanging cable before I test its leverage.

I've more than a bit of practice with whips, obviously.

I plunge from the side of the rooftop the moment my angelic siblings reach me, swinging out and above the waters until I land on top of the taxi's moving roof.

My weight has the exact effect I intended it to, knocking the floating vehicle onto another trajectory, so it's no longer aimed at Charlotte. I manage to pocket the whip I nicked from Jegudiel before he has a chance to reclaim it.

"Lucifer!" Charlotte screams.

I follow her gaze in the direction I'm heading, realizing that the shape of the skyscrapers has funneled the receding water into a pouring basin, so I'm about to cascade down into—

"Fuck!"

I lunge, launching myself from the car's hood and over the flood's ledge toward Charlotte, managing to snag hold of one of the tree's limbs.

The branch cracks, my added weight enough to sever the limb completely.

I throw out my arms, catching both Charlotte and the child she's holding as we all go under. I grit my teeth, a muffled snarl tearing from my throat as an explosion of bubbles bursts forth in my fury. Like the true devil I am, I fight against the current, against the tide—like hell is *this* going to be what ends me—swimming for dear life, just as I manage to wedge the three of us between an adjacent branch and the remains of some broken scaffolding. We resurface, my now mortal lungs screaming.

Maybe my future wife is right.

Maybe I *should* quit smoking.

I use my body to shield Charlotte and the child from the brunt of the current's force as I hold on to Charlotte with one arm and shove the child up and onto a sturdier limb with the other.

The little girl coughs as Charlotte grabs hold of the limb and an incoming bodega awning crashes into me.

"Lucifer!" Charlotte shouts, grabbing for me as I go under.

She may no longer be able to die from being washed out to sea, but the child certainly would have.

And now I might, quite frankly.

I suppose this is what I get for attempting to play the hero, even for my bride's benefit.

It doesn't suit me. It never has.

Redemption is for those worth saving to begin with, and I'd much rather be the villain like I've always been.

But my Mother and fate had different ideas, apparently.

PART TWO | EXODUS

And it came to pass . . .

Azrael

They say that the Garden was perfect, but they lied.

It's too green, too quiet. It smells like ripe things on the verge of rot. Too much sweetness and abundance. The air is thick with humidity. It clings to my skin in ways it shouldn't—hot and wet, like a breath before a moan. This place is alive, verdant and hungry.

And he fits all too well here.

Lucifer moves through the Garden like temptation itself. Languid. Precise.

The shadows of the trees and the light overhead seem to shift around him. As if creation is bending in order to keep its eyes on him.

I know what that's like.

I used to be the only one who looked at him that way, but now . . .

I stay out of sight, watching the way his mouth curves when he sees her—Eve. Soft and luminous, her body made of breath and bone and suggestion. She radiates innocence, unaware of how much she's desired.

And he desires her all right.

What she and her temptation have to offer him.

He eases closer, and Eve's head snaps in our direction.

"Who's there?" she asks, soft, unafraid.

She doesn't yet know what it means to feel fear.

Doesn't understand the danger he poses.

Lucifer slithers closer.

"Little one," he purrs, close enough I can feel the hum in his chest, though I'm still a few yards away. His eyes turn serpentine as he transforms into that damn snake.

"Oh, it's you." Eve blushes, smiling innocently, as Lucifer coils up the length of the tree.

She likes when he does that.

Like a child impressed by a cheap trick.

Lucifer transitions into his usual form, settling beside her, and tips his chin toward the sky as if to indicate who he means. "Do you know what He's afraid of?"

Eve tilts her head curiously, smiling up at him.

Curious is dangerous in a place like this.

And he smells it on her.

Circles it like prey.

"That if you taste the fruit," he says, his voice a slow drawl as he plucks an apple from the tree they stand under, "you'll become more than what He made you. That you shall be as gods."

Eve bites her lip.

A small gesture. But I see it.

And so does he.

Lucifer leans in, not touching her—never touching—his presence alone pressing against her.

Intimate. Suggestive.

He doesn't need to do anything to claim her innocence.

It's already his.

He seduces her with his breath, his gaze.

I watch his throat writhe as he speaks.

I know what it's like to be captivated by him.

Know how it feels to sink my teeth there, in that soft hollow near his throat.

His wounds have mostly healed now. Flesh regrown. He wears the fading scars with practiced ease, but I remember how they looked before, remember the way he cried into my chest the first time I kissed one. The way he trembled when I touched him where his wings used to be.

Now he smiles, laughs.

Even if he still doesn't believe he can be forgiven.

The realm that we built is ours, but it's empty, save for the few of his siblings who've joined us recently, the ones who rebelled alongside him, but I think he could be happy here.

In Eden.

He stands in the Garden with Eve like it was made for him.

And suddenly I hate her for it.

She doesn't know what he is, doesn't understand what it cost him to become this—this beautiful, terrible thing. She just knows that he makes her feel something.

Warm. Daring. Alive.

Nothing close to what I feel when he's with me.

He's still talking. Something about awakening. Power. The fruit he holds between them a promise neither of them fully understands.

And then . . .

He glances over his shoulder.

At me.

I'm in the shadow of the trees, but I let him see me. Let my form shimmer just enough to tighten his breath. Remember who it is who holds him when he comes undone.

We don't need Eve or the souls she offers.

The children she and Adam will have.

Lucifer turns back to Eve. His voice drops. Darkens.

I don't hear what he says to her.

"Is it true?" Eve asks, pulling back, her fingers brushing the low branches of the tree. The Tree of Knowledge, as his Father calls it. "That we'll die if we eat it?"

"You'll die either way." Lucifer turns back to me. "Death is already here."

She follows his gaze toward me, her breath catching. Whether it's from awe or from fear or that strange flicker of something she doesn't yet have a word for—I can't tell. But she recoils all the same. Pulling back into herself like she's seen the future and it's wearing my skin.

Lucifer smirks, watching her fear blossom.

And I let him.

Because I still want him to need me.

"You see him there, don't you? Feel him?" Lucifer whispers, his voice coiling around her spine until she shivers. "That cold feeling? That's Death." And then, softer, "He's the one you should fear most."

He lifts the fruit between them with the reverence of a lover lifting a breast to his mouth.

Temptation in the shape of sweetness.

Sin dressed in sunlight.

Eve reaches out and takes it.

"Go on then," Lucifer hisses, distracting her like he's that damn snake again. He steps behind her, brushing the hair from her neck, and she sighs a little at the pleasure of it. "He only fears that you will become like Him."

"Like you?" She glances over her shoulder.

Lucifer grins.

And then, she bites.

The sound that it makes—the soft crunch of innocence unraveling—shouldn't feel so erotic. But it does.

Like the moment a lover's lips part and don't close again.

Her eyes change.

And Lucifer—fuck—Lucifer glows with something more than light as he moves in front of her.

I step into the clearing, silent as shadow, as Eve runs. "You used me."

He smirks, closing the distance between us until I can feel the heat off his skin. "I needed you."

"Not the same."

He leans in, brushing his lips against the shell of my ear, not kissing, but close enough. "They need something to fear, Azrael. It's the only way they'll crave what I'm offering."

I close my eyes.

I want to kiss him.

I want to tear his damn mouth off his face.

"You're mine," I growl, lower than I mean to.

He presses his forehead to mine for a breathless beat, his fingers curling around the back of my neck like I'm still his lover, not a weapon for his celestial use.

For the pain he so desperately wants to bring his Father.

The only thing he still believes he's good at.

"I'm yours, yes. But so are they."

And it's that—*that*—that undoes me.

Lets me know that I'll never be anything more to him than a deadly tool, because he means it.

He'll touch the world.

And I'll be what it fears.

And neither of us will ever be saved.

CHAPTER NINETEEN

Charlotte

The scream that tears from my throat is barely human.

But the little girl in my arms is counting on me.

I keep one eye on the water, desperate for Lucifer to resurface as I shimmy closer to safety. We're near the sturdier trunk of the tree now, and the rapid waters are starting to deplete, making gravity our newest enemy, until suddenly a familiar pair of hands grab me.

Azrael.

I cling tight to the little girl, pulling her into my chest as we're both flung inside the ether.

When we come out the other side, I land with a wet smack on the penthouse's marble floor, coughing and sputtering, the crying girl still clutched in my arms.

I double over, holding her to me. "Shhh. It's okay. It's okay." I look toward Death, eyes pleading. "Lucifer."

"I'm on it." He's gone again in a blink.

The warmth of the penthouse's heaters seeps into us, the sudden change in temperature barely registering. I'm still shivering from all that freezing water.

The little girl lets out a strangled sob, her arms around my neck tightening as I pull her closer. "Shhh. Shh. It's okay. You're safe now. You're safe."

Though I can't say the same for her mother.

Oh God. Oh God.

What terror did I just wreak on this city?

I rock the little girl back and forth in my arms, holding on to her almost as desperately as she does to me. "Shhh. Shhh. You're safe now. You're safe."

Those seem to be the only words I'm capable of saying.

The same ones I'd always wished had been said to me.

We sit like that for minutes that feel like hours, her small, trembling body wrapped around mine. I'm only vaguely aware of one of the penthouse's staff putting a thermal blanket around our shoulders.

And the other people.

The penthouse is full of them.

Humans. Survivors.

Terrorized by what they've just seen.

The third seal was even bigger than the others. More catastrophic.

I have no doubt New York City wasn't the only place that trembled from God's divine fury.

Azrael returns a few minutes later, his back to us, and my heart stops as I watch him lay out a long, dark body on the penthouse's floor.

Bile rises inside my throat.

No. No. It can't be . . .

And then that version of him is gone again.

"Mommy?" The little girl pulls away from me just as the supine woman coughs and sputters. Her daughter runs toward her.

Several of the staff and a few of the survivors, who clearly have medical training, rush to their sides as I bow my head in relief.

That's one small win at least.

But Lucifer is still nowhere to be seen.

I rise to my feet, my legs wooden and unsteady. As if I'm standing outside of my own body. My eyes comb over the survivors. Their injuries. Their wounds. Those who are stricken with grief and mourning for the loved ones they lost.

So many people. So many people.

But what choice did I have?

What choice did God give me?

It's this or allow even more to suffer.

It's this or the end of everything.

Where *is* He?

I stumble through the first floor of the penthouse, the survivors parting in shock as soon as they spot me—I'm more of a myth to them than anything else now—until I find my face pressed against the freezing glass of one of the floor-to-ceiling windows.

The waters over Madison Avenue have receded mostly.

But the chaos, the destruction and devastation, still lie in their wake.

Wet, watery debris lines the streets, and everywhere I look, cars, taxis, and dumpsters are overturned, their contents scattered about the city. Several nearby parking meters are bent and bowed all the way to the ground from the wave's force. And the people . . .

Oh God, the people.

Already they're turning on one another.

Desperate to survive the societal collapse we all know is coming.

Looters and criminals and others are out on the street, hastily making their way among the shattered glass and the dead.

A plump hand squeezes my shoulder.

I turn, only to find Greed staring back at me, her normally smug expression so solemn it's almost . . . regretful.

And yet, she and the other Originals are completely unscathed.

My anger, my frustration at the injustice of it all, is immediate. This whole situation, the unfairness of how humanity's been forced to suffer at the hands of these uncaring immortals, these out-of-touch billionaires, for so long, all in the name of God's will, just pours out of me.

My power comes rushing back on a tide of vengeance.

A lot like the wave that just decimated our city.

Without warning, I lash out, an unexpected blast of Holy Fire bursting from my hands. It instantly singes the broken Schiaparelli Greed's wearing.

I've never conjured anything like it.

"You angelic bitch!" Mimi stumbles back, glancing down at her now exposed body.

She's nearly as stunned as I am.

Every eye in the penthouse turns toward us.

"Where were you?"

"I don't remotely know what you're—"

"Where. Were. You?" I snarl, the fire in my hands blazing.

Greed's eyes narrow. "For your information, I was trailing Uriel, who—"

But I silence her with the single lift of my burning hand, my fear, my grief for humanity, for Lucifer, compounding until I'm practically glowing with the force of it.

"How could you?" I ask, my voice seeming to echo from everywhere.

My entire body glows like an angelic halo—though I've never actually seen any of the real angels I know with a halo—and the foundation of the penthouse starts to tremble as I stride toward Greed. "How could you leave him when you were supposed to be—"

"Charlotte!"

The familiar reprimand stills me.

Instantly makes me regret what I was doing.

I turn just in time to find Lucifer stumbling from the crowd, his arm slung over Azrael's shoulder. He's balanced on one leg like he can't stand on his own.

All the fight rushes out of me.

My fire's glow dims.

He's pale and wet, his dress shirt completely soaked through with water and blood that doesn't appear to be his. His pant leg is torn. It looks like he's injured his leg, and one of his thighs is bleeding. Several small cuts and bruises mar his cheekbones, but he's alive. He's still breathing.

My heart races.

The next thing I know, I'm wrapped in his arms, crying into his chest as he staggers from where I've just thrown myself at him. He manages to keep hold of me as I start to let out all the grief and sorrow I've been choking back.

"I'm sorry. I shouldn't have gotten angry like that. I'm—"

"It's all right, darling."

All those people. All those people.

"Why?" I whisper to him a few moments later, barely able to speak around the emotions that grip me. "Why would He do this to His own children?"

Lucifer tenses beneath me.

His grip on me tightens as I bury my face into him.

But he doesn't say anything.

He just holds me.

And for once, I'm certain he feels it too.

Humanity's pain. Their anguish.

The one thing that connects him and me . . .

The scars we both carry. Made in the name of an angry God.

One whose love has all too often been used like a weapon by the very people who claim to live for Him.

Somewhere in the back of my mind, I'm vaguely aware of the survivors, all the humans around us, watching, until Ramesh and some of the other staff begin to usher them into the penthouse's gymnasium to be clothed and fed and sheltered until emergency services can arrive.

There's not nearly enough of them to serve the entire city.

My chest tightens.

Finally, when we're alone—Lucifer, me, and Azrael—save for a few of the staff who pass through occasionally, I pull back, gazing up at my devilish future husband.

"I'm sorry," I whisper again.

Lucifer's expression softens. "Whatever for, little dove?"

I meet his eyes. "For everything He did to you."

Lucifer wets his lips before he glances away.

He nods slowly.

Gently, he cups my cheek, pulling me into him until he kisses me.

It's soft at first, not like him, but still confident.

Steady. Sure.

A lot like someone else I know.

His kiss deepens, his tongue overpowering mine as his hold on me becomes darker, hungrier, more like the fallen angel I fell in love with initially. I'm so lost in the destructive pull of it all, in each stroke of his tongue, and the overwhelming devotion I feel for him, that the new feeling of fullness low in my belly tightens with need.

I'm his completely.

With or without my collar.

When we both resurface, I gaze up at him, my pulse racing, certainty expanding inside my chest at the understanding that's just formed between him and me.

All this time I've been looking at him the wrong way. Hoping that maybe someday he would change for me. Learn to love humanity as I do. Or at least, believe they deserve to be saved. But there's no such thing as good and evil in celestial battles. No singular villain.

Immortality exists within the shades of gray.

And if there *is* one villain?

Well, maybe the only one who's been standing in the way of Lucifer defeating Him is me.

I grip both of Lucifer's hands, shaking with regret at how angry I feel as I lean into my devil. "I think I may need to go and see my father again soon."

CHAPTER TWENTY

Azrael

I don't get a chance to point out that a visit to Hell might not be the best idea right now, before Lucifer manages to do it for me.

"Do you think it wise, little dove?"

Considering the apocalyptic nightmare that just destroyed half the city . . .

Recovery is going to be a long time coming, if it ever comes.

I stand off to the side near the penthouse's window, struggling not to fade into the Nothing and break the unexplainable hold the two of them seem to have over me.

I couldn't look away if I tried.

And to be fair, some jealous part of me *wants* to.

To turn away and never look back.

But the vulnerability in his eyes, the tenderness is . . . genuine.

Genuine enough to fool me.

I shake my head, scratching at the stubble on my jaw as I search for an excuse to leave. There's nowhere else I'm supposed to be. Most of the souls inside the city are already gone—I work quickly—and the others, the ones still trapped beneath the rubble or those all over the world who'll meet me as Famine rides and society collapses over the coming days, still have a bit of time left to suffer, unfortunately.

And it is suffering. Their lives. Their existence.

I know that firsthand.

But I seem to be incapable of moving from where I'm standing.

He loves her.

He *actually* loves her.

And it's deeper than I thought.

Because she gave him what I couldn't.

Lucifer cups the back of Charlotte's head, his expression far more tender than anything I thought him capable of. I should've known the moment he gifted his Father's redemption to her. It's the one selfless act he's ever been able to claim, and yet, even then, I was skeptical. But I see it now. In the lines of his face, the way he looks at her . . .

That revelation places a whole new level of hurt on the way he and I ended.

It was bad enough when I thought he couldn't love, but now . . .

Now, the way he's looking at her feels far too private for my viewing.

Personal. Intimate.

Like something that was never meant for me.

Like she never was.

Like he never was, either.

Charlotte leans into him, rising on her toes to kiss him again, and God, I must be seriously fucked in the head if I ever thought we could be . . .

She pulls back, their mouths lingering.

I've seen the two of them together plenty of times before, but never . . . never in the small, vulnerable moments when neither of them seems to realize anyone's looking.

Charlotte's staring up at her Lightbringer like he's the key to her whole fucking world, her everything. Like her next breath, her life, fuck, even her death, the one thing that's *supposed* to be mine, somehow lies in his arms.

And Lucifer . . .

Fuck.

Lucifer, I nearly groan.

I inhale, forcing myself to look away.

How many times did I wish that he would look at me like that? Like *I* was the only thing he needed?

And I was, for a while, anyway.

I thought I'd seen every side of him there was. After a millennium together, there are few surprises left, but clearly, I . . . took him for granted.

It almost reminds me of when he . . .

I can't allow myself to finish the thought.

"Not now. Later," Charlotte whispers, brushing some of Lucifer's dark hair from his forehead. The wet strands fall over his brow again smoothly.

Fuck, they're so effortlessly beautiful together, they're almost painful to look at.

But there's something in Charlotte's voice that lets me know she's not agreeing just because she's eager to please him anymore.

It's because she trusts him completely.

In the way he never could me.

The thought is like a knife to my chest, but I'm not sure which one of them is driving it in. She sounded the same way when I had her pinned beneath me last night, when I fucked her until she came apart. My gaze drifts back toward them.

Fuck, I can't help it.

If only . . .

My whole miserable existence seems to be punctuated in those two damn words.

If only . . .

I shake my head, stomping out that thought before it can begin to take hold. No matter how Lucifer and I might be sharing her, the three of us could never be anything.

The love of my life I can't seem to hate, no matter how hard I try, and the one woman who's ever managed to—

"I want you," Charlotte whispers against his lips, causing my cock to stiffen.

This is not for me. Not for my eyes.

But some invisible force seems to tug at me.

Not fate, but something damn close to it.

Something as powerful as I am.

Suddenly, Charlotte glances over Lucifer's shoulder at me, like I'm no longer alone and she can feel it too.

I press my lips together, swallowing the aroused growl that nearly tears from my throat. I watch her trail a possessive hand over Lucifer's biceps as she stares at me.

A dangerous jealousy strikes hot, clouding my vision.

And I'm torn between whether it's directed toward him or at her.

I'm not sure it fucking matters.

I can't see Lucifer's expression from where his mouth's now buried in the crook of her neck, but the gleam in Charlotte's eyes as she looks at me makes her message loud and clear.

She's not asking for his softness right now.

And she's not content with me sitting on the sidelines either.

She wants *both* of us.

But Lucifer is never going to agree.

"Are you asking to wear my collar for tonight, little dove?" he purrs, pulling back as his thumb traces over the smooth leather of the training one she's wearing like it's jewelry. "For me to make you mine again in every way?" He hooks two fingers underneath it as he yanks her to him.

Mine.

I see red.

A sudden pulse of jealous fury barrels through me.

I prowl forward, prepared to do . . . fuck, I don't even know what.

She's his. She always has been, and yet . . .

I won't let her go that easily.

Charlotte's eyes widen, and she shakes her head, staying me, even as she flicks those innocent doe eyes back toward Lucifer and snakes her arms around his neck.

Like she's *trying* to make a vicious monster out of me.

"Not just yours," she whispers before she looks toward me. "Azrael?"

She puts out her hand, reaching out like she expects me to take it.

But I'm frozen in place.

The taut feeling in my abs hardens, my cock aching.

Lucifer seems to recognize the dilemma she's placed us in as much as I do, and he has just as many reservations about this, because without missing a beat, he clears his throat and says, "Charlotte, darling, I'm not certain it's a wise idea if Azrael and I—"

"Please, Daddy?" she whispers, blinking up at him. "For tonight."

My already stiff cock twitches as Lucifer's gaze rakes over her.

The hunger in his eyes is readily apparent.

My balls tighten.

Lucifer looks toward me then, the hellfire in his irises flaring. He's still furious with me from learning that I put the blade into play, even if I did have my reasons, but what else is new? And I think, for a second, he's going to make some excuse for us both, but then his gaze falls to my lips, and a familiar ache sparks inside my chest.

So sharp, so dangerous and acute, it's almost . . . destructive.

As destructive as he and I together could be.

A moment of tension passes. A momentary truce.

He and I are even now.

It's always a fine line we're walking.

Between love and hate, hope and toxicity.

But now there's one thing that can remain steady.

Our devotion to her.

The words he hurled at me like weapons earlier come rushing back to me. *I would make any deal, destroy anything in my path. Lie, cheat, kill, sin, stop my Father's goddamn apocalypse, and upend the whole fucking universe if that's what it takes to see her happy.*

And I'd do the same. In a heartbeat.

But *this* is different.

It has to be.

I'm not certain I could handle it, if he still had feelings for me.

Lucifer holds my gaze for a long beat, the two of us locked in some kind of eternal battle, and then he gives a curt nod before he looks away quickly.

Like he's afraid I might see too much.

My knees go weak.

"Both of you go to the playroom and wait in position for me," he orders, his voice dropping to that all-too-familiar register he used to use on me.

The one he now uses with *her.*

"Death and I will indulge you in this one time only."

CHAPTER TWENTY-ONE

Charlotte

Neither Azrael nor I manage to say anything as we climb the stairs toward the penthouse's fifth floor. I think we're both in a bit of shock. Over the devastation, the aftermath, the anger I just unleashed, Lucifer, and now this. Neither of us even seems able to look at the other, but I can't help but wonder what the Angel of Death is thinking.

Is he angry? Grateful? Turned on?

All that and more?

Honestly, I can't tell, and the thought concerns me.

I should have consulted him first.

But my own reckless desires got the better of me.

One more reason to keep the rage inside me locked down.

Like my father and his congregation taught me.

Finally, when we're alone inside the playroom, I distract myself from my guilt by retrieving my pillow and placing it where it's supposed to be, at the foot of Lucifer's chair. I know how Azrael still feels about Lucifer despite all the times he's tried to deny it.

Some small part of me can't help but hope that maybe, one day, there might be . . . a future. For the three of us.

I push the thought aside as I settle myself in front of Lucifer's throne. Lowering to my knees, I drop my head and try to mentally place myself into submission. Lucifer said this was one time only, and I have to be okay with that if I want to be with him. I have to be.

I focus on my breathing.

In and out. Slowly.

Azrael wouldn't be here if he didn't want to be. Would he?

I open my eyes, expecting to find him waiting there on the floor beside me.

Instead, he's standing on the throne's dais, wearing a furious expression that reminds me all too much of when we first started training. An odd mix of agitation and desire, and also . . .

Something darker.

Something hungry.

"Aren't you going to—"

"I kneel for no one," he growls, the dark look in his eyes flashing as he assumes his place on the throne's right-hand side, like the perfect soldier at ease. "And you'll call me sir."

I pale slightly.

When we're alone, Daddy Death is one thing, but with Lucifer here, I'm getting two Doms for the price of one, apparently.

What the hell did I just get myself into?

I worry my lower lip, a delicious mix of excitement and a lick of fear overtaking me.

Azrael's made it obvious there's a clear hierarchy to the three of us playing.

And I'm at the very bottom, it seems.

Caught between Death and the devil.

I can think of worse places to be.

"Are you angry with me?" I whisper, gazing up at him.

Azrael's expression remains distant, cold. "Would it matter?" The skeletal side of his face flashes as he looks at me, his scarred brow hitching.

"Yes," I say, eyes pleading.

His resolve softens.

Azrael prowls forward, standing so that I'm eye level with his belt buckle, and the massive swell of his cock is right in my—

Oh. Oh.

I swallow thickly.

My mouth starts to water, and I lick my lips as Azrael tips my chin up, grinning like he knows exactly what he's doing to me. "Be a good girl now and don't get us in trouble with your other daddy. Okay, little siren?"

I nod weakly.

I'm putty in Death's hands.

I'll do whatever he wants. Whatever he asks of me.

I know I'll be rewarded for it later.

Azrael steps away, a smug expression on his face as he climbs back up onto the dais.

My knees loosen, and I have to resist the urge to rock back and forth, rubbing my clit against my pillow at the sight of him, here, in the playroom with me.

This is every fantasy I've had since I first dreamed of him, and more.

My gaze hungrily traces over all the dark ink on his arms.

"Are you going to—"

"I wouldn't be standing here if I didn't want to be, Charlotte," he says without looking at me, like he knows exactly how to quiet my anxious mind.

I nod, hesitating. "About what you said earlier . . ."

"I meant it." Azrael's cool blue eyes turn to me, and the intensity in them is so sharp, so severe, my breath catches. "Nothing's going to change that."

My heart races.

I believe him.

Death's presence in my life is constant.

He's loyal. Without a doubt.

An anchor for when Lucifer untethers me.

I open my mouth to say as much, but the door to the playroom opens, and the devil enters.

I stiffen.

I quickly drop my gaze, looking down at the floor like I'm supposed to.

With Lucifer, I sometimes like to misbehave, test my boundaries, to see what he'll do to punish me, to remind me of his love, but with Azrael, I always want to be a good girl.

A tingling sensation erupts all over my body.

I don't know how to act currently.

The sound of Lucifer's Armanis striking the floor is deliberate, unhurried, if a bit staggered from where his leg was injured from whatever happened beneath the flood's waters. The staff downstairs must have bandaged him and given him a fresh change of clothes, because he's no longer soaked through like Azrael and me.

I try not to think about what it felt like to watch him disappear beneath the waves, how panicked I was thinking that he might be . . .

I push the thought aside, focusing on the here and now.

That's what this is about after all.

I'm not going to waste another moment doubting what I want.

I'm going to grab life by the devil's horns.

Or Death's wings.

Why choose?

I can't speak for Lucifer or Azrael, but the idea of escaping like this, of stepping out of the chaos of the apocalypse, even just for a little while, already has me soaked.

I'm aching for it.

For *both* of them.

Lucifer's Armanis come to a stop as they enter my line of vision, and I can hardly breathe from the relief, the anticipation that fills me.

God, I've needed this.

We've *all* needed this.

"Same protocol as always, darling." Lucifer pats my head like I am his pet, his creature, and no matter what awful and wicked things I might do, I always will be.

And I love it.

Nearly as much as I love him.

I'm devoted to him, truly.

I lean into his touch, sinking into my role eagerly as I lower my head and kiss both of his shoes like he taught me.

The polished smell of the leather fills my nose like a homecoming.

God, I've missed this. Missed him.

It's been too long since I've had him like this.

"And you." Lucifer pivots toward Azrael, and the tension in the room shifts, pulling tighter than one of his piano's strings. "I will remind you only once who's in charge here."

I chance a look from where I'm knelt on my pillow, curiosity getting the better of me.

"And who's that?" Azrael smirks wickedly.

The brief flash of challenge in Azrael's eyes as he meets Lucifer's gaze is palpable.

I feel myself slicken.

Oh, this is going to be good.

Apparently I'm not the only one who's been waiting for this.

They're both just as into this as me.

I sit on my hands to keep from touching myself before one of my daddies lets me.

My daddies . . .

I press my lips together, trying to hide my amusement.

Even if it's the thrill of my husband's punishment I'm craving currently.

"You know better than to keep her waiting," Lucifer growls to Azrael.

"Yes, sir," Azrael quips back, his tone mocking.

I can't help but whimper in need.

I glance down, struggling to hide my eager grin.

This is already so much better than I imagined.

Azrael stares directly at Lucifer, unwilling to yield to him.

Lucifer climbs up and onto the dais, circling Azrael, his gaze raking over Death from head to toe. The corded muscles, the tattoos, the low-hanging jeans that do nothing to hide the massive swell at Azrael's fly.

"Stop smirking like the greedy little slut you've become," Lucifer snarls, his head snapping in my direction.

As if I've been accidentally sending my thoughts to him down our connection.

I pale slightly, dropping my head and my grin.

It's like he can see out of the back of his head or something.

"Yes, sir," I mutter, trying my best to sound obedient.

But I've been dying to be a brat lately.

And it's obvious to us all.

I peek up at him again.

The look Lucifer gives me is one of mild amusement. Like he isn't surprised, but he's also incredibly proud of me.

And that kind of pride in the hands of the devil can be dangerous.

Devastatingly so.

A slow, devious grin spreads across his features, that all-too-familiar grin lighting up my insides in every way.

He's been biding his time, waiting for the exact moment when I'd finally fuck up and give in to my addiction to him again. Just long enough for him to have an excuse to draw out my every dark, wicked desire, every delicious punishment he's been planning ever since the last time he and I were alone in the playroom.

And now he has Death to use as one of his tools against me.

I swallow, my limbs going weak.

I seriously need to stop thinking with my pussy.

Lucifer's chin tips up, and beside him Azrael steps forward, like even without words he knows exactly what he and Lucifer are going to do to me.

Why did I not recognize the monstrous duo I was creating?

Death prowls toward me as the devil smirks at me, and my breath quickens.

Oh fuck.

CHAPTER TWENTY-TWO

Lucifer

My future wife recognizes her fatal mistake the moment Azrael and I move toward her. If she ever dared consider *my* punishments too severe, she will rue the day she ever invited Death into the sanctity of our dynamic.

I will make them both beg for me.

As soon as we're finished with her, at any rate.

Azrael stalks forward, clutching Charlotte by the delicate curve of her throat and yanking her up by my old training collar.

She stands there before us, trembling.

"Undress her," I order.

Our Reaper makes quick work of it, though by my command or because he already intended to do so, I'm not certain. He guides Charlotte to lift her arms, with no more than a gruff grunt before he easily strips her wet dress from her.

I've never seen him this possessive before.

This dangerously intent.

And I'm not certain I like it.

My wife's knees are still raw and red from where they unexpectedly scraped against the rooftop earlier, from when she oh so spectacularly held back my Father's rage.

I could've murdered my lazy excuse for a brother in cold blood for ever daring to subject her to that, but already she's healing.

Thanks to the immortality that *I* gifted her.

I will make Michael suffer like the insignificant leech he is for daring to weaken me so much that she felt bold enough to request this.

But how could I have denied her?

I couldn't have been prouder of her, watching her openly defy my Father like that.

It was practically foreplay for me.

When Azrael's finished, she stands in nothing more than her undergarments, the white lacy material I bought for her soaked through so that her pebbled nipples are now a dusky, seductive pink. Azrael strips off his own shirt without me having to request it, leaving him bare from the waist up, all his corded muscles and black tattoos on display.

I still remember when he first returned to Hell like that, after he'd adorned himself with one of those early primitive art pieces like some of the humans he'd seen.

My response had been, well, properly enthusiastic.

He and Charlotte look positively sinful together.

Like Adam and Eve.

But it's *my* bone she's made of, thankfully.

"Sir?" Charlotte says, as if instead of appreciating the sight of them, I have somehow forgotten what I'm supposed to be doing.

"Don't look at him. Look at me," Azrael growls, gripping her face. "He's not going to help you."

Her gaze darts toward him, and then back again, bouncing between the two of us like she can't decide who intimidates her more.

My cock hardens.

"How many times have I told you not to speak before spoken to, cumslut?" I snarl, stepping forward as I come to Azrael's aid.

This is how it's going to be, apparently.

Death and I are a torturous team again. For tonight only.

Even if she is and always will be *mine.*

"I'm sorry, sir," she whispers, lowering her gaze as I take hold of her collar and Azrael passes her to me. I make quick work of stripping what remains of her clothing, relishing in the way it feels to have her submit to me.

I craved this. Crave her.

The gift that her submission is to me.

Despite the level of cruelty in my tone, eventually I catch her peeking up and over at Azrael again through the thick layer of her dark lashes.

A furious growl tears through me.

The way she's openly defying me, watching him when she thinks I'm no longer looking, is all too familiar to me.

It's the same way she looks at me when she . . .

My spine runs cold.

She loves him.

Without a doubt.

My nostrils flare, the muscles inside my throat constricting as the sudden realization makes it difficult to breathe. The tension that erupts inside my jaw from where I've clenched my teeth so bloody hard I've practically ground them to dust is a new level of mortal pain for me.

I see red.

She was *never* supposed to feel anything for him.

That blasted priest's prophetic warning comes barreling back to me.

Don't make her choose, Sammael.

I pause.

Prophetic.

My eyes widen momentarily.

I tuck that thought away for another time, another place, as an unpleasant tingling sensation skitters through me. Don't make her choose, eh?

Well, bugger that.

Bugger that all the way down to my goddamn realm and back.

I've been handling them both with kid gloves.

But that stops here.

I clutch Charlotte by the throat, my grip tightening, and my gaze darts between them. They want to tempt the wrath of the devil?

Well, they'd best brace themselves for the horns.

I'm ready to play.

I cast Charlotte onto the floor as I turn toward Azrael. "Put her on the spanking bench," I snarl. *"Now."*

"No. No, please, Daddy, I—" Charlotte starts to plead, but I ignore her.

After that little stunt with my Father's blade, she should consider herself lucky that I didn't destroy her deathly paramour permanently.

Let alone now that she expects me to allow him to fuck her inside *my* playroom.

I can put an end to this little charade just as well as I can begin it.

"Did I stutter?" I growl when I realize neither Charlotte nor Azrael has moved.

But then Azrael steps forward again, gripping her by *my* collar and leading her like a kicked dog on a leash toward the bench.

To my shock, she obeys readily. Trailing along behind him like she's almost regretful. Not so much as a hint of fight in her. One of my brows lifts.

Who *is* this docile minx?

Certainly not the brat I've been taming.

Her willingness to submit to him only fuels my resolve as Azrael shoves her face first onto the bench, spreading her legs and chaining her in place. Charlotte's breathing becomes audible in a heady mix of desire and fear, but there's not a hint of protest in her eyes.

And I don't like it.

Not one bloody bit.

For Death she's an obedient little bitch, apparently. Though not for long.

Not if I have anything to say about it.

Locking her in place, Azrael's gaze never leaves her, like she's the most exquisite thing he's ever seen.

That makes two of us.

But it's not *her* punishment I'm plotting currently.

It's his, the impetuous bastard.

Immortal or not, if he ever dares leave her side again against *my* orders, I will make him beg at my feet like the glorified guard dog he is as I force him to watch her come apart for me.

To remind him *exactly* of his place.

Her punishment is just bonus for me.

Once Azrael's finished positioning her, my future wife lies flat upon the slight curve of her stomach, her wrists and ankles shackled upon the lower padded sections of the bench so that she's on all fours. She's been looking a bit peaky in the mornings as of late, but as my brother tactfully reminded me in front of the entire world, there's no possibility that it could mean anything. One more thing I gave up when I gifted her my Father's redemption.

The Righteous will go to Heaven, and I'll sooner sprout wings and fly than my Father would ever allow me to regain my ability to create.

It's one of the many things He took when He stripped my wings from me.

Along with my dignity.

My jaw tightens. Charlotte's simply been feeling ill with the stress of my Father's impending apocalypse, that's all. I cannot allow myself to entertain that it could be anything more than that. Immortality's effects have merely not taken well to her.

But now she's as lush and ripe as ever.

A fresh apple for the taking.

I prowl across the room and position myself behind her, my hand caressing the smooth curves of her bare ass cheeks. "This is for your own good," I growl. "To remind you who exactly who you belong to." I pull back my hand as I snarl, "*Me*."

My hand comes down even harder than usual, and Charlotte screams.

The first blow is always the most shocking, but I don't give her a moment's reprieve.

Her cries fill the playroom as I spank her within an inch of her life for ever daring to get cheeky with me, until her ass is nearly as red as the head of my throbbing cock.

"Are you going to punish her all day, or are we going to do this?" Death asks, once I'm nearly finished with her, purposefully irritating me.

Like he intends for this to be a level playing field between us.

Fat chance that.

"Eager now, are you? Let's see how long your impatience lasts." I round toward Charlotte's head, Death glowering at me as I say to her, "Show me you're worth the next step."

Between the two of them, they'll be lucky if I don't keep them locked inside this room for the next several days. Even without my powers, torturing them wouldn't exactly be a chore. And I will reclaim what is mine again soon enough.

In more ways than one, apparently.

I run my thumb across her lips before I force two of my fingers into her mouth. "Suck, cumslut."

She obeys readily.

Like the perfectly trained whore I taught her to be.

At her core, she is and always will be mine.

And I'm about to prove it to them both.

Azrael has been a mere distraction.

"Your job is to stay quiet like the nasty little slut you've been." I withdraw my fingers from her mouth, lulling her into complacency, before I shove them back in so far she chokes.

Her eyes water.

But she remains silent.

Playing the good girl for me.

Once I remove my hand, she hangs her head, clearly distressed at how thoroughly she's disappointed me. She falls silent, like the obedient submissive she's pretending to be. I retrieve a black silk blindfold from my tool bag. I tie it behind her head, covering her eyes so she can no longer see, before I step back and slip off my shoes.

I won't allow her to recognize me by the sound of my Armanis.

Not for this.

I beckon Azrael forward with a tip of my chin, dropping my voice low as I begin to instruct him on what to do. "Two fingers to start. Keep your pace slow. If she moans before I say, you'll stop and wait until I tell you to resume. You'll praise everything she's doing out loud—no hesitation—or I'll gag the both of you and make you listen instead. You don't get to finish unless she does. If you move too fast, she loses everything. If you get it wrong, I make her wait. Understood?"

He grumbles in the affirmative.

"Good. Follow my instructions."

"And if I don't?" Death's eyes narrow.

I cast him an unamused grin, my gaze raking over him. "Fuck about and find out, why don't you?" I step away, ignoring his futile battle for dominance with me. We both know who's in charge here. "The safe word is inferno," I remind him. "As always."

Azrael tips up his chin in agreement.

And the hellfire in my eyes blazes as Death obeys me.

"Let's begin, shall we?"

CHAPTER TWENTY-THREE

Azrael

Lucifer retrieves one of his vibrators from his tool bag, along with a few other instruments he intends for us to use—a gradient of butt plugs, a leather paddle from the tool rack on the wall, and some luxury brand of lube—before he lays them out on a movable table near me.

"We alternate between us, pleasure and pain," he mutters into my ear.

He doesn't need to specify which one of us will be doing what.

The answer is obvious to me.

I'm pleasure. He's pain.

A part of our old routine.

Back when he and I used to spend as much of our time working over Hell's early victims as we did exploring each other's bodies, while we built his realm together.

With only a modicum of help from his rebellious siblings.

The confusion the two of us will wreak upon Charlotte will be disorienting, heightening every sensation so she never knows what to expect.

Or who, rather.

Only for me to rip away her pleasure or Lucifer to punish her cruelly when the time is right. I'm feeling unusually brutal, considering the circumstances.

But this isn't going to last.

My gaze darts to Lucifer. Every look, every touch, every unspoken feeling is a savage reminder to me.

A reminder of how it was *supposed* to be.

And for what?

Only for him to ruthlessly cut me from his life the moment he learned of the deal his Father made with me.

Our shared devotion to Charlotte may have thrust us back together, may have temporarily mended what had been broken.

But he and I will never be anything to each other.

Not again.

I start with one of the butt plugs, lubing it up, before I yank down Charlotte's thong and rip the flimsy material in two. I insert the first slender gradient into her anus, that sweet, unpenetrated peach puckering as Lucifer massages her head. She rocks back eagerly.

"More," she moans. "More please, Daddy."

"Which one?" I quip.

"Do I need to get out the ball gag?" Lucifer snarls, gripping her hair. "I told you to stay quiet."

He was always so damn quick on the punishment.

I shake my head.

"She's only a brat until you make her forget how to breathe, then she'll be whatever you want her to be." My hand connects with her pussy as I use a bit of my power to remind her who she's fucking with.

She sputters, shrinking forward, unable to breathe. She pushes her blindfolded face against Lucifer's thigh, burying herself into him.

A silent plea for his mercy.

Like the devil might somehow save her from me.

Lucifer tsks, like he's disappointed in how well she behaves for me, but I can see the thick strain of his cock as he undoes his suit pants.

The devil is enjoying himself.

Even if I currently have no plans to ass-fuck him.

I return my attention to Charlotte, releasing her. "Baby girl, I want you to hear me when I say this, okay?"

Charlotte whimpers, gasping for air, and I use one of my fingers to slowly circle her clit.

"This is me being firm. So, I'm giving you permission to be a little messy, okay? But you're still my good girl, even when you're tired, even when you're overwhelmed, even when I punish you, even when that beautiful mind of yours tells you that you're not, understand?"

She nods weakly.

Lucifer growls, digging his fingers into her hair.

"I see how hard you're trying."

He grips her face.

"But remember"—I lick my lips—"you asked for this."

Abruptly, Lucifer yanks her head back, causing her to arch against her cuffed wrists and into my waiting hand.

"Repeat after me, little dove," he orders as I thrust into her pussy. "I will *not* disobey my master."

"I will not disobey my master," Charlotte cries, just as I wrap my arm around her, supporting her enough that Lucifer's given access to her breasts before he brings his nipple clamps down on her, hard, both at once.

To draw out the pain they bring.

Charlotte swallows her scream, fighting to stay quiet.

"Again," Lucifer orders as I lower her onto the bench and thrust into her.

Fuck, she's already soaked for me.

"I will not disobey my master," she whimpers.

"And who's that?" I growl, pausing only long enough to finish stripping out of my clothes before I pump the hardened head of my dick.

I stroke my cock with one hand and finger her with the other.

She's so fucking wet it takes everything I have not to break protocol and fuck her like she needs.

Charlotte doesn't answer at first, but then finally she toys with her lip and in her sassiest tone says, "Me."

Lucifer and I both growl in unison.

"I'm my own master now." She grins, ever the brat Lucifer's been taming.

"There's my wicked, wicked girl." Lucifer smirks as he shoves his now exposed cock into her mouth.

I slide into her pussy.

She's slick and tight and ready, and the hint of resistance I get as I thrust into her, balls deep, is only from my size.

"You want to try that again, little siren?" I growl, Lucifer's grip on her hair tightening as he face fucks from the other end.

My skeletal side flashes.

"Azrael," Lucifer growls in warning, reining me back in, just as Charlotte starts to choke from where I was using a bit of my power to edge her.

The hellfire in Lucifer's eyes blazes. "Control yourself before I do it for you, Reaper."

And he's right.

I tend to get ahead of myself when I'm around her.

Forget my place.

Exactly like I've been doing all along, actually.

I release her again.

"I'm sorry. I'm sorry. Both," Charlotte rasps, lapping and licking at Lucifer's cock like she's still dying to have him in her mouth.

He grins down at her.

"You're both in charge."

My cock stiffens as Lucifer and I share an amused glance.

Now *that's* something he and I can currently agree on.

With Charlotte reminded of her role, Lucifer motions for me to switch positions with him. Reluctantly, I pull out and stand at her head, arms crossed, watching as he takes over.

"You're enjoying this, aren't you, little dove?" Lucifer purrs, painting his cock up and down her seam, until the head of his dick is slick and damp with her heat. "You're nothing but the dirty little slut that I've made you."

"Yes, sir," Charlotte moans from where *my* cock is now slapping against the side of her face. She nuzzles and kisses at it, searching for the head.

Working himself into her, Lucifer traces his hands along her hips, like he's imagining all the things he might do to her if he still had his shadows.

Fuck, we're all so goddamn into this.

And then Charlotte . . .

My sweet little siren shivers—fucking *shivers* beneath Lucifer's touch—just like she did last night when we . . .

My cock throbs painfully.

My breath becomes coarser, more unhinged as she takes me into her mouth.

I throw back my head, trying to convince myself that it doesn't matter. That it's only supposed to be a one-time thing.

But it does matter. Of course, it does.

They *both* matter to me.

Charlotte keens around my cock, her tongue flicking over the underside of the head, and I let out a guttural groan as she spreads her legs wider and starts to rock back onto Lucifer wickedly, seeking him out like a bitch in heat.

A mischievous smile plays on his lips.

"You're a good girl. You're such a good, good girl, aren't you, little siren?" I growl.

Though when she starts to moan around my cock, Lucifer snarls, "Quiet, Charlotte," his grip on her tightening.

The hot and cold is intentional.

Meant to confuse and disorient.

To deepen everything.

More than either of us could ever achieve on our own.

We work her over until she's covered in sweat and shaking, so deep into subspace she'd give or do anything to please us.

"What do you want, little siren?" I ask as Lucifer removes her butt plug and reaches for the next size gradient. Spreading the generous curve of her ass, he rubs his thumb over the tight hole there. "This is your fantasy we're chasing."

She pops off my cock. "I want—"

"I told her to be quiet," Lucifer growls.

"But *I* didn't." I shoot him a narrowed look.

"I'll grant you this one indulgence, but break protocol again and you'll be fucked just like she is." Lucifer's grin turns devious as he thrusts into her like he's proving a point. He presses the next size butt plug into her ass a moment later. He's not going to let me take charge that easily. He knows every button she likes pressed. Every curve of her body.

But he hasn't found a way to keep me in check yet.

And I'm not going to let him.

"Tell us what you want, baby girl," I say.

Charlotte moans. "I want . . . I want both of you."

"Be more specific," Lucifer orders, trying to reassert that he's in charge here.

But I'm not having it.

"Don't listen to him. Listen to me. You're doing perfect, little siren, but be a good girl for your other daddy."

"As if I would ever need your assistance with *my wife*." Hellfire sparks in Lucifer's gaze. "She's only a willful little brat because I allow her to be." He shoves his cock even deeper into her, his grip on her hips digging in like he's aiming for a particular spot.

Charlotte goes wild, seizing and coming all over him.

Lucifer smirks at me. "She's mine. Just like you always were."

My heart stops momentarily.

He thrusts forward, driving into the spot that has Charlotte turning feral, as he tilts his head back, relishing in the feel of her. It's like he's mapped out her entire anatomy, like he did with me, before he grabs the leather paddle on the table and suddenly whaps it onto her ass.

Charlotte rocks forward, the force of it nearly making me cum.

Her teeth pinch down, dragging across my cock, and the slight pain of it has me reeling.

"Do it again," I snarl, fisting her hair.

A sly grin twists the devil's lips, but he indulges me.

The paddle comes down, sending her lurching forward, and Charlotte's teeth run over my shaft.

I nearly lose it right then and there.

Fuck me.

Fuck me, he's playing us both like a goddamn fiddle.

The feeling of her hot mouth on my cock while I know he's toying with me is everything.

"I want one of you in each hole," Charlotte pants, kissing and nipping at me hungrily, so fucking perfect and sweet. Her chest flushes pink. "Oh God. Don't make me say it again, Daddy," she begs Lucifer.

We both thrust into her.

"Not even the Eiffel Tower was ever going to be enough for you, was it, darling?" Lucifer lets out a dark chuckle, teasing her about the name for the position we're in as he strokes a hand over her burning ass cheek.

Their trip to Paris for Fashion Week is approaching quickly.

And with Lucifer fighting hard for their upcoming nuptials, I don't want to imagine what he might have planned to steal her from me while he . . .

"No." I shake my head, running a reverent hand across Charlotte's cheek as I thrust so hard into her mouth her throat clenches around me. Mine and Lucifer's eyes meet. "Nothing is too much for our girl."

Our girl.

Lucifer's nostrils flare like he enjoys the sound of that as much as I do.

Though he's not ever going to fucking admit it.

He licks his lips. "Uncuff her," he orders.

I pull out and follow his instructions before he beckons me with a tip of his chin to lie down on the bench. I lift and position Charlotte over the top of my cock's head, her palms flat on my chest as Lucifer spreads her ass cheeks.

"Now, little dove," he purrs, as he takes hold of her hips, squeezing as we both start to sink into her. "Show Daddy Death how filthy you can be, darling."

CHAPTER TWENTY-FOUR

Charlotte

"So filthy, sir," I moan, answering my husband as I feverishly try to grind my clit against his hand, but I'm so full of Azrael, reaching him is currently impossible.

Azrael sees my need and meets it, rubbing against my clit, first with his fingers and then with some of Lucifer's shadows he conjures, until I'm practically coming apart at the seams.

It's like cool silk slipping over my skin.

Meanwhile, Lucifer's working his way into my ass like it's an even tighter fit than usual, though he's spent the last several weeks building me up to various kinds of anal play, and like the true Dominant he is, he's curated this experience perfectly and is thoroughly lubed up.

But Azrael's already stretching me to the max.

There's no more room, and I'm riding him so hard that I can't think straight.

My blindfold comes off suddenly.

I stare down into Death's face.

His eyes so full of love that I shudder and shake. Lucifer's hands snake up my sides and onto my breasts, unexpectedly removing the nipple clamps, and I cry out as the sensation rushes back to them, making me ache.

My pussy slickens, starting to throb, just as Lucifer manages to shove himself the rest of the way in, so that he's seated all the way to the hilt, and then . . .

Holy hell.

They're both inside me.

My nipples pulse, the clamps' release coupled with the pressure of having them both stretching me is driving me so high that I'm full to the brim.

Lucifer grips my throat before he ruthlessly twists me toward him, cutting off both my orgasm and my airway as he and Azrael stop moving.

"You will *not* come before I tell you. Do I make myself clear?" he snarls into my ear.

"Yes, sir," I rasp as he releases me.

The pain in my lungs sears, sharp and merciless.

His cock gives a sharp jerk inside my ass as he slowly starts to thrust, and in response, Azrael starts to swell inside my pussy.

A gasp tears from my lips, and I try not to moan as they move in tandem, but the sound I make to stop myself from losing it is just as damning.

I sound like the devil's temptress my father always said I'd be.

As I ride both Death and the devil's cocks.

"Well, would you look at that, Lightbringer." Azrael chuckles, clenching his ab muscles so that his dick twitches again. On the other side of that thin wall, Lucifer throbs in response as he thrusts into me balls deep, full force, and I pitch farther forward, bracing myself on Azrael's pecs, whimpering.

"She's not going to last long, Luce," Death growls, his graveled voice making his chest rumble beneath me. "I think she likes that I can feel you there."

In response a gush of heat rushes through me, and I'm certain they can both feel it.

Lucifer chuckles. "Of course she does," he purrs, the heat of his breath trailing over my bruised neck as they both increase their speed, until they're practically pummeling me. "Nothing but the best for my girl."

My girl.

Something inside me aches.

I want to be his again so badly, but why does the sound of that make me heartbroken?

The delicious pressure inside me builds.

Until I'm not sure how much longer I can withstand it.

That full feeling in my belly starts to throb, intensifying the ache, like I might actually be breaking apart.

Without warning, Lucifer rotates my head to steal a quick kiss from me that ends with him deliciously dragging my lower lip between his teeth before he growls, "But if she likes the sight of you on your back, Azrael, wait until she sees you on your knees for me."

Abruptly, I feel Azrael's legs part. I glance over my shoulder, and Lucifer shoves two fingers up into Azrael's ass and curls.

Death's cock turns as hard as stone inside me, the impossible size of him thickening until he feels all-consuming.

I pitch forward again, crying out as Lucifer pounds into *both* our asses, his thrusts punishing as he sends both of us careening over the edge.

I pulse and pulse around Azrael, milking every bit of what he gives me like a shameless little whore.

And I know my future husband can feel it too.

He's never going to let me live this down, is he?

Just as Azrael starts to pull out, Lucifer's hand comes down onto my pussy so hard Death's cum gushes from me. Grinning wickedly, Lucifer licks some of it from his fingers, and then shoves them into my mouth as he snarls, "Now both of you shut the fuck up and come like the nasty little sluts I've taught you to be."

CHAPTER TWENTY-FIVE

Lucifer

I watch the two of them eagerly as they finish, reveling in how easily they come apart for me. Charlotte's so pumped full of us she's praying to me like I'm the goddamn Holy Spirit as I pound into her ass, my fingers thrusting up into Azrael and affecting them both.

The walls of the playroom erupt with the sound of their screams.

But I'm not finished with them yet.

Charlotte collapses on top of her deathly paramour from where she's trapped between us, and I pull out, peeling apart our sweat- and cum-covered bodies only to retrieve the blindfold as Azrael pulls her into his arms.

He's watching me now with narrowed eyes like he's trying to get a read on me and determine exactly what game it is I'm playing.

I've never been this amenable with any of our other lovers before, so he has no idea what to expect, yet he knows better than to assume I don't have anything up my sleeve.

But I'm not prepared to show my full hand just yet.

I toss him a bottle of water from the playroom's mini fridge, and he sips from it, offering a generous portion to Charlotte, before I beckon him to his feet.

"Start again with her pussy. Mind the directions I gave you."

Azrael glances down to where Charlotte is folded in his arms, nuzzling against his chest, as if he's hesitant to let her go. "And if I don't?"

I pull the belt from my discarded pants and snap it between my hands, glancing toward her pointedly. "You may want to fuck about, but does *she*?"

Azrael's expression hardens, but he's up within seconds, more than prepared to protect my future wife from me. I watch as he pumps the massive length of his cock until a few minutes later he grows hard again.

My own cock stiffens painfully.

He's just as divine and delicious as he's always been.

Our years apart haven't changed anything.

He follows my gaze, driving one hand up and down his length as he comforts Charlotte with the other.

She's collapsed onto her stomach atop the spanking bench now.

Not even needing the restraints she was in previously.

He strokes a hand through her hair, gently trailing his fingers down the line of her body as she shivers, before he pushes some of his cum in and out of her opening.

A little move he picked up from me.

The first time I brought some nameless Nephilim back to Hell with us.

Before I've given him the ready, Azrael slips another finger into her, testing how far he can push me.

"Fancy finding out the hard way, do you?" I challenge.

I finish my water and cast the bottle aside, leaving it for the maids, before I move to stand at my fiancée's head. She opens her mouth obediently without me asking, and I shove my cock in before I replace the blindfold over her eyes.

Death's finally hard enough. He takes his place at her other end and thrusts into her. He growls in pleasure, and my balls tighten eagerly.

"Look at you, taking what we give you so well. You're dripping," Azrael purrs to her, his cock coated in the cum leaking from her. "So lush and sweet."

And she is.

The combination of the two of us taking her higher than she's ever been.

Dare I say to Heaven and back?

"More. More please." Charlotte rocks back onto him, moaning so bloody loud I'm certain even my absent Father can hear.

But I am now the one true god she worships on her knees.

We both thrust into her.

Neither one of us blinks as we glare at one another, and Charlotte is such a shameless, cum-filled slut now, I can hardly understand her muffled begging from where she's sucking me.

"Fuck me," she begs, her words clear as she pops off to swirl her tongue over my cock's head.

I thrust back into her, fucking her face the way I know she likes, so that she cries out.

"Which one of us would you prefer, darling?" I smirk in amusement as Azrael chooses that exact moment to tear his gaze from mine and focus his attention upon her.

"She's already soaked again, Lightbringer. Stretched so fucking wide. If she hadn't been such an innocent little virgin when you got a hold of her, I'd glide right out."

Charlotte whimpers, her mouth too full to speak as she sucks my cock, relaxing as she allows me to push all the way to the back of her throat until she's no longer gagging.

I can see the silk of the blindfold growing wet from her tears.

But that's what she wants from me.

For me to ruin her.

"Give me a color, Charlotte," I order, withdrawing only long enough for her to pant a muffled "green" before I thrust back into her.

I throw back my head, breathing hard as her tongue flutters against the thick underside of my prick, and I start to increase my speed. Fuck, I love this woman.

I bring my head upright, and mine and Azrael's eyes meet.

And him, well . . .

A heaviness I cannot place settles inside my chest as I mercilessly thrust my hips forward.

Death is another matter entirely.

CHAPTER TWENTY-SIX

Charlotte

The two of them fall into a surprising rhythm after that, focusing the whole of their attention on me.

Azrael's pleasure. Lucifer's pain.

Azrael's praise. Lucifer's degradation.

Until I'm disoriented by the unexpected thrill of it all.

Once I've almost finished for a third time, before either Lucifer or Azrael has given me permission, Azrael removes me from the spanking bench and Lucifer forces me to my knees.

I drop down onto my pillow, pleading. "Please, Daddy. Please don't stop. I promise I'll be a good girl, if I can just—"

"Leave the blindfold on," Lucifer says, as I assume Azrael's about to remove it.

One of them pads across the room, and whoever it is grips me by the hair.

"You're going to suck on whatever I give you now, understood?"

That's Lucifer. That's definitely Lucifer. It's his voice. That's clear to me, but I'm not certain who's touching me.

A large hand flattens over the smooth strands of my hair, trailing over the tresses and pulling it gently at the base.

Azrael. Definitely Azrael.

I moan eagerly.

Already, I've had both their cocks in my mouth, and my ass, and my pussy, and I'm covered in cum from head to toe just like the greedy little slut Lucifer knew I would be, but with the two of them looming over me like this, I have no idea who's coming at me.

Which I'm pretty sure is what my husband intended.

In a scene like this, he'll exploit any vulnerability that's given to him.

If Azrael doesn't first.

Whichever one of them is holding my hair steps back, releasing me, but I still can't see anything.

I'm flying blind here.

The other steps forward, and whoever it is grips hold of me as Lucifer whispers from above. "Be descriptive," he orders Azrael. "First person only."

I tilt my head, still confused, but I'm blindfolded, so it's not like I know what's happening.

A beat of silence follows as I imagine Azrael quirking that sexy scarred brow. I suspect the scar might've come from Lucifer, based on a few offhand comments, though neither of them has confirmed anything.

I can't anticipate what either one of them is about to do.

Before I can plead for mercy, someone shoves their throbbing cock past my lips, and I choke it down readily.

"What a dirty little slut you're being," I hear from overhead.

That's Lucifer, definitely Lucifer, but I can't tell whether he's in front of or behind me, which means . . .

It must be Azrael's cock I'm sucking.

That tracks.

I run my tongue over the thick, weeping head, gripping the base with my hand.

"Now, little dove, I'm going to step out of the room, and I want you to guzzle Death's cum exactly like you do when the two of you're alone together, darling. Make as much noise as you can."

I quirk a brow, uncertain why Lucifer's staging the scene like this. What pleasure he's deriving from it.

But I'm still relatively new to kink, so maybe I'm missing something?

"Yes, sir," I say, my words muffled around Azrael's cock.

A moment later, I feel someone retreat just like Lucifer said, as a large hand gently grips me.

Azrael.

Lucifer would never touch me so tenderly.

Not when we're in the middle of a rough scene like this.

I tilt back my head, opening my throat and trusting my devilish fiancé at his word.

But that was my very first mistake when I came to this city.

I should have learned better by now.

Clearly there's still some part of that naïve church girl left in me.

I don't know why I ever expected I'd be rid of her.

"You two wanted to tempt the wrath of the devil?" Lucifer's voice grows more distant, and he lets out a dark chuckle like he and Azrael are in on some cruel, sick joke. "Then 'this is my body given to you. Do this in remembrance of me.'"

CHAPTER TWENTY-SEVEN

Azrael

My expression goes cold the moment I realize Lucifer's endgame.

She's going to suck on his cock like it's mine.

Whisper the things she's only ever said to me.

While I can do nothing but stand here, unable to fuck anything but my own hand as I praise and assist in guiding her up and down his length.

To remind me that I will only *ever* be borrowing her from him.

Even if it's my name she's crying.

My gaze hardens, my jaw trembling with the possessive rage filling me.

But like the true soldier I am, I push through it, welcoming whatever pain it brings. I won't allow him the satisfaction of using his safe word.

Not a fucking chance.

I step forward, gripping the back of Charlotte's hair and fisting it gently. My nails dig into my own skin to the point of near pain, but I keep my hold on her light.

I don't dare say anything to reveal what's happening to her as I shove her head forward and onto his length.

The cold resentment in my eyes is obvious.

My ex may not always be able to control me when he and I are outside of the playroom, but inside? Well . . .

The devil always wins, unfortunately.

"Azrael," Charlotte moans as she pops off his cock, kissing and licking it in the same way she does with me. Like she did last night.

She's trying to see what I like.

Trying to be the good girl she so desperately wants to be.

"Don't be shy now, Reaper," Lucifer hisses into my ear, whispering so low over Charlotte's head he's barely speaking. His smirk is fucking diabolical as he nods down to where her lips slide over him. "Give our girl what she's asking for."

I snarl as he thrusts into her mouth readily, leading Charlotte to believe that he's left us alone. I should've expected him to humiliate me like this, but I was too distracted by my own pleasure, my own desire, and all the painful memories that've resurfaced, to see it coming.

Memories I would have much rather kept buried.

"Azrael . . ." Charlotte's soft, breathy moan brings me back into the moment, reminding me that she still expects praise from me.

I glance down to where she's sucking his cock.

Even if my praise is the only thing I can give her, I can't stop myself from wanting to worship her with it. She craves it so desperately. But the humiliation, how similar a situation this is to what I felt with Eve, sears through me.

I'll never be anything more to anyone than the fear of the unknown.

A tool for his use.

No matter what promises she may make me.

"You're doing so well, baby girl. You take my cock so pretty."

Lucifer throws back his head, and I can tell he's getting close. He's the only one of us who hasn't finished recently, so I keep talking.

The sooner we get this over with, the sooner we . . .

Fuck, his face when he's like that is so familiar to me.

"Azrael?" Charlotte whispers again, coming off his cock like she's burning to say something.

"Yeah, baby girl?"

Lucifer pumps up and down his length with his hand, throwing back his head again, and I can't help but think—

"Fuck, you're the most beautiful thing I've ever seen," I confess to him.

My cock throbs painfully.

Fuck me.

How can I hate him and want to be balls deep inside him?

Or him inside me.

It honestly doesn't fucking matter to me.

"About what you said earlier," Charlotte whispers, that sweet voice of hers calling to my ears. Like a true fucking siren. As Lucifer keeps trying to thrust back into her face.

My spine runs cold.

Shit.

I can't let her confess what I think she's about to say in front of him. Not for the first time.

I won't allow him to ruin this for me.

I growl, not having to fake the noises I'm making as I'm forced to watch him thrust even deeper. "I'm not certain right now is the time to—"

She pops off again. "I've been wanting to tell you since last night, but I didn't—"

Lucifer tenses, shoving back into her, his nostrils flaring like he's caught between the mounting orgasm that's about to tear through him and his fury at the confession we both suspect is about to come out of his fiancée's mouth.

My gaze darts between them.

Watching the two of them up close and personal like this is torture.

Sweet fucking torture.

And with those three perfect words poised on her lips and the memory of how it felt to have his fingers inside me fresh in my mind, I . . .

I can't stop it.

This is exactly as fucked as Lucifer wanted it to be, messing with my head.

The pain so sweet there's almost a sick kind of pleasure in it.

I use my free hand to palm my cock, stroking up and down my length. "Baby girl, you don't need to say anything else right now," I grumble, attempting to salvage this as I stare straight into Lucifer's eyes, silently pleading for him to put a stop to this despite that a part of me doesn't want him to. He hasn't looked at me like this in centuries. "I've never met anyone who can pleasure me the way you do." My eyes meet his.

And I mean it.

I'm so close now I might end up coming all over the back of Charlotte's head even before he does, before she drinks down Lucifer's cum like it's a sinful communion.

But she thinks it's me.

She thinks it's me, I remind myself as she nuzzles his cock, those three haunting words still at the edge of her lips.

And that's all that fucking matters.

"Azrael," Charlotte whispers, sliding off him again.

Fuck. I can't stop this.

"I love you," she whispers.

And I nearly lose it.

I arch back, agony searing through me.

Torn apart by the fact I can never get that moment back.

But I also can't seem to resist . . .

"I love you, too, baby girl," I manage between clenched teeth, staring directly into Lucifer's eyes in my shame.

Lucifer reaches across the chasm between us and grips my wrist, stopping my pleasure mid-thrust. "You don't get to come until she does."

I snarl furiously.

"Sir?" Charlotte releases his cock, shocked he's still in the room. There's a part of her that's too goddamn innocent. She fell for his little trick hook, line, and sinker.

And I hate him.

I fucking hate him for it.

I shake my head.

No, I *wish* I could fucking hate him.

But the way Lucifer's eyes meet mine as I shove even harder against the back of Charlotte's head, forcing her to give him one final thrust as he cums inside her throat, complicates everything. His lips part as he growls his pleasure, his eyes never leaving mine.

Charlotte chokes, and the hellfire in Lucifer's eyes flares.

And that's when I know I'm not the only one who's been reminiscing.

The devil has sunk his claws into us both.

And I welcome the pain it brings.

CHAPTER TWENTY-EIGHT

Charlotte

I feel the orgasm Azrael's been working toward build and build, and he gives one final thrust and starts to cum in my mouth.

The blindfold rips off just as I glance up and realize . . .

Lucifer.

I choke, my throat closing around him unexpectedly.

I should have recognized him from the taste alone. Smoky. Malty. Like his favorite whisky, whereas Azrael . . .

Recognition flares.

It's not Azrael who's cum inside my mouth. It's my future husband, despite that I've been—

Oh God, what have I done?

I choke again as Lucifer's balls slap against the underside of my chin. He's now orgasming so hard and pushing so deep into my throat, I can hardly see through my tears. But it's Azrael's name I've been chanting over and over again like a fevered prayer, nuzzling and stroking and licking and whispering to him in all the intimate ways he seemed to like previously.

As I told him that I . . .

Oh God. Oh God.

For the very first time.

And here I was confessing to him on my knees.

All because I stupidly trusted Lucifer when he said Azrael and I would be alone.

How could I have ever thought this was going to be something?

Heat flushes through my cheeks, burning me down to my chest. Now I've not only ruined the intimate weight of that moment with Azrael, but I've unknowingly shown my *primary* Dom all the things I've been doing with his ex behind closed doors.

Humiliation sears through me, white hot and unrelenting.

Like I'm exactly the greedy whore the Righteous or that TMZ article says I am.

I finish choking on Lucifer's cum, swallowing it down out of sheer necessity more than anything, before he abruptly pulls away from me, leaving me coughing and sputtering like the trash I am as I realize that my pussy has now left a large and obvious damp spot on my pillow from where I thought Azrael might be about to make love to me.

A familiar feeling of shame flares through me.

But there's no God left to apologize to anymore.

Only my devilish husband.

My gaze darts toward Azrael, who from the looks of it isn't faring any better with this situation than I am.

His jaw is so clenched I'm almost shocked that it and his closed fists haven't already disappeared into the Nothing alongside what remains of his patience. The edges of his form flicker, and the icy look of fury in his eyes is so cold, so calculated, I . . .

Death's skeletal face turns toward me.

Like *I'm* somehow the one responsible for this.

I sort of am. In part, at least.

I glance desperately between them, watching as Lucifer cleans himself off with his discarded shirt before he drops down into his devil's chair, glaring at us both like he's far from through with us, though I'm not really sure who I should beg for forgiveness first.

Him or Azrael.

This whole situation is fucking disorienting.

Exactly like Lucifer planned it to be.

I turn toward him. "Daddy, I—"

"Quiet, cumslut," he snarls, not so much as looking at me.

He may have been the one to orchestrate this, but his expression is clear.

I brought this punishment upon myself.

And he's furious with me.

My chin starts to quiver as I fight to hold in my tears.

But *he* was the one who first put Azrael in my path.

He made the decision to share me.

The double standard sparks something latent inside me, all the confidence and bravado my upbringing taught me to hold in. That bratty attitude that came out the very first time Lucifer humiliated me in front of the entire Apollyon boardroom before I wrote that furious press release. My resolve strengthens.

Well, not again. Not again, goddammit.

I won't let him get the upper hand on me.

This time, I'm going to make *him* pay.

I turn my gaze toward Azrael. "Sir?" I say in my sweetest, most saccharine voice, looking at him exactly like I would if he were Lucifer.

This situation can go both ways.

Azrael's skeletal expression slowly swings toward me, and something dark flares in his gaze.

He's absolutely livid with me, and Lucifer, and maybe even with himself for getting into this mess, but still, I stare up at him, eyes pleading, willing him to understand what I'm doing. *You want to be in charge, take it,* I silently offer.

The look of fury in Azrael's eyes blazes as he realizes what I'm offering.

Like he's been waiting all eternity for someone to give him this opportunity.

"You're not just his. You're mine, too, aren't you, little siren?" he says, causing an unhinged growl to tear from Lucifer, who leans forward like he's about to come to his feet.

But without his powers, what exactly is he going to do if we *both* defy him?

We're clearly about to find out.

I reposition myself on my knees in front of Azrael just as I use my power to knock Lucifer back down into his seat. Some of my shadows wrap around my husband's wrists, binding him.

"What do you think you're—"

"Is it time to play, Daddy?" I ask Death as Lucifer snarls furiously.

Azrael smirks. "Of course it is, you wicked, wicked girl."

CHAPTER TWENTY-NINE

Lucifer

I did *not* negotiate for the two of them to take over like this, but here we are, unfortunately. My future wife and her deathly paramour have every intention of cuckolding me, and in my own bloody playroom at that.

The tables have turned.

That much is clear.

Charlotte crawls toward Death, orchestrating this whole thing.

Minx.

She-devil.

I snarl.

I might have trained her a little too well, honestly.

Azrael assists her to her feet, lifting her into his arms before he sits upon one of the benches.

"What are you doing?" I snarl, my fingers digging into the plush leather of my throne.

If I weren't trapped in this bloody chair, I'd already be halfway across the room, tearing into him before he—

"Claiming what's *mine*." He positions my wife so that the thick head of his cock is now outside her pussy.

We've already worked her over enough that despite his considerable size, he'll slide in easily. Charlotte lets out a heady moan, trying to ease farther down onto him.

But Death isn't having it.

He grips her hips, his fingers digging into her, drawing the moment out as he stares directly at me.

Death has been waiting for this for a very long time.

And he's going to savor it slowly.

I try and fail to come out of my chair again just as he slides home, seating Charlotte on the length of his cock, so he's fully inside her. An unhinged chuckle tears from my lips as I realize that my wrists are shackled by my own goddamn shadows to my throne.

Whether it's Charlotte or Azrael who wields them, I don't care.

They are *both* going to regret this.

"Very funny, you two." I smirk, despite my lack of amusement, pushing against my bindings again, but they're not moving. My expression goes cold, my gaze narrowing. "I swear on all that is holy, if you touch her without my permission, I will—"

"You already *gave* me your permission, *lover*," Azrael growls, suddenly the untamed version of himself he's been holding back, taunting me as he meets my gaze head-on.

He starts to thrust in and out of Charlotte.

She places her hands on his shoulders, riding him, unaware of the monster she's just unleashed.

"She was part of our deal, remember?"

My soon-to-be wife slides up and down his length, so wet from where she's clearly enjoying this little territorial battle we're having over her that Azrael's shaft is practically gleaming.

"The only permission I need now is hers." Death's attention swings back to her. "And you're so eager to give it to me, aren't you, little siren?"

"Yes, sir," Charlotte moans in agreement.

Calling him by *my* honorific.

I bare my fangs and let out a threatening snarl as Azrael palms her ass, his fingers digging into her skin. Charlotte throws back her head, and her pace starts to increase.

My cock gives an unexpected jerk.

They really are a sinful sight.

But she has no idea the danger she's flirting with, and my jealousy overrides any pleasure I might be feeling. "If you two don't stop this right now, I swear that I'll—"

"Do what? Punish me?" Death chuckles. "Tell me who *you* want in charge, baby girl," Azrael grumbles, speaking over me.

"You, Daddy," she says, before she looks straight at me and grins.

Fucking grins.

Ever the brat she's always been.

But *this* is properly out of line, even for her.

She's furious with me for the punishment I've given them. I can see that now, and now she's going to make me hurt for it.

She slides up and down Azrael's cock, dragging her nails down his back as she stares directly at me, exactly like she does when we make love *outside* the playroom.

I let out a roar so loud, I'm certain my entire realm can hear, my skin tightening. "You want a punishment? I'll fucking give you a punishment, all right. There'll be entire gospels, endless sermons, whole fucking beatitudes warning our future progeny about the pleasure and pain I will bring you."

All with the sole purpose of reminding her of my one and only commandment.

That she is and always will be mine.

For the rest of our immortal eternity.

My voice lowers to its demonic register. "This is your last chance to stop this nonsense, or this will end poorly for both of you."

It's one of the few celestial abilities I've retained, thankfully.

I may no longer have my access to my power, but I'm still the goddamn devil, for Christ's sake, and a devil who's currently being made a mug of by *more than one* of my bratty subs.

"Are you safe-wording, or are you going to finally sit back and enjoy what you've created, lover?" Azrael taunts, his face turning skeletal.

As if *this* were my true intention all along.

The two of them fucking like this.

The fire in my eyes turns molten.

I will give neither of them the satisfaction of besting me.

Especially *him*.

"Both of you will regret this for the rest of your immortal days." I sink back into my seat, expecting Azrael to answer, but it's Charlotte who mutters, "I don't think we will, honestly."

Witch. Vixen.

A furious snarl tears from my throat, even as I lean back, smirking like the devil I am.

They want to play games and dominate *me*?

I'll fucking play.

My wife gazes down at Azrael as she rocks her hips back and forth, just like she does when I have her in my arms.

A lion's roar erupts from my throat as one last time I try and fail to break free of whichever of them is binding me.

My celestial senses grow weaker by the day, waning with each additional moment without my power, and I'm starting to age. Slowly.

For the first time ever.

And now this?

I knew falling in love with her would be the end of me.

I just failed to recognize she'd be the one dancing upon my grave.

Delighted by my distress, Charlotte shakes her head, tsking at me. "Might as well get used to it, Daddy. There's more than one Dom in my life now."

"Like hell there is," I grate out just as I manage to wriggle one of my hands free.

Two can make a game of this.

With or without my powers.

I turn my attention to my ex, focusing upon the weak link. "You've been craving this for a very long time, haven't you, Reaper?"

Azrael turns his gaze toward me, and my lips twist wickedly.

Let her watch him fall.

I won't be the only one love made twice a fool.

CHAPTER THIRTY

Azrael

Mine and Charlotte's rebellion doesn't last long, but it's so fucking sweet, so fucking sinful, and we're both wound so tight from the earlier part of the scene that my ex has no choice but to sit back and give in.

Or make it *look* like he has anyway.

Lucifer watches us hungrily.

I'm so close to finishing, I'm certain I'm only a few thrusts from spilling myself inside her again.

That narcissistic bastard had it coming.

The look of unchecked fury in his eyes is such sweet fucking vengeance, such delicious torture, it almost makes me—

"Reaper," Lucifer purrs, his voice smooth and low and . . . submissive, like it used to be. Like it was so many times when I was inside of him.

Before we both realized he preferred it the other way around.

Before he started to loathe his own vulnerability and recognized that me letting loose was too dangerous. My balls tighten, that familiar tone when I'm already teetering so close to the edge nearly making me cum, but Charlotte's not quite ready.

Her eyes dart back and forth between us as she watches us eagerly. But she's so close to her own finish, her pussy tightening around me like a vise, she doesn't seem capable of doing anything but panting.

Good.

I want her ruined.

I want to ruin her in front of him.

I reach down and finger her clit, giving her the extra stimulation she needs as my other hand comes to one of her breasts.

"Azrael," she moans, not remembering to call me by his address, like she's already long forgotten the purpose of this little game we're playing.

She's so clearly focused on me that her cries only seem to make Lucifer even more furious. The edge of my mouth twists.

Let that devious bastard watch while I fuck his queen.

"Reaper," Lucifer taunts again, that soft, familiar tone calling to me, unleashing something dormant inside of me until I have no choice but to turn and look at him.

He strokes his free hand up and down the length of his cock, from tip to throbbing base. He's not as thick as I am, but he's longer, able to reach places inside me that wring out a pleasure I never would've thought possible.

"Azrael?" Charlotte cups my cheek.

But I'm unable to look away from where Lucifer's hand is still trailing over the swollen head of his cock. The thick vein there. The bead of precum that gathers as he . . .

"Azrael." This time, Charlotte's more insistent.

She tries to guide me back toward the light, toward her, just as Lucifer says, "You're thinking about that time in Pompeii, aren't you?"

My spine stiffens.

"Or Sodom."

"Azrael." Charlotte's voice rises, strained, frustrated. Like we're both hanging over the same cliff, but she's starting to fall and Lucifer's holding on to me.

And I'm torn between two equal parts of myself. The softer side I've given to her recently, and the darker one, the majorly fucked-up one, the Grim Reaper who's always belonged to—

"Or how about that kiss at the CFDA awards?" Lucifer says, driving the final nail in as he crucifies me. "It'd been more than a few centuries since you'd let loose. Did it make you crave it?"

Charlotte goes still in my arms, and I can tell from her sharp intake of breath that whatever she expected Lucifer to say, it wasn't that.

I made a mistake not telling her.

But that was between him and me.

The three of us were barely a thought then.

Charlotte starts to pull off me, but my grip on her tightens.

"No," I snarl, looking back at her and refusing to let go. Not unless she uses her safe word. "Don't let him ruin this."

Her eyes go wide like she never expected I'd refuse her.

I've been intentionally gentle with her up until now, kept myself leashed.

But now the truth's come out to play.

"The Black Plague was another favorite," Lucifer drawls, like he's listing off my greatest accomplishments, rather than all the times when he made me . . .

Goddammit.

Charlotte's eyes go so wide.

Something primal in me awakens.

"If you run, it'll only make it worse," I growl as I drag her back down, impaling her on my swelling cock so hard she cries out.

The fear and the hint of challenge in her eyes nearly undoes me.

But I won't stop.

I don't ever fucking stop.

Not when he's torn off my mask like this.

I grip her face. "You wanted this, little siren."

Charlotte shoves against me, her hands slamming into my chest as she fights me, but I thrust into her even harder, my grip tightening to the point of near pain.

I slam her onto her back on top of the bench and pin her hands above her head before she can manage to get away from me. “Don’t you fucking dare,” I snarl.

But she has her safe word, and she doesn’t use it.

“Daddy?” she pleads, trying a different tactic as she glances toward Lucifer.

Like now that she’s seen this side of me, she’s frightened by it.

“Put her up on the rack once you’re finished with her.” Lucifer smirks, not an ounce of pity in his voice, like he’s the true puppet master of this whole goddamn thing. “You wanted to fuck Death? The Grim Reaper, Charlotte?” That devious grin of his widens. “Now it’s *your* turn to watch, darling.”

CHAPTER THIRTY-ONE

Charlotte

"No," Azrael snarls at Lucifer. "No, I'm not your chained beast anymore."

Death thrusts into me so hard I'm certain I'll be bruised come morning. The way he's pounding into my cervix, like he doesn't give a damn about what Lucifer or I think, is too good to withstand—and also more than my tender heart can take.

He's looking at us both with more than a furious hunger in his eyes, the feeling more intense than any time he's ever looked only at me. The way he's driving into me is so ruthless and unrelenting that I realize he must be reliving what happened between them.

I look toward Lucifer, and I know he feels it too.

Whatever's left of what they once shared is destructive, and it's coming out in the safety of the scene.

Azrael thrusts even harder, so hard I can hear each ruthless smack of his hips against me, the ecstasy inside me building until I feel myself slipping away fast, losing myself too quickly, and this time, I'm not certain Death will catch me. He's so focused on Lucifer, on the pain between them.

My spine runs cold, pleasure and fear mingling, as Azrael reaches up and cuts off my airway. I tense.

Pompeii. Sodom. The Black Plague.

All times when he must have lost control.

Fear grips me, my face turning red.

How many casualties? I ask myself as that familiar feeling of danger shoots through me, heightening everything. *How many people had to die for their love?*

The Angel of Death glowers at me, fucking me like I'm nothing but a useless rag doll, and from his expression, I realize he's enjoying this.

He *enjoys* the sight of me dying.

Everything I thought I knew about Azrael shatters in an instant.

I start to buck, my shock making me fight and strain against him, but he's nearly a foot taller than I am and almost twice my weight.

I'm not sure how I never put two and two together before.

It's one thing to know he's Death incarnate. It's another to see him actively *enjoy* it.

Enjoy hurting people, hurting me.

The pleasure and pain inside me heighten, unlocking my fear, my shame.

Just as Lucifer looks toward him and orders, "Break her open, Reaper."

The command acts like a tripwire inside me, igniting everything. I tip over the edge, clenching all over Azrael.

"Fuck you, you prideful asshole," Death snarls, his grip on my throat tightening as he throws back his head.

"But you fucking love it, don't you?" Lucifer bellows in return, thrashing in his chair, as I pulse and pulse, my eyes rolling back into my head as I feel Azrael cum inside me.

Death comes undone as he and the devil fight over me.

And the implications of that, of what that could mean for the world, for them, are so intense they're triggering.

The anger and shame that floods through me is immediate, even as the pleasure inside me mounts.

How could I have not realized?

How could I have not realized that he . . .

I don't allow myself to finish the thought.

"Let her down now, Reaper," Lucifer growls, reining Death back in.

Azrael's grip on me loosens incrementally.

Like that single command spoken from my future husband's lips holds more sway over Death, over the world, than I *ever* could, despite that I'm the one he's currently fucking.

I shudder and shake, a heady mixture of desire and fury tearing through me.

I thought I was prepared, thought I understood.

But I didn't realize they'd both be my undoing.

My heart shatters in two, all my old trauma coming to the surface.

Azrael releases my throat.

My breath comes back in such a rush, my vision goes dark.

It burns on the way down as I gasp for life.

But Death's still thrusting inside me, his skeletal face thrown back in such pleasure-pain, he looks lost. Wherever he is, it must be a brutal memory, because despite his clenched jaw, there's a bit of moisture gathered at the edge of one of his eye sockets, like he could break any second. He's bleeding grief instead of tears.

And *I* was the one who asked for this.

Who put them both up to this.

Abruptly, I kick Azrael off me, fearing the destruction that'll result if I don't.

I'm barely capable of tearing myself out of Death's grip before I shout, "Inferno!"

The whole scene comes to an abrupt and screeching halt.

"Baby girl?" Azrael breathes, his eyes suddenly open, his face covered in flesh again as he casts a fearful look at me. Like he's concerned I might be terrified now that I've seen the truth of what he is.

I stumble off the bench.

"Charlotte," Lucifer says, the shadows I was wielding falling away from his wrists.

Azrael reaches for me, but I shake my head, pulling away from him.

"Don't," I breathe, panting, still feeling a bit of his cum dripping embarrassingly down my leg. My gaze darts between them.

That's all this ever was, wasn't it?

A ploy for Lucifer to get back with the one immortal who actually matters to him.

"It's not like that, and you know it," Azrael says, as if he can read my mind. And he's right. Of course he's right.

But knowing something and seeing it are two different things.

How could I have been so selfish as to put my own needs first?

"Little dove," Lucifer says, rising from his chair, his voice incredibly soft, tentative, the one he uses during aftercare with me.

Slowly, he moves toward me.

Like it physically pains him to see me this distressed.

As if he wasn't just reminiscing about how many people he—

"No," I say again, turning my full attention and frustration in his direction, feeling suddenly braver than I ever would if Azrael weren't here to support me, like I can let it out. As if the balance of power between Lucifer and me is finally level now that Death's tipped the scales for me. "You don't get to toy with my heart *and* his when you're the one who thrust us together." I swallow, my hands shaking.

I knew what I was getting into with both of them and yet . . .

"Charlotte—"

"And you." I pivot toward Azrael, my gaze softening. "You haven't been being honest with me."

And it shocks me how quickly Death switches back to being the gruff but gentle warrior I trusted so easily.

"Baby girl." Azrael puts his hands up as he slowly moves toward me. "I love you, but we *all* agreed to this, you know that."

"I know," I admit, my breath suddenly uneasy, "but I just didn't realize how . . ."

How selfish I was being.

Acting like my needs matter.

I glance toward Lucifer, my clenched hands trembling.

This was never going to be what I wanted, was it?

I see the second the thought lands, the moment he hears me. The tension in his shoulders coils. They have more shared history, more to work through than I ever could've imagined. How can I ask them to wade through all that, for me?

This can't be what I'd hoped for, can it?

Not without causing both of them pain.

"Charlotte." Lucifer inches even closer, like he means to come after me. He looks just as pained as I am.

Because he had to overhear how Azrael and I . . .

Oh God.

He didn't even *agree* to this, didn't even want to . . .

"I'm sorry," I say to them both, my frustration turning inward.

Just like my upbringing taught me.

I don't bother to grab my clothes before I turn and flee.

Without warning, I plunge into the ether, barreling down into the safety of mine and Lucifer's realm beneath.

It was never going to work between the three of us, was it?

Not when I still feel like asking for more makes me unworthy.

CHAPTER THIRTY-TWO

Charlotte

I don't know where it is I'm going or even what it is I'm running from until I'm already there. I just know I have to get away. I find myself alone on the ledge of the balcony of the palace Lucifer built for me in Hell overlooking a starlit city. The one filled with the souls he feels don't deserve to be here. It's become a safe space for me.

I glance toward Heaven.

"I'm sorry," I hear myself say again, just as I feel someone approach. I glance over my shoulder, expecting to find Azrael.

Lucifer drapes a black silk robe over my shoulders, covering my nude body. "I wish you'd stop saying that." He leans onto the balcony beside me, his presence weighted with that unmistakable certainty that always steadies me. "You've nothing to apologize for."

No matter what else might break, this moment, this connection is ours alone.

I nod, still shaking. "I let my anger out when I shouldn't have. I was just . . . shocked, that's all. Why didn't you tell me that he—"

"Enjoys killing people?" Lucifer snorts. "Honestly, what did you expect, darling? It's far from the worst thing Azrael's ever done." When

I don't respond, he sighs. "We all agreed to the scene, little dove, but I don't ever want you to—"

"There's so much history between you two." I turn away from him. "Knowing that is one thing, but seeing it firsthand is another. I'm not angry with either of you about it. I'm just . . . angry with myself more than anything because I realize how incredibly selfish I've been. For these last few weeks, all I've been thinking about is—"

"Your own desires, your own autonomy?" Lucifer shakes his head. "You are allowed to be angry. Allowed to *feel.* But you're too busy saving everyone else that you sometimes forget you also need to save yourself."

My chest loosens.

"But I shouldn't have lashed out at you," I say, turning toward him and leaning my head into his chest.

He strokes his hand over my hair reverently, using a bit of his shadows, which he can still wield here, to nudge me to him. "I don't ever want you to apologize for making yourself a priority. Not to me. Not to Azrael, and certainly not to my Father. Your human religion may have taught you otherwise, but your desires—your anger—they matter, darling, and I'm sorry if I pushed you and Azrael too far."

"It's not you. You've never done anything to make me think differently. You were doing what a Dom is supposed to do. You're the only reason I'd ever feel brave enough to think I might be . . ."

"Worthy?" he finishes for me. "Of love? Of praise? Of your own acceptance?"

I give a curt nod as he draws me closer, until I'm so surrounded by the familiar scent of him, of the smoke and whisky that clings to him, that it calms me.

"I'm sorry if I hurt you," he says.

A soft smile pulls at my lips. "You know, I think that may be the first time you've ever said that to me."

He nods thoughtfully. "It likely won't be the last. I'm not the easiest chap to love, in case you hadn't noticed."

I snort. "You keep acting like you're beyond saving, but you already proved that was a lie when you saved me." I gaze up at him.

He's so beautiful that sometimes I almost forget who he is.

"I never mean to hurt you."

"I know you don't, except when we're in a scene." I nudge my shoulder against him playfully. "You were *trying* to drive a wedge between Azrael and me."

He smirks, glancing down slightly. Like it amuses him that I can read him so easily but he's not ashamed of it. "Perhaps I miscalculated how much you feel for him. Though you're just as responsible for this as I am, darling."

"I know. I know," I groan. "It's just . . . it feels like with every new choice I make, a new problem arises. A new disappointment. Somebody who's hurt or who—"

"If you attempt to live your life by never disappointing anyone, you're going to be miserable." He steps behind me, pulling me into him again. "On that path lies insanity."

"That's easy for you to say," I whisper, leaning my back against him. "Until recently, you never had to please anyone but yourself."

"Is that so?" He uses his hand to nudge my neck to the side before he kisses across my throat, the feel of his mouth on me sending shivers down my spine until I'm breathing heavy.

He is and always will be my greatest temptation.

He lays a kiss on my shoulder. "You forget there was a time when I lived in service to someone *else's* vision."

"Your Father's?"

I feel him nod, and when I look up at him, he's staring out over the starlit city. "I never wanted to disappoint Him. I just wanted Him to understand how my siblings and I might've . . ." His voice trails off, and I twist in his arms to face him.

He's so much more open with me now than he used to be.

Especially in those early days.

He shakes his head. "Well, we both know how that turned out, at any rate."

I nod thoughtfully, falling silent as I turn and look out over Hell's landscape. It's nothing like what anyone would expect it to be. But then neither is he. "Did Azrael really kill all those people?"

Lucifer chuckles. "Technically, he kills everyone, darling."

I try not to smile at how he acts like that's no big thing. Even without his powers, he's more god than human, and I may be immortal now, but my heart will always belong with humanity, it seems.

And the devil.

"You said that's not the worst thing he's done. What did you—"

"That's his story to tell."

I nod, and we both fall quiet for a beat.

"Did you struggle when God cast you out? With your newfound freedom?"

He brushes some of my hair to the other side of my neck before he presses a kiss to my temple. "In a manner of speaking."

I glance up, willing him to elaborate.

He sighs. "There was someone there to help me."

"Azrael."

He tilts his head in silent agreement.

"We have that in common then." I look away momentarily. I can't blame Azrael for what he's always been, for being Death, even if I failed to fully recognize what that meant until now. "I think he's good for us. He balances us. He makes me feel like I can be brave. Like there's a more level playing field between you and me."

Gently, I pull away from Lucifer, crossing my arms over my chest like I might finally be able to hold myself together without him strengthening me. "You both say you're over one another, but it seems like there might still be—"

"There's not," he says quickly.

Too quick.

"Are you certain?" I look toward him, hoping he doesn't see my uncertainty, the small hint of jealousy I feel even though I know it's unfair. I can't help it. "It'd be okay if there was."

He swallows hard, his eyes flicking toward the shadows, almost like he's wondering if the Angel of Death might be . . .

He shakes his head. "Before you, I'm not certain I was capable of love."

I catch him off guard when I step forward and place a single finger over his lips before he can say anything more. "You promised to be honest with me." My hand falls away. "Do you remember one of the first things you ever said to me? When we met in Gluttony's club?"

Lucifer lifts a brow.

I smile. "'True love is ferocious, vicious, destructive. True love is costly, and humanity knows little of it. It's a price few are willing to pay.'" I pause, those words bringing up an unexpected well of emotion in me. "Back then I thought you were talking about your Father, but you weren't talking about Him only, were you?"

Lucifer hesitates, clearly uncertain how to proceed.

He never intended for me to see right through him.

Past the villain everyone believes him to be.

"I see it," I murmur. "The pain in your eyes when you look at him. It's not just me, is it?"

He hesitates but says nothing.

I glance away from him then, hiding the bit of unwarranted hurt that makes me feel. "Why didn't you tell me he kissed you?"

Lucifer sighs. "I didn't think it was relevant." His shadows reach out, and one of them strokes over my cheek. "My heart belongs only to you. Can you say the same?"

My face falls. "That's not a fair question."

"Isn't it?" he challenges, the edge of his mouth quirking. "I won't apologize for trying to make you mine again, darling, not to you. Not to Azrael. Not even to that goddamn absent bastard you still pray to whenever you think I'm not—"

"Where do you think He is?" I ask, changing the subject as I glance out over the starlit landscape. It's been something I've been meaning to ask him for a while. "God, I mean. And do you think He's listening?"

Lucifer tugs at his shirt collar, clearly uncomfortable with this line of questioning. But ever since he promised to be transparent with me, he's honored his word, and I know, despite any challenge it might present him, he'd move Heaven and Earth for me.

He has every step of the way.

"I couldn't possibly begin to know," he answers.

"Well, if He is listening, I have a few choice words I've been wanting to say to Him." I sigh. "But in the meantime, I need you to make another promise to me."

Lucifer nods, placing his hands in his suit coat pockets. "Anything, little dove."

"Promise me you'll try to mend things with Azrael. Or at least, no more fighting over me."

A slow grin pulls across his lips. "If I say yes, will it persuade you to wear my permanent collar again, to set the wedding date, move back into the penthouse?"

"It's not a no." I smile, teasing him. "But I can't make any guarantees."

I've learned my lesson about making deals with him.

Lucifer chuckles, like that's exactly the response he expected of me. "I'm not certain that promise is mine alone to make."

I meet his gaze, smiling. "Then promise me you'll be the one to take the first step."

"For you, always." He takes my hand, pulling me closer. "For now, and the rest of eternity."

CHAPTER THIRTY-THREE

Lucifer

I find Azrael in the exact spot in Hell I expected he'd be, where he used to retreat whenever we were fighting. He sits on top of the ledge at the Black Plains, overlooking the Abyss, a vast, endless expanse of black obsidian and scorched earth meant to terrify the damned when they first realize they belong to me. The very first part of Hell to take form, actually.

Before the souls, before the hierarchy, before the politics.

Back when he and I were . . .

I tilt my head to the side, squinting. "Looks a bit primitive now, doesn't it?"

Azrael grunts but doesn't say anything.

He leans forward onto his knees, brooding, his posture letting me know in no uncertain terms that he doesn't want company.

I sigh, placing my hands in my pockets. "Charlotte says I'm supposed to—"

"Don't insult me," he tosses over his shoulder.

Like the mere thought of receiving aftercare from me infuriates him.

But unfortunately, I've learned a little more than a thing or two about feelings from Charlotte. Inconvenient as they may be.

Hurt is often a quiet thing.

Nearly as insidious as the temptation he and I created.

I take a seat on the ledge beside him, looking out over the Abyss. "You always loved to stay silent. Like that helped anything."

Azrael's posture stiffens. "It helped you. That night, after the Fall. When you screamed the sky empty and then you just . . . stopped. And I stayed."

"You did," I admit, my mouth unexpectedly dry as an unamused huff escapes me. "I thought you were mocking me, sitting there like one of my shadows."

"No." He shakes his head, before he finally looks toward me. "I was staying so you would know what it felt like—to be seen, even when you're monstrous."

I swallow, my throat writhing. "You never looked at me like I was a monster. Not even when I became one."

He snorts. "Maybe that was part of the problem. I was too afraid of losing you." Reluctantly, he glances toward me. "Still am."

A heavy silence falls, the kind that used to feel companionable but now simply feels like an echo of everything we once were.

I clear my throat. "Do you remember what you said that night? About the Plains?"

He lifts a brow, and I nod to the rock where we're sitting as I reach into my suit coat and offer him a cigarette. He refuses but then conjures a lighter and lights it for me.

"You said we were building for what came after," I mutter in between puffs.

Azrael snorts again. "I lied." He plucks the now lit cigarette from between my lips and takes a long drag, the smoke obscuring his face momentarily. "I was building it for you. I wanted to protect you. It was just you and me. That still matters."

"And my Father?" I accept the cigarette back and flick the ashes, giving him a tight, bitter smile. "You chose to include him, too, remember?" I take a pull before offering it to him again, but he waves it off, and I rise to my feet. "For Charlotte's sake, I suppose we should call a—"

"I'm sorry," he says, causing me to still. "I should've never kept the promise I made to your Father from you, and now Charlotte, but I . . ." He forces a bitter laugh. "I wanted you, and I would've done anything to have you. You might understand what that's like now. Thanks to her."

I swallow. "Anything except tell me how I might finally best Him."

"This isn't about *Him*, Lucifer," Azrael growls. "It never has been."

The end of my cigarette flares and then goes out, leaving nothing but smoke in its place as he rises to stand beside me. His muscled forearms flex, his gaze raking over me. Another reminder of how things used to be.

I wave him off, turning to leave. "If it wasn't about Him, perhaps you should have told me that you—"

"I love you," he says, gripping my shoulder.

I freeze.

"I'm sorry I didn't say it sooner, but I still fucking do, and you know it. We were both just too afraid to—"

"I fear nothing." I step into him, eyes narrowed. "Nothing but having her taken from me."

Azrael's gaze is cruel and mocking as he shakes his head at me. "And what do you think she'll say when she finds out about *our* deal? About the final choice you've been keeping from her? How's that any different?" He draws closer, until he's standing nearly nose to nose with me, so close I fear he . . .

My eyes fall to his lips.

He clocks it, smirking, like I've proven his point.

Goddamn him.

"How is that any different from what I did?" he asks.

"It's not," I admit.

"Then how can you—"

"Because I love her more than you ever loved me," I snarl, my mouth no more than a hairbreadth from his. "You didn't even tell me, and I wasn't capable of it then. How could you have felt anything close to what I feel for her about *me,* when you didn't even—"

He huffs, laughing in my face as a spark of fury ignites in me. "I may have believed that before, but not anymore, Lightbringer. Now, I know better." He leans forward, placing his hands on the side of my face, and I brace myself, expecting . . . but then he thinks better of it, releasing me. "I love her too," he says, the reminder of what they shared in the playroom severing me, "and the three of us could be so much more if you'd just swallow your goddamn pride and—"

"You know exactly why I can't—"

"Can't or won't, Lucifer?" His gaze flicks over me. "The choice has always been up to you. You're just too fucking stubborn to see it."

My body temperature rises, and I start to turn away.

"Kiss me," he growls, grabbing my shoulder.

I snarl. "Why would I?"

"If it didn't mean anything, then show me it didn't."

My mouth goes dry, and something dormant sparks inside my chest.

A thrill. A challenge.

And also . . .

The echo of everything I still loathe about myself.

I grip the back of his neck, pressing him against me. "Eyes on me, Reaper."

I drag my mouth against his so hard I'm certain the earth shakes with the force of it. His taste, the heat of his body, the smell of his skin reminding me of every vulnerable moment I've tried to forget so thoroughly. Of every part of myself I locked away long before my Fall.

He buries his hands in my hair, dragging us both deeper into the kiss.

And I let him.

It seems to go on for an eternity, our tongues intertwining as I'm lost in everything we once were, everything we could be.

Everything I could've been.

Without her.

Abruptly, I pull away from him, my hand dragging across my mouth as if he's poisoned me. But Death just smiles like he's already stolen all that I am.

"It's your decision, Lucifer. Who are you going to be? The Lightbringer or what He made you to be?" He turns and leaves me standing there.

Alone and broken by his venomous love.

And as raw and vulnerable as the day he first met me.

CHAPTER THIRTY-FOUR

Charlotte

When I return to the penthouse, thanks to the slowed time in Hell, it's nearly twenty-four hours later, and I haven't seen or heard from Azrael. Emergency services are still spread too thin throughout the city, so when Lucifer meets me right on time in the foyer, we decide he'll go ahead to Apollyon to assess the damage without me.

The ambulances and other medical staff are serving the most critical parts of the city down near Battery Park and the surrounding piers, triaging those who were severely injured, and searching for some of the victims still trapped beneath the rubble as other crews from farther inland are bused in to assist in other areas.

The penthouse is going to be occupied for a while.

But we have more than enough room.

I work with the staff to coordinate providing bedrolls, blankets, and other necessary toiletries and essentials to those with nowhere else to go, and I even field a video call to the current acting head of FEMA to send additional funding.

Most of the survivors Azrael and the other Originals managed to get out were in the immediate vicinity—Battery Park or somewhere nearby was their home neighborhood—so there's little left for them to return to.

I understand the feeling.

Once I've finished assisting the staff and ensured everyone's as comfortable as they could be, circumstances considered, night has fallen, but I find the strength of mind to snap myself into Apollyon's boardroom. It beats having Dagon drive me uptown. The subway isn't running, nor is it safe for me to ride due to the Righteous and the paparazzi. When I arrive, I'm not surprised to find Lucifer and his siblings arguing.

Lucifer sits at the head of the table with Greed to his left, while Azrael's claimed his usual corner near the window. Wrath, Gluttony, and Envy are there as well, but Lust and Sloth are nowhere to be seen. Az has probably jetted off to Paris, already in prep for Haute Couture week. Good riddance.

Though I'll need to get him back in my corner eventually.

I head straight toward Azrael.

"Are you okay?" I whisper. "If you think I'm scared of you, I'm not. I just—"

"Later." He nods to the executive table.

Neither of us wants an audience for this.

I give his hand a quick, reassuring squeeze before I join Lucifer. He pulls out the chair next to him for me, not missing a beat from laying into Envy like he used to do when he was my boss.

He clasps my hand, and I can't help but think about how strange it is to be back in this room, where he and I started.

So much has changed since then.

"I think we're far past that, don't you?" Gluttony interjects, arguing about the city's dwindling food supply now that Famine is loose.

The city is never going to be the same. We're still standing, but even I can feel the shift, the power structures crumbling.

I lift a brow. "Where's Mia?"

Everyone freezes.

As my assistant, she's always waiting for me outside meetings like this, keeping me on schedule, but I haven't seen her since yesterday morning.

Lucifer lowers his head, but it's Greed who says, "I went back to the studio for her, but the tide had already come in, and so close to the pier, she . . ." Her expression hardens slightly.

My throat closes.

I've never seen Greed this unsettled before, but I think she and Mia might have been . . .

I hang my head, not allowing any tears to fall.

I knew we weren't all going to make it through this. I *knew* and yet . . .

I never expected to lose someone I loved so quickly.

I close my eyes.

There'll be a time and a place to mourn our losses later. When all this is said and done.

If I let myself feel the pain now, I might break completely.

I glance toward Azrael, knowing he can see how I'm struggling to hold myself together. But he's got me. Once this is over.

"And the security team? The other mortals on staff? Evie?"

I haven't seen or heard from her since she ended up back in the hands of her twisted older brother when she called the police to report Jax missing, but according to the paparazzi, she's been spotted a few times down in Brighton Beach, so she's alive at least.

Last I knew anyway.

"Still unaccounted for," Lucifer answers.

I inhale a deep breath, glancing toward him, but he gestures for me to take the lead.

Getting his siblings to help us fight the apocalypse was my idea after all.

Even if it hasn't gone as smoothly as we'd hoped.

Wondering who opened the second seal and why is still irking me.

I sigh, looking at the other Originals. "Today was a mess."

The noise in the room erupts as everyone begins arguing.

"We need a more coordinated effort." Wrath.

"And how exactly do you expect coordination when we don't know which fucking seal Michael's opening?" Greed throws up her hands.

Gluttony rolls his eyes. "The possibilities narrow with each additional seal. We can make contingencies."

"With what knowledge?" Greed shrieks. "None of us even know what Father's demands are going to be."

"And that doesn't do anything to protect the loss of *human* life," I add.

We put as many contingencies in place as we could without sending the public into a mass panic. Every charity in and surrounding the city was overfunded and overstocked, but that doesn't appear to have helped anything.

"We need a different plan." Lucifer leans forward, turning his attention to me. "Opening the seals when they didn't pose a mortal threat to you was one thing, but allowing Michael to play Russian roulette with your life is another. I won't allow you to—"

"No." I slam my hands down on the table and stand.

The whole room goes quiet.

I can feel Azrael's reassuring presence at my back.

"The choice isn't yours to make." I clear my throat. "Until we have a better plan, we stay the course. There's no other option for me." Tentatively, I sit back down.

Lucifer's expression is furious.

But I know Azrael will understand me.

"What did you promise Sloth?" Envy asks suddenly.

I wince. "I might have promised him that whenever I get around to reopening the pearly gates, I would get him back into Heaven."

Lucifer's siblings groan, but I keep my head high.

I'm not going to apologize for making a deal that saved countless people. As bad as the third seal opening was, it would have only been worse if Sloth and I hadn't . . .

I shake my head, not even wanting to consider it.

Lucifer strokes his thumb over my hand in reassurance, capitulating, yet he doesn't look happy about this outcome. But I feel a bit of victory in standing up for myself.

"Great." Greed slouches back in her seat. "And just when I was starting to like you."

"Starting to?" I glance toward Azrael, who's been particularly quiet throughout all this, but he just gives me a heated look like he's proud of me.

My cheeks flush pink.

I return my attention to the room. "I don't see what's so bad about that."

Wrath scoffs, and Envy picks something from beneath his fingernails, looking bored, while Greed sighs dramatically. "Have you taught her absolutely nothing, Lucifer?"

"Taught me what?" I glance between them.

Lucifer leans back in his executive chair. "Reopening the pearly gates isn't like inserting a key into a lock, darling. There's twelve, each gate made of a single pearl, and the pearls are akin to"—he tilts his head, trying to find the right wording—"challenges one must get past."

"Challenges?" I flick a wary look between him and Azrael.

"Living Creatures," Azrael answers, like it's his duty to translate. Among those present, he has the most experience with humans, or former ones in my case, as dark as that experience may be. "Angels aren't the only things that guard God's throne."

"There's cherubim," Greed says.

"And seraphim," her twin adds. "As well as—"

"Our siblings." Lucifer's expression turns grave, and I pale slightly.

I sink back into my seat with a groan.

When am I ever going to stop making every celestial situation worse?

Immortality isn't all it's cracked up to be.

I'm in the learning-curve phase. I'm new to all this, I try to reassure myself, just as a bit of scripture comes back to me.

I've been revisiting it lately. With fresh eyes.

"'One like a lion. One like an ox. One with a face like a man, and one like a flying eagle,'" I mutter, paraphrasing several verses from Revelation, one of many my father and our congregation's Sunday school teachers forced me to memorize. "'Each has six wings and is covered in eyes, even under their wings.'"

"Their eyes are the least of your problems." Wrath snorts.

A warning growl tears from Azrael's throat, sending shivers down my spine, and Lucifer shoots his brother a menacing look.

"What? It's true." Wrath lifts his hands in surrender but stops talking.

This situation is only going from bad to worse.

"Well, one thing at a time, right?" I try to smile, but it's not very convincing. "Michael's clearly out for blood. There's no telling what he'll do next time, and who even knows what Lilith's doing to Jax in the meantime. Not to mention, we still don't know why the Righteous are so hell-bent on targeting me. It can't just be because I'm engaged to Lucifer. It's more personal than that, and if we don't hit back soon, they'll just keep coming. I know them. They'll use this as fuel to convert even more people. It's only a matter of time before they pull something drastic."

"So, what are you proposing, darling?"

I hesitate, thinking of the shocked look on Sloth's face when I held back the seal's flood, of that violent flyer the Righteous posted outside Pier59 Studios, of the fear in Jax's eyes when Ian was keeping her captive.

Maybe holding my anger in isn't protecting anybody.

Maybe it's time to strike first.

"We hit back at the Righteous for abducting Jax. Get information. Remind them who they're up against."

Lucifer smirks in approval, glancing toward Wrath.

Wrath grins. "Leave that to me."

I nod, his enthusiasm making me uneasy. "That doesn't help us with Michael and Lilith though."

"And we all know what the next seal brings," Envy says.

The room goes silent.

Envy continues to pick at a spot on his nail before he glances up, realizing a half second too late that all our attention is on him. He basks in it, the corner of his mouth lifting, but when none of us respond, he sighs. "It's the fourth. The one Mom's been waiting for."

All eyes shift to Azrael.

Of course. The final Horseman. The Pale Rider.

Death.

Why didn't I consider Azrael's role in all this sooner?

"What happens when the fourth seal opens?" I twist my chair toward him.

Azrael shakes his head. "I don't know."

"What do you *mean* you don't know?" Mimi casts him an agitated look.

I'm starting to think she and Death might not be on the best terms.

Azrael glares at her, but I understand him well enough now to recognize it's because he hates being the center of attention like this. Unlike Lucifer. "When God used Lilith's power to create the other Horsemen in my image, there were contingencies in place."

"Contingencies?" I lift a brow.

Azrael nods.

"Those being?"

Sometimes getting Death to mutter more than a few cryptic words is like pulling teeth.

Except when we're alone.

My face flushes.

He lets out a slow breath through his nose and swipes his thumb over the edge of his mouth, his lips tilting upward like he knows what I'm thinking. "The main agreement being, if I remained free, unlike my brothers, I wouldn't know what opening the seals would bring."

A momentary silence falls over the boardroom.

"How's that possible?" Mimi huffs, her gaze narrowing on Azrael as if she doesn't actually believe he's on our side. But Lucifer and I trust him completely.

Don't we?

I glance at Lucifer, but his expression doesn't give anything away.

"That's irrelevant." He waves a hand like it's his job to keep us all on track.

Once a CEO, always a CEO.

But he and Azrael exchange a look.

There's more to that story than either of them is saying, but I know better than to press Lucifer in front of his siblings. Even if he did promise me transparency.

"Back to Sloth," Lucifer says, his grip on my hand tightening.

"I don't see what's so concerning about my deal with him," I say. "I know celestial contracts are governed by divine law, and enforced by Gabriel, but it's not like I have to follow through immediately, right?"

Azrael crosses his arms. "Celestial covenants are like deals with the devil."

I shoot Lucifer a confused look.

He shrugs. "I had to get my inspiration from somewhere, darling."

I roll my eyes, but the arched brow he gives me has me muttering "Sorry, sir" and sinking in my chair.

"They're not *just* enforceable. They can result in exile," Gluttony says.

"Or judgment." Envy.

"And punishment." Lucifer's mouth presses into a flat line.

"Or yours and our brother's personal favorite." Greed looks to Azrael.

"Death," I finish as I look over my shoulder at him.

How did I never realize he was so tangled up in Lucifer's family?

He's more like them than I'll ever be.

Maybe Lucifer would have been better off with . . .

Don't even finish that thought, Lucifer interjects, the hellfire in his eyes blazing.

When he first lost his powers, the bond between us weakened, and I got used to letting my guard down regularly, but lately, I've noticed it's been strengthening again, even though he hasn't reclaimed his powers.

But how?

The question's been plaguing me.

"Be that as it may," Lucifer says, "that's only if you don't complete the covenant in whatever time frame Gabriel deems reasonable."

"But Gabriel's on the angelic side of your family. He's not going to lend me any favors, is he?"

"No," Greed confirms. Like she's reminding me that I'm still in debt to her.

And now Sloth too.

"Okay, so let me get this straight," I say, giving my head a quick shake. "We know that when the next seal opens, Azrael's going to be compelled to do *something*, but we're not sure what, and we also know the next seal will mean all four Horsemen are free, which means Lilith will have finally regained her power, giving her free rein to—"

"Fuck all of us." Lust suddenly appears on the other side of the room, fashionably late to the party as always. He gives me a cheeky wave. "Hey, lovey."

I scowl. "Don't you 'hey, lovey' me. Not after you screwed me."

"With the seal or at your engagement party?"

A deep, irritated grumble barrels from Azrael as I shoot Lust a furious look.

The play party is a sore point, and though Lust is the only Original I actually consider my friend, he's definitely on my shit list.

"Fuck off, Azmodeus," I snap, before I turn back to the others.

"Ooh, I love it when you're bitchy." Azmodeus licks his lips, but Lucifer's nostrils flare, and he leans forward like he's about to—

Azmodeus shrugs. "Jeez. All right already. I know when I'm not wanted."

And then he's gone.

What the hell is with him lately?

"Namely it's our Father that Mother wants to fuck." Greed wrinkles her nose. "In the proverbial sense at least."

Lucifer shrugs. "Not the worst outcome."

"Except that it leads to the end of *all* humanity and no afterlife."

"And we all know Charlotte couldn't handle starting over in another universe," Wrath says.

I give him a disbelieving look.

And to think, I was under the impression I was finally making some progress with him.

Wrath lifts a shoulder. "What? You couldn't."

I roll my eyes.

"Which means our plan isn't going to work, unless Lucifer managed to swing more than—"

"Three."

All eyes in the room turn to him.

I lift a brow. "What do you mean three?"

He ticks off three fingers. "Three is the number of additional archangels that have turned to our side."

I gape at him. "Only *three*?"

He scowls at me, but with him sitting in his executive chair like that, it reminds me a little of how things used to be, and I can't help but smile.

It's all I can do not to lean into him and tempt him.

"You do understand the collective amount of power three archangels hold in addition to having all my legions at the ready?" he says, using that same tone from when I used to be his intern and we'd verbally spar. It was always thinly veiled foreplay, of course. Even when I was convinced our relationship was fake.

Fake is a relative term, it seems.

There's nothing fake about how I feel for him now.

I lean toward him, and he must recognize what I'm thinking, because that perfect mouth of his twists into a knowing grin. He sprawls back in his executive chair, his hips thrust forward, and nods to his lap pointedly.

I'm waiting, little dove, he says into my mind.

My face flames with heat, but I rise from my seat and settle onto his lap shamelessly all the same, kissing him on the cheek. How come he always manages to get the upper hand with me?

Some things don't change, apparently.

"There'll be more," Lucifer says, trying to ease my concern. "Seraph and I targeted these three specifically. They're leaders, influencers, if you will. Next time, more will follow."

"If there even *is* a next time." Greed shakes her head. "Michael isn't going to let you get away with stealing his soldiers that easily."

I look toward her, trying not to feel self-conscious about how her brother's hands are now trailing up to my thighs.

"What are you saying, Mimi?"

Greed's gaze cuts between me and Azrael. "While you two were too busy whining about the fact I left Lucifer's side, all because he had to take a little swim—"

"He's *mortal* now, Mimi." I shake my head as the devil lays a tempting kiss on my shoulder, and Greed waves an annoyed hand at me.

They're all used to me and Lucifer by now.

"A minor detail." She shrugs.

Despite Azrael's early attempts to conceal that knowledge, it didn't take long for the other Originals to figure it out. Celestials are even bigger gossips than the damn tabloids.

"But in the meantime, *I* was following Uriel to the In-Between." Greed puffs out her chest, like she expects us all to be far more impressed than we are.

"The In-Between?" I think back to that strange club Azmodeus took me to. The one that caused the paparazzi to turn on me. "So, it *is* real? Like Limbo? Or is it part of the ether?"

They all seem similar to me.

"The In-Between is a threshold realm, a metaphysical transit zone," Azrael answers. "Limbo is for the unclaimed dead. A construct created when I first came to the world. It's nothing but a holding chamber. The In-Between isn't for souls. It's a realm between realms, a state between chaos and order, like the connective tissue between planes, and the ether is its arterial system."

I blink, trying to take all that in, and also not letting myself consider all the reasons Azrael would have such detailed knowledge of the internal systems of the human body.

"And?" Lucifer's hand comes to my waist, squeezing as he prompts Mimi to hurry up. I can tell he's not going to stay patient much longer.

"And Michael appears to have given him the task of guarding the Heavenly Hosts' most precious treasures."

"The Heavenly Hosts?"

"It's the name of our Father's armies, darling. *My* former army." Lucifer's gaze darkens as he drags me deeper into his lap.

He isn't ashamed to indulge in me, even in front of his siblings.

"And mine," Mimi says, her gaze narrowing.

It's the same look she gives me when she thinks I'm slacking during training.

No wonder the two of them hate Michael. After Lucifer fell, Michael stole more than his place at God's side. He took something from all of them. He claimed their purpose, their friends, their meaning.

"And what kind of treasures are we talking about? Celestial weaponry could be valuable." I think of the whip that's currently in Lucifer's possession, but it's hardly worth risking.

"Your friend and the Holy Lance." Mimi grins.

My mouth goes dry, and Lucifer's hand pauses where he'd just slipped it beneath my Balmain skirt under the table.

"Which means?" A flush creeps up my neck as I look toward Greed, and she smiles at me in that sisterly way she does occasionally.

We have a location.

She knows where Jax is.

And if Greed knows where Jax is, then . . .

"Won't God see Lilith coming?"

"Father's precognitive abilities don't extend to Mother. They're on a level playing field."

"But can Lilith find God and destroy Him without her? Without Jax and her prophecies?" I ask, suddenly shifting forward and pressing my legs closed.

Lucifer grumbles, and I know I'm likely going to be punished for that later, but he leans forward, just as invested in Jax's well-being as I am.

"Later," I promise, kissing his cheek.

He considers my question for a second and then leans back in his chair. "It's possible, but not probable, or she wouldn't have absconded with her in the first place. Not to mention, all I need to restore my powers is a prophet to raise our dear friend Ms. Santiago, the nun, from the dead, remember?"

I nod.

It's all starting to fall into place.

"So, if *we* had Jax before the fourth seal opens, I could find God. Have Him put an end to this, and we could stop opening seals for Michael. No more Armageddon, no more humans would be hurt, and Lilith still wouldn't have her full power, so even if she found God, she wouldn't be able to destroy Him, and you'll no longer be—"

"Powerless." Lucifer smirks at me.

I can't help but want to kiss him. Among other things.

And he sees it.

"All of you out *now*," he orders, his siblings' chairs scraping in response.

He lifts me onto the boardroom table, spreading my legs just as the door closes behind the last of his siblings, and he drops to his knees.

My head falls back as he tears my thong aside, and the fork in his tongue starts to flick over me. I sigh contentedly.

Things are looking up for us, honestly.

Until my gaze snags on where Azrael has faded into the Nothing, and I'm reminded of what all this could cost if we don't pull this off successfully.

CHAPTER THIRTY-FIVE

Charlotte

We reconvene a few hours later to formulate a plan together.

Well, "together" is a relative term when it comes to Lucifer's siblings.

He, Mimi, and Wrath are at each other's throats the entire time, arguing over the particulars of the strategy in passionate Angelic battle terms I can hardly follow, while Gluttony and Envy look increasingly bored, despite that they literally have nowhere else to be and half the city is currently without power.

Azrael and I interject occasionally amid the chaos with considerations about, well, the minor inconvenient detail of how many human deaths might result from some of Lucifer and Greed's more elaborate plans, and it isn't until Imani—or should I say Salome?—stops in to deliver some food and other company-related news that we all get a break from the chaos.

She's quiet mostly, save for a few times when Lucifer directly addresses her, and I don't get a chance to speak to her about what I overheard from Michael, or how the PR coverage might affect our current negotiating. Even if we're no longer opening the seals for Michael, I can't risk the other Originals defecting to his side.

And Azmodeus still hasn't returned after he fucked off to . . . who knows where.

I'm going to have to reconnect with him eventually.

I sit curled up on Lucifer's lap, my head resting on his shoulder as I do my best to follow along, but I'm feeling all warm and fuzzy from what he did to me on top of the boardroom table, and despite what pains in the asses they are, suddenly I'm struck by the fact that this ragtag group of celestial rebels has become my family.

More than my sperm donor could ever be.

I smile.

By the time we're through, I'm all strategized out, and family or not, I'm feeling increasingly concerned at the thought that the bulk of the world's economic and celestial power is not only concentrated in this room but controlled by a bunch of billionaires who can't seem to agree upon anything.

Except that the rest of us are far less important than they are.

But like it or not, they're on board with helping me for now, so I guess I have no choice but to let them off the hook.

Team No Apocalypse is looking up.

We're not all going to die and fade away into the Nothing, so that's something, right?

Granted, it's all contingent on Azrael and me successfully getting Jax out of the In-Between where Lilith's holding her, which is far more complicated than it sounded initially, but it's the best plan we've got. I'm so hopeful about seeing Jax return home that not even Envy's whining about how much he's dreading the rapid approach of Haute Couture week can get me down.

Who hates Paris?

I've never been, and I already know I'll love it.

When our meeting disperses, I manage to catch Imani out in the hall and pull her to the side. "We need to talk."

"I know." She nods. "I know, but . . ." Her gaze darts from the boardroom door to the window and out onto the darkened streets.

Sometimes I forget that her entire life doesn't revolve around Apollyon.

"Wednesday," I say, placing a reassuring hand on her arm. Our usual time.

She nods. "I'll bring coffee."

"Decaf please." I place a tentative hand on my stomach.

I still haven't confirmed anything, but . . .

Imani smiles at me, patting my arm.

No matter what her story is, it doesn't change anything.

She's still helped me more than any other person I know.

I head back into the boardroom.

Greed and Gluttony are the only two Originals who've lingered.

"About the Holy Fire you wielded earlier."

I wince. "I'm sorry about your Schiaparelli."

"Don't." She raises a hand. "I can't stand apologies. They're so . . ." She wrinkles her nose.

"Selfless?" her twin supplies.

She snaps her fingers. "Exactly."

"Well, Lucifer is fine in any case."

"More than fine, I'd say." He pulls me in for a teasing kiss.

He's in a good mood, pleased about the idea of getting his powers back.

When he releases me, I open my mouth, prepared to point out the massive loss of human life that happened today, when Greed suddenly says, "You summoned the Holy Fire far better than any other celestial abilities we've tried." She gives me a pointed look.

"Meaning?"

Lucifer shakes his head, like he's not sure whether to be disappointed or amused. "Those were *holy* powers, Charlotte. Some of our Father's."

"Your Father's?"

Lucifer looks at Azrael, who gives a curt nod before they turn back to me. "We've been training you from the wrong side of the celestial divide, I'm afraid."

"But I can wield your shadows too."

"Not as easily."

He has a point.

Which means I'm . . . more like God than I am like Lucifer.

I'm not sure how I feel about that.

"It might be a better idea for someone else to train you. Someone who's a bit more *angelic*, you might say." Lucifer nods toward the door, and I turn to find . . .

"Seraph," I breathe.

It's the first time I've met one of Lucifer's angelic siblings up close. At least one who wasn't threatening to kill me or who was only there for a few brief moments.

Seraph extends her palms to me, and I round the conference table, taking her hands in mine as I try to stifle a grin. If only my dad and his congregation could see me now.

I'm more holy than they'll ever be.

"I've been praying for this moment." Seraph smiles, but somewhere behind me, I hear Mimi gag dramatically. Seraph squeezes my hands. "I've heard your prayers."

"You've *heard* them?" I glance at Lucifer.

Seraph's lips curve. "I'm the guardian of our Father's throne, so in His absence . . ."

She's been the one answering me.

"I think we'll get along well, Charlotte."

I can't help but grin.

Already, I have a good feeling about this.

"Though you'll still be training with me," Greed adds.

"And me," Lucifer says. "And Azrael, of course."

"Four training schedules. Great." I force a smile, trying not to panic at the thought of all the scheduling. Particularly without Mia.

My heart sinks.

"Our Father's power is fueled by divine justice," Seraph explains.

Divine justice?

I cut a look between Lucifer and Azrael again.

I've been viewing my abilities the wrong way this entire time, trying to connect them to my anger, to the darkness inside me, when what I really needed to connect them to was the injustice underneath.

I exhale.

"Anger can be righteous." Lucifer smirks.

"A powerful force for positive change." Seraph casts him a pointed look. "Or conversely, destructive when turned inward."

Lucifer frowns at her.

Suddenly, Lucifer's rebellion, Eve, the apple, all of who he was *before* makes a whole lot more sense to me. As well as who I'm becoming.

"Divine justice," I repeat, turning toward Seraph and squeezing her hands excitedly. "I like the sound of that."

CHAPTER THIRTY-SIX

Azrael

I don't understand what Charlotte's doing when she finally breaks free from the others, until suddenly she's standing alone in her old office, a nostalgic smile on her face like she's revisiting old memories. I watch over her from the Nothing.

"Take me to your favorite place," she whispers into the silence to me.

My favorite place isn't on this shithole planet, that's for certain, but I don't bother to point that out before I become corporeal and take her into my arms.

When we reappear on top of the building in the cold night air, I'm holding her from behind. "Hang tight, little siren."

I flap my wings, and then we're soaring.

Charlotte lets out a startled shriek.

She covers her eyes the first few minutes, and I chuckle at the thought that mine and Lucifer's little siren might actually be afraid of heights, but once she realizes I've got her, she peeks through her fingers.

I'm never going to let her go.

We soar over the darkened city, stopping on a ledge overlooking Midtown on top of the Empire State Building. It's fucking freezing up here this time of year, and the wind is howling, but I like the view. I prop myself against the building, wrapping my arms and legs around her as I nestle her warmth into me. "You were amazing, standing up for yourself today."

We stare down from the rafters at the city.

"I'm sorry," she whispers, the words so quiet they're almost lost on the wind.

"You don't need to be."

"But I do." She looks at me. "I know you're probably not used to anyone taking your feelings into consideration, Azrael. Lord knows that's not Lucifer's biggest strength, and God and humanity have never been very fair to you, but I see you. I know how you feel about him, and yet I still treated you like you were just a tool for my pleasure." Her voice trails off. "Will you forgive me?"

I allow her to say it, closing my eyes and tipping my head back as I bask in how it feels to be truly seen.

For the first time in my whole fucking existence.

"I forgive you," I say, after we're both quiet for a time. "But only if you forgive me."

Her face falls. "We both consented to the scene. You don't have to apologize for—"

"Not that." I lean down and kiss her deep, our tongues mingling. "For scaring you. For not showing you all of me."

"Do you really enjoy—"

"I'm not a sadist." I shake my head, glancing out at the city lights. "But humanity has always feared the unknown, and I see everyone at their worst points. My purpose, what gives my existence meaning, is . . ."

"Complicated," she finishes.

I nod.

She lets out a long sigh. "Some people only turn toward Heaven in the end. When they fear no one's on the other side." She cups my cheek, guiding me to her. "But at least you're there, waiting for them."

She kisses me, and the desperate feel of her mouth on mine is a cruel thing.

She understands me, and for the first time in a long time I feel . . . hope.

Hope for what this could be.

"And yours and Lucifer's kiss?" she asks when our lips part. "At the CFDA awards?"

My breath stops. "That's not the only time that we—"

"I knew it!" she squeals, a joyous grin blossoming as she wiggles her eyebrows. "I saw how you looked at one another in the playroom."

I can't help but chuckle. Her enthusiasm is . . . heartwarming.

If I had a heart, that is.

"Charlotte, I want you to know I would never—"

"I know. You and I are solid." She leans forward, resting her forehead against mine. "I know you'd never try to take him from me, but that doesn't mean that sometimes I don't wish that the three of us could . . ." Her voice trails off.

We both fall silent.

"Can we have a do-over?" she asks sometime later.

I lift a brow.

"Of what I told you in the playroom."

I nod, my smile widening.

She frames my face with her hands, and the hope in her eyes is soul-baring. More open and honest than Lucifer and I have ever been. "I love you, Azrael."

My eyes fall to her lips. "I love you too, baby girl. More than I would've thought possible." I close the distance between us and capture the sweet taste of her on my tongue. Like milk and honey. Sin and temptation.

Or sunlight cast over a grave.

Everything alive and sweet.

"So, what does this mean? For you and me?"

I quirk my scarred brow. "What do you want it to mean, little siren?"

She turns and relaxes back, and I pull her tighter to my chest, resting my head on top of hers. "I think it means a new beginning," she says, "for all of us."

CHAPTER THIRTY-SEVEN

Lucifer

"I don't see why we couldn't have had this conversation in your office."

"You know I've always had a flair for the dramatic." I shrug.

Seraph and I are alone on the third floor of the New York Public Library in the McGraw Rotunda, the public's access closed due to the current state of emergency. The air is thick with the scent of the library's aged tomes, and it won't be long before this space becomes yet another shelter. Just like my penthouse, unfortunately.

Though using my home to house the apocalypse's victims won't prove to be the publicity stunt I once would've intended it to be.

Christianity is the world's oldest PR campaign, and I've been waging my opposition for some time, obviously.

Seraph glances to the ceiling overhead, taking in the depiction of Prometheus delivering fire to man, though the painting has more than a few distinct similarities to our brother Uriel. "Do you think they would have painted us in this many forms if they'd known what we really look like? In our heavenly bodies?"

Eyes upon eyes. Wheels upon wheels, she means.

In other words, goddamn terrifying.

Monstrous.

"Not likely."

Humanity is nearly as in love with itself as it's always accused me of being.

But at the moment, I couldn't care less about any of that.

"This business with Uriel," I say, prompting my sister to share what she's been withholding. "Is it true? That we can retrieve Charlotte's friend?"

"To the best of my knowledge, yes." Seraph nods. "Michael's furious about how well Charlotte did. That she survived. That your plan's working."

I snort. "It opened his seal in any case."

"But that's not his only endgame. You know that." Seraph's expression turns grave. "He still doesn't know what her death would do to his cause. He intends to hurt her, Lucifer."

"I already have several contingencies in place."

"You mean Azrael?" Seraph wrinkles her nose. She and my other angelic siblings have never been fans of him. The thought of someone, or some*thing*, that precedes our Father's divine order and our Mother's chaos is unconscionable to them. Affronting to their belief. "And what of the next seal? What if Father's word forces Azrael to—"

"He won't," I say, more confident in that now than I've ever been. "We have an alternate plan."

Azrael may be a free agent, may have even hoped to put an end to me by putting the blade into play, but he won't hurt Charlotte.

Not physically, anyway.

My thoughts turn to how he looked at me in the playroom the other day, how he told me he loved me, the way he kissed me. If only he'd said what he did *before* I found out about his little arrangement with my Father, then perhaps he and I would still be . . .

Suddenly, I find myself in desperate need of a change in subject.

"What's Michael's sudden preoccupation with Charlotte?"

I have a few guesses, but targeting her doesn't make sense to me.

Even from my brother's high-handed stance.

Seraph scoffs. "He's jealous of you, of course. Michael will always live within your shadow, Lucy. What other reason does he need?"

"A celestial one, no doubt." I take out one of my cigarettes and stare at it longingly before I sigh and place it back inside my suit coat. I've recently decided to quit whenever I'm topside, but it's not proving so easy. "Michael may be a fool, but he wouldn't dare come for Charlotte over a petty, childish feud."

"And what might his motivation be?"

"To block me from regaining my power."

Seraph rolls her eyes. "Now you're sounding like—"

"Think about it, sister. If Michael truly believes I would use Charlotte for my own gain, gift her some of my power as a fail-safe, that must mean . . ." I gesture for her to continue.

"That he thinks you're incapable of loving her."

"And also," I snap a few times, prompting her further.

"That sacrificing her to regain your abilities was your plan all along."

"Exactly." A feeling of unease shifts through me. This time, I'm unable to resist the urge. I take my cigarettes out of my pocket and light one, finally, having a draw as I allow my head to fall back. Once a devil, always a devil.

I can't even stop bloody smoking, and yet she expects me to turn over a new leaf? To earn my Father's forgiveness?

Not bloody likely.

"It fits. Michael never had any intention for her to survive the seals opening, even from the start."

I exhale, blowing smoke into the darkened air. "And now that she's a bigger threat than he realized?"

Seraph's expression is one of distress. "He won't hesitate to come for her directly."

I end up somewhere down on Seventh a short while later, the church already filled to the brim with the city's survivors. Father Brown doesn't look at me as I approach, but I know he sees me. "A word, Father?"

He nods, reluctantly abandoning the unhoused woman he's currently attending to, and leads me into a small recreation room off the main sanctuary that serves as the church's office. "I'm very busy right now, Lucifer. If this is about—"

"You're a prophet, aren't you?"

His eyes widen. "Pardon?"

"You heard me."

Father Brown shakes his head, tugging at his starched collar as if he's uncomfortable with this particular line of questioning. "I'm sorry. You must have me mistaken for someone else." He tries to leave, but I place my hand upon his chest, backing him against the wall.

The hellfire in my gaze blazes. "You cannot hide from me."

"Can't I?" he asks, the defiance in his features causing me to lift a brow, before he brushes past, clearly dismissing me.

My hand drops.

For a moment, I consider going after him with one of my blades. It would be easy.

But false prophets are everywhere these days. Besides, one misstep and the Righteous will descend like vultures.

Still, there's something off about him. Like something I once knew but have long since forgotten. The same off-balance feeling I had when I saw Michael in front of Charlotte.

Like my power is no longer missing.

Just . . . resisting me.

I shake my head. We're only days away from retrieving Charlotte's friend, and even *I* don't make it a habit of threatening unarmed clergy in one of my Father's sanctuaries.

He'll be at my disposal whenever it suits me.

When the time is right.

I plunge down into my realm shortly thereafter, preferring to avoid the penthouse for the time being. Charlotte's father and I have her upcoming visit to attend to, and when I arrive at his chamber, I'm unsurprised to find Azrael already there, waiting for me.

"He's ready for you."

They're the first words we've spoken to one another since he left me torn open like a lovesick fool outside of the Abyss the other evening.

I give a curt nod. "And have you told her?" I lift a brow as he stalks away. "About your deal with my Father?"

It's the one weapon I still have within my arsenal to ensure she is mine.

He pauses, his back to me. "Not yet. I . . . need more time."

I scoff. "Of course you do."

Azrael heaves a long sigh like my response disappoints him.

Then he fades into the Nothing and is gone.

CHAPTER THIRTY-EIGHT

Azrael

I scour the In-Between and the Nothing, trying to confirm what Greed reported about Uriel and the location of Charlotte's friend, but I don't find anything. Something's keeping her obscured from me.

The thought of that doesn't sit right with me, especially now that we're only a week out from our plan to retrieve her. Charlotte has only just begun training with Seraph, though she's still working with me and Greed—and my ex, unfortunately—but none of us can even begin to know what Michael has planned.

And that makes me uneasy.

Before I can stop myself, I'm at the church on Seventh again. Drawn to the answers I find there like a moth to a damn flame. I don't know what it is about the place that keeps calling to me, but it tugs at me.

Reminds me of His promise.

And I know better than to ignore my instincts.

I find Father Brown almost exactly where I left him a few days ago, in a pew on the left-hand side of the sanctuary. He rests his head back, eyes closed, like he's just taken his last confession for the night and is ready for sleep. I approach silently.

"How did you know about my deal with God?"

He sighs. "Not you too." He opens his eyes, the lines on his face making him look weary. "Lucifer already came to see me."

"He did?" I arch a brow.

The priest huffs. "He accused me of being a prophet."

I snort. "I don't think you're a prophet."

"Then what?" He turns to look at me, but I don't see the flash of something ancient I saw before. Just a tired old priest whose greatest accomplishment is being allowed to live rent-free in the rectory. Lucifer's distrust of the clergy may have rubbed off on me.

I'm the only one the church has given an even worse rap sheet to.

Lucifer may have started it all in the Garden, but humanity *chose* to make me their boogeyman. I can't say I blame them, honestly.

I lift my eyes to the altar the priest is staring at, my thoughts shifting to Charlotte, to the way she looked at me when I had her on the bench inside the playroom the other day. Like the first moment I got a bit rough with her she feared me.

I close my eyes, exhaling.

Even if she's immortal now, not even immortality makes her truly safe from me.

From the fear of the unknown.

"I think you're just a tired old man," I answer eventually. "A tired old man who wants his life to mean something."

He forces a laugh. "Don't we all?"

"Heaven or Hell. Up or down. All life is meaningless in the end."

He chuckles, coming to stand. "I suppose I shouldn't be surprised the Angel of Death is a nihilist."

My head snaps toward him. "And how do you know I'm—"

"I feel it. In here," he says pointing to where his heart beats. "And so I know it in here." He taps the crown of his head.

"So, you *are* a prophet?"

"No, Azrael." He shakes his head as he pats my shoulder. "That's just what it means to have faith."

CHAPTER THIRTY-NINE

Charlotte

That night, when I finally collapse into bed, I have the dream again.

The one I've been having since the very beginning when I met Lucifer.

But it keeps changing.

I run so hard I can feel my heart pumping, though I don't know what exactly it is I'm running from. But when I reach the forest, the darkness no longer feels threatening.

Instead of the gnarled shadows cast by the moonlight chasing me, or the small, fresh-faced girl I expect to see, Lilith is already there, waiting for me.

I turn my head and the setting shifts, so that we're standing in the middle of a darkened orchard, a garden that seems to exist at the edge of the world, the sickly sweet scent of rotting apples all around me.

Lilith's dark skin seems to blend into the night, so that the whites of her eyes and her teeth gleam viciously, and when she speaks, her voice sounds like a shrieking chorus of a thousand furies made one. Of every woman who's ever been scorned.

"The Daughter of Chaos approaches, born to deceive; in blood, she rises in the dragon's name. Birthed of the Holy Mother, against the will of the

Father, she will strike where none dare tread. For within her she shall wield a power yet unseen by the heavens. For as it was written: 'She who was dead shall bring forth the living to the wrath of the Last Judgment.'"

A chill runs down my spine, my breath hitching.

I expect her to stop there, to disappear like she has the last several times I've had this dream, but then she reaches out and touches me. On my belly.

I glance down only to find a generous curve there, and on my wrist, the snake, mine and Lucifer's sigil, the one that marks me as his soulmate, burns suddenly.

I lift my head toward Lilith again, but she's no longer alone.

Four men now stand behind her. The strongholds of the power she needs to unleash.

I recognize them instantly.

Pestilence, Famine, War, and—

"Death," I breathe.

But Azrael refuses to look at me.

"Charlotte," I hear a soft, familiar voice hiss. "Charlotte."

I turn, just in time to find Jax lying beneath one of the trees, a bitten, rotting apple in her hand. It crumbles as she looks toward Azrael and then—

I wake up choking on nothing but dust, the smell of rotting apples still singeing my nose. But I hear the sound of my automated espresso maker running.

I flop back into my pillows with a groan, my heart racing. It was just a dream.

I roll out of bed a moment later.

After Azrael and I called it a night the other evening, I came back to the townhouse, and I've stayed here, hidden away, ever since.

I'm not ready to face the full brunt of the seal's consequences yet.

Padding into the bathroom, I see the CVS bag still on my counter. Before I can lose my nerve, I grab the box and follow the instructions, mentally preparing to wait several minutes like the directions say, but the test turns positive almost immediately.

I drop back onto the toilet with a groan.

Fuck my life. Fuck making my own choices.

Rolling over for fate was honestly easier.

I place my hand to my belly, like I might be able to sense the budding life there, and suddenly I'm centered again. The image of the little girl from my dreams comes to mind. I always thought she was supposed to be Mark's, what could have been if I'd stayed with him, but now that I think about it, I realize her coloring looks a lot like—

"Lucifer." I groan.

How am I supposed to tell him I'm pregnant with everything that's going on between me and Azrael currently?

Within a few months, my life has gone from relatively stable, if a bit stressful, to a full-blown catastrophe. A lot like everyone else in the city.

At least I'm shielded from the worst of it.

I wash my hands and make my way out of the bathroom, the townhouse feeling entirely too empty. I get dressed quickly, but as I'm zipping up one of my dresses that is definitely getting too tight—I let out a noise of defeat—which only has me dreading my fitting on Monday with Xzander for Fashion Week, I notice the black Dior box sitting on my bedside waiting for me.

My collar.

The permanent one.

For a long moment, I just stare at it.

I took it off because I was afraid of losing myself. But now I think what I was really scared of this whole time is my own vulnerability. The way I crave him.

I've never been good at resisting him.

Abruptly, I take the box and shove it into my purse.

If I wait until I'm certain I won't disappoint anyone, I'm never going to be happy. I snap myself back to the penthouse.

"Charlotte."

I turn to find Imani. *Or Salome?*

I'm honestly not sure what to call her.

"Hey." I give her a quick cheek kiss.

"Decaf as requested." She passes me a disposable cup. "Did you—"

"Confirm?" I place a hand on my stomach. "Yeah, but you're the only one who knows. Aside from the tabloid speculations."

She pulls me in for a hug, one that's longer and tighter than usual. "Congratulations."

"Thanks."

She takes in my uncertain expression. "Or are you . . . ?"

"I'm keeping it. I just haven't had a lot of time to process."

"Who would blame you?" She gestures as if to indicate how the world is falling apart all around us.

I haven't bothered to look at today's headlines or at my socials, so I don't know the extent of the damage. I can only take one thing at a time right now.

"Lucifer's study?" I suggest, nodding upstairs.

It's the one place we can still get some privacy. I don't figure she wants the details of her past broadcast to everyone.

She nods.

We climb the stairs together, neither of us saying anything. The staff are even more active than usual, considering they're being paid triple time due to the current circumstances, but the last thing either of us needs is someone overhearing.

When we reach the third floor, I clear my throat. "Did you have any friends or family who . . . ?"

"No, thankfully."

I give a solemn nod.

I can't believe I haven't asked much about her personal life until now. I just assumed Apollyon was her baby, considering the hours she pulls despite being salaried. As close as Imani and I are, our relationship has always been strictly professional.

Well, as professional as working for the devil can be, anyway.

When we finally reach Lucifer's study, I close the door and sink into one of the armchairs. Now that I know I'm pregnant, it's like all the exhaustion I've been feeling has amplified. Or maybe it's the prospect of learning that everything I thought I knew about my mentor was wrong? Or hearing the full extent of the seal's damage?

I'm not sure I'm ready for either of those conversations.

Imani drops into an adjacent chair. "I'm sorry if it hurt you to find out about my identity that way."

"You're only human, right? You don't owe me anything. At this point, what's another celestial secret?" I try to smile, but it fades quickly. "I guess this is why you never wanted to discuss how you started working for Lucifer."

"Yeah, I'm human. It's not that I didn't trust you, Charlotte. It's just . . ." She stares at her coffee. "I like who I am now better than who I was before."

"I understand the feeling."

That's what I've been trying to do this whole time, after all, outrun my past, push down my resentment about who I was forced to be before by becoming something no one ever would have expected from me. Until now, when I've finally arrived and I'm starting to question if I made a wrong turn. I guess it was naïve to believe I could ever escape myself, especially now that I'm being forced to reconcile it with the immortal I'm becoming.

"You don't have to share anything with me that you don't want to."

"I think an explanation is only fair at this point, and I saw how you've been standing up for yourself with the other Originals, with Lucifer. You can handle it." Imani takes a slow sip of her coffee, sighing. "The first time I ever met Lucifer was at the end of my *first* life. I'd been an innocent and scared girl, a lot like you." She grins. "But it was Rome during the Herodian period, and I was royalty, so I was raised in a den of vipers. I learned early how to survive from watching my mother, learned what power seducing a man could bring me."

"You mean the dance of the seven veils?"

My father used the story all the time in his sermons as a warning—the girl who danced for Herod and demanded John the Baptist's head on a platter. To him, she was proof that feminine seduction was the devil's work. But it's hard to believe it's the same woman sitting here in front of me.

She nods. "The truth is less legend and more tragedy. I didn't want John to die. I just wanted my mother to love me. I danced for my stepfather, Herod, at my mother's request. I asked for John the Baptist's head because she told me to. Not because I wanted John to die, but because I was desperate for her approval. I wish I could say that it was more than that, than a young girl so hungry for her mother's love she'd do anything to get it, but it wasn't."

"She took advantage of you, used you for her own purposes."

She glances down. "I've made peace with my choices, tried to move on with my life. I married twice, had two beautiful children"—she smiles at my middle—"lived a long life, but what I did to John still haunted me in the end."

"So, you went to Hell? Because you asked for his head, called for his execution, and you weren't sorry for it. You were angry."

I know this story well. From all my years of Bible school. But the rest I can guess.

She nods. "I begged Lucifer not to punish me, to cut me a deal, and he did."

"But at a price?"

"It's always at a price. Like I tried to warn you in the beginning." She sets down her coffee cup on one of the study's tables. "Deals with the devil are never what they seem."

I snort, suddenly all too aware of the fullness in my belly. "Don't I know it."

Imani leans forward. "I can't tell you much about the time I spent in Hell because now that I've been resurrected into a new body, it's a blur to me. But I do remember the day Lucifer came to see me again." She looks me directly in the eye. "He said he'd come to collect his due, that he needed a soul, someone to help him craft a new image."

I shake my head.

"And why did you—"

"Agree?" She scoots forward. "That's what I wanted to tell you. I'm sure you know by now that he and the other Originals weren't always locked away. Their rebellion against God didn't reach a true defeat until Christ's crucifixion."

"Lucifer never mentioned it, but I always sort of assumed, since . . ."

"'Now is the judgment of this world; now will the ruler of this world be cast out,'" we recite together. John 12:31.

My pulse picks up.

"Even then, there were cracks, loopholes. Lucifer built Hell. It's his domain. God was never going to be able to keep him locked away there. There were ways for him and the others to break through, but never for long. Then when Gabriel came and delivered the news about God's redemption, suddenly the Originals learned what they needed to open the gates of Hell permanently."

I lift a brow.

"A single human soul. That's all that was needed to get through."

My breath comes out in one fell swoop.

"And Lucifer chose you," I say. "The same way he chose me."

She nods. "He thought I could help him win his Father's redemption, even if it technically was only offered to his siblings. That my skills would buy him influence."

I snort. "He wasn't wrong."

Imani is so good at her job, it's terrifying.

Lucifer's mystery, his brand, the mystique. It's all thanks to her.

"No, he wasn't. He hardly ever is."

"So, resurrection must be the only way to permeate a celestial barrier, if you're not of that realm, considering what Lucifer's trying to do with his powers now."

Imani nods, her eyes distant. "From my understanding, before the gates of Hell opened, moving between planes wasn't simple. You needed a prophet to raise someone from the dead, a new body, and then someone with wings to carry them."

"And the person who carried you was . . ."

"Gabriel. On God's decree." She meets my gaze. "But with the gates permanently open, Lucifer and his siblings can walk between Hell and Earth, and the angels can descend from Heaven, but . . ."

"Only Azrael and I can walk between all three."

She gives a curt nod. "I'm loyal to Lucifer, because he gave me a second chance. The kind of second chance God never gave me."

"So why tell me all this? Why now?"

"Information is currency, and I don't know whether my story will be any value to you, but I saw you in that meeting the other day. You're starting to make your own moves. Your own plays."

She's right.

I'm becoming an immortal power player.

Independent from Lucifer.

I reach across the space between us, taking her hand. "Thank you for telling me."

"There's one more thing you should know." She squeezes my hand before we both lean back with our coffee.

"And what's that?"

Imani shrugs. "His feud with Mario Prada is because of me."

I throw back my head and laugh, completely relieved it wasn't something more serious.

"Why did you pick my résumé out of that pile? Was it because of Lilith?" I take another generous sip. "And where does the modeling come in?"

Imani snorts. "The modeling background was just a cover, to create a plausible backstory for how I came to work for Lucifer. It was his idea. Just like his plan to focus Apollyon on luxury goods. You know it's his thing. As for the résumé, yours was as good as any, and I thought there might be a few similarities between you and me. Someone fiery under all the people pleasing."

"Not as many as I'd like there to be." I smile, and she returns it, beaming.

"I'm only going to say this once, girl, but I'm so damn proud of you."

My eyes fill with tears as I lean forward and pull her in for a fierce hug.

We both retreat from the embrace, teary eyed, and for once she's the one who glances at *me* uncertainly. "Does this change anything?"

"Not a chance. If anything, it only makes me love you more."

She and I are alike in so many ways, our stories so similar. A young girl taken advantage of by those around her, forced to make impossible decisions before she was ready.

Forced to become what biblical tales warn of in order to survive.

We sit in silence for a few moments, the weight of everything we've said settling.

"I'm not ready to hear about what this means for the world yet."

She winces. "It's about what you'd expect."

"And the rest?"

"I've got your couture 'resurrection' for Fashion Week well in hand." She winks.

"And my image?" I shake my head. "God, that seems so trivial now, but you know I need for things to go well, so that none of the other Originals try to—"

"It's not as bad as you think." She whips out her phone and turns it toward me. The first image I see is the little girl I saved.

A pang of guilt twinges through me.

I haven't so much as thought about her since.

"Her name's Lily Parker. She's five, and she says you saved her." Imani passes me her phone, and I stare at the headline. At the image of the little girl—Lily—reunited with her mother.

New York City's Guardian Angel.

"But she was just one—"

"You know as well as I do that small acts of kindness can make a big difference when it comes to PR."

I swipe at a few tears that have managed to break free, and Imani smiles at me.

"I see who you are, Charlotte. I've seen who you are from the very beginning, and if you're brave enough, I think that despite all this apocalypse nonsense, despite being engaged to Lucifer, the world is going to see it, too, if you let them."

She squeezes my hand, but I'm no longer capable of saying anything. For the first time in a long time, I feel proud of who I am, of the woman I'm becoming, and the shame I was raised with feels like nothing more than a distant memory.

PART THREE | REVELATION

And then there was silence in heaven . . .

Azrael

There were two sons in the garden that night, but only one would be remembered.

The ground in Gethsemane is dry and coarse, jagged rock over uneven terrain, and tonight the desert air pulses with the promise of blood, of suffering. Somewhere not far off, I can hear the Nazarene praying so hard, sweat breaks through his skin. I feel it spill onto the arid ground, his tears soaking into the gnarled roots like an ancient prophecy.

Lucifer's already waiting for me when I arrive, leaning against one of the terraced slopes, like sin and seduction, his arms crossed, jaw tight.

He tilts his head toward the distant voice. "He's afraid."

I don't answer.

He was afraid before, too—that day in the dirt when he looked up and asked if I'd come to take him. When my name still stung like fresh wounds on his tongue.

That feels like eons ago.

Now, he barely looks at me.

"You'll go to him. When it's time." He nods over his shoulder to indicate the Nazarene.

It isn't a question.

He knows my answer. What it means.

The weight of the night presses against my shoulders. "Yes."

He nods once, solemn, resigned. "You'll be the last thing he sees."

"I'm the last thing everyone sees."

The silence between us stretches. Too big for words. Too sharp for comfort.

Lucifer steps forward. He looks more human now—not in form, but in ache. He's always more godlike when he's furious. But tonight, tonight he just looks . . . tired.

Like he's nearly as broken by this as me.

"You don't belong in this story," he says. "Not with *Him*. Not with them."

Christ's disciples, he means.

"I don't belong anywhere."

A breath escapes him—too close to a laugh, too close to grief. "Except with me?"

I don't answer.

We both know it wouldn't make any difference.

His eyes search mine, sharp and unforgiving. "How long did you know? About the Nazarene? About what He's planned?"

He lifts his chin toward the heavens.

The question cuts deeper than anything else tonight. Not because I don't know what he means, but because I do. Because I made a promise.

Because I broke something between us the moment I kept it.

"I didn't know it would hurt you." It's the closest I can come to an apology. Because it wasn't a mistake. I'd do it again in a heartbeat.

If only he could see what he means to me, what I've sacrificed for him.

"Was it all a lie?"

The words come quiet, but they land like a blow.

He's not asking about the Nazarene anymore.

He's asking about *us*. About everything we built in the dark. About the way I touched him like he was sacred. About how I whispered loyalty between breaths and never told him I'd already given it to someone else.

The space between us sharpens, collapses.

"Was I?" he asks again, voice quieter now. "Was I just another part of His plan?"

"No." My voice doesn't shake. "You were never part of His plan."

Lucifer stares at me, and I see it—the moment something in him shatters clean through.

It's not just heartbreak I see.

It's recognition.

The realization that this was never going to mean anything.

But I was never just his lover.

I was his weapon.

Every time he whispered my name into the hollow of my throat, it was to aim me. Every time he pulled me close, it was to point me at something he wanted destroyed.

A kingdom, a bloodline, a doctrine.

Me.

He used me as his threat—called me beautiful when it suited him, sacred when it served him. And I let him.

Because I thought there was something real underneath.

"If I stay, you'll burn it all down."

His gaze hardens. "If you leave, I'll do it anyway."

The wind moves through the garden, low and wet. It carries the scent of sweat and olives and bleeding men.

Lucifer looks toward the edge of the trees, toward the one who'll die tonight. "He asked our Father to take the cup from him."

"And still he drank."

Lucifer's mouth twitches. "Fool."

I step closer. "I would've followed you anywhere."

"I know."

Place my hand on his chest. "I wanted you to love me."

He closes his eyes. "I did."

"Not like that."

A beat. A breath.

Because we both know he isn't capable of it.

Because he isn't capable of loving himself.

"No," he admits. "Not like that."

I step forward, and he doesn't stop me.

We meet in the space between breath and breaking.

When I kiss him, it's not soft. It just *is*—like gravity. Like memory. His mouth finds mine with a reverence that feels almost cruel. As if he's saying goodbye to something he's already begun to forget.

When we part, his hand lingers on the side of my neck.

It trembles once, then drops away.

The garden's quiet again, but not still.

Somewhere nearby, I feel him preparing to die.

And I'm not allowed to weep.

This is still my duty.

Lucifer turns one last time, his mouth a ruined thing—beautiful, sharp, cruel. "After this," he says, "don't look for me."

"I won't have to."

He leaves without another word. Just a shadow slipping through the trees.

And I stay, as I always do, to watch the end.

CHAPTER FORTY

Charlotte

By the time Monday rolls around and I arrive at Xzander's studio, I'm feeling so hopeful about stepping into my full power and about our plans to save Jax on the near horizon that I've been riding high all weekend. The third seal may have been a level of devastation greater than we anticipated, but I'm confident in the path forward, and training with Seraph has been going so well, I can feel a shift in my energy.

I know who I'm becoming now, and I think I'm actually proud of it.

Azrael and I are solid, each night with him better than the last, and he and Lucifer even seem to have stopped fighting. I've seen their lingering glances, the heated looks, and this morning, after another night spent wrapped in my devil's arms, I felt bold enough to put my permanent collar back on. The one with the pearls and metal eyelets that Lucifer gifted me at our engagement party. Though I haven't shown him yet.

I'm done waiting to have all the answers before I allow myself to be happy. To feel like I have it all figured out. I don't need to earn his love. To please anyone.

I know I'm choosing myself this time. Not hiding in him.

Fate be damned.

This is the right decision for me.

I'm certain of it.

That certainty carries me all the way to Xzander's studio, where I'm feeling light and buoyant until the moment I enter and a hushed silence falls over the room, and I slam back down to earth.

"What's going on?" I glance to where Xzander and his staff are huddled around his iPhone.

Xzander's forehead pinches. "I think you might want to sit down for this, diva."

I cross the room to his side. Nothing the tabloids say about me could possibly be—

I stare down at the words on the screen, the temperature in my body dropping.

> Killing of Five-Year-Old Lily Parker One of Many Tied to Extremist Sect the "Righteous": Open War Declared Against the "Unholy"

Bile burns the back of my throat.

This is retaliation for how I *chose* to strike first.

To punish them for abducting Jax.

Within moments, I'm on my knees in Xzander's bathroom throwing up what little food I managed to keep down this morning.

Xzander—God bless him—orders one of his assistants to hold back my hair for him, so my extensions don't get caught in his nails.

"I'm sorry, Xzander." I pant between retching. "I don't think I can do the fitting today. I—"

"You don't say another word, diva. I'm calling Imani."

By the time Imani arrives with Dagon and the rest of the security team, I'm shaking from head to toe, barely able to speak.

I did this.

I did this because I thought I was strong enough to make a move.

To wield my anger like the divine justice it's supposed to be.

Thought I was strong enough to make moves of my own. That I knew who I was becoming, but clearly, I had no clue.

Imani takes me by the shoulders, urging me to my feet. "You know the drill. Don't say anything." She nods to the flashing cameras outside. The paparazzi are already circling like vultures, leaning in to feed off my pain, my mistakes, like they're hungry.

Hungry to see the end of me.

I shake my head. "Every time I think I've made a right turn, every time I think I've helped someone, it comes back to haunt me. Why give me all this power if He . . . ?"

"You are *not* responsible for this," Imani says fiercely, marching me toward the door.

"She wouldn't have even been on their radar if it weren't for me. If it weren't for how I'd—"

"Charlotte! Charlotte!" the press shout at me.

But it's like I don't even see them.

They're never going to see me like I hoped they would. They never will.

Imani crams me into the back of the Town Car, sliding in alongside me.

We ride to the penthouse in silence.

Until I realize what this means.

"The other Originals," I breathe.

If the Righteous have escalated into killing innocent civilians with only cursory connections to me, it's only a matter of time before they . . .

"The Righteous have connections to Michael, and they already were in possession of celestial weaponry once. The other Originals won't risk their own necks with the Righteous declaring war like this. They'll leave you in the dust. That's how this life works."

This life.

This life of glitz and glamour and celestial power moves that I *chose*.

But when does it all end?

When does all the violence stop?

When am I going to be . . .

That word Lucifer used the other day keeps coming back to me.

Worthy.

I felt so close to it then, but now I just feel like I'm becoming the very thing my father warned I'd be.

"I need you to do a favor for me." I swallow, looking at Imani. My voice sounds wooden, like I'm no longer in my own body.

I feel cold all over.

"Anything."

I nod. "Let Lucifer know we're moving forward with the wedding plans. I want it scheduled just before Haute Couture week. I know it's fast, but it's the last chance we have to shift the narrative in our favor."

Disgust churns through me, a bitter taste burning in my throat.

Is this the immortal I've become?

One who treats human lives like they're just another chess piece?

Imani seems to read my expression. "You're making the right choices, Charlotte. Even if you can't see it currently."

"But at what cost?" I whisper.

We pull up outside the penthouse a moment later, and Dagon opens the door for me. He and Imani fight off the waiting press and paparazzi, leading me inside. But I swear out of the corner of my eye, on the edge of the street corner, I see Gabriel tapping his wrist like the clock on my timer to get Sloth into Heaven is ticking.

The ride to the top floor feels like an eternity, each moment stretching until I feel numb all over.

That sweet girl.

That sweet, sweet little girl.

When we reach the penthouse's foyer, my surroundings don't even register. It's not until I'm standing in front of Azrael and then Seraph inside the training room that I realize I'm simply going through the motions of the day.

This is going to fracture everything.

Our plans.

Humanity.

Azrael takes one look at me and moves to pull me into his arms, but I lift a hand and stop him.

If I allow myself to fall apart right now, I might come undone completely.

Never be able to put myself back together.

"Tell Lucifer I need to see my father *tonight*. It's time we get answers about the Righteous, and we need to consider immediately moving forward with our plans to get Jax."

If our alliance with the other Originals is fracturing because they're covering their own asses, we need to move quickly, and the longer we wait, the more likely Michael and Lilith are to be onto us.

Azrael shakes his head. "Moving ahead right now is too risky. Our plans, the In-Between, it won't be—"

"I didn't ask if it was a good idea, did I?" I snap at him, instantly regretting it. But I double down, the defensive anger I feel at myself for causing this, for making this entire situation worse, coiling like a venomous viper inside my chest. "That's an order, soldier."

Azrael's forehead creases as he frowns. "Yes, my queen."

And then he's gone in a blink.

Disappeared into the Nothing.

I turn toward Seraph.

She's here for training. But I'm not certain I can . . .

"What happened?" she asks, nodding down to where I'm clutching my phone.

An image of Lily Parker. A school photo lit up on the screen.

I show it to her, expecting her to be just as devastated by this as me.

Seraph's expression goes flat, but then her gaze drops, a shadow of grief crossing her face before she shutters it. "This changes nothing."

"What?"

The tightness in my chest aches, and I back away slightly, depositing my phone into my bag.

"You heard me," she says, her expression suddenly unforgiving. "This changes nothing."

I've only been training with her for a little over a week now. But I've never seen her like this before.

Cold and unforgiving.

"You want to fight like an angel? Be one of God's warriors?" She nods toward my hands, a reminder to put my guard up, circling the edge of the lines on the floor we've marked as the training ring. "Then you must trust His will completely."

I shake my head. "I can't."

"You would allow something like *this* to break you? To curb your hope? The death of a single child?"

"I'm not a monster." I wrinkle my nose, staring at her in disgust. "Human life matters."

"Of course it matters." She scoffs, still circling me. "But so do the millions, the billions of other lives that now rest in your hands. And yet you'd allow this to break you?" She straightens, her wings bristling. "You have to use it as fuel."

"I can't."

"You're not thinking like a celestial. Like an immortal. You're still acting like a human, playing small when you're meant for something greater. What are you afraid of?"

"I don't know."

"I said, 'What are you afraid of?'"

I gape at her, not knowing what to say, but then the answer just tumbles out of me. "My anger."

"Why?"

"I don't know. Because I'm not strong enough."

"Why?"

My fists clench. "Because I still fear His judgment."

"Why?"

"Because I'm angry with *Him*!" I shout, the fire in my hands suddenly igniting.

Seraph smiles as I look at her, but all I can feel is my pounding heartbeat, the anger inside me blazing.

"Why would He allow this to happen? Why allow so many innocent people to be hurt in His name? Why is there so much pain and suffering when He claims to love us?" I gesture toward the window, to the city, to the world that's falling apart all around me.

Suddenly, my voice grows small, quiet. "Why would He allow them to hurt me?"

Seraph lifts her chin high, her stance wide. "Good. Now, you're ready." She gives a crisp nod, and I put my guard up. "You think *we* are never angry with God?"

Angels, she means. God's warriors.

"That we never question? Never doubt?" She presses her lips into a hard line.

The fury I feel rising with her every word.

"Do you even *know* my brother?" She thrusts her shoulders out. "He was the best we ever had."

The next thing I know, she's on me, sending a shock wave of burning energy toward me. I manage to roll, diving out of the way, sending a blast of Holy Fire and light back her way.

"But why would He do this?" I clench my fists. "Why me?"

Seraph pulls in a deep breath, a satisfied smile on her face. "Why don't you ask Him yourself when you find Him?"

CHAPTER FORTY-ONE

Lucifer

Charlotte's father is ready for her by the time my wife arrives in Hell for her visit. Azrael and I have been torturing him round the clock for the last several days, leaving little room for him to recover between sessions, in order to make him pliable for her.

But I'll be damned if I allow Death to use it as an excuse to get close to her again.

Not without my being included at least.

I haven't stopped thinking about that goddamn kiss.

The traitorous bastard.

When Charlotte appears outside Hell's Depths right on schedule, her face is a bit flushed from her training with Seraph. She pitches forward, placing her hands upon her knees, panting. My gaze roves over her, noting every detail, every change.

"What?" She glances down at her body. "Do I have something on my dress?"

"No, darling."

She smooths a nervous hand down the front of the Hermès she's wearing, like she somehow fears I might've found something I do not like.

As if I could ever find anything about her unpleasing.

But it's the sight of my collar at her throat that catches my attention readily.

The permanent one. The pearl and leather Dior I gifted her.

I smirk wickedly. "I'm simply entranced by the sight of you, that's all. You look radiant." I pull her into my arms, kissing her to reassure her.

But I can't help but swat her ass as I usher her past me. The way her hips have become the slightest bit fuller as of late hasn't escaped my notice.

And I don't dislike it.

By the time we arrive outside the meat locker's fridge, I'm so bloody bewitched by the sight and sway of them, by the thought that she has *chosen* to be mine again, I'd just as soon abandon the entire thing.

Burying my face in her cunt sounds far more pleasing.

Even if I do enjoy eviscerating her father regularly.

Particularly after the stunt his organization pulled.

I will pick them off one by one until there is nothing left.

Until they can no longer hurt her.

I snatch her into my arms, pressing her up against the nearest wall and caging her beneath me. Her breath becomes shallow as I slowly trail one of my knuckles over her collar. Her eyes widen as she realizes I've noticed, and she shivers, already more than eager for me.

I can smell it on her.

"Are you certain you wouldn't like to—"

"Did you mean what you said?" she asks, gazing helplessly into my face. "A few months back, in the playroom, when you said you'd want to have children with me?"

The question catches me off guard.

"Of course, little dove." My eyes narrow. "Why do you ask?"

She shakes her head. "No reason. I just—"

The distant sound of her father's screams follows, echoing off the tiling.

Azrael emerges from the chamber a moment later, shirtless and sweating, his large body and face covered in blood spray, and his muscled, tattooed arms flexing. He sharpens the edge of one of the freshly cleaned blades he was just using.

He looks positively sinful like that. Downright delectable.

My cock stiffens.

I scowl, glancing away at the reminder of how my body betrayed me the other evening.

The same way it did back at Gethsemane.

"He's ready for you." He turns toward Charlotte.

My wife's gaze roves over him, the amber starbursts in her eyes gleaming, and she flushes a little at the sight of him as his attention falls to *my* collar she's wearing. Death's expression turns cold, but the heat when she watches him couldn't be more obvious to me, and the thought of how thoroughly she still wants him makes me—

Charlotte's father gives another agonized cry from the next room over.

"Do you think he can . . . ?" Charlotte's voice trails off, her expression suddenly panicked.

"Hear us?" I offer, exchanging a quick glance with Azrael. "Why do you ask, darling?"

She looks down, retreating to the same useless denial she tried earlier. "No reason, sir. I just . . ."

I catch her by her collar as she attempts to brush past me. "You know better than to lie to me," I growl.

She stares up into my face, her eyes rife with vulnerability.

But then she glances away, blushing.

My mouth pulls into a slow, twisted grin. "Does it turn you on? The thought of making him listen? Of punishing him like that?"

"What? No," she squeaks, just as Azrael lets out a low growl of approval.

His attention flicks over her before momentarily lingering on me, and my balls tighten. Already, he's hard from torturing her father—I can see it—the thick growing bulge at the front of his trousers. He enjoys breaking them nearly as much as I do.

Just like he did to me when he kissed me the other day.

Told me he loved me.

My nostrils flare, and I turn away again, fixating upon my wife.

Charlotte shakes her head, still heavy in her denial. "Of course not, I just—"

I shove her against the meat locker's wall before she can finish speaking. "Don't lie to me, little dove." My gaze rakes over her. "I trained you better than that."

My grip tightens, and her eyes go wide, but her stare flits to Azrael. "I'm sorry. I just—"

"Don't look at me. I'm not going to help you. You *chose* to put his collar back on. You know what that means." Azrael moves to brush past me.

I stop him with my free hand.

"Are you going to work that out in the scene or keep brooding about the fact that it's *my* collar she's wearing?"

Death hesitates.

"Azrael," Charlotte pleads.

Like she doesn't just want him. She needs him.

To protect her from me.

The thought infuriates me.

Azrael's expression hardens slightly, but then he steps closer. "Tell me what you want, baby girl. Tell me what you want, and I can make it all better."

I snarl at him.

As if she would ever need him to . . .

"Make what better?" she pants, breathlessly casting a quick look between us.

But Azrael's words are like a cruel lash down my spine.

"That ache I know you're feeling." His eyes cut briefly toward me.

I feel pain in my jaw as it clenches. He says it to her, but I feel the weight of it in my balls, know without a doubt that he intends it for me.

And the thought only makes me even more livid.

I focus on Charlotte, pushing all thought of that damn kiss, of how he betrayed me, from my mind as I hike up her skirt. I palm her pussy until she moans so loud I'm certain her father and my whole bloody realm can hear as she grinds against me.

Promising his loyalty to my Father wasn't enough, was it?

Choosing to love *Him* over me?

Now, he wants to steal my woman.

Even when it's *my* collar she's wearing.

"All right, I do," Charlotte pants. "I want him to hear us, sir, but I can't—"

"Can't or won't, little dove?" I ask, tossing out Azrael's words from the other day.

Azrael tenses.

"I'd say if you have to ask, the answer is always *won't*," I growl, the jab cutting sharp as steel.

I feel the moment it lands.

He stiffens.

Azrael snarls. "If we're going to do this, we're going to do it right this time." Azrael turns toward me. "You're not allowed to lie either."

Suddenly, he pulls me in for a harsh, searing kiss, and it feels as if I've been stabbed in the back by my worst enemy.

He kisses me like he's my Judas.

But it's Charlotte's delighted gasp that destroys me.

I lean into him, drawing up to my full height and deepening my position until our tongues are so entangled, I'm able to grip him by the hair. For leverage.

I try to drag him down to the floor, force him to kneel for me.

But he manages to drag me down with him.

The demented laugh that bursts from him the moment his knees hit the floor only infuriates me even more. I stumble to my feet, glaring at him.

I hate him for it.

For all the broken promises he made me.

For that lie he dared to speak.

I glance toward Charlotte, and not only has she stripped off her thong, but she's fingering herself so provocatively that I can tell from the bratty, defiant look in her eye she's *trying* to provoke me. A fury the likes of which I've never known barrels through me as Azrael and I snarl in unison.

"What do you think you're doing touching yourself before we've given you permission to?" I clutch her by the throat, momentarily cutting off her airway.

Azrael's at our side a second later, taking hold of her wrists as he ruthlessly pins them over her head.

"We?" Our little brat grins.

And I see red.

But she'll soon be reminded of why she chose to be *mine*, goddammit.

"Yes, *we*," I answer, doubling down, even as I intend to show her she belongs to me. "Death is only here to help me punish you, little dove, and after this, you will never forget that you are *mine*." I lean closer until I'm hissing into her ear. "No matter how furious you may make me."

CHAPTER FORTY-TWO

Charlotte

Lucifer drags me by my collar, hauling me into a nearby chair with him, and takes me over his knee. His belt is off and in his hand within seconds. Azrael locks my hands in front of me to keep me from fighting. Like a prayer.

A hellish offering.

Lucifer spanks me within an inch of my life, whipping me over and over until I'm screaming. My cries echo off the meat locker's walls until the next thing I know, I'm on the floor, lying on top of that cold tile, my ass burning, my cunt soaked, and Lucifer's mouth is on me.

I cry out.

He's devouring my pussy like it's a new form of punishment, but with my father listening in the next room over, I'm not sure I'm feeling bold enough to—

"Azrael," I gasp, pleading.

He crouches in front of me. "Why did you put his collar on again?" he growls, his jaw tightening as he looks to the Dior calfskin.

I pale slightly.

Death's never been this angry with me before.

"I don't know. I just—"

I traded it out this morning, and now I'm not even sure I really know the reason why. Maybe because I was finally feeling confident in who I was, because I thought Azrael and I were solid, that he would support me making my own choices, that things between him and Lucifer were improving?

But now with Azrael looking at me like this, coupled with the knowledge that my father can overhear me, suddenly I'm not feeling so certain.

All the fear and shame I felt when I was letting out my anger with Seraph earlier heightens.

Finding out I'm pregnant might have had a little something to do with it too.

But I can't tell Azrael, and definitely not Lucifer, when we're in the middle of a scene. They both deserve more than that.

Azrael stares down into my face, the hurt in his eyes nearly gutting me as he waits for an answer.

"It's . . . it's complicated, sir."

"Don't call me sir. Not while you're wearing *his* collar." Azrael's expression hardens, but I know without him saying it that I've hurt him.

And that only makes this whole situation a thousand times worse.

I didn't think putting my collar back on would mean—

"Cum big, cumslut." The cords in his neck pop as he uses Lucifer's nickname for me, instead of his. "Cum big and loud, and let him hear what a rotten slut *he* made you be." He nods to Lucifer.

My breath falters.

Azrael glances down at Lucifer, who's still feasting on me, his grip leaving bruises all over my skin, and the anger and hurt in Azrael's eyes flares. "If it were up to me, I'd punish the both of you."

He'd have every right to, honestly.

My knees go weak. "Even though you're covered in—"

"Do I look like I care?" he snarls, his eyes narrowing.

The vicious way he looks at me then lets me know I've broken his heart in two.

The shame that's thick in my throat is immediate. "I didn't mean for this to be—"

"Quiet, cumslut!"

He shoves his hand over my mouth, using the other to unbuckle his jeans, so that his massive cock breaks free a moment later, and his pants fall.

My throat goes dry.

His cock is more swollen and red than I've ever seen it, so thick and threatening I'm not even certain that he's going to fit inside me.

"You'll take it. You'll take it and you'll fucking like it." He uncovers my mouth and then spits onto Lucifer's back, contempt in his eyes. "And so will he."

I gasp as Lucifer's tongue plunges into me, my breath going ragged.

A rush of delicious heat fills me up, burning from the inside out as Lucifer tongues me like a rabid beast, going feral. He buries the whole of his face even deeper into my cunt like a madman, lapping at my folds like he can't wait to hear me cry his name.

Where he knows my father can hear me.

Oh God.

"Make your choice, darling," Lucifer growls in between thrusts.

Like if I want it, Azrael will be in charge.

"But my father can—"

"You think you have what it takes to punish the both of us, then do it already," Lucifer snarls at Azrael. "Or else get out of my fucking way!"

A deep growl barrels from Azrael, and he pins my hands over my head again. "Challenge accepted, asshole. You know my safe word."

"We need a different one," I pant, trying one last time to fix this.

Azrael lifts his scarred brow.

"One for all three of us."

For what I know we could be, if the two of them would just finally . . .

Death laughs in my face like there's no chance in hell that he and Lucifer and I are ever going to be anything.

My heart shatters.

Lucifer's grip on my ass tightens as he lifts me into a different angle, so that his mouth is now positioned at the top of my upper thigh, and then his fangs sink into me like *I'm* the apple.

I practically come up off the floor from the pleasure and agony.

"The safe word stays the same," Azrael says. "Oblivion or inferno, cumslut. Take your pick."

My breath hitches.

No.

No, no, no, no.

They can't make me.

I didn't want *this*.

I didn't mean . . .

Azrael grips my face. "Do you want this or not?" he snarls.

"Yes," I pant, already edging over into begging from where Lucifer's returned to lashing me with his tongue. "Yes, but not like—"

Not like this.

I want to scream it. I want to shove them both off and claw my way out of this hell, make them feel what I've been swallowing for weeks—years—but the fire catches in my throat and dies like everything else I never let burn.

Azrael's brow hitches. "Did you just talk back to me?"

"No, sir. I just—"

His gaze darkens. "It's him or me, little siren. Pick your poison."

"I . . ."

He snarls, and the shame, the fear inside me heightens until I . . .

I close my eyes in defeat.

If this is the only way I can have them, then I'll swallow it all down, take whatever punishment they give me.

"Oblivion or infer—"

I try one last time to resist it. "I don't—"

"Fucking choose, Charlotte!" Lucifer roars from between my legs.

I feel the pain of what they're forcing me to do rattle inside my bones.

Fate or free will.

Shame or fury.

Love or hate.

"Oblivion!" I shout, only because Azrael's the one standing directly in front of me, because I want to collapse into the numbness, forget all the shame I'm feeling. About this. About Lily. All of it. "Oblivion."

Azrael chuckles, his grin turning wicked as Lucifer glares at me, seething.

"You'll go out of your goddamn mind when I fuck him, won't you?" Azrael nods down to where Lucifer's glowering at me like he doesn't give two flying fucks if he's in charge or not, he's punishing me for this either way.

Heat blossoms in my core, desire pooling between my legs.

Jesus, Azrael's going to make me watch while he—

Lucifer's seething, his face absolutely coated in my wetness, all the way from his chin to his nose. He makes a show of flicking his forked tongue over his lips before he glares at Azrael. "Are you going to fuck us now, or are you going to keep us both waiting?" He unbuckles his pants, hastily dropping them down like a challenge, his perfect ass now ready and bare. "Come on. Discipline me," he taunts Death. "What've you got up your sleeve? Fucking me with your knife? Making me wear panties? Torturing me? Don't threaten me with a good time."

My eyes roll back in my head as his mouth comes down on me again, and I'm pretty sure I almost faint from pleasure at the sight of him like this.

I've never seen him so furious before, so furious and so . . .

Bratty.

A desperate cry escapes me.

I fucking love it.

I fucking love the unfamiliarity of it, but it's also . . . destabilizing.

Lucifer being a sub is the hottest thing I've ever seen.

I'm practically giddy from it.

Even though I'm terrified by the look on Azrael's face and the fact that Lucifer's willing to do this for him; it somehow makes me think I might be not enough for him.

The thought is so familiar, so similar to how that man in the next room over made me feel, to how I used to berate myself every time he forced me onto my knees to pray to *his* God like the "good girl" he taught me to be, I can hardly stand it.

I cry out, all my anger and hurt seeping out of me as I struggle to keep it and my desire under control, until the shadows at the edge of the room morph and the fluorescent lights overhead flicker.

Azrael doesn't waste any time as he starts to pump his hand up and down his length. My mouth waters and I lick my lips, desperate for something to bite down on, a ball gag, a belt, a strap of leather, anything to keep me from screaming how he—

"You want this, cumslut?" Azrael tips his chin toward his cock, and the dip in my belly is instant. "You want to stay quiet and small so you can pretend you're happy being afraid and scared, just like he wanted you to be?"

I nod, whimpering.

"Not until you let him hear you say it." He nods toward the next room over.

I shake my head. "I can't."

"Say it."

I drop my head, desire overtaking my shame. "I want it," I whisper.

"Louder."

"I want it."

"Louder!" Azrael's voice deepens.

"I want—"

"Let that bloody bastard hear it already!" Lucifer bellows from between my legs, and the reminder that he's still my Dom, the same man I love, ignites something in me.

I become liquid fire, so close to climax that all it takes for me to finish is Lucifer shoving two of his fingers up inside me, hissing, "Let him hear who you now call your daddy."

I shatter apart in an instant, wave after wave of pleasure rolling through me.

"I want it. I want it. Please, Daddy!" I beg him.

"Wicked, wicked girl," Lucifer purrs before he's on me again, burying his face in me.

Azrael steps forward, shoving his massive cock into my mouth like it's my reward.

I suck on it like it's candy, licking and lapping and tonguing at the bit of salt I taste there as the last of my orgasm stretches on and on.

I can't get enough of him, of either of them.

Azrael throws his head back with a groan. "That's enough," he grumbles, taking away my prize after only a few licks. No praise.

He's going to make me work for it, I guess.

I stick out my lower lip, pouting, already lost in the heat of the scene, but then Death nods down to Lucifer. "Or I won't have anything left for him."

My eyes go wide, fear and desire gripping me.

I'm about to get a front-row seat to Death and the devil's destructive reunion, and all I can do is sit back and watch helplessly.

As they destroy any chance we might have to be together.

CHAPTER FORTY-THREE

Azrael

Despite how she's just gutted me, my dick is so hard from how Charlotte sucked me off like it was her new favorite treat that I'm not going to last long.

But I'll fucking make myself last if I have to.

I've been waiting a whole fucking millennium to destroy him like this.

And I'm so fucking turned on, I'm almost dizzy from it.

Abruptly, I release Charlotte's wrists and grab her under the arms, hauling her up and over my shoulder.

Lucifer hisses, clutching her hips and attempting to drag her back down like I'm taking his favorite thing away, but he knocks it the fuck off the moment I taunt, "You chickening out, Lightbringer?"

I nod toward his ass.

Who the fuck does he think is in charge here?

His irises narrow, turning serpentine, but then he releases her with a quick shove, muttering under his breath, "If this doesn't prove that I love you, little dove, I don't know what does." He slumps back against the wall before he grabs a cigarette out of the pocket of his suit coat from where it's lying on the tiled floor, and lights it, glaring at me, the hellfire in his eyes blazing. He's the same petulant brat he's always been.

And I can't fucking get enough of it.

"Go ahead." He smirks, blowing out smoke. "Give me the best you've got, Reaper."

But I know he wants this as much as I do.

He's just going to be a dick about it.

"Thought so," I snipe, turning away from him.

I deposit Charlotte onto a nearby cart, shoving aside the torture instruments there in one fell swoop. They clatter to the floor with a crash, but a pair of manacles that hang from the wall remain.

I shackle her wrists in them.

"Sit. Stay," I order.

She looks like a kicked puppy, her attention darting to Lucifer like she's seeking his permission, but when he glares at her, refusing to be her Dom right now, she hangs her head.

She's not sure how she feels about me taking charge just yet.

About him being submissive.

I reassure her with a quick forehead kiss, reminding her that she *likes* being good for me, unlike my asshole ex, before I turn my attention to him. "She's your sub. You gonna go at her again or keep being a brat?"

Lucifer's expression turns furious.

He bares his teeth, his jaw clenching as he starts to stand.

"Don't stand," I order. "Crawl."

The hellfire in his eyes blazes. "If you think for one fucking second, I'm going to—"

"Consider this your penance for Gethsemane."

His nostrils flare. "*My* penance?"

Like he *wasn't* the one who chose his need for vengeance over me.

Wasn't the one who said our love didn't mean anything.

I might've believed that *before* I saw how things could have been, but now . . .

Now, I know the full truth of how he could have chosen me, chosen himself. The same way he's chosen to face himself for *her*. Instead, he put an end to everything we could have had. And for what? The hope of vengeance against his Father?

That he'd come out on top of the apocalypse?

See God dead?

I shake my head.

Whatever twisted reason he used to justify it doesn't matter, because now he can't escape me, and I'm going to get *my* revenge.

For all the ways he doubted me. Told me my love didn't mean anything.

"You heard me," I taunt. "What're you gonna do about it?"

Lucifer rises onto his feet, tossing his still smoldering cigarette onto the floor, and I think for a moment that devilish bastard might actually have the balls to defy me.

The next thing I know, he's shifted forms into that damn snake again, and a massive black python is barreling straight at me, hissing.

Motherfucker!

Charlotte shrieks, pressing closer to the wall.

I'm not certain she's ever seen him like this.

The snake coils at my feet, rising up and up and up until it's nearly eye level before it snaps at me, baring its venomous fangs.

Within the span of a blink, I'm standing nose to nose with Lucifer again.

Sexy dramatic fucking prick.

"You didn't specify *how*, did you, lover?" he says cheekily.

He uses his shadows to retrieve his cigarette, plucking it from midair. He inhales, then blows the smoke at me before he casts it aside again.

I can't tell if I want to punch that damn smirk off his face or fuck him.

Before I can decide, he grabs Charlotte, dragging her still-red ass to the edge of the cart until the manacles at her wrists are pulled taut.

He bends over her, greedily burying his face in her pussy again, his ass bared and level with me.

The devil is a switch. The ultimate brat. That's what he is.

No wonder he gets so much sick pleasure out of taming her.

Her moves are from his own fucking playbook.

"You're going to pay for that," I growl, stepping behind him and spreading his delicious ass cheeks.

I position myself just outside his entrance.

"Are you sure?" he taunts, lifting his face from Charlotte's cunt long enough to mutter, "I can easily top you from the bottom, *lover*."

Unexpectedly, he shoves back into me, like I'm at *his* mercy.

Mother—

I snarl.

I shouldn't be fucking surprised by it, but I am.

I'm nothing but a goddamn tool to him all over again.

But if he wants to use her to run away from me, from himself, to pretend we never meant anything, well then . . .

I chuckle.

We'll see who wins in the end.

Because I don't play fair.

I play forever.

CHAPTER FORTY-FOUR

Lucifer

I thrust back onto Azrael, fully convinced that I'm still capable of taking him bare, but clearly, I overestimated my own abilities. "Bloody fuck!" I swear into Charlotte's pussy.

I'd forgotten exactly how much resistance there could be.

How fucking large he is.

But Death isn't about to give me a moment's reprieve.

His pleasure is as good as his pain.

"You asked for this, *lover*." He spits into his hand, lobbing it onto my arsehole like a crude lube as he thrusts even deeper into me.

I pitch forward, my tongue spearing harder up inside my wife as she starts to whimper in need. I can already tell she's getting close again, the sweet taste of her nectar coating my throat completely.

"Again," she pants, her mouth slamming shut the moment she realizes what she's just said, what that means for me.

Azrael chuckles. "Only if you ask loud enough that bastard can hear it." He nods toward the next room.

"No," she whimpers, eyes darting toward me in regret.

Azrael growls. "Again, or I'll tell him to—"

"Again, please, Daddy!" she cries, just before he thrusts into me.

My cock goes so bloody stiff from where he's hitting my prostate that I think I might be—

Holy fuck!

Azrael's large hand wraps around my front as he takes my length into his hand. "You don't get to come until *she* gives you permission, understand?"

I snarl as Charlotte's eyes go wide.

She knows if she complies, she will pay for it tenfold later.

But if she doesn't, Death will punish her all the same.

Not the worst outcome.

"Azrael. Please, I don't want—"

"You made your choice, little dove." I glare up at her. "And if you think you're not going to pay for this the next time *I'm* in charge, think again," I growl, just before I thrust my tongue into her pussy.

She gushes.

I swear if she fucking squirts in the middle of this, I will chain her to our bed for a week.

"I'm sorry, Daddy," she cries, tears pouring down her cheeks as she looks to Azrael. "I'll do whatever you ask, just don't hurt him." She nods down at me.

I roll my eyes. As if *I*, the goddamn devil, am some fragile thing.

He hasn't even given me his worst yet.

God, I really am fucked up, aren't I?

Though her lack of self-preservation is worse than I feared, honestly.

"I want you to count how many thrusts it takes him before he's begging. Can you do that, baby girl?" Azrael may be fucking furious with us both, but he's clearly enjoying this.

The way he's ruined me.

The pernicious bastard.

"Yes, sir," she says. "Anything for you."

I snarl, her obedience destroying me.

"Then lie back, little siren."

The relief in her face at the name he's given her lighting a match inside of me.

And with him fucking me like this, I'm an immortal powder keg.

Azrael grins. "Don't forget to count for me."

I squeeze one of Charlotte's breasts until she cries out as she thrusts her clit against me.

"One," she whimpers, just as Azrael shoves himself into my ass.

A feral sound claws its way out of me.

"Remember that time in Constantinople, lover?" His hand pumps down my length as he starts to play the same game I did with him the other evening, throwing the moments of immortal lives back into my face like he intends to give me a taste of my own medicine.

But I'm not having it.

"When I drank the blood of a saint and burned down a monastery after I found out you fucking rebounded with *Michael*?"

He snarls. "*I* remember it differently."

My balls tighten as the pressure inside me builds, the feeling of them both so fucking delicious it reminds me of how he used to unravel me.

Azrael's hand runs down my spine. "I remember you begged me not to leave. Swore you'd rip off the wings of every angel if I didn't stay."

I let out a furious roar as I'm reminded of how he tore my heart to shreds, used my vulnerability after my Fall against me, before *she* came along and put me back together.

"Two," Charlotte cries, her voice loud enough there's no doubt that blasted father of hers can hear her. Half of fucking Hell probably can.

Though to my victims, what's another soul screaming?

"Three," Charlotte sobs, as if she cannot possibly stand to see me like this.

How pathetic he makes me.

Azrael's hand pumps over my cock, making me pant. "I remember that you came all over yourself and cried when you swore me your loyalty."

Heat burns through my face.

So, he intends to humiliate me then.

I chuckle darkly.

"Four." Charlotte rocks back and forth against me in a desperate attempt to soothe herself, using her legs to draw my head into her lap and cradling me against her at how much this pains her.

This is nearly destroying her as much as it is me.

Though that's entirely the fucking point.

"I remember exactly how you like it. How you want your hair pulled. Just like what you give to her. Same whimper. Same rhythm when it hits too deep."

"Oh God. Please, Lucifer! Just give him what he wants already." Charlotte tries to claw her way to me desperately, but her hands are still bound.

I look toward my bride, shaking my head at how she still doesn't recognize her own strength. The strength it takes to submit.

"And what's that, darling?" I ask her, my shame a contorted mask of fury.

But it's Death who says, "Admit that you wanted this from the beginning."

I pale slightly. "No."

"Look at her, Lucifer." He grips me by the hair, and I snarl furiously as he forces me to stare at Charlotte. "She isn't going to last much longer. You want her to see you like this? To be punished like this? By *me*?"

I cackle.

As if that could ever be a threat to me.

"I fucking love seeing her punished," I snark back.

"I know you do." Azrael runs his hand over the length of my spine, over the ridges of my scars, and I shiver. "Which is why it's going to hurt you so much when she chooses *me*."

My stomach bottoms out. "What?"

"You heard me." He directs his attention to Charlotte. "Tell him you still love me, baby girl."

"I do, but I—"

"Tell him you didn't mean to be *only* his when you put that collar on again, or else he—"

"Stop! Please, Azrael!" But his safe word doesn't pass her lips. Charlotte stares down into my face, crying. "He's right. I love him. I love him, Daddy, and I know it's your collar I'm wearing, but if that means I have to give him up, I'm not sure that I want to—"

I snarl, gripping her face. "Like bloody hell will I allow you to make a fool out of me." A squeezing sensation ignites in my ribs.

I won't allow her to destroy everything we've built.

Not over the likes of him.

"Don't say another fucking word," I order her.

"Then admit you wanted this from the start," Azrael growls. "Admit you wanted this"—he slides his cock in and out of me—"right from the very beginning."

"I will do no such thing," I hiss, just as Azrael pummels into me even harder, my cock so stiff I'm only a few strokes away from—

I cry out, burying my face in Charlotte's middle from the pleasure-pain of it, wincing.

"Please, Daddy!" Charlotte pleads, nearly as close to unraveling as I am.

But it won't be *his* name on her lips when she does.

Not if I have any say in this.

"Lucifer, please," she begs me. "Please, you *promised*."

To take the first step, she means.

And the way she asks me, as if she fully trusts that I will give her whatever her heart desires despite any hurt it may cause me, humbles me all over again, so that I have no choice but to completely humiliate myself in front of her.

Without pretense.

"I suppose the thought might've . . . crossed my mind," I mutter.

"I knew it!" she squeals, before she leans forward and kisses me.

I smile triumphantly, satisfied with happiness, before I slink back down to her pussy, using the whole of my upper body strength to brace myself to keep Azrael's thrusts from jolting me. "Happy?" I cast over my shoulder toward him.

Charlotte melts into me as I ravish her again.

"Scream for him, sweet girl." Azrael chuckles, releasing one of the manacles. "Scream for him as I fuck your Daddy."

He pounds several more thrusts into my ass, each one more devastating than the last, until with one final stroke, his cock swelling inside me, he—

My eyes roll back in my head as the walls of the meat locker are rent with the sound of our shared screams. I collapse into Charlotte's pussy, her sweet nectar gushing onto my tongue while my cum spills in thick white spurts all over the tiled floor as Azrael finishes in me.

Charlotte pulls my face back up to her mouth, kissing me over and over as she whispers, "I knew you'd keep your promise."

A shiver of dread runs down my spine as Death pulls out of me, his seed dripping from my freshly buggered arsehole onto the floor as he growls, "What promise?"

CHAPTER FORTY-FIVE

Azrael

"It's nothing," Charlotte says quickly.

Too quick.

I see the devious look the moment it forms in Lucifer's eyes, and I realize there's still a new level of hurt he can bring me, a way to walk back his own vulnerability.

A punishment for how I just humiliated him.

The wedge he's chosen to drive between us is a truth I've been refusing to name.

She never saw me as his equal in the first place.

"Tell him, little dove," he orders. "Tell him what you asked of me." He traces a hand over the smooth leather of her collar, a reminder that no matter what I may have coerced her into saying, she still chose him. She always has.

Right from the very start.

And maybe that's the problem—maybe she never saw anything except him.

My eyes narrow, my shoulders tensing, but I want the answer just as much as he does, so I don't say anything. Don't put a stop to it.

I won't give him the satisfaction.

I look at Charlotte, and she pales slightly.

Clearly, I made a mistake thinking he'd be the only one who'd ever hurt me.

She didn't even see the knife in her own hand because loving him made it easy for her to forget that I bleed just like he does. I was just the collateral damage to their gravity.

"I . . ." Her throat writhes as she swallows. "I asked him to take the first step toward mending things between you two, that's all."

"That's all?" I lift a brow.

That's fucking all?

Treating me like I'm nothing more than a pity fuck.

Like my grief was just a bruise she could kiss better.

Like all I needed was a kind word from him to come running back, because what else could I possibly want but *his* attention?

Like my love was always second best.

To both of them.

The whites of Charlotte's eyes grow wide. "I didn't mean to interfere. I just—"

"You didn't mean to interfere?" I chuckle, using my thumb to swipe at the edge of my mouth, before I rake a rough hand through my hair. "That's all you think I was to him? That all it would take for him to mend things with me is a few kind words? Like I was always some background player in *his* story? Someone who'd just be grateful for table scraps?"

"What? No." Charlotte shakes her head, suddenly tugging against the remaining shackle on her wrist. "I just thought if he reached out first, it would mean more. I didn't think—"

"Let me tell you something, baby girl." I prowl toward her, cutting aside any attempt to soften what he and I were. "Before you were here, it was me." I place my hand on either side of her hips, leaning in so that my breath's hot on her face. "*I* was the one who pulled him out of the pit when he broke. I was the one who bore the heat of his rage and the ice of his silence after he fell. I was the one who rebuilt him, made him whole, and I knew the taste of him long before you ever learned to chant his name like a prayer."

Charlotte trembles, her chin quivering.

But the sight of her tears does nothing for me.

I can see the truth of it in her eyes then, how she never viewed me as a real threat.

She never thought I meant anything to him.

Not a threat. Not a partner. Not even part of the equation.

Just the shadow standing behind him—useful, maybe, but never essential.

"And what else didn't you mean, little siren?" I shove off her, starting to pace. "That's what sirens do, isn't it? Sing their sweet songs and never look back at the wreckage they create. What else didn't you mean when you put on his collar? Did you think it wouldn't matter to me? That it wouldn't *cost* anything when you chose him?" I sneer at her. "You never even looked back to see what it took from me."

My gaze cuts to Lucifer, but he seems more than content to stand back and watch the destruction he helped create.

He's letting us bleed for him. That's always been his favorite kind of devotion—worship through suffering.

"I'm sorry, Azrael. I didn't mean to—"

"Do you know why I call you that?" I ask suddenly. "Little siren?"

She casts a reluctant glance toward Lucifer, before she gives the barest shake of her head.

I prowl toward her again, my face transitioning to the skeletal creature I truly am as I place my hands on either side of the wall near her, caging her in.

She turns away from me, wincing in fear.

I chuckle.

I fucking thought so.

I was never going to mean to her what she means to me.

I grip her by the back of the head, crushing my mouth to hers—not a kiss, a punishment—until she pulls away in disgust, and I can't help but laugh. "Because sirens lure men to their death."

Abruptly, I turn my attention to Lucifer, my skeletal face as horrific as it is uncanny. "You want to use our past as a means to toy with her? I'll fucking play."

I snap my fingers, and suddenly, the hall outside the meat locker has been transformed into something he never would have expected to revisit.

His Father's throne room.

Where God carved off his wings like he was nothing.

Lucifer stiffens like the phantom pains on his back have returned in full swing.

A deathly stillness comes over me as his eyes widen.

He shouldn't be surprised by my ability to wield my power inside *our* realm like this, but he still seems to be.

Charlotte glances around the room, her eyes flicking over the white marble walls, the throne of flaming sapphire, its surface gleaming, and the soft white light that seems to emanate from everywhere. Her mouth opens from the shock, but she's free from her shackles now and no longer the focus of my fury.

My anger lies with him.

It's always been him.

How he refused to forgive himself enough that we could be anything.

"Where are we?" she asks.

The Depths and Lucifer's dark palace are the only parts of Hell she's ever seen.

"My Father's throne room, I'm afraid," Lucifer answers, his face paling. "Or a re-creation of it."

The very place where this all started.

Where he fell. Where I destroyed everything.

Made a promise. Swore my loyalty to His father.

Before I even knew him.

All in the hope he'd someday be mine.

And where did it get me?

I turn my gaze to him. "Tell her what you did." I point toward Charlotte. "Tell her what you've been keeping from her, or *I* can."

Charlotte's eyes go wide. "Azrael, you can't—"

"Quiet, cumslut!"

"So, it's to be a restaging then?" Lucifer asks, his jaw tight.

He's afraid of his own vulnerability, loathes it, even now, but he won't allow his precious bride to bear the brunt of it.

"Too much for you, lover?" I taunt.

He bares his teeth. *"Never."*

I prowl forward, and he falls to his knees, allowing me to circle him like we have so many times before. Like we used to do back when we meant something.

Before our love turned into a war we both swore we'd win eventually.

CHAPTER FORTY-SIX

Charlotte

I watch in horror as Azrael circles Lucifer, his hands dropped to his sides, palms up, as if he's about to summon his power and tear into him. I knew whatever happened between them was ancient, brutal, but I never expected that either of them would bleed for it in front of me.

"Azrael, I don't think this is—"

"Quiet, Charlotte," he snarls, silencing me immediately.

Tears prickle at the edges of my eyes, but I don't allow them to fall.

I hurt him.

I know I did, and I've never been on the receiving end of Death's anger before, but I can tell from the way he and Lucifer are glaring at one another that this isn't about me.

This is about them.

About what happened to them.

The origin story I'd been hoping they'd tell me.

But not like this.

I want to scream it. I want to tell them that if they'd just stop fighting, they'd realize they love one another. But I stay quiet, swallowing it down, trying to make myself as small as possible as I retreat into the nearest corner of the room.

It's something I used to do whenever my father would get angry with me, hide away until his rage had passed and I felt certain that he wouldn't hurt me.

At least until the next time he lost control.

I can't tell them what I want to say at the moment.

My own anger has caused enough hurt for today.

But I'm not worried for myself.

Or even about the wounds seeing them like this opens inside me.

I'm worried they'll destroy any possibility of mending everything that's been broken today.

But I've learned my lesson about coming between them, about interfering, so I sit on my knees, silently muttering as I clasp my hands in front of myself.

And pray.

I pray silently that they can use this to work out all the remaining hurt between them.

So that it doesn't end like this.

Azrael prowls around Lucifer, circling him over and over like a predator, like he's trying to decide how exactly he's going to start this whole thing, and Lucifer . . .

Oh God, Lucifer.

He looks more furious than I've ever seen him before.

Like he's angry at *himself*.

Why is he going to subject himself to this?

Unless he doesn't want me to know whatever Azrael thinks he's been keeping from me. Unless he hasn't been . . .

My stomach drops.

He made a promise to be transparent with me. That everything between us would be built on truth.

The pain in my throat constricts suddenly, my body temperature rising.

But he *hasn't* been transparent with me, like he said he would, like I thought he was, has he?

He broke his promise.

What could he possibly want to keep from me so badly?

"Do you know why I want to punish him, Charlotte?" Azrael says, like he can hear exactly what I'm thinking.

I shoot him a nervous look. "No."

The pain of how he put me in my place earlier is still aching. He'll *always* know Lucifer better than I do. I feel the truth in that like a jagged shard inside my chest.

"He's been lying to you," Azrael says. "Right from the very start."

Lucifer's nostrils flare. "Say another word, Reaper, and I swear I'll—"

"You'll do what? Use me?" Azrael shakes his head, chuckling, though the sound is crueler than it is amused. "You already have. Over and over again."

"Azrael, I don't think this is—"

"Ask him about the deal he and I made, Charlotte."

My spine runs cold. "What?" I breathe.

"Ask him about the choice he took from you."

Lucifer glares at him, his voice low and firm. "If you dare try to come between us, I will—"

"What's he talking about, Lucifer?" I say, rising to my feet, my legs unsteady. "What did you promise?"

I sound just as lost, just as timid as I did at the start of all this.

Before he went and made me his queen.

Before I became the monster I always feared I'd be.

For what feels like the first time ever, Lucifer looks . . . panicked.

His gaze darts to me, face pale, eyes haunted. "Darling, you have to understand, you're the only thing keeping me decent. Without you, the world would've burned anyway."

"Tell her," Azrael snarls, lip curling, his stance stiff. "Tell her what you took from her, or I will."

Lucifer looks at me then, and what he says in that moment is a thousand times worse than anything I could have imagined. Any other trauma I've ever endured.

Including my father.

"There was only ever one fail-safe way to save humanity, darling. One sacrifice that could stop the seals from opening. A sacrifice that could rebalance the cosmic paradox that allowed the seals to be opened in the first place, a sacrifice that could end everything." He swallows. "And you're it."

My heart shatters, my stomach clenching.

And the pain, the agony of my husband's betrayal, is immediate.

He lied.

My vision blurs, the sharp pain in my womb tightening.

I thought he'd changed. Thought he'd given up everything for me.

But he was still letting the world burn this entire time. For me.

"When you saved me, you . . . started all of this?"

Azrael releases a slow, furious breath. "He made me promise to try and keep you alive at all costs, regardless of what happens to humanity."

Regardless of what happened to . . .

The whole world sacrificed, because he loves me.

Even as I was trying to save it.

My life. My immortality. My choice whether to live or die.

All taken from me.

By a lie of omission.

Lucifer's eyes meet mine, not with regret, but with a horrible, haunted certainty. Like he *knows* what he's done, and he still believes he had every right to do it. "No wife of mine will ever play the hero," he says, his voice low and final. "You would've chosen to die, Charlotte. I couldn't let that happen. I was protecting you from yourself."

I choke.

"You didn't just lie," I whisper. "You decided my life was worth more than the world. You let me put your collar back on, knowing you'd already taken my choice away. That isn't love, Lucifer. That's ownership."

And I agreed to it.

Oh God.

Walked right back into it willingly.

My collar suddenly feels tighter around my throat.

Pain ignites in the center of my palms as my nails dig into my skin and the ground begins to shake.

I start forward, legs trembling as the room blurs, the anger inside me consuming everything until I collapse, unable to control it anymore.

And everything fades to black.

CHAPTER FORTY-SEVEN

Charlotte

I'm falling so fast it feels like I'm fragmented. Like a part of me is broken and I'll never be able to get it back again. The sound of my own agony rings in my ears as I scream and scream and scream. Until I scream myself hoarse. Suddenly I'm jerked out of midair by an invisible force, and I'm standing on my own two feet again.

I'm in the middle of a desolate landscape, the sky stretching as far as the eye can see.

There's nothing but ground here.

Like primitive Earth.

It's no more than a hastily molded lump of clay.

Lucifer lies in the mud and the muck nearby, curled in on himself and bleeding, but despite the pain of betrayal I feel, I stagger toward him.

But I pass straight through him.

"Lucifer?" I ask, but he doesn't hear me.

He stirs slightly.

I turn and find Azrael crouching over him, his hair uncut, his arms and chest bare of all his tattoos. He reaches out, but then Lucifer lashes at him with his hand.

Above his eye, like I always suspected.

Then the scene shifts, and I'm in the middle of a lush garden, the smell of fresh apples all around me. The best I've ever tasted. I know that without even eating any.

Lucifer stands in front of a woman in the shade of a towering tree, and I can feel Azrael in the near distance, watching, the cold shiver of his power rushing over us. I can't help the hint of jealousy I feel—it twists like a knife in my gut, igniting a flash of anger as I see the way Lucifer looks at her, and then Azrael. And I realize that she must be . . .

Eve.

The scene shifts again.

It's the scent of olives I notice first, the scent putrid on the dry desert air. I've never been to this part of Jerusalem before, but I'd recognize the gnarled roots of the ancient trees anywhere.

Gethsemane.

Lucifer and Azrael are kissing, but it seems like a goodbye, and somewhere nearby in what I guess is Aramaic, I think I hear what must be . . . Christ.

A shiver runs through me.

The scenes go on and on.

An endless stretch of stories, of moments, of memories, spanning out over the whole of time, the knowledge of each one gleaned in only a few seconds.

A kingdom. A bloodline. A doctrine.

Destruction. Death. A creed.

Like I've bitten into the apple, and now it's given me all the knowledge I've been missing.

Azrael's voice rings loud and clear, clanging around in my skull like it might be his memories I'm seeing.

Each moment that led to when he first saw me.

The scene shifts abruptly.

He holds me in his arms, cradling me, on the floor of Grand Central as Lucifer prowls toward us.

But then I blink, and we're somewhere else.

"If that's the case," I hear Death saying, "then I think that I may have a better offer that suits you."

We're standing in an old, abandoned mall now, sometime within the last century, the decaying relics of a forgotten era making the atmosphere eerie, but it's the devious grin Lucifer gives Azrael in response that chills me.

"What exactly are you offering, Reaper?"

The sequence shifts again. It doesn't allow me to stick around long enough to hear anything. But I know already what Lucifer agreed.

My body shared with Death in exchange for his protection.

Until the right time, until sacrificing me could no longer mean saving humanity.

So Lucifer wouldn't lose me.

No matter the cost.

When I come to a stop again a few moments later, I'm standing in the middle of a familiar orchard, the sickly sweet smell of rotting apples all around me, like in my dream, but this time, I recognize where it is.

Eden.

But the Garden's dying.

And it isn't Lilith that greets me.

It's Jax.

I rush toward her, throwing myself into her arms.

I want to cry. I want to scream. I want to collapse in relief, but something makes me hesitate.

She pulls back from the hug. "We don't have much time."

I glance over the familiar planes of her face. "What do you mean?"

"Charlotte, whenever they demand you open the fourth seal, I need you to know you can't stop it."

My brow furrows. "What do you mean I can't stop it?"

"What's going to happen. It's a part of God's plan."

"God's plan?" I only seem capable of echoing her words back at her.

My mind feels distant, fuzzy, like the weight of all those memories is drowning me, like I might be in the middle of a . . .

A dream.

Is that what this is?

"This isn't just a dream," Jax says. "It's a prophecy. I've been trying to send it to you, to show you. In the orchard. What's going to happen when he—"

"Charlotte," a sharp voice hisses, rattling inside my skull.

Lucifer.

I'm certain it's him, but for some reason, I don't want it to be.

"Don't leave me," I say, grasping Jax's hands.

"I have to." She squeezes them and then places a protective hand over my belly. Clearly, she already knows about the potential life growing there. "I'll see you again soon."

"But what am I supposed to—"

"It'll all be okay. Just let it happen," she says. "Just let God's plan unfold."

I shake my head. "But what does that mean?"

How can I stand by and do nothing? I need answers.

"Charlotte!" Lucifer's voice hisses inside my head again.

"I have to go," she says, glancing over her shoulder, her eyes wide like she's suddenly panicked. "Lilith's coming."

"Lilith?" I pale at the thought of what she might do to her.

"Charlotte!" Lucifer's voice echoes.

I try to grip Jax's hand. "I don't want anything to happen to you."

"I know, but I'll be okay," she says. "Go."

"But I need you to—"

"Charlotte!"

I come to on a gasp, surging forward before I immediately turn and vomit all over the floor. I realize only seconds later that I'm no longer in the re-creation of God's throne room. Instead, I'm on all fours in the hall leading into my father's torture chamber. Like I was only out for a few seconds.

But it felt like a whole eternity to me.

Lucifer has a hold of me.

He grips me by the shoulders, his face as white as a sheet and contorted with worry, but I have a vague memory of Azrael forcing him to confess his sins, of how he broke his promise before he—

But there's no time for that.

I shove him off me, trying to surge to my feet.

But he grabs my hand. "Charlotte, please. I don't think it's the best idea right now if you—"

"You don't get to make my choices for me," I hiss, unbuckling my collar and tossing it onto the floor in front of him. "Not ever again." I turn to Azrael, addressing him like the celestial soldier he's always been. "I need to see my father. *Now.*"

CHAPTER FORTY-EIGHT

Charlotte

My fingers dig into my palms from all my pent-up anger at *both* of them, but I shake my head, brushing past them easily.

If they're allowed to make unilateral decisions about whether I live or die, about whether I'm allowed to *sacrifice* myself to save all of humanity, then at least I can decide for myself that I want to pay my father a visit.

I prowl forward.

The interior of the meat locker is as cold as it was last time, the scent of blood and the smell of rotten flesh lingering. I struggle not to gag, thankful that my morning sickness isn't acting up, other than for that dizzying prophecy, but the smell still gets to me. I'm pretty sure I'm far enough along I'm starting to get past the worst of the nausea, but I'm still not certain how I'm going to tell Lucifer and Azrael.

Especially not after this.

Not after they *both* took my choice away from me.

I glance in their direction.

Azrael crosses his arms over his chest, standing guard by the door like if I decide to run, he'll be there to catch me, though I'd just as soon use my powers to plow him over, like he's done to me so many times in training, and Lucifer—my gaze snags on my fiancé, and I nearly scream—fucking Lucifer leans against one of the refrigerators, looking like he's just as irate about this whole situation as me.

How dare he.

How dare he make decisions about my life *for* me. When I hadn't asked him to.

I know him better by now than to assume he'd sacrifice me to win some war against his Father—if he didn't love me, he wouldn't have given up his redemption for me in the first place—which means he must have had some *other* reason. For making me think I could win this apocalyptic battle, could save humanity, when the whole time he was keeping the one damn blue chip that could save all of humanity from me.

He doesn't want to lose me. Isn't sure he could live without me.

But that doesn't lessen the sting of what he kept from me.

It's like fate and free will have finally converged, and both paths have led here.

To this moment.

I face my father.

As far as I know, this dingy, disgusting meat locker that looks like it's straight out of a horror movie isn't Hell's worst accommodations, but it's not ideal either, and I'm pretty sure Lucifer chose it with a clear purpose in mind.

For the drains.

Torturing hypocrites is one of his favorite things, and sometimes when he comes home, he can be a bit . . . messy.

Just like I'm about to get.

I'm finally furious enough to put an end to this whole thing.

Let out everything I've previously been holding in.

No matter how sinful it makes me.

I step forward, standing confidently in front of my father much faster than I did the last time, and the steady, self-assured way I'm able to hold his gaze sends an unexpected shock of fear through me.

Something's changed since our last visit.

But I haven't quite put my finger on what it is yet.

My father lifts his head, looking at me wearily, clearly disgusted by everything he was just forced to overhear. But I don't care.

I no longer give a damn what he and his followers have to say about me.

Imani's right.

People will see me for who I am if I let them.

And if they don't?

Then they were never really looking.

I've wasted enough of my life trying to be palatable.

I'm going to start living for *myself* now.

Everyone else already is.

His lip curls. "'And behold, there met him a woman with the attire of a harlot, and subtil of heart,'" my sperm donor rasps, his gaze sweeping over me.

"That's a misquote, actually," Lucifer murmurs.

I cast him a furious look, and he stops talking.

I'm learning all sorts of new things about my husband tonight.

Including that he's memorized more parts of the Bible than I have.

"I make it a habit to study my enemies," he offers, clearly having read my thoughts through our connection. I haven't been very good about safeguarding them lately.

I'm going to have to change that.

Azrael huffs like he doesn't believe him.

I just shake my head, my mouth pinched as I turn back to my father, claiming the space I need. The two of them are here as more of a courtesy than anything. I don't need either of them to catch me if I fall anymore.

I'm going to be my own safety.

This time, I'm ready.

I'm certain of it.

"You're right," I say to my father, shocking all three of them.

My lovers grumble in disapproval.

They may call me worse in the middle of a scene, but never outside of it.

And they've been trying to rid me of my shame and self-loathing from the start.

I nod, starting again. "You're right, I *am* a shameless whore. But I'm *his* whore." I nod toward Lucifer. "And also, his." I shoot an irate look to Azrael.

He could have told me himself about his and Lucifer's deal, but he didn't.

"And nothing you could do or say is going to take that away from me." I lift my chin high. "I'm not scared of you anymore."

I summon a bit of Holy Fire into one of my palms to prove my point, and my father stiffens. The sight of his fear galvanizes me.

"I'm more angelic than you'll ever be."

My first question comes easy.

"Who among the Righteous's leadership made the deal with Michael?"

I think of Lucifer, of how, whatever his reason, he broke his promise to me, of all the transparency I thought that he was giving me.

"'For such men are false apostles, deceitful workmen, disguising themselves as apostles of Christ.'" My father's voice drips with self-righteous venom. "'And no wonder, for even Satan disguises himself as an angel of light.'"

"2 Corinthians," Lucifer mutters without looking up. "You really are obsessed with my greatest hits."

"And me." I shake my head. "What exactly is it that the Righteous are working toward? What's your endgame?"

I think of Azrael, of how he came barreling back into mine and Lucifer's life like the force of nature he is, upending everything, only to make me fall in love with him, while the whole time he was keeping Lucifer's secrets from me.

My chest aches.

"Did you target Jax specifically, or was it because she was *my* friend? And how did you get Ian on board? I know he really *was* the one who drugged Jax at Lust's club, so was he just a creep, or was he one of you all from the start?"

"'Woe to those who call evil good and good evil,'" my father hisses, straining against his restraints, "'who put darkness for light and light for darkness—who put bitter for sweet and sweet for bitter!'"

I think of Jax, of the terrified look on her face when she thought Lilith was coming for her. We need to get to her, fast.

"What about the bombs at the Met Gala? Were those just so Mark could kidnap me, or were you planning something bigger? Why couldn't you just let me live?"

My father leans forward, eyes wild. "'They will throw their silver into the streets, and their gold will be treated as unclean. Their silver and gold will not be able to deliver them on the day of the wrath of the Lord—'"

"Ezekiel 7:19," I snap, showing him I didn't forget everything, just the parts that are no longer relevant to me, to allowing myself to live. "And you still believe Michael's silver will buy your way into Heaven?"

The silence that follows is bitter enough to curdle blood.

And then I think of him, the monster before me.

Of how he taught me to abandon myself, become smaller.

"I just can't understand why you're obsessed with—"

"It was never about you!" he spits. "You think Michael came to *us*? We went to *him*. Long before the first seal cracked. We saw the signs. The chaos rising. The world slipping. We made the deal years ago, long before you ever whored yourself to Hell. We arranged everything. The club. The drugs. Ian was one of ours from the start. The gala was a smokescreen, meant to draw your fire. While you were busy protecting yourself, *we* delivered the prophet straight into the hands of the Most High."

My stomach clenches.

"Why?" I breathe. "Why would you target my friend all because I didn't believe in your twisted doctrine?"

My father shakes his head, like he doesn't believe I still don't get it. "You were never the prize." His pale lips curl into a disgusting grin. "She is. *She* is the key to the fourth seal, and thanks to Michael, her death will be our Rapture."

Her death . . .

I stand there, frozen in shock as the weight of my father's words sinks into me.

As I recognize the full extent of everything he's done.

It was never about me.

I was just a distraction, collateral damage on his path to eternity.

My palms start to burn, the feeling reminding me of my husband's hellfire. It's one of his favorites, obviously, but I can wield Holy Fire far better now.

My hands ignite like a torch, the warm, ethereal glow illuminating my face, and when I speak, it's a demonic voice that comes out of me. The one Lucifer's powers gifted me.

"I want you to know I'll do whatever it takes to ensure you *never* get into Heaven."

My father's eyes twitch, and I know in that moment I have him right where I want him.

He's more disgusted by me than he is by Lucifer.

And that tells me everything.

Nothing I ever could've done would have pleased him. Would've been enough.

"That's what you want after all, isn't it? Why you've been keeping up this ridiculous routine, staying silent, like His word actually means something to you." I step forward, gesturing with one of my fiery hands toward the ceiling. "So, what exactly did Michael promise you? Eternal salvation? A place in Heaven? That he'd liberate you and all your persecuted friends from Hell?"

I watch, unsurprised, as his face contorts with rage and he becomes the vicious monster he's always been.

If only the members of our congregation had seen it more readily.

But they're just as blind as he is.

And I don't shy away.

Because I'm not afraid of him anymore.

My anger may have been locked away for a long time, but now I'm going to let it out to play.

Because now I'm a more vicious creature than he'll ever be.

CHAPTER FORTY-NINE

Lucifer

I see the moment my wife's fear of what she could become makes her hesitate, as she begins to question if what she's about to do will make her like him, like me. A vicious creature whose only true focus has ever been on what benefits him. I take that as my cue to step in. This is what I've been training her for from the very start, and I'll be damned if I allow my Father and his blasted teachings to ruin it for me.

She hesitates, caught between who she was and the terror of what she could transform into.

Her father's eyes narrow. "'For the Lord knoweth the way of the righteous: but the way of the ungodly shall—'"

"Oh, stop with the bloody Bible verses!" I sneer.

My wife's hands start to glow as they clench into fists, and I can feel her anger, her wrath, barely leashed, my Father's divine justice fading as she tries to bury it again. But I won't let her hide from herself. From her power.

Not any longer.

"We all know they never actually meant anything to you, or you wouldn't have hurt her. You wouldn't have ignored the parts of His word that didn't serve you. The parts all of you ignore about love, forgiveness, mercy"—I shoot a furious look toward Azrael—"about feeding the sick, housing the poor, loving thy fucking neighbor."

I shake my head, the words pouring out like they've been trapped inside my throat this whole bloody time.

"Christ never turned away from the whores, the lepers, the sinners. He would've flipped every damn one of your tables, yet you ignore that to justify your own hate, your own bigotry." I wrinkle my nose, sounding like what I once was. My Father's warrior. "There's nothing Christlike about you, and if it's up to me, *none* of you are going to escape me. That's why you're here, after all." I gesture to my realm all around us. "So, why don't all you pathetic humans actually start to fight for your own salvation? The best thing you can do for yourself now is to—"

"Michael will deliver the Righteous to the Kingdom of God!" her father roars, thrashing about against his bindings like if he could break free, he would do whatever it took to annihilate her, to silence her again.

My eyes turn serpentine, and Azrael snarls, stepping forward. I think I feel her rage waning, her shadows retreating to the edges of the room, but then she suddenly throws her head back and laughs, the pitch high and shocking.

And despite that her hatred for him is delicious, it sends a chill down my spine.

Because she sounds like *me.*

Furious and in control.

My she-devil really *has* come out to play.

"You really don't know, do you?" She chuckles, shaking her head in between breaths. "Of course you don't. You've been down here this whole time, so why would you?" She steps forward, brazen again as she places her hands on top of his shackles, leaning into his space. "Michael has already betrayed you," she hisses.

Her father's eyes widen, his face a furious red. "No." His features harden. "No, it's not in his scripture. 'And then there was war in heaven: Michael and his angels fought against the dragon—'"

"'And the dragon and his angels fought back,'" Charlotte snarls before she starts to circle him, her expression twisted in fury. "Michael used you. Just like *you* used me."

"No."

"The Righteous are all going to Hell, just like I warned you."

"No!" her father roars.

"God's gone, and He isn't coming back."

"Whore of Babylon! Daughter of perdition!"

"You and your religion mean nothing to me anymore! Nothing!" she screams.

I step forward, pressing one of Azrael's blades into her shaking hand. She takes it before she stands in front of him again, trembling in her fury.

"I was your daughter," she whispers, her voice breaking as she places a hand on her stomach like the thought makes her sick. "All I ever wanted was for you to love me."

Her father sneers. "'A woman should learn in quietness and full submission. Do not permit a woman to teach, to assume authority over a man. She must be—'"

"And yet you've never wondered where I learned to want all this? How your verses made me the perfect victim—perfect for him!" she shrieks, gesturing toward me. "You drilled obedience into me until it became holy."

I pinch my thumb and forefinger tight, drawing it like a thread over his mouth, and his lips disappear. I may not have my power whenever I'm topside, but it remains here.

I take my bride by the shoulders as I lean down and whisper into her ear just as I did with Eve. "Think of all he's done, Charlotte," I hiss, joining the fray as I tempt her, call out that dark power inside her with my own. Her father's eyes bulge and his face contorts as he recognizes what it is I'm doing, as he witnesses how thoroughly I've seduced her. "All the times he hurt you."

Her tears come hard and fast as she trembles from the memory. "Too many."

Her father thrashes in his chair, his screams muffled.

"Think of every moment he chose to forsake you!" I shout over him. "Every doubt he ever created."

Her muscles quiver, the temperature in her body rising, anger simmering.

I can feel it. Her desire to end him.

"Then think of how I've worshipped you."

She draws in a harsh breath, her chin held high, her eyes closed at the thought of the pain I've brought to her this evening. At what I have kept from her.

At the twisted love I have captured her with. Right from the start.

At the recognition that her life was mine from the very beginning.

"And then consider how it might have been different, what you would do." My grip on her tightens, my hand caressing her throat as I remove her collar from inside my suit coat and place it around her neck again. "If only he'd done the same."

I snap the buckle closed and release her, shoving her between her shoulders so that when she stumbles forward, we might as well be in another scene.

I know without a doubt from the way she staggers and then straightens, the muscles of her spine lengthening in a slow, deliberate movement, that the vicious creature I've been training her to be is here.

I've made her into the kind of monster my Father made me.

One day, she's going to thank me for it.

"Tell him how you really feel, darling," I order.

She shakes her head, still fighting it, despite how I can feel her rage simmering.

"Do it *now*, Charlotte!" I bellow, commanding her as I have so many times before.

But this isn't a scene. It's her father's torture.

The exorcism of her demons.

It's the crux of this whole goddamn thing.

"Show him how you feel!" I bellow.

"I can't!"

"Show him or I'll—"

She lets out a furious battle cry, screaming her rage out to the heavens, the fluorescent lights overhead bursting, and I see it then.

The moment she steps into her power.

The moment she becomes my queen.

She turns toward her father, her eyes now serpentine and glowing with hellfire as she says in a demonic voice, "Are you afraid, Daddy?"

And then she lunges, plunging the blade ruthlessly into his throat.

My cock gives an excited jerk at the sight of it, and Azrael's eyes turn feral with bloodlust at the destruction he knows is coming.

But her abuser deserves so much more than the minor lash she's given him, so I keep pushing, each command snapping like the crack of a whip as I drive her to be the largest, most hateful, most sinful version of herself she could possibly be.

"He stole your virtue!"

She shrieks, gripping the sides of his face, her hands igniting as his skin begins to singe and rot.

"Your innocence."

She lets out another furious cry, the rage in it searing us both as she lunges into him, knocking over his chair. Her father writhes, bleeding beneath her, but if anything, she only grows more frenzied, more bloodthirsty.

My commands energize her.

She throws herself on top of him, shrieking as she claws at his face, over and over again, each blow a twisted memory.

My cock stiffens.

I've never wanted her more.

"Your virginity," I say, marveling at how all the shadows in the room start to bend toward her, pointed and hovering, her rage sharpening them like daggers. Hundreds upon hundreds of them, one for every time he raised a hand to her. Azrael lets out a dark, haunting chuckle.

"And most importantly," I hiss, driving the final nail in. "Your self-worth."

The cry Charlotte releases is demonic, the sound of her rage like she's channeling my Mother as she throws out her arms, the gesture bringing down all her shadows at once.

Her father's blood sprays over the entire room like the splash of a baptism as she eviscerates him in one fell swoop, collapsing onto what little remains.

She curls in upon herself, sobbing.

I'm at her side a moment later, pulling her into my arms.

"Look at what you've done, darling. Look at all you've wrought."

"I destroyed him," she whimpers. "I—"

"No," I say, gripping her face and forcing her to look at me. "You've freed yourself. *I've* freed you."

A haunted look clouds her eyes, and my blood runs cold as she turns that demonic voice on me and says, "What have you done to me?"

CHAPTER FIFTY

Azrael

The sight of Charlotte absolutely eviscerating her father might be one of the most erotic things I've ever seen. But I don't plan on telling her that.

Not with that haunted look in her eye.

The divine fury she's wielding.

Like she's just broken apart completely.

She turns her anger to Lucifer, the look of judgment, of divine justice, contorting her pretty features as she lifts her hand and then—

"No!" I shout, diving for her, pulling her into my arms, and spinning us both away from Lucifer.

The blast of white light that bursts from her takes out a large chunk of the ceiling, no longer aimed toward our lover.

Ours.

I may be fucking furious with him at the moment, but the word acts like a kind of anchor for me. Despite what he may think, I've never wanted to end him.

Not even when I put the blade into play.

And no matter what we may have broken tonight, they both still mean something to me.

Even if I can hardly stand to look at them.

Charlotte thrashes and fights, furiously battling against my hold. But if it's Lucifer's job to ramp her up, push her to be all she can be, then it's mine to drag her back down again, to ground her. Make her remember what it means to be human.

Remind her of why she keeps coming back to me.

"Shhh. Shhh, little siren. I've got you," I rasp into her ear, even as I pin her against the wall. Like I did the first time she faced her father.

When standing in front of him nearly tore her apart.

But this time, she's broken completely.

We're lucky she didn't burn the world down with all the rage she's just unleashed.

But this is what she needs to heal, to let all that toxicity out.

She collapses beneath me, crying harder than I've ever heard her before.

"It's okay, baby girl. You burned it all down, and we're still here. You're allowed to feel it. What he did to you doesn't own you. Not anymore."

That seems to be the key, what puts her back together slightly, soothes her.

Reminds her of her own humanity.

She comes back into herself slowly, her breath deepening and her pulse fading as she gradually becomes more still in my arms.

"That's it, baby girl," I purr. "Let it out. Just breathe."

Lucifer's watching us with an uncertain look in his eyes, like he never actually expected her to *need* me. For me to be an integral part of this.

"It wasn't about me," she whispers, the words soft, broken.

"No, it wasn't."

I may not have what anyone would consider parents, but I've seen enough deaths, enough life, to know that the only thing worse than their hate is their apathy.

And the scars they leave.

"Jax," she whispers, tensing in my arms. "The Righteous. We have to—"

"Lilith's been keeping her obscured from me."

Charlotte's eyes go wide. "If her death is the key to the fourth seal, then Lilith, the Righteous, Michael . . ." She scrambles off me. "We have to—"

Lucifer steps into her path. "Darling, rushing in unprepared to face my Mother might not be—"

"No," she says to him, refusing to step aside. "You forfeited the right to make decisions for me." She turns and looks at me like she's giving me this one last opportunity to be her choice.

To support her.

"Are you coming with me or not?"

CHAPTER FIFTY-ONE

Charlotte

I don't have time to fully process the metaphysical mindfuck that's the In-Between or everything that's at stake—Lucifer's powers, the end of humanity, God, the afterlife—all I know is that my best friend is in danger, and my crazy three-headed goddess of a Mother-in-Law has her.

I can't waste another second waiting.

When Azrael snaps us all topside and we appear in the Whispering Gallery in Grand Central, I'm as confused as I've ever been.

"I thought you said Limbo and the In-Between weren't the same thing?" I say, my voice echoing. I glance at the time on my iPhone.

It's nearly three in the morning.

Long past when the city's night owls have gone home and well before the morning commute begins, so the station is empty. Only a few routes have resumed after the third seal flooded mass parts of the subway, and crime's been getting out of hand since the third seal collapsed everything.

"Not everyone's limbo is Grand Central Station." Azrael gives me a pointed look.

I flush, looking away. If I'd bothered to consider how he felt, considered a different perspective than my own, maybe I wouldn't have hurt him. I should have told him where my head was at before putting my collar back on, that it didn't change anything for me and him. Hurting him wasn't intentional, but clearly, I need to be more mindful of my own blind spots.

I take an interest in a spot on the floor near my feet as he turns to Lucifer. "It might be best for you to wait here. Let me and Charlotte take the lead like we'd planned."

"Like hell am I going to—"

"Enough." I step between them, suddenly aware of how they both tower over me. "There's no time for your bickering right now. Every second counts. Save it for Lilith."

I glance around the empty space, to the nearby Oyster Bar and Restaurant, and the echoing halls.

At this time of night, there's almost something eerie about it.

"What are we supposed to do? Shouldn't there be some kind of door?"

Lucifer lifts a brow at me, like he's uncertain how I'd know this.

"There was this door when Azmodeus took me to the In-Between from this gallery in Brooklyn. Transmitter, I think?"

"When the fuck did my brother take you to—"

"When the paparazzi caught us in that club, remember?" I shoot him a reproachful glance. "I might've neglected to mention it was the In-Between at the time, but it's just because I didn't fully understand it was in another dimension. Besides, you have no place to talk with the secrets you've been keeping."

Lucifer frowns, but he doesn't argue.

My attention cuts to Azrael. "So how do we get in? And why not go straight from Hell?"

He and Lucifer exchange a meaningful look.

"We built Hell with very few connections to the In-Between," he answers.

My gaze darts between them. "Because . . . ?"

Azrael's brow furrows as he says to Lucifer, "She's *your* sub."

Lucifer's mouth pinches, but then he turns to me. "There are, in fact, some truths that are better left unspoken."

I frown at him.

Azrael shakes his head. "Let's just say we weren't keen on the idea of unexpected wanderers."

So, either they were trying to keep Hell's souls from getting out or they were trying to stop something from getting *in*.

I pale a little.

Azrael runs his hand over the stone of a nearby wall, like he's searching for a clue he can't seem to locate.

"Do humans sometimes . . . wander into the In-Between?" I think back to the odd mix of the dance club's patrons, and how the hell the paparazzi might have found me.

"Sometimes," Azrael answers.

"Among other things." Lucifer shrugs.

My pulse picks up. "Other things?"

Azrael crosses his arms over his chest. Clearly, I'm no longer his responsibility.

Lucifer scowls at him. "My Father's lesser-known creations, what some might call his creative failures."

His creative failures?

I don't particularly like the sound of that.

My thoughts turn to some of the patrons Azmodeus and I encountered in that club. Their glowing eyes, how otherworldly they seemed.

Even more otherworldly than Azrael.

I shudder.

"And what happens to the humans who wander in?"

Azrael grunts noncommittally.

"That's enough questions, darling." Lucifer steps toward one of the archways and begins searching, his hands trailing over the tile.

"But couldn't we just go to the one in—"

"The entrances move," Lucifer mutters.

I want to ask exactly how they know there's an entrance *here*, but I fall silent. Like my Dom told me. My hand flits to my collar.

I should take it off. I should rip it from my neck and drop it at his feet.

But I don't.

Because I'm not ready to stop being his. My hand falls to my belly.

Even if he broke his promise.

My gaze flits to Azrael, my limbs suddenly feeling heavy.

"Should we have brought your siblings?" I ask Lucifer a few moments later. "Whichever ones haven't abandoned us, I mean."

"If your friend is in as much danger as we think she is, there's no time." Azrael switches to another arch. "We stick to the original plan."

Sneak in. Get Jax. And get the hell outta Dodge.

Before Lilith or Uriel or anyone else standing guard can suspect anything.

I turn and start searching over the nearest stone archway, like they are, even though I have no idea what I'm looking for. There must be a switch or a lever or who knows what, but then my eyes snag on a small phrase etched into the stone tiling, the letters carved so small and haphazardly that if I weren't looking, I'd never see it.

I run my fingers across the inscription, reading it aloud. "'I'm still here.'"

Something in the air shifts then, and for a moment, I swear I hear the echo of another whisper, of someone answering back, but I can't make out what they're saying.

When I turn and glance over my shoulder to look for them, the hairs on the back of my neck rise on end, and the arch opposite me seems farther away. The white tiles have shifted, and a heavy feeling settles into my stomach. There's a supply cabinet door that wasn't there previously. A door marked in large red, spray-painted letters.

NO ACCESS.

I cross the Whispering Gallery toward it and try the handle.

At first, it's locked, the handle not even moving.

"Can you hear me?" I whisper to it, wondering if that voice will answer back, but when I try the handle again, it turns, and the door creaks open.

The sound draws both Lucifer's and Azrael's attention.

"I . . . think I might've found it." I shrug helplessly.

Lucifer's smirk turns wicked. "Clever girl." He steps past me, bringing my hand to his lips and kissing it as he looks me directly in the eye. A heavy weight settles in my chest, the fullness in my belly aching.

How can I still want him, even when he betrayed my trust?

Even if it *was* because he loves me.

Didn't want to lose me.

Lucifer releases me, forging ahead, and I glance away, trying not to let Azrael see how Lucifer's praise still affects me.

I fail miserably.

Azrael's jaw goes suddenly taut, and he brushes past me.

He takes out one of his blades a moment later, gripping it as he moves in front of me and Lucifer like the well-trained soldier he is.

My ribs tighten.

Even after everything that's happened tonight, he'd still put himself on the line for us.

My shoulders drop, the pressure feeling too heavy.

"Follow me." Azrael steps into the darkness.

Lucifer beckons me forward, ushering me past him, like he means to put me in the middle, but I place my hand on his wrist. We need to go about this strategically.

"Maybe I should—"

"I may be mortal now, darling, but it's *my* powers on the line, and I'm considerably more trained in celestial combat than you are. Don't insult me." He nudges me forward.

I drop my chin. "Yes, sir."

I step into the darkened stairwell, and he follows, closing the door behind us.

We descend into the darkness with me caught between the two of them, Azrael at my front and Lucifer protecting my back. My attention ping-pongs between them.

Maybe that's been the problem all along—me being caught in the middle.

Between Lucifer and Azrael. Heaven and Hell. God and humanity.

Maybe Lucifer's right. Maybe that's why removing myself from the equation, sacrificing myself, sounds so appealing—because it's just another form of self-abandonment.

What I've been fighting against all along, actually.

But how do I make a choice when every road leads to an imperfect outcome?

To losing what I have?

The pressure inside my head builds and builds exactly like it did when I unknowingly came here with Azmodeus, making it hard to think. I press my palm to my head, trying to stop the ache, but just when I think I can't possibly stand it for another second, the staircase levels and the feeling dissipates.

We're standing in the middle of what I'm fairly certain is an abandoned subway tunnel. The darkness around us encompasses everything.

A sporadic drip of water echoes nearby, followed by the sound of a falling pebble.

I use a bit of my Holy Fire to light both of my hands like torches, lifting them high, the ethereal glow flickering.

"This way." Azrael nods.

Lucifer and I follow him.

We walk for what feels like hours, the tunnel gradually growing narrower and narrower, until my feet start to hurt and I'm grateful I switched into sneakers for training with Seraph this afternoon despite the Hermès I'm wearing. Greed insists that training in athletic wear is counterintuitive since I'll never know when I'll find myself in a celestial battle and heels are what I'm usually wearing. She's right in any case.

But at least Seraph gave my feet a break.

"How do we know when we—"

Azrael hushes me, and a moment later we come to a stop outside another door, this one labeled in large, spray-painted block letters: **RESTRICTED ZONE**.

My stomach cinches into a knot.

I hold up my hands, allowing Azrael to use my firelight to examine it.

"This isn't right." He glances to Lucifer. "Do you think Greed lied?"

Lucifer gives a slow tilt of his head. "Not likely. She'd never admit it, but she's attached to Charlotte, and I had Seraph confirm."

If Greed's "attached" to me, I don't want to know what she's like when she *doesn't* like someone.

Azrael lifts his scarred brow, the firelight making it appear even more jagged.

I drop my chin to my chest, forcing myself to look away.

What I saw in Jax's prophecy feels . . . intrusive. Intimate.

"Could Seraph be working both sides?"

"Not likely. It'd be too great a risk for her."

Azrael shakes his head. "Something's wrong." Then to me. "I should be able to sense Uriel and the others standing guard."

There's no one here but us.

"Do you think that means—"

"They knew we were coming." He looks to Lucifer. "Whichever of your siblings went rogue must've sold us out already. She might not even be here."

Adrenaline shoots through me.

But if she's not here and Lilith has no more use for her, then she . . .

"It's not too late to turn back now. Recalculate." Lucifer places a hand on my shoulder.

Like he's leaving the decision up to me.

My heart clenches. He didn't mean to hurt me either. Just like I didn't mean to hurt Azrael.

He loves me. He doesn't want to lose me.

But that doesn't make this any easier.

"Your friend would understand, little dove. She'd never want you to place yourself at unnecessary risk." He gives me a pointed look.

If the roles were reversed, if it were *his* life at stake, would I have done the same? Made the decision for him? So that he didn't have to?

"Maybe he's right." I glance at Azrael, and he gives a reluctant nod.

Better to waste time and come prepared than walk into a known trap.

Resigned, we turn to head back in the other direction.

Only to find a dead-end wall where we just entered.

Lucifer mutters a few choice curse words. "I fucking hate the In-Between."

Azrael swallows, nodding toward the door. "Looks like it's decided the only way out is through."

"It?" I extinguish my fire, just as Azrael opens the door.

We step inside, and I instantly regret it.

My stomach pitches into my feet as I relight my hands. "Where are we?"

"The Vestibule, it looks like," Azrael says quietly, like saying it too loud might wake something ancient.

The space beyond the door isn't a room exactly, but it *feels* enclosed—like we've stepped into the forgotten pause between heartbeats.

A hall stretches out in front of us, open and unending. It's not *dark* exactly, but the light here doesn't feel real either. It's gray and flickering, like a dying fluorescent bulb, but none of it connects right. Angles refuse to align. Doorframes hang midair without walls to anchor them, and a cracked mirror leans next to an old discarded vending machine. On the far wall, there's a flickering sign that reads: **NOT AN EXIT**.

"Seriously, what *is* this place?" I ask, though my voice sounds smaller than I want it to.

I can't help the goose bumps that start to prickle over my skin.

"A non-place," Azrael says, as if that's supposed to make sense. "It's a threshold. Grown out of memory. Things people tried to forget. It's the heart of the In-Between."

"So what? Like a purgatory for unfinished thoughts?" I spin in a slow circle.

Lucifer gestures around us, jaw tight. "More like a waiting room for the cosmically fucked."

Azrael lets out a slow breath. "The Vestibule isn't here to help us. It's here to make us hesitate."

"Hesitate about what?"

"About *everything*." He turns to face me. "There're no real doors here. Only choices that *look* like doors."

"What does that even mean?" I look again at the doorframes, but none of them seem like they actually *go anywhere*.

They're just shapes, suggestions.

"There's no way out, is there?"

"Not a real one," Lucifer says. "Just choices. Until it's done with us."

I glance around.

They're all labeled in past tense.

YOU CHOSE THIS.

YOU LEFT.

YOU WANTED TO KNOW.

The worst part is I think some of them might be right.

On the nearest, the words **THIS IS NOT A DOOR** have been scrawled in black marker. Another not far to its left says **YOU LEFT HER**.

I hate this place already.

"It has to be that one," I say, pointing toward the one labeled **YOU LEFT HER**.

Lucifer scowls. "Of course you'd pick that one."

I frown at him. "Why wouldn't I? It's obviously talking about Jax."

Lucifer's expression hardens. "Not for me."

My eyes dart to Azrael, and I lift a brow.

"It says different things for different people."

My breath catches. "And what does yours say?"

He swallows. "'She chose him,'" he admits.

My eyes widen. "And yours?" I ask Lucifer.

Lucifer tugs uncomfortably at his tie. "I'd prefer not to say."

I huff. "Oh, come on. Azrael and I both—"

"It says 'This is what he meant,'" he snaps. He looks away, running a ragged hand through his hair.

The silence that stretches between us is deafening.

My gaze flits to Azrael, but I ask Lucifer, "Which he?"

But my husband doesn't answer before he crosses the space in three quick strides and wrenches the door open, plowing through.

It doesn't swing open so much as unravel.

Azrael ushers me through a moment later, following right behind me, and then we're standing on a marble floor that's slick with blood.

Though I have no idea whose.

The Vestibule is gone. No more flickering gray. No more whispers. Just a wide, cathedral-like chamber, lit by light that doesn't seem to have a source. The air hums with something ancient and wrong.

A familiar form lies on the floor nearby.

Jax!

My heart races.

She's crumpled beneath one of the high arches, her hands bound and chained by some filament-like material that glows blue. Her face is bruised, one cheekbone swollen and split, but she's breathing, barely, and I move to—

Azrael grabs my wrist. "Wait."

His voice is so tight it freezes me.

Because Jax isn't alone.

Across from her, standing like the messiah he thinks he is, is Michael.

I shouldn't be shocked by the sight of him. "Where's Lilith?"

Michael tsks. "Not exactly the friendliest way to greet your future brother-in-law, is it?"

He's holding the Holy Lance, twirling it in his hands. Something deep in me recoils.

That thing isn't just celestial. It's final.

I try not to consider Azrael's connection to it.

Michael glances down to where my gaze leads, like he sees my fear and he's amused by it. "Mother bowed out for this. She's on her hunt for Father."

"Azrael, can you—"

"On it."

Like searching the universe for the Goddess of all Creation while also simultaneously standing ready to defend us is no big thing.

"Jumping the gun a little?" Lucifer asks Michael.

My gaze flits to Jax again.

My heart races.

I've never seen her look so sickly. Not even after Ian nearly . . .

"Mother won't have her full power unless we open the fourth seal for you, and why would we do that?" Lucifer says, showing our full hand.

Michael's already onto our plan, so I guess what's the point of keeping up the pretense any longer? I trust Lucifer's judgment.

He's a brilliant strategist.

And he hates Michael more than anyone.

He'll do whatever it takes to win this.

Michael chuckles. "And what do you think this is, brother? Teatime? I wasn't about to let you turn any more of my army against me." He shoots a resentful look in Lucifer's direction, then faces me. "But unfortunately, I still need you."

"I'm not opening any more seals, and neither are the other Originals. Not if I can help it."

Especially if there's no longer the benefit of getting more of Lucifer's old army on our side.

Michael smirks. "Oh, but I think you are."

"And what'll you do when Mother destroys Him before your little apocalypse can even truly begin? Before He has a chance to return?" Lucifer asks.

Michael laughs like the question amuses him. "You truly think Mother will be able to find Father? To best Him?"

Lucifer shakes his head. "You underestimate her. You always have."

Azrael steps forward. "Let her go, Mikey." He nods toward Jax. "You want the fourth seal open? Let her go, and we'll consider it."

Michael scowls like Azrael's personally disappointed him. "You were a great fuck, Azrael. We could've been good together. Too bad you've always been such a lovestruck fool for him." Michael clicks his tongue and gestures to Lucifer. "And you're not in a position to make any demands this time." He spins the lance once, almost lazily.

The gesture makes my stomach twist.

Even Jax winces in her sleep, like the weapon hums at a frequency none of us can stomach.

I drop down by her side, no longer heeding Azrael's warning. "Shhh, it's okay," I whisper to her, running a soothing hand over her hair.

I'm going to do whatever it takes to get her out of here.

"She's human. She's no threat to you, and if Lilith's already used her for her prophecy, to find God, she's no longer valuable to you. Let her go."

Michael's smile is terrifying in how gentle it is. "Oh, but she *is* valuable. Because she matters to you."

A sour taste coats the inside of my mouth.

I don't like where this is heading.

My fists clench. "What do you want?"

Michael tilts his head. "The same thing you want, Charlotte. For our Father to return, and for His broken toys to stop trying to put themselves back together." He casts a glare toward Lucifer and steps down from the dais. "You're going to open the next seal for me."

"We've already been through this. I'm not going to—"

Azrael shifts. I can feel his tension, see the way his hand hovers near his blade. It's not just the threat of the lance. It's something else.

Something's wrong.

"Charlotte, don't move," Lucifer orders.

I can tell from the tone of his voice that if there were ever a time to listen, this is it.

When Lucifer speaks, his voice is low and dangerous, like he's already connected the dots. "This place—this isn't part of the Vestibule."

Michael's smile widens. "No. This is something older."

My adrenaline spikes. "Older than what?"

"Older than doors. Older than choice." Michael gestures wide, and the walls seem to pulse like they're breathing. "You didn't choose this door," he says softly. "It chose you."

And behind him, something stirs in the dark.

A shape. A *presence*.

Watching.

Waiting.

My heart races.

Oh fuck.

CHAPTER FIFTY-TWO

Charlotte

"Here's what's going to happen, Charlotte," Michael continues, advancing toward me. "You're going to open the next seal for me, and it's up to *you* whether or not I let your friend go."

My mouth hardens into a thin line. "Of course you're going to let her go. Otherwise, I'm not going to—"

"Just listen to him, Charlotte," Lucifer says, nodding to whatever's on the other side of the darkness. "You don't want to make him angry."

Him.

I have a sneaking suspicion he isn't talking about Michael.

I swallow. "What do I have to do? Stop another flood? Wave off another plague of locusts? Or fight whatever this—"

"Don't insult it," Azrael warns.

Act as if it isn't there, Lucifer sends down the line between us.

But what is—

Not now, *Charlotte.* He gives the barest shake of his head.

My stomach clenches.

What could possibly be in that darkness that he . . . ?

I don't allow the thought to continue. I can't let my panic get the better of me.

I need to stay focused.

Michael shakes his head, grinning like whatever he has up his sleeve for the seal, this time it's far better. "No," he says. "All you have to do is choose."

"Choose?"

My gaze darts between Lucifer and Azrael.

The threat of what'll happen if I don't is clear.

Michael and the lance.

Or whatever that thing is.

I don't want to come face-to-face with one of . . . God's failures.

My palms slicken.

The thought alone is the thing of nightmares.

Michael waves a hand, seemingly unconcerned with the beast at his back, and suddenly there's a scroll in his hand and two goblets sit on a small table beside him. I have a feeling neither of them contains anything I'd want to drink.

"Pick your poison, Charlotte," he says, popping the scroll open unceremoniously. "One grants you absolution. The other, clarity. But neither spares you the truth."

Pick your poison.

The words are all too similar to what Azrael said to me outside my father's torture chamber only a few short hours ago. But it feels like a lifetime.

"I don't—"

"Come on now, Char. Even Judas took the cup," Michael taunts. "The one on the left saves your friend. The one on the right spares humanity."

My eyes widen. "Spares humanity?"

"From the pain of the fourth seal." His gaze darts to Azrael, and my blood runs cold.

With the fourth seal, Death will be unleashed on the world, and I'm not sure I want to gamble with what that means for humanity. Or what Azrael would be forced to do if I . . .

I glance toward him, and he gives the barest shake of his head.

He still doesn't know. That was part of it. A condition for his freedom.

My gaze falls to the cup on the right.

But if I drink it, doesn't that mean Jax dies?

"Which one of the Originals is this seal for?" I ask, wishing we'd brought along Lucifer's siblings. That they hadn't turncoated on me the moment the Righteous posed a threat to them. It's probably the only time in my immortal life I'll *ever* think that.

Michael lifts a brow. "You can't tell?"

"Greed," Lucifer mutters.

Greed.

My eyes widen.

Meaning to open the seal, I *have* to choose to help the world, instead of save my—

"But for you, it'll open either way," Michael clarifies. "The choice is yours."

I look to Jax.

She's still barely conscious, but I can see her eyelids flickering, and the words she said to me during that prophecy come rushing back to me.

It's okay. Just let it happen.

Is this what she meant? To let God's plan unfold?

She couldn't have possibly meant that she was okay with dying.

"It should be an easy choice for someone as righteous as you, shouldn't it, Charlotte?" Michael taunts. "Save the one you love or save countless others?"

My heart pounds.

And then I look toward Lucifer and realize . . .

"I'm sorry," I say, a lump of remorse forming inside my throat. "I would've done the same thing if I were you in your position, and had I known, I wouldn't have chosen any differently."

I would've let him burn the world down for me. For us.

Lucifer's chest puffs out, and the hellfire in his eyes blazes.

He's been willing to admit to himself all along what I refused to see.

He wouldn't just burn the world for me.

We'd burn it *all* down for each other.

Lies of omission are still lies, but they're easier to forgive, it seems.

And he'd never wish that decision on me. Not within a thousand lifetimes.

But this *is* my decision.

My choice.

I turn back to the cups.

I don't want to help Michael any more than I have to, and with none of the other angels here, opening the seal for him doesn't benefit us. But if I don't—

That thing in the dark stirs.

It's okay. Just let it happen.

I glance at Azrael. "If I choose her, will you be able to—"

"I don't know, baby girl," he says, and the tormented expression on his face nearly destroys me.

This is what it means to love Death.

To not fear uncertainty.

My gaze falls to Jax again.

That had to be what she meant. That Azrael would be able to save her. I have to trust in what she told me. In her prophecy. That's the only option.

I can't condemn countless people to death. Even to save my friend.

Even if the choice doesn't feel easy.

Slowly, I step forward, taking the cup on the right into my hands. I look toward her, her eyes now open slightly.

"It's okay," she rasps. "Let it happen."

And that seals my fate.

I lift the cup to my lips and drink deep, draining it of the communion wine I find there.

When I'm finished, I swipe the back of my hand over my lips, facing Michael as I feel more than sense the fourth seal cracking. "Are you going to let us go now?"

My attention flits to where that monster waits in the dark.

Michael laughs and tips his chin toward the scroll he's holding like it's his instruction manual. "Father didn't say anything about letting you go, now did He?"

He snaps his fingers, and then he's gone.

The beast in the dark stirs.

And there's nothing I can do but back away slowly.

CHAPTER FIFTY-THREE

Lucifer

I fucking hate my brother and everything that self-righteous bastard stands for. Mother and I are going to have words over this. But I don't have time to consider what I might do once I get hold of him.

That *thing* within the darkness moves, coming to its feet.

Only a handful of meters away from my bride.

"Charlotte, darling," I say, struggling to keep my voice even as I inch closer to her. Azrael has his blade well in hand, following my lead. "Keep your eyes on the floor and retreat slowly. Do you understand?"

"Yes, sir," she whispers, starting to inch toward me.

As I've told her dozens of times before, she may be immortal, but that does not mean there is nothing within my Mother's chaotic universe or my Father's divine order that can pose a threat to her.

It simply means that when it does happen, it will be a lot more dramatic.

Charlotte does exactly as I instruct her, knowing better than to defy me at a moment like this. She's nearly in the clear, nearly within my reach, but then her friend enters her line of vision, the girl rasping for her last breath.

"Jax!" My wife drops to her knees.

Chaos erupts inside the chamber.

Just as Azrael and I lunge for her and her friend, the creature bursts forth from the dark, its massive jaws roaring.

I'm going to be punishing her for this for the rest of eternity, unfortunately.

If any of us bloody survive this.

Her self-preservation skills are seriously lacking.

When we both come out of the dive, I've got hold of her friend behind one pillar and Azrael has Charlotte behind the other.

The creature prowls about in the darkened chamber, searching for us stupidly.

"What the hell is that?!" Charlotte shrieks.

"It's a Living Creature." Azrael hushes her.

The beast roars, searching for where we might have gone, but it relies on sight and smell alone. It has thousands of eyes, but it cannot hear us.

"Or one of my Father's early attempts, I'd say."

"*That's* what's guarding the pearly gates?"

She says it as if she's just fully come to understand the kind of celestial deals she's been making. Particularly the one she'll soon have to settle with Sloth.

"And yet you've been telling me to let you make your own choices," I snark back.

"I've changed my mind, sir," she cries, hearing that thing growling in the dark as it scuffles about. "You're in charge now, I promise."

I roll my eyes. "Day late, dollar short, darling."

The creature is roaming, but since it cannot see us, it's uncertain what to do.

It's only a matter of time before it sniffs us out.

"Would the both of you shut up, so I can focus?" Azrael growls. Trying to get a line of sight on where it might be, he leans around the corner.

I twist, peering around the pillar as it steps into the faint light, and I get a proper look at it. It's all wings and eyes and muscle, stitched together by divine ego and whatever nightmares my Father might've had lying about at the time.

Four faces curl around one skull—lion, man, eagle, ox—like my Father couldn't decide what the fuck He wanted it to be when it grew up, so He just said "yes" and decided to be done with everything. There are too many wings, eyes everywhere, and none of them blink, giving us no reprieve. The beast doesn't breathe so much as radiate judgment, the kind that gets cities leveled and souls bartered, but its four maws promise divine retribution.

How the fuck my brother managed to tame it is beyond me.

"On the left. Near the opening of the antechamber," I whisper to Azrael.

He nods. "On the count of three, I want you both to run for the door."

My eyes narrow. "What are you going to—"

"Just fucking *trust* me for once in your goddamn existence," he snarls. "I've never done anything without your best interest at heart."

He means more than this moment—the blade. The lance, the one he used against me.

"One."

His deal with my Father. How he betrayed me at Gethsemane. Didn't warn me about His plans to sacrifice the Nazarene, how I was to be locked away.

"Two."

My grip on Charlotte's friend tightens. And now, how he's fallen in love with *my* woman. Ruined whatever chance I might've had to keep her safe from herself.

Though it seems as if she might be coming around at any rate.

For a moment, I fear I might have misjudged him.

But then my gaze snags upon Charlotte's friend lying in my arms, desperately grasping to the last breaths of her life. Her death is going to destroy Charlotte.

My jaw tightens.

I know then without a doubt that I am not ready to forgive him just yet.

"Three!"

I lunge for the door, Charlotte's friend clutched in my arms. The weight of her doesn't slow me, no matter what that blasted door might say.

Because if she dies, the possibility of me regaining my powers, my immortality, all that I am, also dies.

And that is an outcome I refuse to live with, frankly.

CHAPTER FIFTY-FOUR

Azrael

I split myself in two, becoming noncorporeal and then reforming on the spot in front of the beast, just as Charlotte starts to—

"Run!" I shout, distracting the Creature.

Charlotte's eyes are wide in fear like she's considering coming after me, but then she and my ex barrel toward the door labeled **YOU CHOSE THIS**.

I don't want to consider what that might mean, and I'm too busy to do anything but exist in the moment right now anyway.

Eyes upon eyes stare down at me.

Fucking thousands of them.

"Come at me, motherfucker," I growl to the beast, and it lunges.

I become Nothing again, reforming a second later and plunging one of my blades into its side. It rears up on its hind legs, its four jagged maws screeching. The raw force of it rattles my bones, the echo vibrating through the cathedral ceiling so hard that parts of it start to fall. Like its cry can shake creation at its seams.

But that's all the distraction I need.

I'm through the door and slamming it shut on the other side a moment later.

The choice we've made begins to unravel it, the door slowly disappearing.

We're back in the Vestibule again.

"Do you think it can come through?" Charlotte nods toward the door shape as it slowly fades away.

"I don't know." And I don't want to stick around long enough to find out.

My eyes fall to Charlotte's friend, where Lucifer's now knelt on the floor, laying her out in front of him. I feel that familiar tug inside me, which must mean . . .

Charlotte exchanges a horrified glance with me, and I know she must feel it too.

"No," she whispers. "No, she can't . . ."

Time seems to slow to a crawl as Charlotte runs to her friend. She falls to her knees in front of her, pulling the other woman into her arms. The cry that rakes through her body nearly rends me in two, my worst nightmare come to fruition.

"Azrael!" I vaguely hear her screaming, her voice like a distant echo. "Azrael, you have to—"

"He won't," Lucifer says.

Time seems to collapse in on itself again, catching up to normal speed.

"He won't." Lucifer faces me, his jaw set and a bitter look in his eye. "Will you?"

I feel the resentment in his words like a knife in my chest.

Know without a doubt what this is going to be.

The end of her and me.

"Because of the deal you made with God? Because of the seal?" Charlotte glances desperately toward me. "But you can break it, can't you? You can—"

"He won't, Charlotte," Lucifer repeats, the sharp hurt in his eyes nearly driving me to my knees. "You accused *me* of wanting to play games with her heart? But you still haven't told her, have you?"

He's right.

I didn't.

I avoided it.

Like a coward.

Because I knew what the truth would lead to.

Because it already led there once before.

"Tell me what? Azrael, what didn't you—"

Lucifer's voice turns cold, his expression sour. "Ask him about the promise he made with my Father, darling."

"Your Father?" Charlotte looks so lost, so confused, that the sight of her pain feels like its own kind of death to me.

The death of everything she thought I was previously.

She turns to me. "What is he talking about, Azrael? What have you—"

"I made a promise to God." I swallow. "That I would . . . be there, at the ending."

"That you would . . ." Charlotte's voice trails off as she glances between her friend and Lucifer. "But she said . . . she said everything was going to be okay. In her prophecy. She said you'd be able to save her. I don't understand why you—"

"He's known how this would end from the very beginning," Lucifer says. "Haven't you, Azrael? But you were bound by His word to let it happen."

"To let it happen," Charlotte repeats, like the words hold some greater meaning for her, her features contorting as she realizes what he . . .

"You knew she would die?" She looks down at her friend. The prophet's still breathing, but just barely. "You knew she would die and yet you . . ."

I shake my head. "I didn't know it would be her for certain, but I—"

"But a prophet all the same," Lucifer suggests, his voice taking on a hard edge. "You knew the broad strokes of bloody all of it. Of this. Of my Father's plans. Whether Charlotte and I live or die in the end. It doesn't take a genius to infer the prophet who would die would be her"—he nods toward Jax—"which means you suspected it right from when you put the blade into play, didn't you? Just like you knew He was going to lock me away, knew He was going to make a monster out of me, take my powers away, and yet you said *nothing*, whispered promises of loyalty to me while the whole time you were stabbing me in the back."

"I did it for you," I growl, the anger and hurt at how he's refused to *trust* me for the last several millennia shaking me to my core. "I did it for you, even if you still can't see it yet."

I turn toward Charlotte.

But the way she looks at me then is everything I feared.

A mix of horror, hurt, and a deep understanding.

An understanding of what it means to love me.

The end of all things.

And regret.

The regret that inevitably comes anytime someone gets too close to me.

Because I'm more than just the unknown they fear.

I'm the reason this ends the way it always had to.

"I trusted you," she whispers. "I trusted you, and you lied to me."

"I couldn't tell you how it ends even if I wanted to, Charlotte. Not without changing His plans. And even if I could, it wouldn't have made a—"

"Why?" she breathes, the tears falling down her face cutting into me like knives.

"Because you already made your choice back when I first held you in Grand Central." I nod toward her collar. "So, I never really had a chance to begin with."

CHAPTER FIFTY-FIVE

Charlotte

I stare up at Azrael, fully understanding what was missing from every interaction, every memory I saw between him and Lucifer.

The knowledge that he was never truly on our side to begin with.

Of how his promise to God pitted him against me, against Lucifer.

And the fact that Lucifer had been my choice, right from the start.

"Why?" I ask, trying to understand what would cause him to hurt us both like this, what could possibly cause him to stay loyal to God throughout all this, choose his promise over me, over Lucifer. "Why would you—"

"If I could tell you, I would, Charlotte."

But he can't.

He swore himself to secrecy. In devotion to the Creator.

A choice he refuses to unmake.

He still believes that the cause he stands for, whatever it is, is more important than me. Than Lucifer.

I stare down at my friend.

Than her.

The tears clouding my eyes start to fall like raindrops onto her face.

"You're just like them," I whisper to him. "You're just like them."

When I glance up, Azrael doesn't seem to understand what I mean.

"The Righteous."

He pales slightly.

He knows how this ends.

Whether I live or die.

Whether we defeat Michael. Stop Lilith.

And whether Lucifer ever gets to be free.

From the pain, from what his fall cost him.

"I'm sorry," I mutter to Jax, swiping one of my tears from where it's fallen onto her cheek, my voice breaking. "I should've come sooner."

I don't know that it would have made any difference, not with what Michael and the Righteous and Lilith had planned, but I still wish things could be different.

That I could save her.

Jax's hand shakes as she tries to point toward the ceiling, but then it drops again. "He wept when He showed me this moment," she whispers, staring off, unfocused, into the distance as though she's seeing past the dark ceiling overhead and into the starry night sky. "He wept, but He never said I could change it."

God, she means.

Something inside me finally breaks clean through.

My hope. My humanity. My faith.

I don't know what.

All I know is that I'll do whatever it takes for this to never happen again.

For Him to sacrifice someone I love in the name of His fucked-up plan.

Me included.

Lucifer was right.

I'm going to live for me.

Morality be damned.

I hold her close, cradling her in my arms.

"Do you remember when you took me to my first party on the Lower East Side?" I ask, struggling to keep my voice steady, to comfort her in the only way I can. "The one where I kept tripping over my own two feet?"

She smiles up at the ceiling but doesn't look at me.

"Do you remember what you said when we ducked out onto the balcony? When I told you that I didn't feel like the city was ever going to be my home?"

She shakes her head.

"You told me that home isn't a place. It's the people who see you when you can't see yourself."

"I remember." A shallow breath escapes her. "Maybe that's why He was crying."

My voice catches, and a strange stillness settles over her face, like a kind of peace.

"I love you." I drop my head onto hers, our foreheads touching, her skin already cooler than it should be. "You're my home. My best friend. You always have been. Please don't leave me."

Her chest stutters.

Once.

Then stills.

I hold her tight as she gradually grows colder in my arms. Until I feel the last shudder of her breath as she leaves me.

When she's finally gone, with trembling hands, I brush her eyes closed, shaking as I lift my head.

Azrael doesn't appear to take any enjoyment in this, at least.

He just watches. Quiet. Unmoving.

And does nothing.

Just like Him.

The thought sickens me.

He crouches in front of me sometime later, and reluctantly I pass her to him, unable to even look at him as he cradles her in his arms. I can only grieve one thing at a time, currently.

Lucifer helps me to my feet, pulling me into him and tucking me into his chest as I turn my back on Death, on my friend, on everything I thought we could be.

"Please," I whisper to my devil. "Please just take me home."

Even if there's nothing left of it.

CHAPTER FIFTY-SIX

Charlotte

It feels strange being alone like this. Just me and Lucifer.

Hollow in a way I don't have words for.

I don't know how I know Azrael isn't following us, that he's no longer watching.

I just do.

When we finally reach the Whispering Gallery, the In-Between having clearly decided it's taken enough from us, it's early morning.

I can tell from the commuters. The people bustling about the city. They don't pay us any mind. The foot traffic moves around us, people rushing past with coffee cups and unread text messages and lives they still get to live. Like they don't even notice that something essential's been ripped away from me. That she died.

That he's gone.

And the world didn't even pause.

The **NO ACCESS** door closes behind us, and soon enough, it's gone too. I glance at the adjacent wall, but it's blocked by a group of well-meaning tourists who are testing the acoustics and taking selfies, so I don't know if the inscription is still there.

It doesn't matter, I guess.

Lucifer puts his arm around me, slowly leading me toward the exit before the tourists or anyone else can spot us. He doesn't say anything, but I know he feels it.

The loss, the grief I'm feeling.

If he could've spared me from it, he would've done whatever it took to save her for me.

Without a doubt.

But Azrael . . .

I shake my head.

No.

No, this can't be about morality for him either. I know him better than that.

So, what *is* it about?

I don't have time to fully let myself process that question before we climb the staircase together, entering the main rotunda. "I'm sorry about your powers," I hear myself saying.

That's another thing that was lost in all this too.

Our one last hope for saving humanity.

And if the world ends before Lucifer regains his immortality, then he'll . . .

"There'll be no more dying today." Lucifer pulls me close. "Naturally, I have a backup plan."

I gaze up at him, and he pauses, taking hold of my hands.

"Do you . . . ?" He hesitates. "Do you still love him, little dove?"

Azrael, he means.

I nod.

I think that's the worst part of all this.

That I do.

That I have so much love for him, for Jax, and now there's nowhere for it to go.

I think that might be all that grief is.

Love with no place to go.

"Do you really have a backup plan?" I ask. The hope I feel at that thought is tenuous, fractured even, but I can't help but notice that we're standing in nearly the same spot where this all started.

In the same spot where I chose to be his.

As though fate led us here.

I close my eyes for a moment.

Now that I know everything, I know I'd still make the same choice.

Even if all our options feel shitty currently.

But I remember how it felt then.

The hope I had for something better.

Even if my heart aches for my friend, my home.

The other celestial I wish I could share this with.

But how can we find a way back to each other after all this?

I don't know the answer to that, but there's got to be a way. There's got to be.

Because if there's one thing loving the devil has taught me, it's that love finds a way.

No matter how dark and twisted.

Lucifer doesn't say anything, but he smiles a little, like he knows what I'm thinking, even if I haven't put it into words yet, and I know that, regardless of what happens, he and I are going to make it another day. He's been my choice since the very beginning.

The best one I ever made.

"So, what's the next step, sir?" I lean onto my toes and kiss him, trusting him to take the lead. His choice *is* my choice, and that's all that matters.

"Our way, little dove," he says. "The way will always be ours."

I smile then, even though it's hard, even though it hurts, because I know without a doubt that this is one promise he's going to keep.

He has from the start. In every change he's made for me.

In every dark word he's whispered.

Even if it means that the devil is now in love with humanity's guardian angel.

Because that's the one key similarity between him and me.

That we'll both love each other ferociously, viciously, destructively, until the end of time.

And God help whatever gets in our way.

He leans down and kisses me, softly, gently, before he leads us both out of the building. But still, I wonder if it's enough.

If love is enough to fill the emptiness I'm feeling.

Or if all we'll have left at the end is the ruins.

And the ashes of a world we've burned together.

CHAPTER FIFTY-SEVEN

Charlotte

Lucifer calls Dagon to pick us up in the Town Car outside Grand Central, because apparently, I'm in "no condition" to walk the several blocks down to Seventh. My limbs feel so heavy with grief and fatigue that I don't have the energy to argue with him. I don't want to risk an unwanted encounter with the media right now anyway. I'm in no state.

It's one thing for Azrael to have hurt me.

It's another for him to have hurt her. Hurt *him* again.

I'm not certain I'll ever be able to forgive him.

We're inside the sanctuary, waiting for Father Brown to see us as he prepares for his first morning service, when for what must be the fifth time, I ask, "Are you *sure* Father Brown is a prophet?"

"I'm not certain, but it's likely."

I rub my forehead. "And you've been seeing him?"

"Yes, darling."

"And he took your confession, before you . . ." My voice trails off.

"Why is *that* the part that's so bloody hard to believe? I wasn't always the devil, you know." Lucifer sits down in the pew next to me.

"I know. Believe me." I bite my lip apprehensively. "Did you know initially that saving me, giving me God's redemption, would allow the seals to be opened?"

"No." He shakes his head. "But if I had, it wouldn't have mattered, darling. There's nothing I wouldn't do for you."

My heart races. "There's just a few things on my mind, that's all."

I recount to him my theories, all the inconsistencies I've been thinking about lately. How our connection has been growing stronger, how he's the only one of his siblings who lost his power when his seal opened, how saving me changed, well, everything.

"I just can't help but think there's something we're missing in all this."

"And because of Azrael?" he asks, the hellfire in his eyes gleaming.

My face falls.

I glance down at my hands. "I want there to be a reason that explains why he did this to us, I guess."

Why he didn't choose Lucifer and me.

We both fall silent for a beat.

"What you said in the scene was true, wasn't it? That you never intended to be *only* mine?"

I look toward him then, eyes watering. "I want to be yours. I do. But I also want to be . . ." I lower my head. "Does that make me a bad wife? That I . . . love someone other than you?"

Lucifer sighs, leaning forward. "No, darling. I don't think it does."

His eyes are so full of grief, of uncertainty and hurt, that I don't think I realized how much this was tearing him up inside. "Is there something he gives you?" He ducks his chin, staring intently at a spot on the floor. "Something that I . . . can't?"

When he does finally look at me again, the longing in his expression is so raw, I can't help but ache for him. "Is that what you've thought, what you've been worried about this whole time?"

He nods slightly, and I can't help but want to throw myself into him. I wrap my arms around his neck, kissing him for all he's worth. It's pain and shared sorrow and longing all in one, but when I pull back, I hold his face in my hands. "No," I whisper against his lips, shaking my head. "No. It's not about that. It never was."

"And yet you still—"

"Want him?" I hang my head. "Don't you?" I give him a knowing smile.

He huffs, like he still can't see what it is I'm seeing, or at least he still refuses to admit it. That for better or worse, Azrael is a sin that belongs to us both.

"I don't love you in spite of your sins, Charlotte. I love you *for* them."

"And Azrael?"

His expression hardens. "His sins are a bit different."

"Are they?" I stare up at the stained glass image overhead. The image of Christ ascending. "Or are they just something neither of us wants to see?"

Lucifer arches a brow.

I inhale an unsteady breath, finally confessing what I've been thinking. "At first, I thought I cared for Azrael because of the choice he offered me, but now I realize it was never really about that. You were already my choice. You were *always* my choice." I let out a long sigh. "But I think the reason we've both been so reluctant to trust Azrael, to treat him like an equal partner in the way he deserves, is because, well, Death shows us parts of ourselves that we don't want to see."

Lucifer releases a slow exhale, his gaze holding steady on me. "And what's that, darling?"

I swallow. "Your anger with God, with yourself, your desire to hurt Him how He hurt you. How you've allowed your pride to get in the way of your vulnerability. And the . . . shame I know you still feel underneath all that. The regret." I hesitate. "You don't need to forgive Him, Lucifer, but I think you might need to forgive yourself."

Lucifer's breath becomes shallow, his eyes widening slightly like he's struggling to hold my gaze, and then he glances away.

The vulnerability I see in him then is frightening to me.

I'm not sure if I'll be strong enough to hold him together if he breaks.

Not when he's the one I've always counted on to hold me.

But Azrael . . .

"And you, little dove?" He wets his lips, his throat writhing. "What does Death force you to see?"

I inhale, struggling to admit my sins out loud. "That there are limits to my faith. That there are more similarities between you and me than I was ready to see, but that's not a bad thing. That sometimes I lose myself in you, and also . . ." I swallow. "That there are some sacrifices I'm not willing to make."

The pride, the knowing grin he gives me, makes me smile in spite of the pain. He taught me that.

How to respect myself.

To value my own desires. My own wants and needs.

I won't allow my trauma to make me abandon myself anymore.

He pulls me into his arms and kisses me deeply, our tongues mingling like he's reminding me of all I'm worth. I only wish he could see the same for himself.

That he deserves God's forgiveness just as much as me.

When we break apart a short while later, I'm dizzy and breathless, and feeling more than a little lost in him, but there's still an underlying feeling of grief, of sadness that hangs over me. It'll be there for a long time, I'm certain.

I recount to him what I saw in Jax's prophecy. What I thought it meant.

My insides knot.

"It's my fault she's dead," I whisper.

Lucifer scoffs, taking my chin between his fingers. "Did you *want* to open the fourth seal, little dove, or did my brother?"

"You know what I mean." I hang my head. "I'm still sorry for it."

"So am I."

We sit in silence for a few moments, my head resting on his shoulder.

"You understand why I might have been a bit salty when I found out Azrael put the Holy Lance into play?" He strokes my hair gently.

I nod. "I figured you would be."

"You knew?"

Another nod. "I already forgave him for it."

I recount all that's happened between Azrael and me, all we've shared. He deserves to know, I think.

"And what about this? Your friend? Will you forgive him for that?"

I shake my head, still unsure how to answer that or about how to tell him what sparked me putting my collar back on to begin with. I shift slightly in his lap, and his hand steadies me instinctively, his touch warm through the fabric of my dress.

His body surrounds mine, and I wonder if he can feel it too. The quiet ache in my belly that lets me know I'm his.

My hand flits to my collar. "I'm not certain it matters anymore."

We're both unable to say anything else as Father Brown leans into the sanctuary. "I'll be with you both in a moment."

He disappears, and I stare after him. "I don't understand why you waited."

One of Lucifer's brows ticks upward.

"If Father Brown *is* a prophet, why not just use him right when you knew? Forget all about . . ." I stumble over Jax's name. It feels like if I say it out loud, if I speak it, she'll really be gone.

"I'd never ignore something that matters to you, darling. We're in this together. Even if it appears I haven't always acted that way."

"And if Father Brown isn't a prophet? If there's no other way to stop your family than . . . sacrificing myself?"

Rebalancing the cosmic paradox that started all this in the first place.

Cutting the seals off at the root.

Lucifer shakes his head. "I won't live without you."

"Neither will I." I take his hand. "Would you really choose to die alongside me? For humanity?"

"For humanity, no." He cups my cheek. "But for you, I'd do anything, Charlotte."

My hands start trembling. "And if it comes to that?"

Lucifer's expression turns grave. "Then we do what I've always done from the start, little dove." He squeezes my hand. "We give my family hell, and we go down fighting."

"Together." I smile at him, though there's a bit of grief in it. I'd rather spend what little's left of eternity in Hell with him before it all comes to an end than imagine any immortal life without him. I glance up at the image of Christ overhead. "Do you want to get married?"

Lucifer blinks. "Pardon?"

"Do you want to get married? Right now?" I nod toward the altar. "We can still have the wedding, of course, since it's already in the works. Humanity might need all the pomp and circumstance to distract them from the world burning, and if we're going to go down fighting, our wedding would make a great last stand, to give Michael hell, to wave a big middle finger at your Father, but considering all the press there'll be, I thought you might want to . . ."

"Of course, little dove." He chuckles. "I thought you'd never ask."

The ceremony is private and fast, and I force Lucifer to make a pretty obscene donation to Father Brown and his congregation, but that doesn't lessen the gravity of the moment.

Father Brown's voice is steady as he leads us through the vows, though I barely hear him over the pounding of my own heart.

But Lucifer's hand never leaves mine, his thumb brushing over my knuckles, calm, certain, like he's branding me with his touch.

When he says "I do," his eyes burn so fiercely into mine I almost forget the world outside these walls is ending.

When I repeat the words, I don't falter.

I feel confident in this decision.

It's the one I was always going to make from the start.

Even if the current circumstances are filled with uncertainty.

When it's over, we wait in the sanctuary alone for Father Brown to retrieve extra copies of the paperwork.

My eyes flit toward the confessional. "You know, I've always wanted to—"

Lucifer hauls me up by my collar and into his arms. "No need to say another word, darling."

The love he makes to me then is heated and quick, fueled by our shared grief of the end we both fear is coming.

When we both stumble out of the confessional, despite my grief, I feel almost . . . happy.

Peaceful.

He tugs me into his arms, pressing me against the outside of the confessional, until I'm once again heated and panting, aching for him, but then I glance over his shoulder, my eyes going wide as I yank him back inside immediately.

"Lucifer," I whisper, hurriedly closing the door.

He drops down onto the confessional bench, pulling me into his lap. "Already ready for another round, darling?" He nips at my ear.

"No," I hiss, a hint of panic shooting through me. "No, my father's congregation is here."

The Righteous? he says through our connection.

I nod, not wanting to speak.

I don't want to draw any attention to the fact that we're here, not now that they've declared open war against us. Especially since Lucifer is still mortal.

A sudden sense of panic overtakes me.

It was bad enough losing Jax, but I can't even consider what I'd do if, before all this is said and done, I were to lose . . .

No. I shake my head.

No, I can't allow myself to go down that road.

Not without losing my focus completely.

What are they even doing *here?* I think, more to myself than anything.

But I'm not exactly great about not broadcasting my thoughts loud and clear to Lucifer, so he still answers.

Father Brown, I presume.

We both exchange a meaningful look.

If the Righteous suspect he's a prophet, and if they've been following me and Lucifer, then they . . .

The image of that flyer at the pier comes back to me.

The school photo of Lily Parker.

The fact that they've been threatening anyone who stands in their way. Anyone who supports us.

My eyes go wide.

If Father Brown dies . . .

Lucifer gives a stiff nod, his expression suddenly grave.

This is our last chance.

Or we both die, together.

And I've had enough death for today.

I place a finger to my lips, even though I'm certain I don't have to tell Lucifer. I open the door to the confessional just wide enough to see Father Brown and a member of my father's old congregation talking.

John Whitaker.

He's a bit older than Mark was. Nearing middle age. With a bit of paunch.

By all appearances, he's nonthreatening. A middle-aged white guy. Like most American evangelicals.

But I still remember how he'd clap Mark on the back every time I flinched when he moved too quickly and say, "*A firm hand makes a godly wife.*"

Then glance at me like he was checking to see if the lesson had stuck.

Or how his hand would linger on my shoulder just a little too long as he smiled.

Always smiling. Just enough to make me question if the subtle threat I perceived in it was even really happening.

I bet he and so many others from my old life wonder what drove me to Lucifer.

I won't allow what they did to me to control me anymore.

I slip the confessional door back closed, pressing myself against it.

They're just talking. Maybe it's just a casual visit?

Lucifer's eyes narrow, and I don't have to hear him inside my mind to know what he's thinking.

I can fight.

No, he says. *And that's final.* He touches my collar, reminding me of who exactly is in charge. *After what happened today, you're in no mental state to. Your life is not the only thing I would burn this world to protect, little dove. I'm unhinged for you.*

He traces a finger down my collar to between my breasts, stopping just above my heart.

And I shiver.

Then what do we do, sir? I nod toward the door. *We can't just hide here. They could kill you. I can get you to—*

Go get my sister, he orders. *She still owes you a favor, and you no longer need it for her seal. She won't turn you away.*

And what are you going to do if they . . . ?

He unbuttons his suit coat and reaches inside his shoulder holster, removing one of the celestial blades he carries. *I have a plan, obviously.*

CHAPTER FIFTY-EIGHT

Lucifer

The moment my wife is safely distracted by the task I have given her, I slip from the confessional, my blade at the ready. Immortal or not, I would never allow her to face off against her father's soldiers like this. She's already freed herself from them, no need to revisit old wounds, and considering her former congregation have been working alongside my brother for some time now, there's no telling the true threat they pose.

If I'm going to die on my wedding day, it's not about to be in some bloody confessional in a church near Broadway.

I ease around the confessional's edge, pressing myself against the far side where I'm unlikely to be seen. It's not exactly difficult to remain stealthy to human ears.

Even when I am not in my top form.

I will destroy every one of the Righteous and feast upon their entrails before I allow them to steal my last chance to regain my power.

My last chance at immortal life with Charlotte.

There are other prophets, other avenues, to be certain, but none I'm likely to locate before my goddamn family do what they always do and cock it all up.

My wife won't be forced into relocating to another universe.

With or without me.

I grip my blade, holding it at the ready as I slip toward the far side of the room. Father Brown and his companion are on the other side of the sanctuary now, still talking, but the menace is facing away from me.

"You don't understand, Father. He doesn't deserve a pew. He deserves the pit. You'd seat Satan among your flock and call it grace, but all he'll do is poison the well and laugh while your church burns from the inside. Renounce him. Tell us where he is, and no harm will come to you."

"Satan is his brother, actually," Father Brown says, his face giving nothing away when he spots me.

I place a finger to my lips, approaching slowly.

"You don't understand. The serpent is no longer an angel."

Father Brown presses his lips into a fine line. "I think he'd disagree."

His aggressor's voice grows even more hostile. "He's the rot in creation, the whisper in Cain's ear, the thing that watches when you think even God has turned His face away."

I've never had someone flatter me so thoroughly. I cast a smug look toward Father Brown, and he smiles at me. "You don't say?"

"If you won't tell us where he is, won't join us, then I'll have to—"

The cultist reaches for the gun at his back.

I raise my blade, and it's only then that Father Brown notices the celestial knife in my hand. "Sammael, no!"

The congregant spins, his gun lifted.

I gut him in one swift blow, stabbing my blade into his stomach and using the whole of my strength to grip his shoulder and drive it up into his sternum. A pulse of satisfaction runs through me. I see the moment the realization settles in, the moment he realizes his soul is mine. "See you in Hell."

I watch the light fade from his eyes, the last few beats of his heart pulsing. I shove him off the end of my blade, wiping the blood on my suit's pant leg.

Thankfully, black covers everything.

"That was entirely too easy." I stare down at him.

The priest looks down at the man almost regretfully. The brown of his face is slightly ashen, but he's not as horrified as I expected he'd be.

"He could've repented."

I scoff. "Before or *after* he killed you?" I roll my eyes, crouching to check my victim's pockets. No doubt Charlotte will be able to ID him, but that doesn't mean I'll make it easy on the NYPD. Though many of them are already in my pocket.

"You killed him," Father Brown says, like he's confused by it.

"Yes, I believe we've established that."

"To protect *me*? An unarmed priest?"

I shoot him an incredulous look. "Of fucking course, I did. I *need* you. To restore my powers, and I—"

His gaze hardens. "I'm not a prophet, Lucifer."

I huff. "If you're not a prophet, then I'm a monkey's uncle."

"I'm *not* a prophet, Sammael." He holds my gaze, but it's the way he says that old name that gives me pause.

My eyes narrow.

"You're more like your Mother than I ever expected you'd be."

My stomach drops. "Pardon?"

A round of shouts on the far side of the sanctuary follows.

Our unwanted guest wasn't alone, obviously.

Of course, he wasn't.

I stand, quickly ushering Father Brown past the bleeding corpse. "We need to get you out of here. *Now.*"

"But I'm going to be late for morning—"

"Do you want to live or not?" I grip him by the shoulder as we reach the door, and I hear my sister's high-pitched cackle on the far side of the sanctuary.

"Mimi," he says.

She's going to love tearing into those fools.

Though how in the bloody hell he knows the nickname I've called her since we were cherubs, I don't know.

I open the door, shoving Father Brown through, but that's when I see an unmarked car waiting just outside the building.

The window rolls down.

The car moves forward.

The barrel of a semiautomatic emerges.

And Father Brown does the most disgustingly sanctimonious, self-sacrificing thing he could possibly do. He steps in front of me.

"Your redemption isn't as far-fetched as you think it is, Sammael."

And it's only then, from the disappointed look he gives me, that I recognize him for who he is. Without a doubt. The sound of gunfire rings out.

My Father casts me a pained expression as He crumples onto the church steps in front of me. As He uses Himself as a human shield to protect *me*.

Fucking bastard.

And to think, I was certain He couldn't make me hate myself more.

CHAPTER FIFTY-NINE

Azrael

I follow Lilith as closely as I can, determined to put a stop to wherever this leads. I don't know if it'll be enough to redeem me to Charlotte—to show her and Lucifer that every promise I've made, every step I've taken throughout this whole fucking thing, has been for them, for *their* shared life—but it doesn't make a goddamn bit of difference.

I love them. I love both of them.

And they'll know it in the end.

Even if it's the last thing I make them understand.

Lilith pours herself through dimensions like oil over fire. Where she passes, reality frays. Galaxies spiral harder, stars flicker with second thoughts, and the rigid math of the cosmos collectively loosens its collar. She's birth and decay in the same breath, and time skips around her ankles like a frightened child. Seductive. Luminous. Lethal.

She's not destruction. She's unraveling with purpose.

Because she's understood only by what came *before* understanding. Just like I am.

I don't know how I sense there's something wrong, but I know without a doubt that things aren't going according to her plan when I end up down at that damn church on Seventh again before I can even blink. There's another end near. A significant one.

I see Lucifer and Father Brown on the steps first.

The unmarked car second.

The barrel of the gun aiming.

And then I see the priest step in front of Lucifer, just before the gunfire comes loud and hot. Several rounds in quick succession.

From a tactical standpoint, I'm not familiar with human weaponry, but I've reaped enough victims of this kind to know what it means.

To know it's rare for a mortal to survive.

And Lucifer is . . .

Lilith screams as the priest falls. Her fury ripples out like a tear of fabric through the universe, too primal to be grief, but there'll be another time to chase her.

I'm at Lucifer's side a moment later, realizing within seconds that he might be . . .

He clutches his now bleeding shoulder, staring down at the priest.

One of the bullets grazed him, but Father Brown, on the other hand, is . . .

I stare down at the priest's body, expecting to see the soul, the shimmer of what was once there for me to reap. But there's nothing.

Lucifer's white as a sheet.

And that's when I realize that Father Brown must be . . . his Father.

"He died for me," Lucifer says, his gaze unfocused like he isn't seeing anything. But this is a twist even *I* didn't see coming.

I knew that Fucker left out several key details, but *this*?

It only makes the promise He made me seem cruel. Hollow. Like a lie.

Charlotte appears in the doorway alongside Greed a moment later, unscathed, though Greed is covered from head to toe in . . .

"Yours?" I nod to the blood coating her.

Mimi makes a show of licking some of it from her too-plump lips. "What do you think, Reaper?" She grins at me.

Gluttony appears behind them, nearly as drenched in it as she is.

Charlotte's hand flies to her mouth as she notices Father Brown. "Oh, Lucifer."

"He was . . . my Father," Lucifer mutters, voice broken.

Greed seems to catch on before anyone else. "What?" Her gaze falls to the priest, and immediately she drops to her knees. Her hands flit over His prone form, and the small sound that whimpers out of her is all too familiar to me.

Grief. Regret.

"No. No, He can't possibly *die* like this, can He?"

There's something desperate in her voice, like she needs Him to exist to stay anchored to herself.

Charlotte places her hand on the doorframe, struggling to remain steady. "The Righteous . . . killed God?"

"In His earthly form. But He can't die. Not like this."

Lucifer's expression morphs from one of shock to fury. "He does *this* on our goddamn wedding day? This"—he gestures wildly at the corpse—"this self-serving, sanctimonious bullshit?"

"Wedding day?" My breath stops.

She really *has* chosen him then.

Charlotte shoots me a regretful look, and for the span of a heartbeat, it almost softens something sharp in me.

She loves me. Even if she's chosen him.

I know she does.

But that love won't be enough to save us. Not from what's coming.

"I didn't think you were coming back," she whispers.

As if it would've made any difference.

I shake my head, stepping toward her. "I'm not going anywhere, little siren."

I'll guard her and Lucifer for the rest of my days.

She stares up at me, her expression reluctant. There's a hesitation behind her eyes now, like she's waiting for permission from someone else. Her eyes dart to Lucifer. "I'm sorry, Azrael." But she doesn't move closer. Doesn't reach for me.

I grip the back of her neck, noting the way she shivers, holding her steady. But it's not enough. I know that instinctually.

I don't know what changed when she put his collar back on.

Only that I'm no longer a part of it.

"So, Father Brown was . . . God?" Charlotte steps back, giving me an almost wary look. "Did you know?"

"No."

No wonder that bastard knew exactly what to say to make me hope for more.

My face turns to stone.

Charlotte's eyes go cloudy as she stares down at the corpse. She sways slightly, blinking hard, like she's trying not to come apart.

"I followed Lilith here," I say.

"Mother was here too?" Greed sniffles, her eyes narrowing on me.

She's never trusted me. Not after I broke up with Lucifer. Locked her and the other Originals in a cage right along with him.

And for what? Because I was ordered to?

Because I made a promise?

Only for God to fuck all of it and abandon me right near the finish line?

Charlotte's eyes widen. "But if this is where Jax prophesized God would be, and now He's gone, then—"

"Lilith will tear apart the universe searching for Him," I finish.

Charlotte pales. "And with our plan for Michael, with the seals already ruined, Lucifer's power is . . ."

The sentence doesn't need finishing.

Lucifer stands, his tie hanging loose in his fingers, like he forgot what it was for. He stares through the blood on the steps, through the priest's body, through all of us.

He's unraveling.

But it's Charlotte I look to.

She takes a half step toward him, instinctive, gentle. She doesn't touch him, but she doesn't need to. Her body knows where she belongs.

And it's not with me.

I feel it land, sharp and slow.

I was never first. I always knew that.

But I thought maybe I could be last.

Thought maybe I could *matter* enough to change the ending.

Charlotte's gaze flicks briefly toward me like she senses the shift—like some quiet part of her still cares—and for one thin breath, I want to believe that's enough.

But she doesn't move.

Not toward me.

The silence between us is heavier than any scream. I take a step back, trying not to show the way it tears something open in me.

I glance down at the priest's bleeding body.

Why come here? Why toy with us if He planned to leave again?

Greed huffs, suddenly rising to her feet. "Well, this has all been fun, but I'd prefer not to stick around, especially now that my seal doesn't need opening." She casts Charlotte an almost regretful look. "I wasn't too fond of the idea of potentially losing my powers."

"It appears *I'm* the only one Father chose to fuck in that particular way." Lucifer crumples his tie and casts it onto the ground, glaring at it like he doesn't know how it got there.

The universe is tilting and bleeding around us, and they're still squabbling like it's a sport.

"Well, you always were His and Mother's favorite." Greed rolls her eyes, her mouth flattened, then looks to Charlotte. "I'd rather live in another universe than end up dead thanks to some self-righteous human fools. No more deals for me, and I think I speak for all our siblings when I say, you're fired, Charlotte."

Charlotte's face reddens, her hands clenching, but she doesn't say anything.

Signaling their leave, Greed snaps at Gluttony, but then pauses and says, "Oh, I almost forgot." Gluttony passes her a blood-sprayed dossier, and she shoves it into Charlotte's chest. "Consider it an early wedding gift." She walks off, her designer heels clicking down the stone steps and leaving blood prints in her wake, her twin trailing behind her.

Charlotte stares at the dossier with shaking hands, opening it, only to see . . .

"Lust." I growl at the image of Azmodeus's face staring back at us.

I knew that fucker would screw her eventually.

She shuffles through image after image of him with Michael, Gabriel, all the angelic members of the family, flinching at the betrayal in each one.

Lust opened the second seal. We know that now, at least.

But it doesn't make a goddamn bit of difference.

I glance at the priest's body.

At the blood. At the absence where the soul should've been.

Even He's gone now. Without a goodbye. Without a purpose left for me to serve.

Why bring me this far just to leave me?

I look at Charlotte again, one last time.

But even now that she's closed the dossier, she isn't looking back. Not at me.

I step into the shadow, becoming Nothing.

And for the first time in my existence, I wonder what happens to a reaper when there's nothing left to reap.

CHAPTER SIXTY

Charlotte

We're on Apollyon's private jet, the promise of Paris looming before I'm even able to fully process what's happened. We're headed to the wedding, to my debut at Paris Fashion Week. I'm supposed to look happy, to pretend that the world isn't falling apart all around us. But I can't muster the will. I haven't had the heart to tell Xzander and the other members of the team that most of what we packed for Haute Couture week is pointless. We won't be needing it. I just . . . need some time to think.

It's not long after takeoff, and I stare out the window, looking at the Manhattan skyline.

Why would God choose to be *here* in the city, only to vanish the moment He revealed Himself to Lucifer?

I shake my head.

I guess it doesn't make a difference now.

It's only a matter of time until Lilith tracks Him down. Until she tears apart every inch of the universe, of reality, looking for Him. The wedding may distract humanity temporarily, allow us to take one last stand against Lucifer's family, but regardless of what we do, Lilith and Michael aren't going to stop, and even if we *could* get Lucifer's siblings back on our side, then what?

It's starting to feel like we've been fighting a losing battle right from the start.

I watch the city grow smaller and smaller in the distance. With Jax gone, it somehow feels right to be saying goodbye to New York like this. Paris will be my debut on the international stage, and though I've been looking forward to this for months, I can't bring myself to feel anything even close to happy.

Paris isn't going to be the resurrection I'd hoped it'd be.

It's a stage built for glamour and bloodshed.

All I can hope is that Lucifer and I meet the end on our feet.

"Why?" I whisper, pressing my hand to the window's glass and watching the heat imprint that forms there. Maybe, wherever He is, God can hear me.

Though I'm not sure I have any hope left that He'll answer.

That's been the problem this whole time, honestly.

The door to the main lounge bursts open, and I jump, startled by the noise.

Lucifer staggers inside a moment later, swaying with each step. "Talking to my Father again?" He shuffles toward the bar, an empty tumbler in his hand, his speech slurred. "Apparently, we've *both* been doing that a lot lately." He snorts.

He's cleaned up from where the bullet grazed him, in a fresh suit with his hair wet and effortlessly messy in a way that makes my knees weak. He's stripped down to just his dress shirt and pants, his shirt chaotically hanging untucked on one side, and his tie is dangling over his shoulders like he's forgotten he took it off in the first place.

"Are you drunk?"

He lifts a finger, hesitating for a beat too long. "No." He grabs an entire bottle of whisky from the cabinet and uncorks it, taking a swig.

"You *are* drunk."

He looks at me, pawing at the five o'clock shadow on his jaw as he weaves slightly. "I thought you'd be with him."

"With who?"

"Our lllover," he says, overexaggerating the *l*. He swaggers across the lounge and drops down into the seat beside me, shoving the bottle too close to my face, but I wave it away.

"Suit yourself." He tips it back, chugging for so long it's concerning, before he swipes his mouth with the back of his hand and gives me a bleary-eyed look. "No powers. No creation. Maybe you *would* be better off with him."

I shake my head, playing the good girl. "I'm yours, sir. There's nothing Azrael can give me that you—"

He chuckles too loud like I've just said something extremely funny. "Oh, but there is." He scoots forward, precariously propping the bottle in the chair and muttering "stay" as if it might actually listen, and then the next thing I know, he's on his knees in front of me, kissing my stomach before he flops his head into my lap. "If it wasn't for Him, I'd have already put a baby there." He runs his hand over my belly.

The dip inside me is instant.

I blush, a rush of heat igniting in me. "You mean Azrael?"

"No." He presses another kiss to my middle. His hand comes to my neck, and he brushes his thumb over my collar affectionately, before he rises to his feet, unsteadily pointing toward the ceiling. "Our Father who art in fucking Heaven." He reclaims the bottle and collapses into his seat again, sprawling out. "He took my ability to create *and* sacrificed Himself for me on our wedding day." He snorts, taking another swig. "Make it make sense."

I blink at him. "He took . . . your ability to create?"

"Don't worry, love." He kisses me on top of the head, then the tip of my nose without explaining. "Maybe Azrael can knock you up."

He rises from his chair. His lips press flat in thought, like he's considering going to tell Azrael about that genius idea, before he staggers off to who knows where.

I likely couldn't locate him if I tried. This plane is so freaking huge it's like Air Force One, with multiple levels. I can't wrap my head around it.

I sit there in silence, calculating dates, adding up months and weeks and questioning if Lucifer might not be . . .

No.

I shake my head. No, there's no way.

I was pregnant long before I ever slept with Azrael.

This is just one more thing on a long list of celestial improbabilities that don't make any sense when it comes to Lucifer.

I place a hand on my belly, wondering what this could possibly mean.

But then Azrael appears in the doorway.

"Hey." My hand falls away.

He tips his chin in greeting. "I see you've had a visit from the Prince of Tipsiness." He nods to where Lucifer left the bar cabinet open, a few bottles scattered in disarray.

My lips flatten, and I try not to grin. "More like the Prince of Drunkness."

Azrael sighs. "He's like this whenever he has a run-in with his Father. I'll keep an eye on him." He moves to follow Lucifer, but I grab his wrist.

"Azrael."

I stare up at him, not knowing what to say.

We haven't had a moment alone together since . . .

"Please." I pat the seat next to me. "Sit with me?"

He nods, lowering down into it, but once I feel him there, the warmth of his body, the intense sensation his nearness brings, doesn't do anything but make my chest ache.

"He's not a good man, but he's better than he believes he can be, deep down. You should know he didn't want to lie to you. But he'd do anything to protect you."

"I know."

I'm not certain what else to say.

I swallow. "I've never been to Paris." I nod to the window.

Azrael grunts. "You'll like it."

I wring my hands together, glancing at them. "Do you think Azmodeus will . . . ?"

"He already picked a side, and it wasn't ours."

I nod slowly. That betrayal stings more than I want it to, but I don't even have the space to feel it right now. Not with everything falling apart around me. I hold Azrael's gaze for a beat, staring into those endless blue orbs like liquid ice, and I can see the frustration, the hurt inside him freezing over. Like he's trying to lock it down, stay steady for me.

Even after everything.

I bite my lip, locking my hands together to keep them from shaking. "Maybe he was forced to. Maybe Michael *made* him do his bidding."

Reluctantly, I glance toward him.

Neither of us is talking about Lust anymore.

The light in his eyes dims, and he lets out a long exhale. "He made a choice." His brows gather, elbows propped on his knees as he stares at his feet. "Even if he might regret it."

I take his hand in mine, my breath bottling up inside my chest. "Sometimes we make choices without understanding what they mean, without knowing what the consequences are." I lock his hand tighter in mine. "People make choices all the time, but if we love them, we have to trust that they—"

"I knew the reasons." Azrael holds my gaze, his certainty cutting through me. "I knew the consequences, and I still chose Him."

My throat closes. "Why?"

Azrael huffs, shaking his head. "If I told you, would it make a difference?"

I open my mouth, trying to find the right words, but I'm not certain how to answer him.

Resigned, he nods. "Didn't think so." He rises from his chair. "I'll always be here when you need me, little siren. I just won't be . . ."

The one you chose.

Even if you love me.

He turns to head in the same direction as Lucifer.

But then I grab his hand again and . . . "I'm pregnant."

Azrael's eyes go wide, his gaze combing over me, and I think he might be wondering if he . . .

"It's Lucifer's." I nod to where my husband went. "I just assumed . . ."

"I can't."

I nod. I figured as much.

Death can't create life.

Though I'm a lot further along than that anyway. I avoided that pregnancy test for a while. Buried my head in the sand.

A crease forms between his brows, not in anger, but in thought.

"Why do you look so . . . ?" I struggle to find the right word. "Concerned?"

Azrael sighs. "Charlotte, you know that any child of Lucifer's would be—"

"Don't." I lift a hand. "Don't even say it. She's going to be baptized the minute she's born." I place a hand on my belly, frowning. "For sentimental reasons more than anything."

"She?" Azrael lifts a brow.

"I just . . . have a feeling, I guess."

He gazes at my midsection like he might be able to see the thread of her life there.

"Do you want to feel her?" I ask. "I'm not sure if she'll be immortal, but Death or not, your touch hasn't seemed to hurt anything."

Slowly, he draws closer, sitting down next to me. Hesitating, he reaches out his hand, but then he . . .

"It's okay." I grab it just before it falls. "You won't hurt us." I press his large palm to my belly.

I don't know how I know that. I just do.

It's instinct, it seems.

Azrael rubs his hand over me, his touch gentle and reverent, and his eyes widen slightly like he—

"I can feel her there," he says, his gaze darting to mine.

I smile, eyes shining.

She's not big enough to feel from the outside yet, but I know that he means . . .

Her essence. Her potential.

Until she draws her first breath and her life begins.

And he eventually becomes her ending.

If we even make it that far.

"This is why you put your collar back on." He stares down at where he touches me, his eyes filled with a longing so intense, my breath quickens. "Does Lucifer—"

"He doesn't know. Not yet." I shake my head.

"You told me first," Azrael says, not breathing.

It's a statement, not a question.

"Yes." My eyes fill with tears.

"Because this means . . ."

I nod once, sharp, trembling. I don't want to admit that this changes things. Already what happened with Jax nearly tore us apart, but once Lucifer learns about this, he's going to be more protective of me than he's ever been.

If Lucifer learns about this.

If I have the heart to tell him now that we're both headed toward the end.

Azrael's face falls. "That's not something I can compete with."

"No," I admit.

My tears start to fall in earnest, and deep in my soul, I know this is the end of him and me.

Even though I don't want it to be.

"I understand." He steps away.

"Azrael." I reach for him again. One last time.

"Yeah, baby girl?"

That nickname sends a fresh ache through me.

"If the wedding is our final stand, if Lucifer and I are injured, or if it comes to that, will you . . . ?" My voice trails off.

I feel him tense beneath my grip, like despite who he is, *what* he is, he'd never want that for me, but then he grumbles, "I'll make it a mercy."

And then he's gone, disappeared into the Nothing.

Leaving me sitting there, belly full, but with my heart smashed to pieces. Like I've lost not only one life but two in the same breath.

PART FOUR | APOCRYPHA

For God so loved the world . . .

Azrael

A weeping God isn't something you forget.

I pace outside Heaven's throne room like a caged animal, prowling in the spaces between stars. A silent observer. That's the role He gave me. The role I never fucking asked for.

And tonight, I hate it. I hate all of it.

The sound of His cries aren't thunderous. They're quiet. Like a nail carved through flesh.

Tonight, Heaven bleeds sorrow. The kind of pain that doesn't wash off easily. He stares down at that godforsaken hill, at Golgotha's crucifix.

But it isn't *that* son who deserves His tears.

The one who died willingly.

I tear into His throne room, unable to stop myself, furious, seething. God kneels on the marble steps, His hands trembling, His eyes heavy with tears. The sacred drops pour down His face, carving silent rivers into the ground, but I've stopped mistaking His tears for truth.

His tears mean nothing to me.

Just like His fucking promises.

As I approach, His shoulders tense. Like He expected my rage, even before I came here. He's stripped bare, raw and exposed, a father losing not one son, but two, broken in ways even the stars can't carry. The architect of all things is crumbling in grief.

But as far as I'm concerned, He can fucking wallow in it.

I swallow, voice rough. "You swore this wasn't the end."

"It isn't." He shakes his head. "This is how he's redeemed."

Lucifer, he means. The love of my entire existence.

The one who just ripped out my heart down in Gethsemane like it was nothing.

Like I didn't even matter.

Like he and I didn't mean . . .

I shake my head, rage coiled tight in my fists. "He's fallen too far. You have to end this. You *swore* to me." I let out a guttural growl, my anger barely leashed.

But I'm not scared of this Fucker.

I've ended greater gods for less.

"You think he's lost?" He asks over His shoulder, voice suddenly cold. He doesn't turn to look at me.

My ribs tighten slightly. "Even *I* can't bring him back. Not from this."

From locking him in a cage. He's going to be furious when he gets out.

God scoffs. "You underestimate love."

"Or maybe I just no longer trust *this*." I gesture between us. "This pact. This vow I swore. You said he'd be redeemed. Said he'd know mercy. Said that one day he'd be . . ."

Mine.

I can't bring myself to say it.

It feels too much like a lie now.

Like an impossibility wrapped in divine promise. What He calls a blessing.

I huff, throwing my head back with a hollow chuckle. Lucifer was right. This Fucker was never going to keep His word to me.

Not when those words were carved from *my* sacrifice.

My response is quiet. More revealing than I want it to be.

"I'm the end. What good am I to the living? What chance do I have in keeping him?"

Down below, the Nazarene shudders and then his head falls, his crown of thorns bleeding.

God sighs. "You keep him because you believe he can be more than what he's been."

"You mean more than you *made* him to be." I scoff. "I'm tired of believing in broken things. Tired of carrying promises that feel like chains."

"Then let them weigh on you." His voice echoes off the edges of the cosmos with His fury, then softer, "You're the only one who can carry this."

I lift my chin in challenge. "And if I don't?"

He steps closer, and the air thickens, dense and pulsing like the moment before a supernova. My fists clench as gravity bends around Him, like the universe itself is bracing.

But I meet his gaze head-on, eyes narrowed in fury.

Locked in a soundless war with the shape of mourning that still holds the stars in orbit.

"Would you risk a different end?" he asks.

Than the one where Lucifer's mine, the one where he and the woman he'll come to love, the one who isn't even a thought yet, *choose* me, see me as no one ever has before.

He turns away, already knowing the answer.

I smother a flinch.

"Keep thy faith, Azrael. Keep thy faith, and I shall unbind their fates, and then you shall have love everlasting."

I lock my jaw and stare past Him, into the burn of a sky that won't stop bleeding.

Every part of me wants to rage, to scream, to refuse.

I draw in a breath that tastes like blood and ash. My jaw locks. My wings twitch like they want to tear at something, anything.

But my refusal won't save him. And neither will my pride.

The Creator asks for faith, but all I have left is grief shaped like obedience.

And a rage sharp enough to cut Heaven in half.

"For him, I'll carry it. Even if it kills me."

He nods. "I know."

I laugh, bitter and quiet, because I've seen what Lucifer has become—a ruin, a shadow of what he once was. "Beginnings shouldn't look like this. Not when everything's burning."

God's face hardens, distant, fixed on that hill far below.

The cross that stands silhouetted against a bloodred sky.

He nods, slow and heavy. "I made a promise to him, to all of creation, that even in darkness, there will be light."

"Then what do I do?"

Lightning fractures. In the distance, the Nazarene gasps his last breath. God's shoulders flinch—not from surprise, but from pain older than time.

But He chose this.

And I did too.

Over and over again.

The silence thickens, and an unspoken command hums.

And something in me shifts.

"So, I carry this burden. Alone."

I know it's the truth before I even say it.

I'm Death. Destroyer. Reaper. Ender of Worlds.

But I've become something else too. The keeper of a fragile hope. The bearer of a secret too heavy for even the highest angels to bear.

"You won't be alone. I'll be with you. And near the end, so will she."

I feel it then. The tremor beneath all things, the faintest pulse of something not yet born.

Lucifer's redemption.

I lift my gaze, past the weeping God, past the aching stars—to the place where his fate waits. For the moment I know he needs.

And I vow to see it through.

Because even in Hell, even in ruin, there's promise.

And I'm the one who keeps it.

Through silence and exile.

Through every broken vow and whispered lie, I carry the weight of His mercy in my chest like a secret blade.

Unseen, unheard.

Until the day the devil himself can bear it.

This is my truth. This is my burden.

That even in a world where angels fall and gods weep, a thread of hope remains.

And I bear it. Alone.

For him.

CHAPTER SIXTY-ONE

Lucifer

I meet my sister on the Rue du Charlemagne in the fourth arrondissement, in the Le Marais near Saint-Paul and the Seine. The streets are narrow, the frozen cobblestones and petite crêperies providing little protection from the winter wind, but such human novelties hold little interest for me. To the west, the Seine glimmers faintly, its waters nearly frozen with cold. But I enjoy the cold, despite the hellfire humanity's come to expect of me.

Though not for much longer, obviously.

Not if my family has their way.

Seraph appears next to a closing shop, examining the hand-painted menu written in fading chalk, like it interests her greatly. She's always been amused by humanity's inventions. It's like watching a monkey learn to ride a bike, honestly.

"What are these?" she says, as I pass her the mound of vellum and ribboned cardstock my wife sent with me.

"Wedding invitations. Charlotte insisted."

She glances down at the Angelic inscriptions my wife begged me to hastily scribble upon each. "You mean to die alongside her?" My sister is quick on the uptake.

I give a curt nod.

"Seems like a waste."

I huff, taking out a cigarette and lighting it. There's no point in attempting to quit now. Might as well destroy what's left of this mortal body while I still can. "A waste of what? Money? I could burn mounds of it and still have enough to buy Heaven."

Money is the religion of power.

And I am the true god of it.

She shrugs, tucking the invitations under one of her wings. "Of life? Of potential? I don't know. But I'll fight with you." She sighs before she turns to leave.

She crosses a few meters down the cobblestones, the tips of her dual feathered wings trailing on the ground behind her. They're nearly larger than she is.

Not that it's ever stopped her from fighting our Father's battles more fiercely than any other angel I've ever known. Save for me, at least.

Back in my angelic heyday.

Now look at me.

"Why now?" I ask, calling after her.

The question nearly dies on the wind.

But it's something I've been wondering for some time, frankly.

She gives me a hesitant look.

"Why stand by me now and not when I rebelled?"

She sighs, striding back to me. "Your rebellion was foolish. Fueled by your own pride, your fear of losing Father's love and little else." The words come quick. Like they've been sitting upon the tip of her tongue for eons.

But it's nothing I haven't said to myself already. Or heard dozens of times before. In every dialect in every tongue and language known to man. My shame is nearly as public as my image.

Thanks to the villain they've made me.

"But you weren't wrong about humanity." She drops her chin, gesturing to the empty street about us, her brows lowering. "They don't deserve His love, His mercy. But I think that might be the point." She lifts her gaze to me. "And what came after . . ."

For a moment, I think she may leave it at that, walk away without admitting what she truly thinks, but then she looks me directly in the eye, an unexpected certainty in her gaze. "Father was cruel. Unkind. The punishment didn't fit the sin, and what He made of you after, the way He cast you out like you were a monster, like you hadn't always been His most devoted, His most loyal son since the dawn of time." She shakes her head. "It wasn't right. It wasn't fair, Lucy."

I place my hands in my pockets. "Thank you, Seraph."

She smiles, but there's a bit of pity in it.

And I hate that I understand it.

Hate that I'm aware of all I'm missing.

Of all He stole from me.

"And now?" I ask.

Her sigh is long and weighted, like she feared I'd ask this, given enough time. "You're still my favorite brother. But I suppose I'd hoped there might've been a chance you could still be . . ."

"Redeemed?" I let out a chuckle, but it doesn't hurt like it used to. I flick some of my still smoldering ashes onto the stones. "I hate to break it to you, sister, but if there *were* a path, I'd have already tried it. I spent hundreds, thousands of years searching."

Her mouth pops open. "You did?"

I nod. What's the point in putting up a front anymore?

I've already sunk to my lowest low.

Preparing to die. To save fucking humanity.

My wife has made certain anyone who'll listen knows the pathetic truth of me.

That I bled for Him in the way He never bled for me.

Not until recently, at least. I scoff.

"I did," I admit, blowing out smoke as I think back to all the time I wasted. All the schemes I planned that never panned out. "And do you know what that bloody Bastard said to me? Before He died on the steps of that church near fucking Broadway, of all places?" I wrinkle my nose in disgust. "He said, 'Your redemption isn't as far-fetched as you think it is, Sammael,'" I mimic in his voice, my tone mocking. "What self-righteous horseshit."

Seraph tilts her head at me, eyes narrowed, but I'm uncertain what it is she sees. "Perhaps you don't need it. Perhaps you can give yourself what you need. I don't think you've been looking in the right place, Lucy."

I chuckle, unamused. "Oh, and where's that? Timbuktu?"

"No." She repositions the invitations she's holding so that they're no longer pressed to her chest. "The part you've always tried to keep under lock and key." She drums her fingertips overtop her heart. And then she flies off.

I cast what remains of my cigarette onto the ground, asking myself the same questions I've been asking myself for eternity. But if there is one strategy, one outcome that has always eluded me, it's this.

I will never know my Father's forgiveness. His mercy.

And I think it might be high time I make peace with that, finally.

CHAPTER SIXTY-TWO

Charlotte

I slip from the Suite Imperial at the Ritz without a sound, the blades Azrael's been training me with strapped beneath my coat. I'm not the best with them, but I'm good enough, and I know without a doubt Death's going to follow me. I should find that reassuring, comforting even, considering what lies in store. But tonight, I need all the self-confidence I can get.

Outside, the city's caught between late night and the stretch of early morning, the cobblestones echoing under my Maison Margiela boots as I cut through Place Vendôme. The sky overhead is a predawn blue that makes everything feel like a secret, but if I really wanted to hide, I could snap myself where I'm headed instead of walking.

I just . . . need to clear my head.

Prepare for what's coming.

I pull my Saint Laurent coat tighter against the cold, trying to make myself as small and inconspicuous as possible. Thankfully, the paparazzi aren't as awful about following us here as they are in Manhattan.

As I round onto Rue de Castiglione, the wind carries the scent of fresh baguettes and croissants from a nearby boulangerie, and I sigh a little.

Azrael was right. I do love it here.

Even with the violence I know is coming.

I pass a row of shuttered shops with window displays so beautiful I can't help but pause every few feet to look at them. Everything here is perfect, polished, pristine.

Better than a dream.

But I've lived in this glittering world long enough to know that glamour isn't always what it seems.

Sometimes it's dying while the world watches and cheers.

By the time I cross into the courtyard of the Louvre, the city's just beginning to yawn and stretch. A few lights flicker on behind framed dark windows, and in the distance the Louvre's glass pyramid rises out of the ground like a knife.

I try not to think about Michael's knife, about what it might feel like to have the Holy Lance sticking out of me like in the Righteous's flyer, and *not* in the fun kind of way with Azrael.

The wedding is still a few days off, I remind myself.

But I don't want to consider that this might be the only time I get to see the city.

I shake my head. I don't know why I've placed what little fractured hope I have left in Azmodeus. Maybe I'm being naïve.

Or maybe I'm just that desperate.

I'm not ashamed to admit I'm afraid of dying.

What it means for the life growing inside me. For mine and Lucifer's daughter.

I stop in the center of the square, pausing to take in the rare moment of freedom. No cameras. No paparazzi. Just me.

And Death.

Azrael's out there, watching. I can feel the weight of his eyes between my shoulder blades. The subtle chill his nearness brings. It's comforting, in a twisted way, to know he'll be our end.

Even if it makes my heart ache.

Slipping inside, I pay off the guard I spoke with earlier just like I've seen the other Originals do so many times before. The museum is currently closed, but the lights are still on, and I head toward the first floor, the Denon Wing, to Room 711, where the *Mona Lisa*'s waiting.

I snap a quick selfie—#MonaLisaSmile—and schedule it to post in the next few days.

After I'm gone.

I stiffen.

Pushing the thought from my mind, I head to the next room and stop in front of a painting labeled **SALOME RECEIVING THE HEAD OF JOHN THE BAPTIST**.

The placard reads: **BERNARDINO LUINI. C. 1520**.

I take a photo and type a text to Imani.

Accurate? with a smirk emoji, and press send.

Footsteps approach.

Azmodeus enters the gallery with a woman, who looks like she could be a French supermodel, on one arm and her equally gorgeous identical twin on the other. He kisses both of them *adieu* so long it has heat rising to my face.

I clear my throat.

Lust is the ultimate playboy.

It should honestly be a crime for someone to be that beautiful.

He grins at my interruption, then dismisses them, watching them appreciatively as they go, before he turns his attention to me. Despite all the ways he's hurt me, I can't help that my heart races a little.

My brother-in-law is a walking wet dream.

And a devious traitor.

"Hey, lovey."

He joins me in front of the painting of Salome, relaxed and easy. Like we've always been. The hurt of how he destroyed our plans is still raw.

If he hadn't opened the second seal, there might still be a chance Lucifer and I could make it through this. We'd still be one seal away from Lilith's powers, we'd have flipped more angels to our side, and Jax might still be . . .

My jaw tightens. "How do you think she felt then?" I nod to the painting.

Art galleries have become mine and Azmodeus's thing, and there's a lot of paintings of Salome, but this one has her almost smirking.

As she's handed John's head on a platter.

The side of his mouth curves. "Why don't you ask her?"

I blow out an irritated breath.

Apparently, I'm the only one who *wasn't* in on that secret.

I never expected Lucifer's other siblings to have any loyalty, but with Az . . .

With him, I let my guard down. Thought he was my friend.

I was wrong, clearly.

He moves to the next painting, watching how I'm staring at him and casting me the devastating smirk that the media practically salivates over.

But I've seen Lust up close and personal before. Know what it's like to have his mouth on my breasts, his hands all over my body until I'm out of my mind with need, even if it was because Lucifer was sharing me. Outside that, our relationship has always been platonic. Harmless flirting.

But I trusted Him too, didn't I?

And look where it got me.

Without warning, I draw one of my blades, slashing at Azmodeus before I can change my mind. My knife slices his shirt, almost nicking him, but he dodges it, his deviant grin widening.

"Is this your idea of foreplay? Usually, this kind of fun's reserved for my exes, but I love it when you're feisty."

"You fucked me." I lunge, letting out all the frustration I've been feeling.

But I miss. Just barely.

"In the playroom, or are you hungry for a repeat?" His eyes fall to my chest, and my nipples harden. "You're a simp for me, Charlotte."

I throw myself at him, letting out a furious shriek, but he grabs my wrist easily, twisting until my blade is pointed at my throat. "I'm all for knife play, but this is hardly the place, sweetheart." He casts my blade to the floor and releases me.

I growl, grabbing the other strapped to my thigh. "You opened the second seal."

Az's smile falls. "Oh, that."

I swing low, another surge of frustration cutting through me, but he doesn't rise to the bait. He lets out a dark chuckle.

The mask he wears is suddenly gone. Lust isn't just the queer best friend or the seductive playboy I've always known him to be.

He's something far more dangerous.

I come at him again, throwing round after round of celestial fire at him from one hand and letting my blade sing with the other. I'm pretty good now, even Azrael says so, but a part of me is holding back. I don't really want to hurt him.

And he doesn't fight me.

He just dodges every blow.

"Fight me."

"No."

I swing left, then right, advancing on him, trying to push him into a corner. "I said fight me, you slut!"

Azmodeus's smirk is wicked. "For the record, I'm not *a* slut. I'm *the* slut. Try again."

I abandon my blade, dropping it onto the floor. It clatters against the marble, and I send a blast of shadow in his direction, but Azmodeus just spins out of reach like it's nothing, and I let out a frustrated growl.

He raises his hands. "Finally letting out some of that pent-up rage, huh, lovey?"

I snarl, charging at him, sloppy and losing focus. He grabs me, capturing one of my arms until I'm forced to break free.

As soon as I do, he backs away, putting some distance between us.

"Can you even *do* anything other than make people horny?"

"Hey, now." Az snatches one of my blades off the floor. "That was below the belt. You really don't want to fight me, Charlotte. My sin's your favorite, and you know it. All those offerings you make me?" He tsks, nodding to how tight my dress is. "Though that breeding kink you've got going with my brother has gotten you into a bit of a tight spot recently, hasn't it?"

I let out a furious shout and come at him again. I lash at him relentlessly, this time with fire, driving him even farther back. "You *used* me!"

I catch the edge of his pant leg, making it smolder, and the smell of burned fabric fills the air.

"Goddammit it, Charlotte. I know the pregnancy hormones are making you crazy, but I'm *trying* to help you." His eyes flash to a supernatural green, like he really doesn't want to do this, but I'm backing him into a corner.

I inch closer.

"I don't fight fair," he warns.

"I'll take my chances." I advance again.

"All right. You asked for it." Azmodeus's eyes darken.

Abruptly, he surges forward, my knife in his hand. In three quick moves, he has it up against my throat and is pressing me into the wall until I'm pinned beneath his large body.

I try to pull away, but the glowing green in his eyes flares.

His touch is too . . . everything.

Too intense. Too delicious. Too . . .

Out of my control.

And I want it.

Even though he doesn't remove the knife.

Instead, he cups my face, like he's about to kiss me, and the world blurs at the edges, my focus narrowing to nothing but him.

Every want, every need, every desire is his for the taking.

Heat pools between my legs, liquefying my insides.

I want him. I want him so bad that I can't . . .

"Oh, sweetheart," he purrs, his heated gaze flicking over me like he can already taste the desire on me, because he created it. "You thought it was bad when my brother got inside that little pretty head of yours?" He leans in so close his lips brush mine, my breath hitching. "I *am* desire."

He loosens his grip, starting to step away, but I use my foot to drag the other blade toward me. Azmodeus frowns, kicking the knife across the floor, and then he's on me, positioning his muscled thigh between my legs so that I'm riding it.

I can't help but want to rock my clit against him eagerly.

It's like he's in control of my entire body.

In charge of every desire.

This is what he does. Makes people impulsive, unable to resist.

He licks his lips, his gaze growing impossibly hot as it sweeps over me, and my body responds like a traitor. "I'll play nice this time. Won't make you ache too hard. Which version would you like, sweetheart?" He drops his head, and when he lifts it again, suddenly it's Lucifer, staring back at me, caressing my collar.

Except it's not him. I *know* it's not him.

It's still Azmodeus.

But my body betrays me all the same.

"My brother?" Lust asks, though it's Lucifer's voice I hear.

I stiffen.

He rolls his shoulders, his thigh still pressing between my legs, making me throb with need, and I flinch because then it's Death I'm looking at. "Or Azrael?"

My desire flares, craving what I haven't had in days.

He presses closer, Azrael's massive frame coming over me, and I welcome his touch willingly. He places a hand on my thigh, dragging up my skirt so torturously slow that my insides twist in mortification, even though I'm panting.

I can't control it, but I don't want to, and then Azrael's large, firm hand settles on my belly, a familiar need pooling there, and it's *his* voice I hear when he says, "Does Lucifer know that you wish it was me?" He nods down to where he touches me. "That you wish it was me who'd filled you until you leaked?"

I press my eyes closed, a tear slipping free.

But it's not Azrael.

"Stop it, Az," I hiss. "Whatever this is, stop it."

Abruptly, Azmodeus releases me, shrugging away from me, and when I open my eyes, it's his own too-handsome face he's wearing.

Lust is a weapon.

All my desire turned against me.

I tremble from head to toe. "You're an asshole."

Azmodeus swipes his thumb over his lips. "I am, but you love it."

I wince.

I wish he were wrong.

I haven't felt this powerless, this exposed, since Lucifer first threw my employment contract at me.

"I hate you," I mutter, but even as it comes out of my mouth, I know it isn't true.

I just hate what he does to me. What a shameless slut his sin makes me.

Lust huffs. "Who's the liar now, lovey?"

He turns to leave.

"You were my friend."

The words come out more broken than I want them to be.

Azmodeus slowly twists toward me, the emerald of his eyes gleaming. I don't think I've ever seen him truly angry before, but the fiery look he gives me then is unnerving.

"I *am* your friend." His nostrils flare. "And because I'm your friend, because I care about you, I had to teach you about our world the hard way." He huffs. "You think I want to hurt you like this? Like my brother used to do?" He tries to brush a stray hair from my cheek.

But I swat his hand away.

His face hardens.

"Look around, Charlotte. Who do you see standing here? As you wait for your death?"

I inhale, more tears running down my cheeks. "No one. I see no one."

Not even Azrael.

Azmodeus's eyes soften, like he really *does* care for me, in his own twisted way. "In our world, the only one you can ever fully rely on is yourself. You think love is going to get you anywhere with our siblings? With *Lucifer*?" He shakes his head. "Love's not going to help you."

My breath stutters. "Of course, you'd think that."

I don't know how I didn't see it before.

Lust doesn't do love.

He does obsession, desire, possession.

But not love.

Never that.

"And what *is* going to help me? Fucking the people who care for me? Like you?"

"Putting yourself first," he mutters. "Putting your own desires before everything. That's the only way you're going to survive this."

"So, you decided to serve me up to Michael? To teach me a lesson?"

"No." He swipes a thumb over those perfect lips again. "No, that wasn't the only reason. But that doesn't concern you."

He says it like it's a dark promise of what's to come, and it sends a chill through me. I don't know what he means, and I'm not sure I want to find out.

"Like it or not, I activated you, Charlotte. Maybe someday you'll thank me for it." He cups my cheek, and the desire, the longing it ignites in me makes me shiver. "Even if it makes you hate me."

I shudder.

But he releases me, and I recoil in disgust.

If he weren't so fucked up, he'd make someone out of their mind in love with him.

Their heart wouldn't even stand a chance.

I stare up into his face, into those haunted emerald eyes. He's even more broken than Lucifer.

Azmodeus steps away, and Azrael appears at my side a moment later. The *real* one.

Lust must've blocked him from getting to me.

He moves in front of me, shielding me protectively, and I start to shake.

This really *is* the end.

Azmodeus isn't going to help me, save me.

"Why?" I ask as Lust walks away.

The selfishness I get. The desire, the impulsive decision-making. The possession.

Lust is all those things.

But why hurt me?

Azmodeus glances over his shoulder, like he wrote the playbook on seduction, on manipulation, and he expects me to thank him for it. "You're the only person who's ever tried to love me." He shrugs.

He really thinks he was *helping* me? Like this was some divine favor? Or some twisted expression of love? But this *is* his idea of love, isn't it?

Dark. Devious. Seductive.

Devastating.

I collapse into Azrael's arms, the last of my hope torn out of me. "But what am I supposed to do?" I call after him. "What am I—"

"You're one of us now. Figure it out for yourself, Charlotte," he calls back, not even looking at me.

I shiver, because I don't want to admit it, but he's right.

I belong in this glittering, vicious world.

And like it or not, maybe it's time to start seeing how wicked I can be.

CHAPTER SIXTY-THREE

Azrael

When Charlotte and I stumble out of the Louvre, she's so broken, so full of grief, she's shaking. The sun is starting to crest over the horizon, lighting up the Parisian streets like a lost memory, but we make our way through the courtyard, heading back toward the Ritz on foot. She needs some air to clear her head, but she's supposed to be with *him*, not me, and that's when I turn toward her and say, "Is it true? What Lust said?"

I tip my chin toward the Louvre.

I overheard. I saw. Even when that slippery bastard made it so I couldn't get to her.

Charlotte looks a bit lost, but then she nods. Just barely.

My cock stiffens, and it takes everything in me not to touch her, to pull her into my arms and give her exactly what she wants. The fact that I can't makes it feel like I've been gutted from head to toe.

"I wanted this, with Lucifer"—she places a hand on her belly—"and I know things with us are still new, but someday, I . . . also wanted it with you," she whispers, her voice small and broken.

Wanted. Not want.

Past tense.

I swallow, my throat writhing.

"I need a minute." I turn away from her, raking a hand through my hair, uncertain what to say. She's his now. I know that.

Touching her would be a violation of the little trust Lucifer's placed in me.

And I still love him too.

I know creating life won't ever be a possibility for me, but . . .

She wanted it to be.

She wanted it to be.

And all I know is this fucking changes things.

Fuck, I can't do this.

I can't stand by her side, wanting her while he . . .

My shoulders stiffen. "And if I could?" I ask, turning toward her, a newfound hope sparking in me. "If I could give that to you?"

"Azrael, I—"

"Answer me." I grip her by the back of the neck, dragging her to me. Collar be damned.

Our mouths are so close I can practically taste her on my tongue, feel the moment when her knees go weak. She melts into me.

"Be honest, baby girl."

She inhales, shuddering slightly. "How couldn't I?" she whispers, her lips parting. She closes her eyes, another tear slipping free. "I love him, but I love you too. I didn't want you to leave me."

My grip on the back of her neck tightens, my breathing uneasy.

I want so badly to kiss her, but I can't.

She glances away. "Azrael, I . . ."

"It's okay, little siren. It's okay." I pull her into me, wrapping her up tight, her head resting against my chest.

Just for a moment, just long enough to ease the ache inside me.

But that's when I see Gabriel standing on the corner, waiting for us.

I sweep her behind my back in one swift move, positioning myself in front of her.

Ever her guardian. *Their* guardian.

Always.

"Go back to the hotel now, Charlotte," I order.

The clock on her deal with Sloth is still ticking, and Lust already fucked with her enough.

But she doesn't move. She's still staring at Gabriel, her eyes narrow and angry.

"Charlotte," I growl, my tone laced with warning.

I may not be her Dom anymore, but I don't need to be in order to get her to listen to me.

She disappears into the ether, leaving me and Gabriel alone.

For a moment, I just glare at him, neither of us saying anything.

Our stares clash in a silent war.

He and I are supposed to be on the same side, technically.

And yet . . .

I've never actually been on God's side. Have I?

I drop my hands, the chill in the courtyard plummeting several degrees as my face turns skeletal before I become Nothing.

I barrel toward Gabriel like a phantom, his eyes going wide at what he knows is coming. I'll end that fucker with a single touch for even looking at her wrong. But he hightails it out of there at the last second before I reach him, like the little bitch he's always been.

He races into the sky, clearly deciding that whatever I'm going through right now, he doesn't want to fuck with me.

I don't blame him.

Nothing on this goddamn planet could survive me right now.

I stare up into the endless blue after him, a furious look on my face.

"Why?" I snarl, uncharacteristically shouting at the heavens like the sound of my voice alone can bring them down. The same way Lucifer did that night outside of the Abyss. "Why abandon me right at the fucking end like this? After all I did for you? I guarded your secret, kept it all in for you, for him, even when it destroyed me!"

A few passersby on the street start to gawk, turning away in fear, but I don't care. I'm furious. Furious and . . .

Done.

I am so fucking done.

I won't be His celestial errand boy.

I turn away, stalking back toward the glass spire outside the Louvre, unable to stop myself from thinking about how it felt. When she told me she loved me on the Empire State Building, when she shivered in my arms, when he left in Gethsemane, the longing in my chest when she let me touch that tiny thread of life in her.

No one's ever trusted me enough to let me hold a life at its very beginning before.

At its creation.

And if He lied, if He really did fail me, I'm not only going to lose them, but they're both going to lose . . .

Something ignites inside me.

Something primitive, terrifying, furious, and . . .

Life altering.

This has gone too far.

I've been loyal to Him long enough. I was too much of a coward to risk losing them before, but now . . .

Now I'd cut out my own heart if it'd ensure they wouldn't bleed.

I shatter apart, one part of me barreling toward the edges of the universe as the others work to fulfill their duty.

An old woman in a nursing home.

A newlywed in India.

A sick little girl in Tokyo who cries when she sees me.

So many lives. So many endings.

And never once did I stop to question.

Never once did I succumb to my own grief.

Every order. Everything He asked.

The Garden. Gethsemane. Grand Central. The lance. Her friend.

And for what? For Him to do *this*?

To fucking abandon me right as we reach the finish line?

No.

I am Death. Destroyer of Worlds. Reaper of unjust gods.

And *this* ends here.

I find Lilith at the edge of existence, where form forgets itself. She spills through the silence like a fault line—not arriving, but *unmaking arrival.* The void clings to her like memory to a dream. Near her, even light dims, ashamed of its simplicity.

She smiles, not in welcome, but in a prophecy fulfilled, as she turns toward me. "I had a feeling you'd be coming to see me."

"I hear you want grandchildren." I step forward, the void reluctantly parting.

Her grin widens. "I do."

"If that's the case . . ." I swipe my hand over my lips. "Then I think I might have an offer that suits you."

CHAPTER SIXTY-FOUR

Lucifer

The evening before the wedding, when I return from picking up my tuxedo, my wife is wearing nothing but one of my dress shirts and is already on her knees for me.

My cock stiffens.

"What a good, good girl you're being, little dove," I purr, stepping toward her.

She glows from my praise, lowering her head for a moment and blushing prettily. "Is it time to play, Daddy?" Her long lashes flick up at me hopefully.

She's a complete hellion.

She knows exactly what she's doing to me.

And I cannot resist her.

I hang my tux on the valet stand, unbuttoning my cufflinks as I ease toward her. She's a picture, the image of sin, sitting there like that. Everything I want and more, and yet . . .

Something, or some*one* rather, is missing.

I pause, noting how her smile doesn't quite reach her eyes.

"Give me a color, Charlotte."

She stiffens, knowing I've seen right through her. "Green, sir," she says, but I can taste the lie easily.

I step closer.

She tracks me eagerly, waiting to see what I'll do. She wants this, that much is clear, but our play, my punishment, isn't what she needs.

I shake my head. "No." I turn away from her, stripping off my suit coat. "No, not tonight." I glance over my shoulder at her, and the look she gives me is devastating.

Heartbroken.

I can hardly deny her.

What in God's name has she done to me?

I chuckle. "After all this time, you cannot possibly think I'm saying no because I do not want you."

She glances down at her hands uncertainly. "I can, sir."

My expression softens.

Releasing her rage upon her father may have begun to heal her, but the scars will remain for some time. I remove my shirt and brush my fingers along the ridges on my spine—raised, uneven, a map of the wound He left behind.

I know that all too well.

I cross the room to her in two quick strides, gently leading her by her collar to her feet.

"I want you, always. I can hardly stand the moments I'm without you, the ache it creates in me, and I will never say no because I do not want you, little dove. But I will when there's something more important I can give you." Slowly, I tangle my hand into the base of her hair, drawing her up onto her toes as I kiss her.

The world narrows to the space between us, quiet and reverent. I tilt her chin up with care, my lips brushing over hers like a vow—slow, lingering, full of the things I haven't yet found the words to say. She leans into me, soft and trusting, and I kiss her deeper, trying to memorize the shape of her mouth, the way she sighs into the moment like it's home.

When I pull back, her gaze flits to mine uncertainly. "Sir?"

My thumb traces across her collar affectionately. I reach for the fastener, unbuckling it as I whisper, "Inferno."

Her eyes widen.

It's the only time I've ever used our safe word.

The only time I've ever put a stop to one of our scenes.

"This isn't what you need right now, is it, little dove? What you really want? You're just hiding in it." I pull her closer, knowing she understands what I mean.

My punishment isn't all that I can give her.

Right now, it's my love she needs.

She stares up at me, eyes shining with unshed tears, at the way I see her, know her, intimately. "You've never told me no before."

Never been the one to demand she join me in our shared vulnerability.

Outside of one of our scenes.

"Some things don't change." I hold up her collar, a reminder that she is and always will be mine as I lay it out upon the bed. "But others can. Like you've done for me." I pull her into my arms, pressing her against me. "You loved me, trusted me, even when I was at my most monstrous. Woke up parts of me no one else could. It's high time I care for you as you've always cared for me."

A tear slips down her cheek. "You already have, Lucifer. You already have cared for me."

When I kiss her then, it feels nothing like it did the first time—it's a soft brush of tongue and lips and teeth. I kiss the tip of her nose, then her temple, her cheeks, suckle upon the hollow of her throat until she's panting, writhing beneath me, and only then do I claim her lips. It's a thousand times better than it was at the start, infinite and unending.

She and I may die tomorrow, may greet Death readily, but this, the way she's changed me, loved me, humbled and broken open parts of me I would've never dared to look at, that will remain long after we're both gone.

I lead her down onto the bed with me then, catching her in my arms as we both fall. Our hands rove over one another in a desperate need. I nip at her collarbone, and she laughs when I growl, tearing my shirt from her so readily one of the buttons pops free.

The love I make to her is slow and reverent. Soul shattering. Life ending.

Charged with all the hope she's given me.

When she lies in my arms sometime later, naked and spent, my hands tangled in her hair, her curved frame soft and sated against me, I realize that *this* is what I will miss the most.

The moments where she unravels me.

Makes me soft in ways I didn't think were possible.

"Do you think it'll hurt?" she whispers, lazily tracing a finger over the scarred sigil on my chest.

Dying, she means.

I shake my head. "No. I don't think Azrael will let it. Not for you, anyway."

At the mere mention of his name, she stiffens slightly, glancing away.

But I don't want her to hide from me. Not tonight.

Gently, I grab her by her chin, turning her to look at me. "You miss him, don't you?"

She nods. "Don't you?"

I inhale a deep breath. There could never be anything more sacred, more holy, than the trust she has placed in me, in our dynamic, than what she means to me, but I don't have it in me to lie anymore.

To myself. To her.

"I do," I confess. "I'll admit having him around was a bit fun, perhaps, but I suppose it doesn't make any difference now."

She smiles, though there's a bit of pain in it, before she suddenly separates from me, wiggling her way toward the end of the bed.

When she returns a moment later, my collar is in her hands, and she's looking at me expectantly, a hopeful gleam in her eyes. "Please, sir? I . . . don't like being without it now."

"Still as eager to be mine as the day you first walked into my boardroom, I see." I chuckle. "All right, darling. Turn 'round."

She kneels upon the mattress, her supple back facing me, and I brush some of her golden hair over her shoulder. Slowly, I fasten it at her throat, before I kiss her neck. She tilts her head to the side as my tongue caresses over her pulse, and she shivers for me.

"Why did you choose to put it back on, little dove?" I ask her, whispering across her skin. "Before everything."

She sighs softly, melting into my touch. "I wanted to be yours again. I've always wanted to be yours." She turns and places her hand on my cheek. "I was just afraid of losing myself in it, in you. I thought I needed to have all the answers, figure out who I was, but I think deep down, I was really afraid of how exposed it made me to you."

My pulse quickens.

She takes my face in her hands. "I love you, Lucifer Apollyon. I love you with an ache I can't hide from, an ache that reminds me I'm not whole, but you give me hope that I could be."

I smile, the words wrapping around my heart, sealing every fracture I once thought permanent. In her smile, I find the best of me. "I love you too, little dove"—I kiss her—"and at the end, there's no one else I'd rather have beside me."

CHAPTER SIXTY-FIVE

Charlotte

It's the morning of the wedding, and I couldn't feel more miserable.

I spend the better part of the first hour I'm awake throwing up what feels like everything I've eaten since we came to Paris and then some. I don't think it has anything to do with my morning sickness, but when I come out of the bathroom, pale and shaking, on my pillow I find a small ginger candy that looks like it might've come from the other side of the world.

Japan maybe?

Azrael.

I haven't seen him much since outside the Louvre the other day, but I've felt him nearby, lingering. I know he's waiting for us.

"Thanks," I mumble, knowing he'll hear, before I pop it into my mouth.

I glance around the suite, feeling aimless and uncertain what to do. I spent all night—awake mostly—in Lucifer's arms, enjoying what little time we have left, but he's been restless, up and down whenever I sleep, and clearly, he's already started the day without me.

We're both mourning in our own ways, I guess.

I sigh, getting dressed and mentally preparing myself.

Sleep is the one mortal habit I still have left. I like the break. From everything, from thinking, especially lately. From wondering what it'll feel like to die.

Maybe it won't actually be that bad. Like Lucifer said.

Not if it's anything like being in Azrael's arms.

And I trust that no matter what happens today, he'll make it good for me.

A mercy. Like he said.

I get dressed in a loose-fitting Brunello Cucinelli turtleneck and a warm pair of leggings and head upstairs to the Suite Mansart, where my bridal party's waiting. It won't be long before I'm changing into my wedding dress anyway.

The late-morning air in Paris in January is cold, but as I pass by one of the Suite Imperial's many windows, I realize there's a blanket of snow over the city. It rarely snows this time of year in Paris, but a layer of white still glitters overtop everything. Untouched and pristine.

I smile, thinking of that first night in the graveyard with Azrael.

Of so many nights spent on the penthouse balcony with Lucifer.

Of when he cast the aurora borealis over the city. The first night I realized I was in love with him.

I may be walking to my own death, but joy can be found in unexpected places, it seems.

When I reach the Suite Mansart on the top floor, the atmosphere is more somber than anything. Greed's here, and so is Imani, along with Xzander, Sophie, and a few other acquaintances, but several key people are missing.

Jax, Evie, Mia.

Along with any distant female relatives I might've once called family.

And Azmodeus.

I frown at the thought.

I want to dismiss what he said to me as the ravings of a madman, someone so fucked up he might never actually love somebody.

But I can't help thinking there's some . . . truth in it.

I *have* been inactive. Relying on others to save me.

Lucifer. Azrael. The other Originals.

What if I relied on myself, was as wicked and devious as any of Lucifer's siblings?

I can't see any other way out.

How do I fight for myself when I'm not even certain what it is I'm saving?

At least I'm not alone. I'm pretty sure Imani, Dagon, and the other demonic members of the security team have a rough idea of what's going on, and I know the other Originals do. Lucifer's legions are at the ready, prepared to fight for us, but numerous as they are, they won't be able to best a whole army of archangels, and Greed can't keep a secret to save her life. Even if seeing Lucifer and me at our lowest low hadn't tipped her and the others off, the guest list would have.

All of Lucifer's family is here.

All six other Originals, all seven archangels, including Michael and Gabriel—I guess Sloth isn't going to be getting his little vacay to Heaven after all—along with at least fifty others whose classifications and angelic taxonomies I can't begin to keep straight.

Our guest list is a mile long. Every angel, demon, celebrity, and power player known to man and then some. We're going to take out as many of them as we can.

Michael would be a complete fool if he didn't realize why we invited him here.

But he's here all the same.

To watch us go down in flames.

Sophie spends most of the morning fussing over mine and Greed's hair and makeup, since with Jax gone and Evie still under her brother's lock and key, Greed's my only bridesmaid. Despite the dark cloud hanging over me, I manage to find a bit of joy buried beneath the chaos. If this is my last day, I'm going to spend it happy, goddammit.

By the time it's midafternoon and we're less than an hour from the ceremony, I'm standing in front of the trumeau mirror in the Marie Antoinette room in one of our suites. A four-poster canopy bed waits behind me, the gilded balustrades and the antique-style furniture making me feel like I've been transported to a different time.

One when another extravagant, hellish queen was waiting for the gallows.

At the hands of her own people.

The Righteous and the press are those really responsible for our current situation, after all. No matter how Azmodeus may have screwed me.

I sigh. "At least it's not death by guillotine."

I smooth a gentle hand down my dress. It's a Ralph and Russo ball gown, designed specifically for me, the arms covered in lace and the bodice coated in diamonds.

Simple. Elegant.

"You look beautiful."

I spin to find Seraph entering the room. I haven't seen her much in the last few days, since there's no real point in training. Not when we're outmatched.

"Thank you." I cast her a half-hearted smile.

She sits on the bed, patting the spot beside her, and I smooth out my skirt and join her.

"I'm sorry it has to end this way." She takes hold of my hand.

She's the first one to acknowledge what's actually happening today.

That I'm going to die.

"I'm sorry too." I squeeze her hand.

I've only been training with Seraph a short time, but I like her. She was the first of Lucifer's angelic siblings to join our side, and despite how it went wrong with Azrael, I know taking the first step isn't easy.

Leaving behind the only way of life you've ever known takes enormous strength.

"Are you going to fight with Michael? Maintain your cover?"

It seems like the obvious thing to do.

Why join us when we're in a losing battle?

She shakes her head. "No. I stand by my conviction. Father wouldn't want this."

"So, you'll die? For our cause? For humanity?"

She nods, and I grip her hand tighter, understanding.

She releases it, and I draw it into my lap, staring down at my engagement ring. "I've been trying to wrap my head around all this. To make sense of what my life could mean, asking myself if there's anything I would've done differently, and I've also been thinking a lot about what you said. About how you have doubts, about how that doesn't change your faith, but lately my doubts outweigh everything."

"Mine too," she admits.

She rubs my leg, giving my knee a reassuring squeeze, before she stands.

But what Azmodeus said has been nagging at me at the back of my mind, like an itch I can't scratch.

Figure it out for yourself, Charlotte.

Seraph's almost at the door when I call her name. "Seraph?"

She turns to look at me.

"Lucifer said something the other day I've been wondering about."

"Oh?"

"He said that when God took his wings, your Father also took his ability to create."

She nods. "He did. Only a few of our siblings know."

Which means Azrael might not have known either. It would've been before they met.

"So, it's true then? That Lucifer can't have children?"

Seraph places her hand on the doorframe, her expression full of regret. "Yes, it's true."

I hesitate, but then I think back to that memory turned prophecy. The one Jax sent me.

To the sight of Lucifer lying there, bleeding and alone in the dirt just after his fall when Azrael found him, and the way he was . . . pleading for God's forgiveness.

My eyes go wide.

Azrael's been guarding him, all this time, despite being God's soldier, but why guard him? Why try to keep bringing him back to the light, unless God believed he could be . . .

It all falls into place in an instant.

"Was Lucifer ever a part of God's original redemption competition?" I stand suddenly, desperately looking at Seraph. "The one Gabriel issued at the start of all this? When the Originals were first brought topside."

Seraph's brow furrows, but she shakes her head. "I don't believe so. Why?"

"And if it was true," I say, stepping toward her. "If Lucifer *could* have children, what would that mean?"

She looks me up and down, and I turn to the side, relaxing so she can see the slight swell there, and the spark of hope in her eyes is immediate.

"It would mean that Lucifer already had Father's redemption, right from the very start."

Hope and joy jolt through me, and my grin widens. "Seraph, is there any chance that I could borrow the extra pair of your wings?"

CHAPTER SIXTY-SIX

Lucifer

Contrary to popular belief, I fucking hate parties, even when *I* am the center of everyone's attention. I sit at the edge of the bar, nursing my final drink in between entertaining guests before the ceremony, but the smoke and peat flavor I normally relish does little for me. I am a lit match in a gas tank.

The promise of what's to come hangs heavy in the air.

My last pleasure will be their pain.

I throw back what remains of my glass, prepared to summon Azrael, my best man, so we can get this show on the road, but then I feel a familiar presence slink up behind me.

Michael.

I face him.

"I should've expected the vultures would start to circle before I even took my vows." I lift my empty glass to him before abandoning it.

Michael huffs, signaling for the bartender. "I'm not here to scavenge, Lucy. I just came to see the groom before he damns himself a little further." He grins at me before he orders a bourbon and water. "You *are* my brother after all."

"Can't take it straight?" I nod after the bartender.

Michael chuckles. "Some of us have no desire to get drunk on our own delusions."

"Funny. You've been high on your own virtue since I fell. How's that working out for you? Does Father know you exist yet?"

Michael's grip on his glass tightens incrementally, and he sets it down, the veins in his neck straining. "I look forward to stabbing the Holy Lance into that beautiful bride of yours while you watch."

If only he realized that doing so will be the bitter end of this little apocalypse he's waging. I will feast on his entrails before I allow him to destroy Charlotte. If I cannot have her, no one can.

I smirk. "Don't act like that wasn't always your plan. You've been sharpening that flaming sword of yours since long before the invitations went out." I lean onto the bar top beside him, my voice dropping low. "Tell the Hosts to bring everything they have. I want the sky to bleed before the cake's even cut."

Michael's jaw tenses, his face mottled with his fury as I turn away from him.

But he won't let me have the last word that easily.

"Play with me?" He nods toward the nearby grand piano. "For old times' sake?"

My nostrils flare, but I nod, capitulating.

The guests will fucking eat it up.

I sit down on the bench first, claiming the high keys so I can control the melody, even if he sets the pace.

Michael drops down onto the bench next to me, purposefully nudging my shoulder with one of his wings. I pluck the nearest feather, causing him to startle before I begin playing.

My fingers move deftly across the keys, setting the tone as Michael claims the bass.

"You always played too fast. No patience for the sad parts," I mutter through clenched teeth, smiling as the cameras begin to flash.

He huffs. "You always dragged them out like you were trying to make the notes bleed."

I smirk, adding an unexpected flare, and the cameras flash wildly.

They're here for me and Charlotte.

Not him.

He'll always be second best. Even when I'm dying.

For once, I feel an unexpected bit of pity for him.

Michael lets out a shallow sigh, the bitterness in his expression fading as the song goes on. "Do you remember when Father made the stars, and you tried to rearrange them into your own constellations?"

"'Tried'?" I scoff. "Mine were better. People still name their gods after them."

Michael huffs, his lip twitching. "You always needed to leave your mark. Even on perfection."

"And you always needed everything to stay *exactly* the way He made it. Even when it didn't work." I reach across him, knocking his hands out of the way and claiming the lower octave for myself. "A word of advice, brother. If you want Father's attention so badly, perhaps you should do something unexpected for once."

Abruptly, I end the song on a cheeky, flourished note.

The crowd of guests clap, and I stand, giving a jaunty little bow as I prepare to leave. But Michael is far from finished yet.

"Gabriel says he saw Azrael yesterday."

My shoulders tighten, the possibility of what that could mean not lost on me, but I keep smiling for the cameras. "Must've been a short visit. He's been afraid of him since Babylon."

"He says he saw Azrael with Mother."

My spine runs cold. "You're lying."

"You hope I am."

"Spare me the cryptic buildup. I'm not in the mood." I glance over at him. "What did she say?"

Michael shrugs. "I wasn't there. I was too busy being uninteresting." He stands, casting me a deadpan look. "But let's just say Gabriel said they weren't arguing. They were far too busy *enjoying* one another, if you know what I mean." He laughs.

The burning sensation in my chest doesn't shock me.

But the jealousy does.

Though I no longer have any claim on Death.

"Of course," I mutter, my expression betraying nothing. "She always preferred him. All spine and silence. Just her type."

I button my tux coat, moving to step away.

"I heard she might come today. She's angry you didn't invite her yourself."

I pause. "You're joking."

"Do I look like the funny one?" Michael quirks a brow. "Maybe she wants to see which of her sons she's burying."

I chuckle darkly, straightening my sleeves as I step into his space. "You think you'll win today, but I hate to break it to you, brother—that battle you're fighting? I've already won."

Michael's eyes narrow.

"Self-righteous or not, Father will never take a bullet for you." I clap him on the shoulder as I pull back. "Enjoy the ceremony. The end always makes a good show."

I take my leave, snaking my way throughout the party and shrugging off a few of the guests who try to deter me, before I duck into the Ritz's inner courtyard.

"Azrael," I hiss into the silence, knowing he'll come whenever I call.

The Reaper appears on the other side of the garden a moment later, and my pulse races.

In a tux, he cuts a mean figure, all smolder and bone and ruthless grace, and it's a bloody shame he'll never sink into me again, but considering the gossip I just overheard from Michael . . .

"You fucked my Mother?"

The accusation is a bit more petulant than I'd hope for, really.

Like a child scolding his guardian.

"I know she's been after you since the dawn of time, but honestly, Azrael?"

Death has the audacity to appear unashamed, and his eyes drag over me, cataloging every inch he used to own. He rolls his shoulders, cracking his large, tattooed neck like he's unused to wearing something that constrains him so tightly. I hate how easily my eyes follow the motion, how familiar his body still is to me, how much I want to trace those lines with my tongue instead of my memory.

"We weren't corporeal."

I blink. "How do you even—" I put up a hand, stopping mid-sentence. "No, don't answer that."

I turn my back on him, grimacing at the thought, before I spin to face him again. I sound like my ruddy Father as I begin lecturing him. "I know you are no longer involved with me and Charlotte, but for her sake, I thought you might choose to be—"

Death chuckles at me. "You devious little bastard."

Unexpectedly, he prowls toward me, closing the distance between us and crowding my space until I'm unwillingly forced to take a step back, so he cannot see how he—

"You're jealous, aren't you?"

Pain ignites in my jaw as I glance down. "I have no idea what you're talking about. I—"

"You don't have to admit it, Lightbringer. I know you. You're so fucking jealous you can't stand it." A slow smile builds over his lips. "I thought you'd go back to pretending, now that she's yours, but all it takes is one meaningless fuck with someone else, and you can't even hide how much you miss me, can you?"

My mouth moistens, my breath quickening, the temperature in my body rising.

But I have always been a complete mess for him, and he knows it.

"So, this is how you choose to take your revenge over the fact that she chose *me*?" I sneer, my contempt obvious. "And just before my goddamn wedding day."

I try to leave, but he catches my arm.

"I made a deal with her."

"You what?"

"You heard me." His grip on my arm tightens, then loosens slightly, and I shrug him off. "I made a deal to protect you and Charlotte."

The fury that ignites in me is white hot, laced with the pain of so many times before when he didn't choose me.

"Of course you did, because Father couldn't possibly allow me to end this on my own terms. Jesus Christ, Azrael, what's it going to take for you—"

"I didn't do it on His orders," Death growls, backing me up against an ivy-covered wall until I'm reaching for one of my blades. "I don't know where He is any more than you do." He shakes his head. "But now Lilith's taken care of. Temporarily. She's going to help you and Charlotte, so that you—"

I shake my head. He cannot possibly be serious. "You went behind my back again. Without consulting me. Without—"

"Asking permission from you?" he finishes. "Like Charlotte?" He drops his head, chuckling like he's disappointed in me. "I'm not your sub, Lucifer. But that's always what scared you the most, isn't it? You've never been able to control me, and I know you fucking hate that, but I swear everything I've ever done has been for you and—"

"Oh, not this ruddy nonsense again. You—"

He grabs me, shoving me against the wall, until I have no choice but to face him or give in. And I will not go down without a fight. Ever.

"Why now?" I snap, blade suddenly at his throat. "I'm about to walk down the bloody aisle, and *now* is when you decide to choose something different? To choose *me*?"

"I know you don't trust it, but I've been telling you this whole time, everything I've ever done, everything I've ever been, even acting as your Father's servant, has been for you." Roughly, he grips my face, his gaze raking over me appreciatively. "I love you, you fucking bastard. Even if you can't see it yet." He leans in like he means to kiss me again, but I shove him, then throw my hands in the air.

"It doesn't fucking matter now, does it? Not when we both know I'm going to choose—"

"I don't care that you love her more. I love her too. But what are you afraid of, Lucifer?" He steps closer, leaning into my blade, using his proximity like a weapon against me.

My balls tighten, my cock stiffens, and my mouth waters at the thought of how he—

"Nothing would make Charlotte happier than the three of us together, so what are you—"

"Because I don't deserve it!" I shout, my voice suddenly shaking, even as my hands clench into fists. "You? The love who *betrayed* me?" I huff. "Perhaps. But her? The *both* of you?" I shake my head. "I'm not sure I could ever—"

He grabs me then, dragging me into him, and kisses me.

My blade clatters uselessly to the ground.

It's a kiss for the ages.

The kind that's been written about since the dawn of time.

Ferocious. Vicious. Destructive.

And it costs me everything.

For a moment, I simply melt for him, allow him to lay siege upon my mouth, savoring the way he's brought an end to me. Stripped me of what little pride I had left. But then he fists his hand into the base of my hair, and I'm moaning, bloody moaning, meeting him tongue for tongue, lash for lash, like it was never going to end any differently.

When he releases me, I'm ruined, panting and breathless.

And I feel more than a little put out that I have so often done the same to Charlotte.

She's never going to let me live this down, is she?

Azrael grips both sides of my face, nipping at my bottom lip, and the space behind my ribs hollows like I'm being starved. The pull I feel for him is one I've never been very good at resisting. "You're going to be amazing at it," he whispers, kissing my jaw.

"At what?" I pant.

He steps back, grinning. "I'll leave it to Charlotte to tell you."

I sigh, struggling to regain my composure. "She's going to give us both hell, you know."

Azrael grins, clapping me on the back. "She won't be the only one."

I lift a brow, but he just chuckles like he has a secret he can't wait to tell me. I smile and clap him on the shoulder, relenting. "Let's go get our girl, Reaper."

CHAPTER SIXTY-SEVEN

Charlotte

The limo takes what feels like forever to reach the Château de Versailles—where we've rented out the chapel and several halls for the ceremony—and I'm already running late. Seraph and I had to figure out the whole wings situation, and there was way more blood involved than I expected there would be, but we managed to do it without ruining my hair, makeup, or dress, so that's something.

The moments stretch until they feel like hours, every second dragging on for a lifetime, though in truth, the ride is only about forty minutes. I don't know what exactly I'll say to Lucifer to convince him he's had God's redemption all along, or if he'll even believe me, and if it were any other day, I would've just snapped myself to his side immediately. But I'm not risking traveling through the ether with a wedding train of this length, even if it is removable, and if I wasn't already worried about dying at the altar, Sophie would kill me if I messed up my hair.

But I'm not dying.

Not if I can help it.

As we drive down the Avenue de Paris that leads directly into Place d'Armes, I ask Dagon to head past the main entrance at Grille d'Honneur to the Queen's Gate to avoid the cameras. He parks at a side service entrance that leads to the royal apartments, bowing as he opens the door for me. "My queen."

If there were ever a time I felt the weight of that title, this is it.

I give him a small smile and hurry inside, taking the servant passages up the narrow staircase and bypassing the formal Cour d'Honneur completely.

I need to find my husband and fast.

Slipping into the Queen's Antechamber and avoiding the main entrance, I navigate through the dim, narrow passages behind the queen's enfilade, my massive train trailing behind me. I should have had Seraph or Greed come to help me with it considering how unwieldy it is, but there's no time for second thoughts now.

I'm safely inside the Hall of Mirrors before I allow myself to take a breath, but I can still hear the celebration happening downstairs. My exhales cloud in the chilled air, and I'm about to call out in hopes that Azrael might hear me through the Nothing, but then I turn and find Michael.

The Holy Lance is in his hand, and he twirls it once, almost lazily, like he did in the In-Between.

I glance back to the door I came from, and for a moment, I consider trying to make a run for it, but this dress isn't conducive to fast movement. Though I plan on ripping the train off after the ceremony and photos, and I'm armed to the teeth underneath, I wouldn't stand a chance against Michael, and my in-laws are not about to ruin my wedding day.

Not if I can help it.

I face him, subtly dropping my hands.

All my training has made it so I can defend myself, hold my own, but it's going to take a lifetime for me to catch up in skill to Lucifer and his siblings. Azrael still regularly wipes the floor with me. A warrior I am not.

But I've learned how to handle celestial bullies, and that's all Michael really is.

An immortal bully with a childish score to settle.

"Well, Dad works in mysterious ways, doesn't He?" Michael presses his hands together in prayer and gestures toward the ceiling.

I take a step back.

But there's nowhere to go. I'm already backed into a corner, and this dress is going to be the death of me. I made a mistake asking Azrael for privacy today, but I didn't want him to see me before the ceremony. I'm going to have to talk my way out of this.

Like I would with any good PR story.

"Michael." I give a little curtsy in greeting.

"Charlotte." The archangel grins like the cat who just swallowed the canary.

"Thanks so much for coming, but I really need to get to the chapel." I try to walk past him, pretend this is a casual conversation with any guest, but he blocks my path easily.

"Going somewhere, princess?"

The hairs on the back of my neck rise on end.

I switch tactics.

"Lucifer and Death are looking for me."

"Are they?" Michael smirks. "How long do you think it'll take them to find you?"

My spine runs cold, but I gesture to the lance. "Oh, and you're welcome by the way."

Distract. Reframe. Refocus.

Michael lifts a brow.

"You know, for giving you what you want. If it weren't for me, you wouldn't have nearly as many seals open, and now with Lucifer and me bowing out, it'll be easy for you to get the other Originals on your side, won't it?" I plaster on my best Sunday-morning-greeting grin.

Not to mention killing me puts a complete stop to your apocalypse plans.

But he still doesn't know that yet.

I tuck that ace up my sleeve for later, faking a smile, but Michael just laughs like he thinks I'm genuinely funny.

My ribs tighten.

"Cute." He gestures over the length of my body. "The whole media bit. I see why my brother likes you. Lucy's always had a soft spot for anything he could corrupt." He drags the Holy Lance across one of the marble pilasters near him, and it lets out a deafening scrape.

My mouth runs dry.

He tosses it to his other hand like it's nothing, juggling it effortlessly. "Did you know when we were cherubs, I used to look up to Lucifer?"

I force a shrug. "That doesn't surprise me. You're obsessed with everything he does."

Almost as obsessed with him as me.

I couldn't love my husband more, and falling in love with Azrael has only reaffirmed my commitment to him, to both of them.

Together, they're my everything.

Michael smirks wickedly, like he's legitimately enjoying this. "He's the oldest, you know. Mother and Father's clear favorite, and with so many of us, I used to have to fight just to be in his shadow, clamor after whatever scraps he'd give me."

My pulse races, adrenaline shooting through me with each additional step he takes. I *really* don't want to ruin my dress. "I get it. What it feels like to be overlooked. I was a human nobody until Lucifer plucked me out of obscurity, and it's addicting, isn't it? The limelight, the attention, being allowed to stand in even a sliver of his shade?"

And terrifying.

Our fans would dump me on my ass in a minute if I were ever to leave Lucifer. Many almost did the moment the paparazzi got ahold of those photos of me and Azrael. The public eye is fickle. Nearly as fickle as immortals.

They'd turn on me in an instant.

But it's not them I'm here for.

It's me.

My heart speeds up, the thought lighting an unexpected buoyant sensation inside my chest.

Lust was right.

All this time I thought I was fighting for humanity. For something greater than myself.

And that's true. But I've also been fighting for me. To be my fullest, most sinful self.

God and my father's judgment be damned.

I smile, suddenly standing taller as my lungs expand.

Just like that, I know who I am.

I am the woman who fights for her own salvation.

No matter how wicked it may make me.

I glance at Michael, my lips twisting into a satisfied grin. I can't say I'm no longer afraid of him, but I'm not going to cower in fear at the thought of what he, the Righteous, my father, or hell, even the devil can do to me.

No matter what it is, I'm confident I can recover from it.

Regardless of the scars it might leave.

Michael draws closer, only a few feet away from me now.

I could try to blast him, use my powers.

But I don't need to.

"You really don't know, do you?" I say, trying the same line that worked on my dad. Abusers are all the same, honestly. "Lucifer's already two steps ahead of you. He was this entire time. If you kill me, your apocalypse dies too. The seals will be closed off, and God won't come back anytime soon to thank you."

Michael waves a hand. "Oh, I've known that since before you killed your friend."

I wince. My grief over Jax is still raw.

Michael spreads his wings wide, their feathered tips extending out, then dropping down. "The Righteous have had their eye on you and your 'prophet' for a while, and while most of them turned on me when I didn't deliver their Rapture, there were others who remained faithful, hopeful, willing to talk to anyone with wings. When I found out about Him, I paid Him a little visit, and lo and behold, I recognized who He was instantly. I couldn't have mistaken Him anywhere. Unlike you and Lucy."

My stomach clenches. "So, you had the Righteous kill God?"

He chuckles. "No, I wouldn't do that to Dad. That was their own doing. Humans are just monkeys with a faulty conscience and a knack for inventing interesting ways to kill each other, but Father said He didn't want the apocalypse, said that wasn't why He left. You can imagine I felt a bit"—he tilts his head back and forth—"fucked over by that. I was still planning to open the remaining seals anyway, for the fun of it, as a fuck-you to Dad—Lucifer and I may have a bit more in common than I thought—but then I changed plans, though killing you serves my goal all the same. Lucifer won't ever get his powers back if you're dead. Not if I can help it."

Changed plans?

My mind starts to connect the dots, the patterns, put conclusions together.

"So, you teamed up with Lilith before the fourth seal opened? Switched teams?"

No wonder Lilith wasn't in the In-Between. Michael wasn't underestimating her. She was trusting *him* to do her bidding.

But to what end?

Michael spins the lance, a prideful gleam in his eye. "Mother plans to create a new universe, and while she may have made the mistake of originally intending for its god to be Lucy, she changed her tune the moment I was willing to deliver her what she wanted."

My stomach drops.

It all makes sense now.

Why Lilith destined me for Lucifer. Why she played him and Michael off one another. Helped Michael get the lance. All to convince her favorite son that this world was unsafe, that her new universe would be the safer option for me.

For me and his child.

She was gifting her new god a goddess.

That haunting prophecy of hers comes rushing back to me.

For as it is written, she who was dead shall bring forth the living to the wrath of the Last Judgment. And she thought I was going to play right into her plans.

I shake my head.

No. No, I'm not going anywhere, and neither is Lucifer.

Not when this world is still worth saving.

Michael lifts the blade.

"Don't." I shake my head, my palms suddenly glowing with white light. "Lucifer will scorch you where you stand." He doesn't even need his hellish powers to do it anymore.

Not after I tell him he's had God's redemption, his angelic powers, this whole time.

"Michael!" I hear a familiar voice hiss.

The voice of a mother scorning her child.

Lilith.

Michael whirls, shoving the lance behind his back guiltily. "Mom." Unlike me, he doesn't exactly look surprised to see her, just nervous.

My pulse races.

Lilith stalks toward us, her dark hair lifting with each step like it's electrified from her fury. "I swear, Michael Apollyon, if you touch a single hair on her head, I will . . ."

The sentence doesn't need finishing.

Lilith's threat is clear.

Michael sighs. "Mom, be reasonable. I opened the fourth seal for you, got your powers back. We're on the same—"

"*This* is why I'm still going to make you fight for your place with Lucifer. Do you understand?" Lilith turns from one to many, the voices of all three terrifying versions of her echoing off the hall mirrors. "If you must settle this petty score with your brother, you'll have it out with *him*. Not Charlotte."

"But, Mom, I—"

"Do I make myself clear, Michael?"

Michael's shoulders sink. That's a battle we both know he can't win. Lilith is a goddess. The Mother of everything. More powerful than God Himself.

Michael casts me a scathing look, but then he tucks the Holy Lance back into his tux and leaves, the sound of his footsteps echoing after him.

Lilith turns from three to one again, her hair settling.

Mother. Maiden. Crone.

But she's back to being Mother again.

Holy fuck.

I face her.

I'm not feeling much better about the idea of being alone with her than I did with Michael.

"I hear you have something I want." She smiles at me, beckoning me with the crook of a single finger, and without moving my feet, I'm halfway across the room, so fast it's like the edges of reality bent me in her direction.

My breath comes in quick, heady pants, swirling around my face.

"May I?" the Goddess asks, nodding down to my bodice.

It's laced tight enough I'm not showing, but that's starting to become a struggle. It won't be long before I can't hide it anymore, and I still need to tell Lucifer, but how exactly do you tell your Mother-in-Law, the Goddess of all Creation, that she can't touch your baby bump?

Before I can stop myself, I give a reluctant nod.

I don't think Lilith will hurt me, especially since she knows I'm pregnant.

She *really* wants grandchildren.

She draws closer, and the moment the Goddess presses her hand to my belly, I feel the first flutter of movement there.

My eyes go wide.

Lilith's grin is so triumphant it reminds me way too much of Lucifer whenever we're in the playroom, which is a large part of how we got here, honestly.

I'd do anything for him and that damn grin.

"A girl." Lilith smiles.

A statement, not a question.

The prideful gleam in her eyes is confident. "Oh, she's going to be something."

Daughter of the devil. Granddaughter to God and Lilith.

I force a nervous smile.

Yeah, she's going to be something all right.

A complete hellion most likely.

"She'll look like the prophecies I've sent to you." Lilith removes her hand, clasping her palms together like she's willing it into existence, and because she's said it, it'll be so.

My pulse races. So, that beautiful little girl, the one with the dark curls and the upturned nose and the fiery amber eyes, really is mine and Lucifer's daughter.

I try not to choke on the well of emotion that creates in me.

But I'm too terrified to enjoy it right now.

I knew Lilith had been sending me those dreams since the moment I found out she'd fated us, but hearing her confirm it is a whole different level of messed up.

"You'll make a wonderful mother." She pats my tummy, her eyes shining, before she steps away. "You won't have to worry. When I find my Husband, this universe will end, and we'll make a new one. I'll even restore Lucifer's more hellish powers. Michael may have insisted he get his chance at playing God, but Lucifer will find a way to best him like he always does. Don't you worry your pretty little head over it. My bets are on him for a reason. He's my pride and joy after all, my first and greatest love. Even if things didn't work out with his Father."

I give the slightest shake of my head. "I don't want a new one." My voice is barely audible.

"Pardon?" She turns to look at me.

My shoulders stiffen. "I said I don't want a new universe."

Lilith's smile fades. "You'd choose to have my granddaughter here? In *this* world? The one my Husband sculpted from the scraps of my creation?" She says the word *husband* like it's the most despicable thing. "In this place where men claim to be leaders, but then use His word to rape, to maim, to pillage, to abuse? To take the power of those created in *my* image, despite that *I* was who birthed them? Who birthed all of them?" The ends of her hair start to electrify again.

"I get it." I lift my hands in surrender. "And I agree with you. He locked your babies away. Took your power for His apocalypse and then didn't give you any of the credit."

"Exactly," she hisses, those electrified ends settling a little. "I knew we'd see eye to eye."

"But punishing Him isn't going to heal you."

I can say that with certainty now.

Torturing my father may have helped release the pent-up emotions that were blocking me from healing, but it didn't *fix* anything.

The scars are still there.

What I really needed to do was give him the one thing he never gave me—mercy—to believe in myself, to reclaim my power. Just like Lucifer needs to do.

She casts me a wistful smile. "I'm a goddess, Charlotte. I've no interest in healing."

"Humanity doesn't deserve to die in the crossfire." I step forward. "If you go after God, I'm going to try to stop you."

I can't allow her to destroy the entire universe.

As fucked up as it may be, there's beauty in it too.

Beauty that's worth saving.

Lilith's smile spreads, slow, knowing. It's the same smile Lucifer gives me when he thinks I've done something "quaintly mortal." "I'd love to see you try." She steps closer, the air bending with her like gravity itself leans in to obey her. "You make a beautiful bride. It's almost as if I handpicked you for my son myself. I could choose another." She smirks wickedly, patting my cheek before she turns to head downstairs toward the ceremony.

Leaving me shaking from head to toe.

She thinks I'm optional. That she could replace me.

But I'm confident in Lucifer's love for me now.

"There's one thing I don't understand," I call after her.

She pauses, glancing over her shoulder.

"If you knew Lucifer had God's redemption this whole time? That he could have children, and you wanted him to take God's place? Why not tell him?"

She smiles. "Clearly, you have a lot to learn about being a mother, Charlotte." She smiles wistfully. "I did tell him, back in that clearing. But our children rarely listen until they're ready."

CHAPTER SIXTY-EIGHT

Azrael

When Lucifer tasks me with searching for his missing bride, I hear Charlotte call out to me from the Hall of Mirrors. I'm at her side in an instant. She asked for privacy, for me to give her space today, and even though it was a risk, I granted it, because she didn't want me to see her before she walked down the aisle.

She stands in the middle of the hall in her wedding dress, and the sight of her hits me like an electrical jolt through my body.

The stillness in me shifts, almost alive.

Fuck, I love her.

And she's mine now too. Even if she doesn't know it yet.

My smile builds slowly. "You've never looked more beautiful, little siren."

She blushes, her gaze sweeping over me. "You don't clean up half bad yourself."

I grin. I don't particularly love how the tux I'm wearing stifles my movement, clings a little too tight to the width of my shoulders, but I smooth a hand down the front all the same.

Her gaze follows it hungrily, but then she glances away, like she still thinks she shouldn't want me. "Lilith was just—"

"I know."

I prowl toward her, closing the distance between us as I recount the details of mine and Lilith's deal. The blood oath I made.

Charlotte's eyes grow wide, her long lashes fluttering. "So, you broke your covenant with God to save . . ."

"You and Lucifer. And also . . ." I tip my chin toward her bodice, to what she's hiding.

"That's the real reason why Michael gave up opening the seals? Because Lilith's already locked them? Thanks to the deal you made with her?"

I nod. "She'll still try to get Lucifer to agree to relocating, but only *after* he and Michael have it out. She's still hell-bent on finding God, destroying everything."

We're not in the clear entirely.

But one enemy is better than two.

Charlotte takes it all in, the hope in her eyes building. "And how did you manage to . . . ?"

I blush, pawing at the back of my neck sheepishly. "Don't ask."

Charlotte laughs. "Azrael, you devil."

I chuckle. "There's a reason my brothers, her little harem of Horsemen, were designed after me, and why she never much liked me with Lucifer, aside from the fact that I couldn't give her grandchildren."

She suppresses a smile. "A part of me thinks I should be jealous, but I guess I no longer have a claim on you, do I? And when you're immortal, it seems like everybody ends up fucking everybody."

"Something like that." I grin.

We both fall silent for a beat, the space between us charged with everything left unsaid.

"Azrael."

She steps forward, and for a moment I think she might tell me that she . . .

She places her hand on my chest. "I know what you've been guarding all these years."

My breath comes out in one fell swoop.

A knot forms in my stomach as my limbs turn heavy.

She can't possibly mean that she knows the secret I've been guarding.

"When Jax sent me her prophecy, I saw . . . a lot of moments between you and Lucifer, including when you first met, when he was pleading for . . ."

God's mercy.

I keep my face blank, my breath bottling in my chest.

She's so close, so fucking close, but I can't allow myself to hope that she'll figure it out.

"You've been safeguarding Lucifer's redemption this whole time, haven't you?"

I exhale everything I've been holding in.

A weight lifts from my shoulders, and I stand tall, a rush of adrenaline swelling in me.

"Lucifer told me that when he lost his wings, God also took his ability to create," she says, practically reading my mind, "and then when I asked Seraph, she said Lucifer was never included in God's original redemption competition in the first place, but that's not because God doesn't love him, is it? It's because Lucifer already had God's redemption this whole time. He's just been waiting for you to guide him, to help him see."

I bow my head in a silent prayer, glancing toward the heavens as I mutter, "You mangy Mother Fucker."

All this time and He wasn't just waiting on my Lightbringer.

He was waiting on me too.

To show Him I was willing to risk everything for the son He's always loved.

For the daughter who believed in Him.

I close the distance between her and me in two quick strides, needing to move. To release some of this . . . this euphoria I'm feeling.

I grip her by the back of her neck, my gaze combing over her appreciatively. Fuck, she's breathtaking. Everything I could ever want, though I thought she'd never put it together.

"You clever, clever girl," I praise her.

She blushes, glancing down shyly. "You stood by Lucifer for all of eternity, hoping that one day he'd see the good in himself."

I nod, my face feeling stretched from where I can't stop smiling. "If I'd have told him, he would have never believed me, and he would've risked losing . . ."

"You," she finishes.

"No." I draw in a large breath, my chest expanding. "You. Lilith may have fated you for him, but God chose you to help him heal."

Charlotte beams at me, the love in her eyes washing over me like a wave of peace, of contentment. "You've been guarding us both, at all costs, right from the very beginning."

I place a hand on her lower back, pulling her close, until she can feel my need pressed against her. She gasps, still thinking I'm forbidden fruit to her, but the bit of amber in her eyes turns molten.

"It seems God makes good on some of His promises after all."

I want to lean down and kiss her, show her she's *ours*, rip this dress off her and fuck her until she's full of me, but I'll leave that final revelation to Lucifer. I run my thumb over the diamond collar she's wearing.

Our collar.

Or it's going to be.

Even if we'll only have a short time for her to wear it, if Lilith has her way with God.

"What are we going to do about Lilith?" she asks, her thoughts mirroring mine. "I have some ideas, but I'm going to need your help."

"I'll safeguard your plan however I can, little siren. Trust me." I cast her a lighthearted grin, filled with the promise that from now on, she and her devil will have my undying loyalty.

For now and the rest of our shared eternities.

CHAPTER SIXTY-NINE

Charlotte

When I slip out of the Salon de Diane, the room that Azrael and I ducked into for me to direct him on my plan, Greed intercepts me in the vestibule leading toward the Royal Chapel, brandishing my bouquet.

"Where the hell have you been?" she hisses. "The photographers. All the guests. Everyone is waiting for you downstairs."

I shake my head. "I got held up by Michael and then your Mother. Where's Lucifer?"

"Already waiting at the altar for you. He sent Azrael to look for you."

Oh, Azrael came looking for me all right.

Every moment near him knowing I'm not allowed to touch him is torture.

How badly would Lucifer punish me if I had Azrael freeze time and fucked his best man before the wedding without his permission?

I push the fantasy aside.

If my husband's already at the altar, then we're going to have to improvise.

Greed ushers me along the corridor, trying to hurry me toward the chapel, but I grab her arm, staying her. "Mimi, I want you to know that whatever happens today, I appreciate you giving me that dossier." It's better than any other wedding gift I'm likely to get.

Though I specifically asked all the guests to make generous donations to a list of global charities around the world. I think philanthropy might be my next undertaking anyway.

I am *so* over PR.

Greed waves a dismissive hand. "My brothers had a bit of a hand in it, too, though if we're going to die, I'm happy to hoard all the credit, of course."

"We?" I lift a brow. "You and the other Originals changed your mind? You're going to fight with us?"

My heart stops.

Lucifer was right.

The winds of celestial battles *do* shift quickly.

Greed blows out an annoyed breath like I'm asking about yesterday's news. "I talked the others into it this morning. I'm a far superior negotiator to you."

"And what kind of deal do you expect in—"

Greed huffs. "Not everything I do is for my own gain, you know. Just most of it." She shrugs.

"Then why . . . ?"

"For Mia, and because you're my sister. That's why." Her plump red lips press together in confusion. "What other reason do I need?"

Without warning, I fling myself into her arms, pulling her in for a hug.

And though she grumbles a little, to my surprise, she lets me.

When we break apart, I'm beaming from ear to ear, smiling as wide as any bride should be and hoping my mascara and setting spray hold as she passes me my bouquet.

Pulling her into a nearby alcove, I quickly catch her up to speed.

"*That's* your plan?" she says when I'm finished.

I cringe. Well, when she puts it like that, it does seem a little . . . haphazard.

But I'm still new to this, and it's the best I've got, unfortunately.

"Well, that's some of it anyway, and you're not going to like this next part, but"—I take her hands in mine—"I also need you to help me give Sloth a pair of wings."

CHAPTER SEVENTY

Lucifer

When Azrael returns from tracking down Charlotte, he prowls down the aisle like a primal beast, pausing only when he reaches one of the first pews. He heaves my brother to his feet by one arm, hauling Belphegor up to the front of the chapel with us and depositing him at the altar beside me.

"What the hell are you doing?" I hiss.

If I'm going to fucking die today, I'm not going to spend my last moments with my siblings. Mother may have chosen to momentarily lend a hand to our cause, but there is a zero-sum chance a fight won't break out at the reception. This room is a lit celestial powder keg, and despite whatever delay of the inevitable Azrael may have buggered out of my Mother, I am still, unfortunately, mortal.

And I am done keeping my siblings in line for all of eternity.

Let them be someone else's problem now.

"You'll thank me later," Azrael grumbles, brushing his hands over the front of my Versace tux as he straightens my jacket for me. He hasn't stopped grinning since he had his way with me in the garden earlier, and the joy he clearly takes in this is a bit disturbing.

I never expected he'd be this eager to end me.

Though I suppose the lance should've been my first clue.

Bel blinks slowly, like he might have pregamed a whole fucking field of cannabis in order to get through this. He's always hated family gatherings. "Why did you drag me up—"

"Just shut up and stand there," Azrael growls.

"Did you find her?" I ask, my muscles tightening. A small part of me is furious at the thought that sending him might've meant that she enjoyed him without me.

"You may be her primary Dom, but she's *ours* now, remember, Lightbringer?" Death claps my shoulder. "Don't worry, she's coming."

Death looks a little too pleased with himself for my comfort, at the moment.

But I suppose I have no choice but to trust him now that he's finally broken his covenant with my Father. Who else has been beside me since my Fall?

"What were the terms of the deal you made with Father, anyway?" I glance toward him.

Azrael grins. "You'll find out soon enough."

But then the music swells, the crowd stands, and I find my bride standing at the start of the aisle, and my heart stops beating.

She's an absolute picture. Perfection embodied. More angelic than I could ever be.

She's already my wife. Already mine in every way. But seeing her like this tightens something in my throat.

"It's okay if you cry, Lightbringer," Azrael mumbles.

"I don't bloody cry," I hiss.

Azrael snorts.

"Not in public, at least," I grumble.

Charlotte makes her way down the aisle, all our guests watching and the cameras flashing. For a moment, I hope no part of this is tainted for her by the fact that, even if I hadn't killed him, her father would never have been deserving of handing her away to me.

I am the only one she calls Daddy now.

Azrael will need a different honorific, honestly.

She belongs to me.

Has given me her heart.

Even when I didn't deserve it.

Even when I manipulated her for my own means.

The trust she's placed in me will be what humbles me for the rest of my days.

When Charlotte reaches my side, she passes her bouquet to my sister, who quickly exchanges it with Azmodeus, who's sitting in the front row, in favor of a large rucksack I've just now noticed he's holding. A bit of crimson pools at the bottom.

My brother just looks down at the bouquet, smirking, like he finds all of this an epic waste when we could skip the whole romance and go straight to the shagging.

I might have once agreed with him, but I'm still furious from how he fucked Charlotte and me over, and after I allowed him to touch her no less, so I glance down at the bouquet pointedly, my tone mocking. "You think love has brought me low?" I chuckle darkly, the hellfire in my eyes blazing. "You're next, brother," I hiss.

Lust pales a little.

I turn toward my bride, taking her hands in mine as the priest begins to chant in Latin. Angelic wasn't exactly an option, unfortunately.

"Lucifer," Charlotte whispers, the words spilling out of her when I lift her veil, her eyes fierce with something she can't hold back.

I don't typically stand on ceremony, but she seems completely unaware of all the guests and cameras watching us.

"Yes, darling?" I mutter through my teeth.

"There's something I need to tell you." She grips my hands.

"Whatever it is, little dove, I think it can wait until—"

"I'm pregnant, sir."

The words come out a little louder than she intended, and a hushed whisper tears through the crowd.

But I can't possibly have heard her correctly.

I glance over my shoulder at Azrael, eyes narrowed, but Charlotte pulls my attention back to her.

"I'm pregnant," she repeats, reading the confusion in my expression easily. "And it's yours, not Azrael's," she adds. "I'm certain."

I stand there, feeling frozen and lightheaded.

And then what she said connects, and without warning, I drop to my knees in front of her, pulling her to me and kissing her belly. Over and over again. Where my child is . . .

"You perfect, perfect girl," I worship her. "Look what you've given me."

My heart races, a tingling sensation starting at my chest and expanding outward so fast I can hardly wrap my head around it.

When I stagger to my feet a moment later, I pull her into my arms, kissing her for all she's worth—which is everything—everything I own, my billions, my power, all of it.

She can take all of it for all I care.

Once we resurface, the chapel is so quiet I could hear a pin drop, and even the priest has stopped chanting.

I look out over our myriad of guests, scowling. "Oh, don't look so bloody shocked. No bride of mine was ever going to be a virgin."

"I don't think that's what they're shocked about, Lucifer," Charlotte mutters, her eyes darting to the crowd.

My brother and several of my angelic siblings now stand, their weapons drawn, their wings spread, and that's when I realize that I'm going to be a . . .

A father.

I'm going to be a father.

Like *Him*.

And yet I have no idea how to be . . .

My gaze shoots to Azrael as I sway slightly, a bit of color draining from my face. "Azrael," I mutter desperately.

Death grips me by the shoulder, steadying me.

As he always has.

"I've got you, Lightbringer." He smiles, wide and knowing. "You had it all along. I was just waiting for you to see."

All this time, he's been . . .

I turn toward him and grab him by both sides of his face, kissing him in front of the crowd. A shocked gasp tears from all the humans and media present as the cameras begin flashing. But Charlotte's adorable squeal of delight is all that matters to me.

This moment will be plastered all over the world within minutes, across every newsstand and digital screen, but I don't fucking care.

Let humanity see what they both mean to me.

Charlotte grabs my hand, squeezing it in approval, and I pull back, my heart swelling over how she's beaming from ear to ear. She saw this coming all along, didn't she?

I don't know how I never recognized it before.

But redemption, I realize, feels a lot like the moment she first told me she loved me.

The moment she set me free.

The sound of a blade drawn from its sheath echoes from the other side of the chapel as my brother draws the Holy Lance, stepping forth as the humans amongst the crowd begin to scream and flee.

My Mother watches from the back of the crowd, a slow grin spreading, like she intends for us to have a proper row, and I realize with a start what her true endgame must be.

But I have no intention of being a god.

I prefer being the villain He made me.

I throw back my head and laugh wickedly, casting out my arms wide. "Guess who's back, Mikey?" I chuckle fiendishly, before I glance toward Azrael. "Right then. Shall we?"

Abruptly, I slam my fist into the ground, the few human guests left shrieking as I use the whole of my angelic strength to tear open a fissure all the way down to my realm beneath. Prophet be damned. I'll fucking break the rules like I always have.

Azrael has hold of the nun's soul in a second, promptly stuffing it into the body of a fresh corpse that one of his other versions has just procured. The nun sputters back to life, and the remaining crowd gasps.

"Welcome back, Ms. Santiago. Now if you don't mind, once I'm through with you, you may want to make yourself scarce quickly." I crook two fingers in a slow, deliberate beckon, as if I were drawing a thread from her spine, a smirk playing at the corner of my mouth. "I believe there's something of mine you've been keeping."

She coughs, sputtering for air, and a cloud of black smoke-like shadows pour from inside her. Within seconds, my hellish power rushes to me like a force. The nun collapses to the floor, passing out, and then I am whole again.

I would never give up my sins because my Father forgives me.

He can fuck right off if He expects that.

I glance at Azrael, at Charlotte, pressing my hand protectively over her womb as I sweep her behind me—I don't know how I didn't recognize it before; she's glowing—and then back to the lance in my brother's hand.

I'll be damned if I allow something as trivial as that blood-soaked blade to best me.

It's time to play.

"I may be redeemed now, but make no mistake, brother." Hellfire coils beneath my skin, erupting across the chapel floor, ready to strike. "I will always be the villain in your story."

CHAPTER SEVENTY-ONE

Charlotte

If the sight of Lucifer in his wedding tux wasn't doing it for me, the defiant smirk on his lips as he faces Michael would be.

I'm glad I'm already pregnant, because if I weren't, this moment would've sealed it.

A rush of warm heat pulses through me, my breath quickening.

Maybe Azmodeus was right.

Maybe I really *do* need to get this breeding kink under control.

Lucifer steps forward, positioning himself in front of me as Michael strides down the aisle toward us, the lance in his hand. The human guests trying to escape are the only thing slowing Michael down, but it's Azrael I look toward.

I reach out, gripping Death's palm.

"You ready, baby girl?" His skeletal face flashes, but I lean in, kissing him in spite of it. He's death and decay and destruction and the delicious end of everything Lucifer and I have known previously. But he's ours.

And that's all that matters.

I nod, taking hold of Lucifer's shoulders from behind, as I rise on my toes so I can whisper into my Dom's ear. "You can punish me for this the next time we're in the playroom, sir."

"I look forward to it, little dove." He stiffens, not knowing what I'm about to do, but trusting me. As his equal. "Be safe, my queen."

The next thing I know, Azrael has me in his arms, kissing me like I'm *his* too. Like Lucifer isn't the only one claiming his bride today. I rip off my train, eager to get as close to him as possible and barely even caring about the eyes of the crowd when he sweeps me into a bridal carry.

I smile up at him, sighing, knowing he's got me.

He's got us both.

Suddenly, Greed grabs Sloth, wrenching him to her from behind. She tears off his tux jacket, ripping it in two easily, before pulling Seraph's extra pair of severed wings from the large bag in her hand and slapping the bloodied stumps onto Sloth's back. She mutters under her breath as she uses a bit of her power to weave and fuse them into his spine like they're his stolen birthright, sealing them into place.

"Ow! Oooow!" Sloth howls, glancing over his shoulder at her like he's so stoned he's just now noticed what she's doing.

Why did *he* have to be the one I agreed to get past the pearly gates?

His eyes widen as he realizes what's on his back, and his new wings flex as he mumbles, "Bro. No fucking way."

"You're lucky I like it enough on this pathetic excuse of a rock that I didn't hoard them for myself, you lazy asshole," Mimi snipes, swatting him upside the head affectionately as Bel stretches out his new wings.

"You're going to have to carry me when we get closer to the gates," I say to him, thinking back to that bit of knowledge Salome gave me—all we need is a tear in the realm large enough for a soul to get through, mine, and someone with wings to carry me. I just hope Sloth having me with him is enough of a shield for his sins so he can sneak into Heaven.

But like a true brat, I'm not asking for God's permission.

I'll beg for forgiveness later.

I glance to Lucifer. "I love you."

“I love you too, little dove.” He squeezes my hand, trusting me to act as his queen. Then to Azrael. “Keep her safe, Reaper.”

Azrael grins. “Always.”

Abruptly, I throw out a hand, causing a bit of light to shoot up through the ceiling right above Michael’s head. A hole crumbles in the roof of the chapel, and he dives out of the way.

Azrael flaps his wings, and then we’re shooting skyward out of the chapel, barreling toward Heaven.

My gaze falls to the back of the building, to where I see Lilith let out an amused laugh the moment she realizes what I’m doing. She said she wanted to see me try, so I’m going to try goddammit. In true bratty fashion.

I give her a devilish smirk as we go.

The devil may be her son, but he’s *mine* now.

Race on, bitch.

CHAPTER SEVENTY-TWO

Azrael

Charlotte and I barrel toward Heaven, Sloth in tow, his stolen wings beating against the air. He's not clumsy, just unfamiliar with them after a few millennia, like a weapon reclaimed after centuries of disuse. But he was once made for this. Just like Lucifer was.

And now, for better or worse, he is again.

The wind bites.

The sky thins.

The pressure of the atmosphere increases until I can feel where Heaven looms.

Behind us, the atmosphere crackles with incoming force—Lucifer's siblings, some of the angels that followed, are gaining on us. Radiant and wrathful, they streak through the sky like divine missiles. They're not chasing us. They're hunting.

Like the ruthless warriors they were always meant to be.

Their presence scrapes against my spine, a celestial gravity all its own.

But Charlotte's warm in my arms, her heartbeat pounding against my ribs like a war drum. Her fingers curl lightly through the hair at my nape, and she buries her face in my shoulder. Like she's chosen me, trusts me completely.

With her life. With their daughter's.

So, I push harder.

We're climbing fast, cutting through the atmosphere within seconds.

Still another me stands beside Lucifer as I summon my scythe into my hand, his shadows curling around his Armanis. Michael and the others storm toward us.

Above, the sky splits, and the angels hunting us gain on us like judgment itself, their divine light bleeding at their backs, wings drawn and weapons lit with Heaven's fury. Fuck, there's too many of them.

"Stay with her, Reaper," Lucifer hisses down below, but I'm no longer his weapon to command. "I've no need of you."

I shake my head. "I've waited nearly two thousand years to fight by your side again. I'm not going anywhere. I've got enough for both of you."

"That's an order, Endbringer," Lucifer snarls.

I glance at Charlotte in my arms—her eyes locked on the rift ahead, her mouth parted slightly, radiant with purpose and fury.

She can do this.

She'll find God before Lilith.

This girl who shouldn't have survived.

This woman who made Death and the devil fall hard.

This new immortal carrying a child with more power than half His angels could ever bear.

My little siren. My death wish.

Our future.

And below, Lucifer laughs.

That laugh—the one I've missed. The one that used to echo against my skin whenever I'd take him in the Garden, back when we weren't trying to destroy each other.

He looks glorious in that tux, hellfire licking at his feet.

And he's right.

Right now, he doesn't need me.

Michael will never touch him again.

Not after this.

We're going to make Heaven and Earth tremble.

I follow his order, focusing the whole of myself on Charlotte.

The gates to Heaven begin to shimmer—like a mirage in the distance, a flickering wound that doesn't want to heal. There may be twelve locks keeping it closed, but we're going to split the sky wide fucking open.

"You ready, baby girl?" I murmur into her ear, my voice battling against the wind.

She smiles, clinging tighter to me.

I rise like a storm, like a plague, wings stretched to the limit, and she screams as together, we rip through Heaven's gates like we were always meant to.

CHAPTER SEVENTY-THREE

Lucifer

My wife and our Reaper vanish like twin bolts, their ascent vibrating through the atmosphere until the air bleeds with a raw, celestial pressure. My shadows coil and thrash after them, reluctant to let her go, but I force them down. Grind my heel into the scorched floor.

Let her throw open Heaven's gates. Rip apart the home that was once stolen from me.

I've other divine business to handle.

Michael steps forward, the Holy Lance in his grip, the blade glinting in all his pathetic, righteous fury. His wings are unfurled, spread wide and white in all their gilded glory, and oh, how he must fucking relish that mine will never return.

Even with our Father's redemption.

Charlotte and I are going to have a little chat about her gifting Seraph's extra pair to Sloth. But I've never needed them.

Not for tearing down whatever holy roller might stand in front of me.

Near one of the shattered pews, Azmodeus leans against a scorched column, idly drawing sigils with his finger through the dust and ash.

"Are you two going to keep measuring holiness, or can we fast-forward to the part where Mikey bleeds?" He grins, all teeth and danger. "I'm placing bets with Mammon on who cries first."

Michael ignores him.

I smirk wickedly.

My siblings are going to join me after all.

I'd expect nothing less.

They crave angelic blood just as much as me.

Heaven's downfall.

Michael's jaw sets. His eyes narrow. "When I'm god, I will show you no mercy."

I chuckle. "Look around, Mikey." I gesture to the flaming chapel. "I already am a god." I point toward Heaven. "And even He loves what a devil I can be."

Michael lunges.

I meet him head-on, our blades clashing—his Lance against the infernal edge I summon into the heat of my palm. He shoves me back, throwing Holy Fire like it's a goddamn curse, but I spin out of the way. The blast knocks a few of the pews clear across the room.

This may not be Armageddon, but both of us are bloodthirsty.

Our siblings scatter.

And I push harder, still laughing.

"You think you can kill me?" I spit, eyes blazing. "Even your own army thinks you're second best." I gesture to where some of the Hosts are still dithering about the room, clearly questioning where their loyalties lie now that Father has chosen me.

Michael has never been anything more than second fiddle.

Unworthy of being His adversary.

With a furious war cry, I drive back at him with a blast of light, forcing him to shield himself with one wing as its heat scorches the air. We clash again, my shadows to his blade, and the lance sings with a sacred wrath, but I've fought worse.

I've fought Him. Fought for His mercy.

And this time, I've got every reason to win.

Charlotte.

Azrael.

Our child.

Our future.

The Hell on Earth that will be our making.

Michael stumbles, tripping over my foot. He lashes out, blade slicing toward my side, but I twist, the tip grazing only the edge of my shirt.

The fabric hisses as it burns, smoke curling like incense.

"That was Versace, you fool." I grab him by his tux collar and slam him into the marble floor, my face inches from his. "I was never the one afraid of falling," I hiss, voice low and venomous. "And this time, I'm dragging you down to Hell with me."

Michael shoves me off and flips backward, wings flaring out, fury writ across every line of his face. But I see it now. The smallest sliver of doubt. A crack in the mask of his divinity. Because deep down, he knows as well as I do.

I've already won.

I smile coldly and draw myself to my full height, fire dancing along my skin. My shadows curl about my legs, my true form bleeding through the seams of this skin.

"You were a prideful fool!" Michael roars, glancing about at the unmoving Hosts in his rage. "We all saw the mockery Father made of you."

"Looks like Dad changed His mind." I chuckle. "I never needed to be His favorite. Not like you did. And yet everyone believes *I'm* the one with daddy issues?"

Michael roars and charges me again.

This time, I don't hold back.

I become everything He feared and more.

Hellfire and brimstone.

Shadow and fury.

Pain and punishment.

My shadows meet the lance in a blinding clash, heat and light, sin and destruction rippling outward like a force, shattering what's left of the chapel windows and sending debris raining from the rafters like falling stars.

In my periphery, I'm vaguely aware of my closest siblings charging toward the angelic Hosts in a divine combat for the ages.

Chaos incarnate echoes through the chapel.

Wrath clashes with Raphael, furious ego and healing magic colliding in bursts of crimson and gold. Wrath barrels straight into him, their fight a storm of fists and fire. No grace, just raw, righteous fury. And anger sharp enough to make the sky bleed.

Lust charges at Gabriel, every move a deadly seduction, blades flashing like silver tongues.

Even Envy circles Ramiel, snarling, never satisfied and never still until he's stolen his opponent's most cherished ability. Gluttony rips through Sariel's holy light with an unholy hunger that devours the spells of his angelic counterparts in midair, laughing through the ash.

And Greed—dear, radiant Mimi—spins with the grace of a dancer through it all, her golden blades slashing through Uriel's defenses before he can blink. Her eyes gleam with the promise of *more*, as she snatches his power from him with every strike, like it's owed to her.

Only Sloth is missing, but he has his own war to wage.

They're devils just like I am, the whole lot of them.

Pains in the arse though they might be.

Michael and I go round for round, toe for toe, my legions and his armies joining the fray. Heads roll. Limbs sever. Blood sprays. Until the palace is little more than shambles around us. Until we are both panting in our never-ending fury.

Michael fights as if he has something to save—Heaven, his legacy, himself maybe.

But *I* fight like I've got nothing to lose.

Because I'm not afraid of burning.

Even if I now have everything to live for.

His blade slices across my chest, driving me back, but I barely feel it. My fist slams into his jaw, and he staggers, wings flaring wildly to catch his balance.

I follow, ever relentless, the ground blackening beneath my feet with every step. My power coils tighter with each blow, each block, each strike.

My righteous fury, my heavenly powers, burst out of me—my light, my divinity, nearly blinding everyone in the vicinity. I steal the moment to my advantage, driving Michael back and into the broken altar furiously as I manage to claw the lance free of his hand.

The holy relics crack.

The gold fractures.

And somewhere nearby, I swear I can hear one of my siblings scream. Seraph, perhaps.

I lean in close, pressing the infernal edge of *my* blade to Michael's throat.

He sputters, paling in fear. "All right. All right, you win, Lucy. But for Christ's sake, Mother's here, show some mercy."

"Mercy?" I murmur, voice like embers. "Mercy?" I let out a fiendish chuckle. I knew it wouldn't take much for him to beg. "Only if you plead for it."

Michael's eyes narrow, but he opens his mouth, prepared to relent just as I shove the blade harder against his throat. Blood pools there, calling to me.

Reminds me of every wicked thing I've ever been.

I want nothing more than to see him bleed.

I lean in close, hissing, "You forfeited the right to my mercy the moment you threatened my *wife*." I bring the blade up.

Michael is breathing hard, blood trickling from the corner of his mouth.

But his eyes burn with fear, with fury.

The remains of the chapel tremble around us.

Powers converge, like something divine unraveling at the seams.

Above, I can *feel* Charlotte and Azrael tearing through the gates. Heaven rupturing.

And below, Hell waits for me with open arms.

And here, at the center of it all, I stand, unchained.

Free.

I raise my hand, power gathering at my fingertips, ready to strike the final blow.

"You don't deserve His forgiveness," Michael spits.

"Perhaps." I smirk. "But for the record," I say, voice like thunder, "I never fell. You did."

I bring the blade down with all my might.

But my Mother's power stops me mid-stab, barring me from moving.

"Enough!" she shouts, stepping forth from the shadows and freezing us all. With a flick of her wrist, the lance flies from my hand to hers, and she casts it aside ruthlessly. I'm unable to stop her.

There is only one thing more powerful in this universe than I am.

And it's my Mother.

"That's enough," she says. "You've had your fun now, sweetheart."

I glare at her. "He threatened Charlotte."

"And when *you* are the god of our new universe, you can punish him accordingly." Mother waves her hand, and begrudgingly, I'm forced off him, coming to my feet. "But until then, you will let your brother live. Death isn't the worst thing you could possibly do to him." She grins, unabashed, in her little secret. But she's not the only one who's fucked mine and Charlotte's boyfriend. I glare down at Michael furiously.

I've gutted greater creatures for less.

Ended countless lives over a mere whisper of treason.

But my Mother is right. For him, I can do worse.

I can show him exactly why I deserve Father's mercy.

With a furious grumble, I reach down, tugging him to his feet.

The rest of our siblings stare in awe, their own battles long forgotten.

I wrench Michael in close, lowering my voice as I hiss, "Perhaps *this* is why He chose me." Abruptly, I release him, turning my attention to our Mother.

"Don't worry, sweetheart." She pats my cheek affectionately. "Everything will be better in our new universe."

"I'm not going anywhere, Mother, and neither is Charlotte." I brush ash from my chest, eyes flicking to the heavens. Perhaps this is what He had in mind all along.

Perhaps He may have foreseen . . .

No, I'm not going to give that Bastard even a shred of my credit.

I am a being of my own making.

"You'd choose to remain here? In your Father's world?"

I nod. "I have no interest in being a god. Not beyond what He's made me."

She looks at me as if she's never seen me before. Or perhaps, it's that I've changed recently. Love really has made me its fool. "You'd give up your place, your chance to take your Father's role, for *them*?" She gestures to the human nun, collapsed among the debris.

As if she alone represents the whole of humanity.

As Charlotte once did for me.

"Of fucking course not." I shake my head. "I'd give it all up for *her*. For my wife."

"For the woman *I* gifted you?" my Mother practically shrieks. "You'd choose her? Over your own fate? Over me?"

I shrug. "It's the natural order of things."

She scoffs. "Now, you sound like your Father."

I wince.

Perhaps I am a little more like Him than I thought previously.

Though that sparks an entirely new conflict inside me.

I have no fucking idea how to be a father.

I pale slightly.

"Don't worry, darling. I can fix this. Make it all go away. You'll be just like your old self."

"Don't you fucking dare," I snarl, surprised at how readily the words come to me. "I do not *want* to go back to who I was before her, and there is no universe you could possibly create that I wouldn't burn to the ground in order to get back to her."

"You . . . love her?" My Mother says it as if it's something even she thought I was no longer capable of.

"Of course, I do. And fated or not, the outcome would've been the same." Charlotte may have struggled with it, but I've known that with complete certainty right from the start.

From the moment I gifted my Father's redemption to her.

She is mine.

As is he.

Always.

For the rest of our immortal eternities.

"Well, where does that leave me?" Mother pouts, sticking out her lip like the divine child she's currently being. "In a new universe with no god? With *Michael* to lead?" She gestures toward my brother, who's finally stumbled to his feet, his mouth still bleeding.

And I find that I understand my brother's hatred of me.

Even if I'd gut him as soon as look at him.

If only our Mother weren't watching.

"You could give the job to someone far more deserving." I nod toward Seraph.

She stands at the edge of the crowd, her sword in her hand, the whites of her single pair of wings sprayed with red.

I can think of no one better. More willing to make sacrifices for the ones they love. Even when they don't deserve it.

For a moment, Mother looks as if she might consider it. Ever since our Father stole her power, the concept of a divine feminine universe has always appealed to her.

But then Michael stomps his foot, like the petulant brat he is, ruining the whole goddamn thing. "No," he snarls. "No, no, no, no, no. That's not fair, Mother."

I roll my eyes. "I'm not certain fairness has ever had anything to do with it."

Clearly, we were not raised in the same celestial Heaven.

Fair?

Our family is right fucked.

"Quiet, Michael," Mother snaps, eager to dismiss him.

Out of the corner of my eye, I see my brother retrieve the blade from the floor and lunge for me.

"Lucifer!" Mimi shouts.

I turn, just seconds before the blade reaches me.

A blast that shakes the foundations of the chapel nearly levels everything.

Michael stands, swaying for a moment, staring down at the smoldering hole Mother's just burned into his chest like he can't believe that she would ever choose to destroy her own son.

"Does anyone *else* want to disobey me?" Mother shrieks, glancing about the rubble in her fury.

Michael drops, as dead as if I'd been the one who ended him, while I stand over him, unscathed. "Well, that was anticlimactic." I pluck the Holy Lance from his still-warm hand, depositing it in the interior pocket of my tux. "You never did learn."

The number one rule of our dysfunctional divine family.

Don't anger Mother at all costs.

I return my attention to her. It seems I might've broken my own protocol, I'm afraid.

Mother's eyes narrow. "If *you* won't listen to reason, then perhaps your wife will." She snaps her fingers, and then she's gone, racing toward Heaven, no doubt.

Not a single tear shed over the son she lost.

My spine runs cold.

And I may no longer be mortal, but I'm still just as powerless.

As she chases after my new wife and her grandbaby.

Into the one realm where I will never be free.

CHAPTER SEVENTY-FOUR

Charlotte

When Azrael and I finally touch down on what feels like solid ground, my eyes are closed, and my hands covering them are still shaking. I don't know why I'm more terrified by the thought of seeing Heaven than I was of seeing Hell, but some part of me doesn't want it to be a disappointment, maybe?

It feels like I've been training my whole life for this.

I sort of have been, I guess.

"It's all right, little siren. You can open your eyes." Azrael lowers my hands for me, holding me steady.

I blink, finally feeling brave enough with his support. My eyes slowly adjust to the bright white light.

My heart swells.

We're standing in the middle of a vast field of flowers, the vivid purple blooms around us seemingly unending. Sloth lands silently beside us.

I never imagined Heaven would look like this.

Like the most beautiful places on Earth I've ever seen.

All the spots that've been left untouched by humanity.

Heaven isn't a palace, a floating city in the sky.

It's mountains carved into the universe's highest peaks.

Sharp, pale-pink ridges rise from the ground, ancient and wild, their jagged edges cutting into the fabric of the universe and softened by a blue sky. The light hangs low behind us, painting the stones in hues of rose and lavender beyond the stretch of lush green. The air feels pure, sacred, like an endless rush of spring. Like I'm breathing in something older than time.

I notice the gates in the distance.

They're unspeakably beautiful.

They shimmer as iridescent as mother-of-pearl, vast and curved like open wings, their surface sparkling with a light that shifts, half-memory, half-dream. Colors ripple over them that I don't even have names for, and their nearness feels like music. Like the first note of a lullaby or the last breath before sleep.

This isn't at all what I expected.

Heaven isn't a place.

It's a feeling of finally coming home.

Azrael holds me tight, steady as ever, but I'm barely aware of his dark wings brushing over me. My eyes are on those gates. The way they don't swing open. Instead, they just . . . glow.

My hand drifts to my stomach, the smallest flutter beneath my palm reminding me why I'm here. Why I have to do this.

"I never thought it would feel like this," I whisper.

Like I could stand here forever in this field and be happy.

Azrael presses his mouth to my ear. "It's always been beautiful," he murmurs. "That's why he misses it."

Lucifer, he means.

I take a heavy breath, shaky and full, my heart aching.

My husband will never get to relive this.

My heart breaks for him.

I step forward, leaning down and brushing one of those vibrant purple blooms until it shivers in the wind.

A sudden roar echoes off in the distance, from the mountains.

"The Living Creatures," Azrael says. "They've summoned them."

The angels who were chasing us.

I'd hoped we'd somehow managed to throw them off.

But they took a detour for a different reason, it seems.

I glance at Sloth.

He seems almost as incapable of speaking as I am. Like he can't believe he's finally home, but now that he is, he's paralyzed by the sight. "I didn't think you'd ever actually get me here," he mutters, his voice breaking.

"You can thank Salome the next time you see her." I look at the gate before I turn toward Azrael. "I thought you said we were going to blow through them all."

He nods, the contentment in his expression fading. "I went through as many as I could, but even I have my limits, little siren. This is the last of the twelve. The seraphim and cherubim are still hot on our tail. It won't be long before they find us here."

I nod, struggling to determine what to do next.

I'll never complain about traveling through the ether ever again.

Breaking into Heaven was like being shattered apart, only to find all the pieces of myself I'd thought I'd lost and have them molded back together.

Now I feel more whole and complete than when I started.

I glance around at the gorgeous mountains.

This place may be beautiful, but I'll take Hell over this any day.

All the real fun's down there.

My gaze sweeps over the landscape. Over Sloth.

He belonged here. Just like Lucifer.

Once upon a time.

In this place of divine beauty so unmatched it almost makes me weep.

It only makes the way God cast them all out seem even crueler. More devastating.

"How are we supposed to—"

"Go through the gate." Azrael nods toward it. "I'll hold them off. It'll open for you. You're the only reason I was able to break through the others, remember?"

"But I don't want to do this without—"

"You can, little siren." He cups my neck, his calloused thumb gently tracing along my jawline. "You can, and you will. End of story. Once you're past the gate, you'll be safe. All you have to do is find Him."

Find God.

The guy who's abandoned us all this whole time.

Easier said than done, I think.

Another roar echoes.

This time, closer.

It sends a chill down my spine.

I've seen what kind of creature that noise is attached to. Or an early version, at least.

I'm not eager for a repeat.

"Go." Azrael releases me, nudging me toward the gate like he's delivered so many others here so many times before. "Time moves faster here. You won't have long. Remember that."

"And what am I supposed to do if I—"

"You'll find Him, Charlotte. I have every faith in you, and Lucifer does too, and when you're ready to come home, I'll be here at the gates, waiting."

Sloth takes my hand, like even if Azrael can't go with me, he will.

For now, at least.

So, I allow him to lead the way as I watch Azrael fly off, dark wings spread like shadows against the sky, and I wonder how Lucifer and I ever thought we could do this without him in the first place. I don't want to imagine a different ending.

CHAPTER SEVENTY-FIVE

Charlotte

Sloth leads me toward the pearly gates, my eyes transfixed on them the entire way. We walk for what feels like only a handful of minutes, though the distance we crossed makes it look like it would take a lot longer, but when we finally reach them, I realize I don't exactly have a plan for what I'm doing.

I delivered Sloth here, blew the gates open.

Now what?

They look as if I should be able to walk straight through them, but I know it can't possibly be that easy.

"What am I supposed to do?" I glance to Bel, hoping he might have the answers.

He shrugs. "I don't know." He's busy admiring his new wings like he still can't believe they're there. "I've never needed to open one. Before Dad cast us out, they always just opened on their own."

Of course they did.

God and Lilith clearly never made him work for anything.

"Do you think they would now?" I ask.

He shrugs again. "Only one way to find out." At least he's willing to help me now.

Or maybe it's something about this place. Maybe it heals a part of what was broken previously.

You taste like Heaven.

Lucifer's words. He's whispered that to me so many times. Into the hollow of my throat, against my stomach, my lips, between my legs.

Now I realize what he was always trying to tell me.

Heaven wasn't just his home.

It's the feeling of something being healed in him.

My eyes fill with tears, but I don't allow them to fall. I wish he were here beside me.

I have to do this.

If not for us, then our daughter.

So she knows there's more to humanity than it seems.

Just like her father learned when he fell in love with me.

Sloth steps forward, and the moment he reaches out his hand, dipping it past the open air of the gate, thunder sounds and lightning strikes, the crack so loud it's practically right on top of us. When Sloth pulls back his hand, his skin's steaming.

"Holy fuck!" he howls.

Okay, so apparently there *are* some parts of Heaven that feel like the God of the Old Testament, and I'm not particularly thrilled at the idea that my Father-in-Law might smite me.

I place a hand on Bel's shoulder, gently urging him back. "Let me try instead." I step forward, my heart racing at the idea of getting anywhere near that open space.

But there's no other option.

Like in the In-Between, the only way out is through.

I think about what Azrael said when he left, about how time moves faster here, and how I'm supposed to be racing against Lilith, finding God before she can destroy everything. I don't have time to hesitate. I'm the key.

The cosmic paradox that was never meant to exist, if not for Lucifer.

Inhaling a deep breath, I plunge my hand through the empty space.

At first, nothing happens.

Tentatively, I take another step through.

On the other side of the gate something speaks:

I am not born, yet I do grow,
I bind the high, I break the low.
I cannot die, though I am lost—
And only truth can pay my cost. What am I?

I glance at Sloth. "Did you hear that?"

He runs a hand through his beach-blond hair. "Vaguely. I wasn't really paying attention."

I roll my eyes. "It's a riddle."

Bel shrugs like there's nothing at all odd about that. "Have you seen Earth? It's all contradictions. Dad loves riddles."

I shrug. Fair point.

I turn back toward the voice. It's neither male nor female, angelic nor human, at least as far as I can tell.

It feels older, like it came from the root of the wind.

The vibration of it echoes in the space between us, the sound humming over my skin like it's searching for something inside me.

I repeat the words back to myself.

For a moment, I'm frozen.

Because the gates don't shimmer with golden light.

They don't swing open at the touch of divine blood.

They ask. They wait.

For something real.

From me.

I stare through them and think of Lucifer—of his laugh, his lips, that devilish smirk, his shadows curling around me like a caress, despite that he was never taught softness.

Then I think of Azrael, his voice in the dark, the feel of his skeletal hand in mine, of how he kept his word, even when he'd never known love before Lucifer, didn't know what it would bring for an eternity.

Then I think of mine and Lucifer's daughter growing inside me.

A miracle born of a being Heaven rejected.

But still I don't know the answer.

"Well, it's obvious, isn't it?" Bel scrunches his face.

I lift a brow, prompting him.

"Faith."

The moment he says it, I know he's right.

It's what brought me here.

What *keeps* bringing me here, despite how impossible this all should be.

"Faith," I whisper, my voice breaking against the soft light as I glance down at my belly.

Not the kind in a church. Not the kind my father used to preach about.

Not the hymns or the commandments or the holy fear.

But a faith that led me to kiss the devil, to love Death.

The kind you give when the whole world tells you you shouldn't.

"I don't know who or what made you," I say into the quiet, my words catching on the wind as I speak, "but I think . . . I think you've been waiting for someone like me."

The silence stretches.

And then the gate breathes.

It shimmers with an impossible color, light cascading outward in threads of gold, like silk stitched through the sky, unraveling every lie I've been told about who belongs here.

Heaven is open to anyone who has faith, regardless of its doctrine or creed.

The last gate parts.

Not violently. Just gently.

Like it's been waiting for me the whole time.

Like I belong here.

I reach back, extending my hand to Sloth, confident he can come through now, but he shakes his head reluctantly. "I wanted to come home, but now that I'm here, I'm . . . not certain I'm meant to be."

My heart breaks for him.

Because I know what it's like to feel that way.

To be cast out.

I vow right then and there that if I do find God and beat Lilith, I'm going to give Him a stern talking to. About practicing what He preaches.

And not just with Lucifer.

Sloth turns away, his wings spreading wide like he's prepared to take flight.

"Wait!" I call after him.

He glances over his shoulder at me.

"How am I supposed to find Him?"

"How does anyone find Him, Char?" Sloth laughs. "You just start looking."

CHAPTER SEVENTY-SIX

Azrael

When I return from Heaven a few hours later, only a handful of minutes have passed on Earth. But mortal concepts of time mean little to me. The battle is over, Lucifer's family's blood shed, and he's won his latest fight with his angelic siblings, even if it wasn't Armageddon.

Now, my Lightbringer stands among the wreckage of the chapel, his eyes unseeing.

Seraph approaches him slowly, offering him Michael's flaming sword like it's the spoils of war. Lucifer takes it, staring straight through it, down to the corpse lying at his feet. He sees it now. How broken everything's always been.

I retrieve the sword without a word, stowing it away in the Nothing for him for another time. I look down at Michael.

He wouldn't have been half bad in bed, if he hadn't had such a raging inferiority complex. But his is one soul I might . . . hold off on reaping.

For now, at least.

"Was it you?" I nod to the corpse.

"No." Lucifer huffs like that fact still disappoints him. "Mother, unfortunately."

Lilith always did know how to make an exit.

Even if fucking her is like a crash course in chaos theory.

I glance about the wreckage. Save for Versailles, the battle was mostly contained. Nothing near what it could've been. But Earth will never be the same.

The first four seals are still open.

The Horsemen, my siblings, the ones created in my image, roam free.

Humanity will feel their effects for generations to come.

But they chose their fate, and they'll reap what they sowed.

Even if Charlotte thinks they deserve forgiveness.

I step toward Lucifer.

He's covered in blood spray and ash from his hellfire, his hair is deliciously scruffy, a downright mess, but he's never looked more beautiful to me.

Because I know what comes next.

His reckoning.

"I . . . don't know what to do with it," he whispers, voice broken.

His father's redemption, he means.

I let out a small huff through my nose, nodding. This has been a long time coming. But some things need to break, to end, before they can find a new beginning. "You do what you've already been doing, Lightbringer. You keep living in spite of it."

"And my sins?"

I chuckle. "I don't think they're going anywhere any time soon, do you?"

"No." He shakes his head. "But I'm still not sure what it means to be . . ."

Free.

Of hate. Of anger. Of resentment.

What it means to be capable of being redeemed.

Charlotte isn't the only one who needed to find a new identity.

"I can't fall apart," he says, still shaking his head, like he knows this with complete certainty. This lie he's told himself since he first started to fear his own vulnerability. What first made him crave dominance. "I have to remain steady for her. For my siblings, I—"

"Do you have to? Or are you scared not to?"

I grip his shoulder, steadying him, but just when I move my hand to allow it to fall away, he whispers, "If you love me, don't let go."

My hold tightens.

I've been waiting a whole eternity for him to trust me like this. To bare his soul to me.

"I'm afraid for her," he admits, his eyes slowly lifting toward Heaven.

"You have to trust her. The same way you've trusted me."

He gives a reluctant nod. "I . . . don't know how to be a father."

I suppress a small smile. "You'll figure it out. I have faith in you. Always have."

"Will you help me?" He looks toward me, desperate and unguarded. "I've never built anything you didn't help create."

I cup the back of his head with both hands, our foreheads meeting. "I'll be here in whatever way you need me, Lightbringer."

He exhales, long and deep. "I lied, you know." He swallows, throat writhing. "I lied every time I said I didn't love you."

I chuckle. "I know."

From the other side of the wreckage, Lust lets out a sudden wolf whistle. "Would you two fools kiss and get to the fucking already? The only way this ends is with sword crossing."

I shoot him a furious look, but then Lucifer pulls me into his arms, whispering, "Let's go home, Reaper."

And just like that, the end becomes a beginning.

CHAPTER SEVENTY-SEVEN

Charlotte

I wander for what feels like days, though it must be a lot longer. Time passes more quickly here. Like how the minutes slip by in the playroom when I'm completely lost in my own pleasure. Night never comes, though there's occasionally stars overhead, and the sky and the landscape is like an endless stretch of infinity.

I pass terraced mountains, rainbow deserts, the layered sediment flowing from red to orange to yellow with pops of cactus green. There are glacial lakes with the bluest water I've ever seen. Trees covered in pink cherry blossoms that float through the breeze and coasts lined with endless white sand. I'm never hungry, never tired.

I'm never anything but at peace.

But I know time is passing quickly here.

I mark it in the changes in my body.

The way my breasts are a little fuller, my belly a little rounder as I reach each new landscape.

Until I can feel mine and Lucifer's daughter regularly squirming inside me.

Faith. I think that's going to be her name, if Lucifer approves.

She's a hellion all right. Like her dad. Like Death.

Kicking me in the ribs every chance she gets.

But it doesn't feel like pain. Just contentment.

And even though I'm alone, I'm happy.

I walk and walk and walk. I could go on like this forever, if I weren't vaguely aware there was something even greater out there waiting for me. I wander until I'm drawn toward . . . something, though I don't exactly know what.

Occasionally, I change direction, switch paths, but I don't know where any of them lead.

I let my intuition guide me.

Count our baby's kicks.

Eventually, I reach a rocky coast, and though I'm not tired, if I stay here much longer, Lucifer and Azrael are going to miss my entire pregnancy. With how quickly time's passing, I'm way further along than when I arrived here, but just when I'm considering turning back, in the distance I see a figure standing on the edge of the coast.

It's the first person I've seen all day. Days? Weeks maybe?

I'm not sure, honestly.

I pick up my pace, jogging a little to catch up to them before they disappear. I'm not so big that I can't move easily, but there's no hiding my bump now.

It's going to be obvious to everybody.

I draw closer and closer to the edge, the landscape dipping and then rising so that I lose my view. The crest over the hill seems to take ages, until I'm hoping, praying with all my might, that when I reach the other side, I'll find Him there.

But when I reach the cliff's edge, it isn't God.

It's His prophet.

Jax.

She turns and looks at me, her smile wide and her dark hair swept back from her face. I'm not certain if I say anything. I just pull her into my arms, clinging to her, and she lets me.

If Heaven is a place where nothing hurts, then all our loved ones must already be there.

She pulls back, placing her hand on my bump. "Look at you. You're adorable. You're glowing."

"You are too." I laugh.

She looks like an angel, but without the wings.

Like she belongs here.

"I'm sorry. I—"

"Don't." She shakes her head. "This was always how it was meant to be. You did exactly what you were supposed to."

"Except find God." My face falls. If I don't turn back soon, then what? "Lilith's going to destroy everything."

Jax smiles. "I think He likes to turn up when you least expect Him to." She nods over my shoulder, and I turn to find God standing there.

Or Father Brown, what He calls Himself when He's in His earthly form, anyway.

"Charlotte."

He offers me His hand.

I don't know whether to take it or whether I want to scream.

To rage for all the ways He's failed me.

Failed us. But I'm too at peace to do anything but stand there.

A part of me also wants to thank Him for . . . everything.

He seems to catch on to my dilemma, nodding like He understands, before He gestures over His shoulder. "Walk with me?" He looks toward the coast.

I give a reluctant glance toward Jax.

"I'll see you again," she says. "Even if you're Hell's queen."

I trust her. She hasn't steered me wrong previously.

I pull her in for a hug, muttering a quick, "I love you."

"I love you too." She rubs my belly one last time for good measure. "You'll be an amazing mom. Don't let Lucifer make you have too many. You know he comes from a huge family." She laughs, smiling at me and then God, like they're old friends.

Maybe they are, I guess.

I squeeze her hand, reluctant to let go, but the moment I set her free, her glowing form disappears entirely. I turn toward God.

We set off down the coastline together, walking in silence.

At first, it's comfortable.

Companionable even.

But then it stretches on for too long, and I open my mouth, about to say—

"I know why you're here, Charlotte," He says, stopping near an outcropping of rocks and running His hand along the ridged surface.

His presence is calm and steady, the order to Lilith's divine chaos.

Despite the wrath I know He's capable of.

"How did you know? I thought your precognitive abilities didn't extend to Lilith?"

He smiles like the term *precognitive abilities* is somehow amusing.

I suppose to a god, it would be.

"I don't need to see what fate has in store to know what my wife is planning." He nods to the edge of the cliff, to where Jax was.

Of course. Jax is one of His prophets. She would've told Him.

Though she wouldn't have been able to come here, where she was supposed to be, if Azrael and I hadn't smashed open the pearly gates. She would've had to stay in Hell with us.

It's hard to not let that make me regret opening them.

"I'm not particularly happy about my gates being destroyed," God says, reading my thoughts. "Even if it was a bit fun to watch."

"I'm sorry."

"Azrael's still angry with me."

I nod. "Probably."

"Rightfully so." He turns away for a moment before He asks, "And Lucifer?"

We both already know the answer.

"I think some part of him always will be."

God's solemn agreement is silent, a slight dip of His chin.

"Why'd you do it?" I tilt my head to the side, wondering what it must be like to be the Creator. The architect of all of Lilith's raw materials.

"You want to know why I punished Lucifer? Why he fell, if I'd always planned for him to be redeemed?"

I nod.

"Isn't it obvious?" He asks.

I shake my head. "Not to me at least."

He smiles. "I've made mistakes. Just like you. I created humanity in my image, Charlotte, and I'm not perfect."

I exhale, trying to suppress a smile.

He's just as fucked up as we are.

I don't know why, but that makes me feel a little better.

"Well, I don't know that I'd exactly put it in those terms," He says, reading my mind.

We both fall silent for a beat.

"So, you know Lilith's coming for you, but you're not going to hide?"

"No."

"Why?"

If He loves us in spite of our flaws, I don't see what would make Him want to end humanity that way.

"I deserve what she gives me. This is my penance. For how I've wronged my wife, wronged Lucifer."

"But if you die, then . . ."

Humanity ceases to exist.

How come I seem to be the only immortal who can see that?

The answer comes to me in a second.

Because that's the part of my humanity that remains. My hope that we can still be redeemed.

Just like Lucifer was.

"That doesn't matter to you any more than it would matter to Lucifer, to Michael, or even Lilith, does it?" I ask.

God may have made us in His image, but to Him we're just one small speck of stardust in an ever-expanding universe. A footnote in His celestial ending.

Unimportant.

But not to me.

"What can I say to change your mind? To stop you from handing yourself over to Lilith?"

God shakes His head. "There's nothing you could do to convince me."

And to think, I figured His wife was the unreasonable one.

Suddenly, Lilith appears behind God, her smile slow and wide, like I led her right to Him.

Why the hell had I not thought of that possibility?

I place myself between them.

Like I did with Lucifer and his siblings.

Though I don't know exactly what it is I'm supposed to do to stop a battle between two creators. My attention darts back and forth as panic sears through me.

No. This can't be the ending.

I can't die without one last time in Lucifer's arms. Or one more night with Azrael.

"Lovely of you to do the work for me, Charlotte. I have so little faith in Him anymore it would've been a struggle to find Him on my own." Lilith looks at God, eyes narrowing. "Husband."

"Wife."

Their greeting to one another couldn't be colder.

But there had to have been a time when . . .

"You both love your children," I say, my voice smaller than I want it to be. "In particular, your son." God may have kicked him out, given him a chip on his shoulder, but my husband is absolutely the golden boy of his family, and no one can convince me otherwise.

Maybe that's why he's so determined to make the world his stage.

Lilith's expression turns accusing. "You threw him out at the first sign of struggle."

God's brow furrows. "You coddled him, even when he defied me."

"What if you're both right?" I shrug helplessly, feeling like I'm standing between Lucifer and Azrael all over again. I think they'd *both* punish me if I told them they argue like an old married couple. "What if you both need each other? There's no order without chaos. No light without dark. No pleasure without pain."

Just a lot of endless nothingness.

Void of meaning.

"I created Him." Lilith sneers.

I huff.

Well, there goes that idea.

She steps forward as I scramble to find another way. Another path to resolve this.

This is a celestial minefield.

"But you also *chose* to surrender your power to Him, didn't you?"

Lilith's head whips toward me. "What are you trying to say, human?"

My stomach drops, and if it weren't for the fact that I'm carrying her grandchild, I'm pretty sure she'd smite me. The ends of her hair blaze.

"He took advantage of you, yes, and that was wrong." I shoot God a chastising look. "But I think what you're really angry about is the fact you let Him, that in the aftermath, you lost sight of your own power for a while, and now you don't know how to reclaim it." Shaking, I try to take her hand, and to my surprise, she lets me. "You think being angry will get you back to that power, and it might for a while, but that won't get you any closer to where you're heading."

I'm speaking to myself as much as I am to her. If PR has taught me anything, it's that the best narratives come from a place of honesty, of shared experience.

I think about what I've missed the most during the time that's passed here. From the gleam in Lucifer's eye whenever he tells me to get on my knees to the devious grin on Azrael's face whenever I make him feel seen.

That's what Heaven's missing.

Joy.

It has peace, contentment.

But it's nothing without joy.

And joy can't happen without healing, without moving forward, without moving on from dwelling on the past, long enough to recognize there's no meaning to be found in something that's senseless and unfair. Dwelling doesn't reclaim anything.

And that's where the true power lies.

In mercy. In forgiveness.

In reclaiming joy.

Even if it's undeserved.

That's the piece Lucifer and I have been missing all along.

We need to stop looking back.

We need to start looking forward.

I squeeze Lilith's hands tight. "You don't need Him," I say, nodding over my shoulder toward God. "You don't need Him to be happy. You don't need His apologies, or His forgiveness, or His explanations. But you do need to give Him mercy, for yourself. You already have all the power you need. All you have to do is reach out and take it." I hold her gaze. "Take it and don't look back. Take it and create a new universe. One filled with life and abundance and joy and all the things He made you think you could never have. A life filled with every wicked thing He couldn't take from you. That's the real way to punish Him. To not let yourself be defined by what happened, but to thrive in spite of it."

God clears His throat. "As interesting as that little speech was—"

"Quiet, Jehovah," Lilith snaps, holding my palms tight. "I suppose since Lucifer is still digging his feet in, Seraph will do. Perhaps you're right, my creation. Perhaps I don't need to destroy Him, but only if you—"

"Lucifer and I will come visit." I latch on to that small thread of hope and pull. "And we'll have plenty more babies, I promise." I glance between them. "Though maybe not as many as you two."

Lilith laughs.

When the Goddess isn't raging, isn't trapped by her own fury, she's beautiful, joyful.

"All right, my child. You win. For now. But when humanity has finally fallen . . ." She glares at God, the darkness in her eyes flaring as she turns from one to three. "Don't think I won't still come for you."

She fades into the fabric of the universe.

And then she's gone, released from her fury, into the joyous chaos she was always supposed to be.

I look at God, my hand resting over my belly as I shake my head. "You owe me."

CHAPTER SEVENTY-EIGHT

Charlotte

When I finally stumble back through the pearly gates, it's like stepping out of a dream. The gates tower above me, brilliant and blinding. My knees nearly buckle from the weight of everything that's happened.

But then Azrael is there by my side like he sensed the exact moment I came back to him, his hand firm at my elbow, anchoring me.

For a heartbeat, we just stand there, his eyes flickering with pride. His gaze falls to my bump, and he licks his lips, his expression full of longing. I want to say something, anything, but all that escapes me is his name.

"Azrael . . ."

The sound of it on my lips feels like home.

"You perfect, clever girl," he breathes.

I collapse into his arms, his hand falling protectively to my belly like I'm his, and his mouth twists into a smile. At first, he just looks at me, like he's trying to memorize me all over again, his eyes shining. Then he tugs me to him, claiming my lips.

His kiss is fierce, desperate, unrelenting.

When he releases me, I wrap myself in him, my tears dampening his shoulder as I cling to him. For the first time in what feels like forever, I relax completely, allowing myself to believe we survived.

"Lucifer?" I ask, pulling back from him.

"He's at Fashion Week. You've been gone about a week and a half." Azrael cups my cheek. "I'll take you to him."

Only a little over a week?

It feels like a whole lifetime has passed for me. I glance down at my bump.

Or a few months at least.

Azrael chuckles like he can see all the wheels inside my head turning, before he rubs a hand over my belly. "I didn't think you could be any more beautiful, little siren." He leans down and kisses me, long and deep.

Death draws me to him, my toes curling in pleasure, until I'm panting.

He holds me tight, barely any space between us, and I feel a rush of wind as his wings flap, and then the next thing I know, we're standing backstage at the Grand Palais Éphémère.

"Go." He swats me on the ass, grinning. "I'll be in the playroom when you both get back."

"Do I have to?" I whine, even though I'm eager to see my husband.

He gives me a stern look. "You'll regret it if you miss it. Be a good girl for me."

I blush, ready to obey, eager to please him.

The only thing more terrifying to a brat than a hard Dom is a pleasure Dom.

And I've been getting the best of both lately.

Azrael rubs a hand over Faith, dropping a quick kiss there, too, like she and I are just as much his as we are Lucifer's. A kinky, immortal family.

But what else is new?

He nods to the stage. "I'll keep an eye on you until you're back."

I smile. "Of course you will, you freaking stalker."

I give him one last kiss, reluctant to let him go.

But Lucifer and I will be home in only a few hours.

His wings beat again, and then he's gone, leaving me standing among the backstage chaos.

I'm still in the tattered remains of my wedding dress, the back of my bodice hanging open from where I had to unlace it, and I'm pretty sure my makeup has long gone to hell and back. I look a lot like I do whenever Lucifer and Azrael have had their way with me in the playroom. But I don't care.

I'm here for me.

No one else.

To take my victory lap for quietly saving humanity.

I navigate backstage until I spot Xzander. He's pacing back and forth in front of Imani, looking as if he's about to lose it—he's likely terrified that I won't show—but when he catches sight of me, his eyes go wide, his gaze darting over me, and then, "Diva!" he shrieks.

Clearly, he doesn't even know where to begin.

I shrug. "The show's celestial themed. This is what being a celestial looks like."

He places a hand on Imani's shoulder like he needs her to give him strength. Imani just shakes her head. "You're on in five, Charlotte."

The next few minutes are a flurry of hair and makeup. Xzander furiously cuts and stitches and throws together what remaining pieces he can salvage from his original design, and to be honest, it looks almost the same, other than the artfully placed midsection to accommodate my baby bump, since he didn't know I was expecting.

All in all, it's not my worst look.

But I would have gone out there in my wedding dress if he'd let me, honestly.

Imani was right.

The world will see who I am if I let them see.

But it's a minute before I'm about to go on, and I still haven't spotted my husband.

"Where's Lucifer?" I ask Imani.

"He's closing out the men's show just before you. You'll cross paths on the catwalk."

Of course we will.

"You're on, Charlotte." Imani moves to usher me out onto the stage.

I grip her hand. "Thank you, Imani. For everything."

She grins, waving me forward. "Girl, get out there already."

I head onto the stage. It may not be the most elegant strut that Imani's taught me, but I don't really care.

I'm confident in who I am.

In who the devil's made me.

When I reach the main runway, I spot Lucifer at the other end, his back turned to me, and I grin from ear to ear.

I can't wait to see the look on his face when . . .

He turns and spots me, his eyes roving every inch of me. He strides toward me, his stare never leaving mine as I walk toward him.

I expect to brush hands with him, meet him in the middle, but as soon as he reaches me, he snatches me into his arms, viciously kissing me.

The crowd goes wild, the cameras flashing.

The next thing I know, he's hauling me offstage by my collar, not even allowing me to finish. But I don't particularly want to.

I'd much rather be in the devil's arms than in the public eye any day.

The moment he has me backstage, he pins me to the wall, knocking over a rack of clothes and shoving everything in our path aside in order to get to me.

He has me caged beneath him, my leg over his hip so that his erection's pressed against me, and the only bit of space between us is because of my belly.

His gaze sweeps over me hungrily. "Oh, darling. What a right mess I've made of you," he growls.

He tangles his other hand in my hair, gripping it roughly at the base as he kisses me. He snaps his fingers, and we become shadow, and then we're standing in the middle of the playroom.

Azrael's already there waiting for us, a slow grin pulling on his lips, like it's no surprise to him that we're back so quickly.

Lucifer palms my breasts, moaning slightly at how they've grown in size. "Look at how gorgeous our girl is, Reaper."

Azrael's large form approaches at my back, his massive cock pushing between my ass cheeks as he takes hold of my hips, leaning over me in order to kiss Lucifer. "She's perfect."

"She's—"

"Ours," they say in unison.

That word goes straight to my pussy, making me hotter.

The hormones are driving me wild.

Thank God I have both of them.

Azrael walks me backward toward one of the benches, lowering down onto it behind me so that I'm propped against him, my ass positioned at the edge of the seat. His hands come to my breasts as he peels down the costume I'm wearing, kneading and touching and palming me until I'm practically feral with need.

Meanwhile, Lucifer strips off his own costume, and then he's standing before us in all his glory. He drops to his knees in front of me, touching and playing with me until, between the two of them, I'm nearly coming apart.

"Be gentle with her, Lightbringer," Azrael warns as Lucifer positions his cock just outside my entrance.

"He is, sir," I breathe. "He always is."

In his own way.

Lucifer eases into me, rocking his hips as he throws back his head with a groan. "My wicked, wicked girl," he purrs. "You're soaked for me."

"For us," Azrael mutters, kissing me deep, his hands still working over my breasts. "She's already losing it, Lightbringer."

And he's right.

I feel a flutter, an ache igniting inside me.

"Such a greedy little siren, aren't you?" Azrael kisses my neck.

I groan as Lucifer pushes deeper and deeper, my head dropping back onto Azrael's shoulder. "Give me more. Please, Daddy," I beg.

Lucifer growls in approval. "You're going to be calling me that both in and outside the playroom now, little dove." He rubs a hand over my belly as he thrusts into me, until I'm practically mewling.

The pressure inside me builds, my whole world narrowing to where Death and the devil touch me.

I'm never going to survive eternity with the two of them.

But I'll take all the pleasure they give me with the pain.

CHAPTER SEVENTY-NINE

Lucifer

When Azrael and I have finished working over my wife one at a time, as gently and carefully as possible for her and our child's shared safety, I lead them back to the bedroom for aftercare. Azrael kicks the bedroom door open, prowling inside like the absolute brute he is, before I can stop either of them from seeing what a disaster they've made me.

Charlotte's eyes go wide in shock, since clearly the maids haven't yet been in, and Azrael, the devious bastard, starts laughing so hard, I don't think I've seen him this gleeful in all our days.

"I . . . might be working through some things." I paw sheepishly at the back of my neck.

Various infant paraphernalia is scattered about our room: an assortment of bottles, varying sizes of designer baby clothing, and a half-assembled crib with instructions that are written in a language even *I* seem incapable of understanding.

"Oh, Lucifer." Charlotte sighs, but she smiles up at me.

"Don't." I lift a hand, silencing them. "Do not say anything. Either one of you. Do you hear me?" Azrael is still chuckling like he doesn't need to breathe, which he doesn't. I rake a rough hand through my hair.

"I'm well aware this is the one area of our lives where I have no idea what I'm doing, and if I turn out to be anything like my own Father, I'm going to be awful at it, despite my enthusiasm."

Charlotte's gaze softens. "You're not going to be—"

I shoot her a warning look.

"Sorry, sir," she mutters, suppressing a grin.

Azrael finally settles, shaking his head at me. "It's all right, Lightbringer. You can tell us what you're going through."

I glance between them, tempted to stuff it down, to lie through my teeth like I always have, to make everyone believe there is nothing that ever terrifies me.

But I don't have it in me to put up a front anymore.

I let out a frustrated snarl, my shadows whipping about the room as I start to pace. "How am I supposed to be a bloody father when I've barely begun to work through my issues with my own Father? This is torture, honestly."

My wife and Azrael exchange a meaningful look.

"What?"

I don't much appreciate the devilish gleam in their eyes.

Charlotte hesitates, but then Azrael gives her an encouraging nod, and she extends a hand to me. "I think I might have an idea of how you could work through some of those issues, sir."

It's two days later, and after much negotiating and a lot of grumbling on my part, the tables have turned considerably.

I sit on my devil's chair inside the playroom, waiting for my wife to make an appearance.

Azrael stands at my side, already at the ready, stripped down to nothing but his jeans.

If I have my way, they won't be staying on for long.

But my wife is the one who's in charge today.

When Charlotte sweeps into the room, she's wearing a gauzy black nightgown that covers her almost completely, but when she strips it off, depositing it onto one of the play benches, it reveals the fetish gear she has on beneath.

I growl appreciatively.

Azrael just snarls, "Quiet, cumslut."

But he's not talking to Charlotte.

He's talking to me.

I crack my neck, a wide, devious grin on my lips, as I lean back in my chair. "Is that the best you've got, Reaper?" I sneer up at him. "Punish me like you mean it."

"Oh, he's going to," my wife says, her Prada heels clicking against the playroom's floor as she comes to stand in front of me. She's holding a riding crop, and my cock stiffens as she uses it to tip my chin toward her, the devilish hellfire in her eyes gleaming as she purrs, "Tonight, you will call me Lady Death."

EPILOGUE

Charlotte

Eleven months later . . .

"Tell me again why you won't allow us to do this for you, darling?" Lucifer trails a bead of sweat from my shoulder to between my breasts with his finger, like he's wishing he could lick me clean. But he knows I'm too hell-bent on this for him to deter me, so he doesn't push me.

"I already told you," I say, striding toward the meat locker's entrance as I pass Faith to him.

He cradles her in one arm effortlessly, already a pro at caring for her.

She's less than a year old, but he absolutely refuses to leave her alone with a nanny.

Nothing but the best for the devil's daughter.

She's going to be the most spoiled little princess Hell has ever seen.

Seeing the way he loves her has healed me in a way I didn't realize I'd still needed, until now at least. Faith starts to fuss, squirming to get back to me, and more importantly, my boobs, which she's in a constant—if slightly one-sided—battle with her dad for. But she always wins.

Azrael swoops in unexpectedly, stealing her out of Lucifer's arms.

If I didn't know any better, I'd say she's just as much his as she is Lucifer's.

He dotes on her with a level of praise he doesn't even give me. "I've got her," he grumbles, kissing her chubby cherubic cheeks until she's giggling.

She somehow looks a bit like him, despite being the spitting image of Lucifer.

I think it's the black feathered wings.

Lucifer seizes the baby-free moment to pull me into his arms, kissing my forehead gently. "We no longer ***need*** him, little dove." He nods toward my father's meat locker. "Might as well forget about him and be done with it."

He dips his head lower, that devious mouth of his trailing down to my neck, as his hand dips over the curve of my ass.

He's already vying for another baby soon, and I'm losing that battle quickly.

My devilish husband gets what he wants. Always.

One way or another.

And I can't get enough of how devoted he is to me.

"If you keep doing that, I won't be able to focus, and then I'll lose my nerve." I press a quick kiss to his lips and then Azrael's, unsurprised he's stayed silent about this.

He knows this is my choice, and he's not about to take it from me.

Though neither is Lucifer, even if he might nudge me in whatever direction he sees fit.

"I already told you. I feel like I have to prove something. It'll be quick. I promise."

Lucifer huffs, reluctantly releasing me, but I don't miss the devious gleam as his eyes flit over my collar.

Their collar.

The next time he gets me and Azrael alone in the playroom, we're in for it.

"Who do you feel you have something to prove to, darling? To Azrael? To *me*?"

"To herself, Lucifer." Azrael inhales a deep breath, tossing Faith up in the air so she giggles slightly. He passes her back to Lucifer and wraps his arms around me, burying his face into my neck as he inhales the scent of me.

Lucifer lets out an appreciative growl, enjoying the sight of us together.

He no longer tries to hide how he's feeling.

Something changed after the wedding.

Like the rift that was once between them is a thing of distant memory.

I take their hands in mine. "I need you to support me in this, okay? Help me through this."

Lucifer gives a derisive huff but then frowns, patting Faith until she starts to fall asleep in his arms, and Azrael just nods at me, urging me on.

Fortunately, I know that when push comes to shove, Lucifer will give me anything I ask for, because he loves me.

Death included.

"I love you," I say to them.

"We'll be waiting, little dove." My devil nods, and then I turn and walk into my father's chamber alone.

The meat locker is the same as the last time I visited.

But no one's been down here much lately, and it shows.

A few cobwebs hang in the corners and a layer of dust—ash, maybe? considering we're in Hell—has settled over everything.

When I enter, my father lifts his head unsteadily, his gaze combing over me, taking in the wider width of my hips, the changes in me. I'm not sure if he knows I'm a mother now, and I don't care enough about him to tell him.

Faith will not know either of her grandfathers, and Lucifer and I plan to keep it that way.

To my surprise, my father doesn't start in with his usual Bible quotes, though I'm pretty certain there's nothing he could say that could hurt me.

I know who I am now.

Who I'm becoming.

Who I've always been.

And there's nothing I'm ashamed of.

Except for one thing.

"Come to take your pound of flesh again, she-devil?" he hisses, more serpentine and crueler than the devil could ever be.

I shake my head. "No. That's not what I'm here for."

I'm here to exorcise the last demon he seems to have left in me.

My father quirks a brow but doesn't say anything.

I inhale a deep breath. "I'm going to give you the one thing you could never give me."

His eyes narrow. "And what's that?"

"My mercy," I say, a proud tear running down my cheek as I turn on my Louboutin heel and walk out of his chamber, smiling wickedly, my head held high.

Never once do I feel tempted to look back.

ABOUT CONSENSUAL KINK

The depictions of BDSM in this book are for fantasy entertainment purposes only and are not intended as an accurate representation of the BDSM/kink community. For many, BDSM and its queer history is sacred, hallowed ground, but I hope readers feel I've used it to appropriately and thematically fuck with the power structures that be.

For those interested in learning more, please seek out resources on risk-aware, consensual kink.

ACKNOWLEDGMENTS

I've received so much incredible support throughout writing this series, but I am particularly grateful to those who were in my corner for *Beautiful Redeemer*. I wrote this book during a particularly tumultuous time in my life, and as such, this book would not have happened without the amazing team of people behind me.

To my agents, Lesley Sabga and Nicole Resciniti, for the constant support and for believing in this idea from start to finish. I'm so grateful to have you in my corner.

To my editor, Maria Gomez, for always believing in my vision and championing this series, and Sasha Knight, for finding all the ways to make this story better.

To Christian Bentulan for the amazing covers, and to the whole Montlake team for promoting and producing this series.

To Brilliance for the amazing audio production, and to my audiobook narrators—Ethan Reid for being the perfect Lucifer, Isabelle Turner for bringing Charlotte to life, and Troy Duran, whose voice lived rent-free in my head whenever I was writing Azrael.

To my mom, for taking care of the boys and dinner so that this book could happen, and to my boys for believing in me and celebrating with me when I typed "The End."

To my MAKE friends for holding me when I cried and for telling me I could do this, even when I thought I couldn't. To Abigail Owen, for taking the pressure off and for believing me, always. To Mariah

Ankenman for the In-Between suggestions and the "daddy issues." And to Elm Jed for being my resident BDSM-brainstorming buddy and enjoying my unhinged texts even first thing in the morning. Those two fingers belong to you, my friend.

To Dolly for helping me start the journey, to Danielle for pushing me out of my "comfort" zone, but most especially to Yma for helping me finish it. For reminding me that Charlotte's victory was also my victory, and that I'm breaking cycles too.

And to my readers, loyal and new, for following Charlotte and Lucifer and Azrael to the finish and for your endless enthusiasm. Thank you for going on this journey with me.

ABOUT THE AUTHOR

Photo © 2025 Yuliya Panchenko

Kait Ballenger is an award-winning author of dark romantasy and paranormal romance. She is obsessed with tales of morally gray, sometimes villainous heroes and can't resist a spicy redemption arc. When she's not busy writing kinky paranormal fantasy, she can usually be found with her nose buried in someone *else's* naughty books. Kait lives in Florida's Bible Belt with her two adorable sons—but she'll gladly use that belt to whip you.

For more information and the latest news, connect with the author on TikTok (@kaitballenger) and Instagram (@kait.ballenger), or sign up for her newsletter at www.kaitballenger.com.